THE NEXT TIME YOU SEE ME

This Large Print Book carries the
Seal of Approval of N.A.V.H.

THE NEXT TIME YOU SEE ME

HOLLY GODDARD JONES

THORNDIKE PRESS

A part of Gale, Cengage Learning

GALE
CENGAGE Learning·

Detroit • New York • San Francisco • New Haven, Conn • Waterville, Maine • London

LIBRARY OF CONGRESS CATALOGING-IN-PUBLICATION DATA

Jones, Holly Goddard.
    The next time you see me / by Holly Goddard Jones. — Large print edition.
        pages ; cm. — (Thorndike Press large print core)
    ISBN 978-1-4104-6031-8 (hardcover) — ISBN 1-4104-6031-2 (hardcover) 1. Murder—Investigation—Fiction. 2. Kentucky—Fiction. 3. Large type books. I. Title.
    PS3610.O6253N49 2013b
    813'.6—dc23   2013017255

Published in 2013 by arrangement with Touchstone, a division of Simon & Schuster, Inc.

Printed in Mexico
1 2 3 4 5 6 7 17 16 15 14 13

For my mother, Ruth; in memory of her mother, Evelyn Elizabeth Ezell, 1917–2011

PART ONE

CHAPTER ONE

1.

Emily Houchens watched as Christopher Shelton, who sat in a desk two rows up and one over from her own, leaned back and smoothly slid his notebook over his shoulder, so that the boy sitting behind him could read what was written there. This second boy, Monty, began to quake with suppressed laughter. The notebook retracted; an open hand took its place, waiting expectantly, and Monty softly gave him five: *Good one.* Mrs. Mitchell, who was pacing in her predictable way up and down the aisles while the students worked, had missed the whole exchange, and Emily tucked her chin into her chest to hide the smile on her face. Christopher had the easy luck of an action hero in a movie. Things always worked out for him.

"Five more minutes," Mrs. Mitchell announced, and Emily dragged her attention back to the sheet of paper on her desktop and the meager lines she had written in response to the prompt. It was a Friday, the day their English class focused on test-taking strategies, which everyone hated — even Mrs. Mitchell, Emily suspected. The prompt read:

Painters, like writers, use images, tone, and even characters to convey a theme or emotion in their work.

a. Select an important emotion or image communicated in the novel *A Separate Peace.*

b. Imagine how a painter might render this same emotion or image on a canvas. Describe this imagined painting, detailing how and why this emotion or symbol is conveyed by choices related to space, color, texture, and shape.

"It's all bullshit," she had heard Christopher tell his friends at lunch one day. She had taken her usual seat — not at the popular table but at one nearby, where she could eat with her back to the group and listen, unbothered and unnoticed, to its conversation. Lunch immediately followed English, and so the subject of Christopher's diatribes was often Mrs. Mitchell, perhaps the only teacher in the seventh- and eighth-grade wings who seemed unimpressed by the charming, handsome boy who'd moved to Roma, Kentucky, last year from Michigan. "I never got a B in Ann Arbor. And that was *Ann Arbor.* How can some English teacher from the boonies give me a B? You don't even speak English here."

The kids at the table had laughed agreeably.

Now, as Mrs. Mitchell resumed her place at the front of the classroom, Emily brought her paragraph to a hasty conclusion and set her pencil down. Her underarms prickled with heat, and a lump of anxiety formed in her throat. Stupid, stupid to let herself get distracted again by Christopher. The open-response questions were for a grade.

"Cross your t's and dot your i's," Mrs. Mitchell said. The chairs squeaked as students shifted, and there was a chorus of sighs. "Let's read some of these aloud today and discuss them. Can I get a volunteer?"

Emily let her hair hang over her face. *Not me, not me, not me,* she willed.

She heard snickering and peeked through her bangs. Monty was poking Christopher between the shoulder blades with the eraser end of his pencil, and Christopher jerked in his seat. His hand shot up.

11

Mrs. Mitchell looked at him warily. "Yes, Christopher?"

"I'll read mine," he said, shooting a satisfied glance back at Monty, who put his head down on the desktop as if a game of Seven-Up had started. Emily could hear him wheezing with laughter.

"Go ahead," said Mrs. Mitchell.

Christopher stood and held his notebook in front of him like an orator. "In *A Separate Peace,* Finny decides to wear a pink shirt. Some say this is an expression of individuality but I see it as a sign that he is gay. Pink shirt equals gay. Also the name Finny: very gay. So my painter would paint a picture of a gay man in a pink shirt symbolizing one hundred percent gay."

There was a stunned silence. The students exchanged glances, delighted and disbelieving, then shifted their attention back to Mrs. Mitchell, primed for the inevitable explosion. Her face had gotten very red, as it always did when she was flustered, and her hands were shaking. Emily ached with secondhand embarrassment.

"Go to the back of the room and take a seat," Mrs. Mitchell said in a quavering voice. "Stay there. Don't leave when the bell rings."

Christopher's neck glowed suddenly with

its own bright heat, and he moved as if to hunch down and grab his books from beneath his desk.

"Go on," Mrs. Mitchell said. "Leave your books."

"OK. *God,*" he said. He made a jaunty about-face, mouth set in a smirk, and stuck his fingers into the front pockets of his jeans, so that his thumbs rested easily on his narrow hipbones. He sauntered down the aisle between his row and Emily's, and she couldn't help but watch him. His skin, which hadn't yet lost its summer color, was golden against the white cuffs of his oxford shirt, and a lock of his thick, dark brown hair hung over his eye, so that he had to cock his head to shake it out of his vision. He had always been kind to her — that is, unlike others in their grade, he had never been cruel to her. They'd shared a table for a semester in seventh-grade science class, both of them smart enough and serious enough to complete Mr. Wieland's assignments successfully, with time left over for catching up on homework due in the next period. He'd even helped her with her science project, "The Effects of Ultraviolet Light on Tadpoles," staying after class with her a few times to look at the tadpoles getting exposed to the UV lamp, cracking jokes

13

about tadpole fricassee and tadpoles with suntans, helping her sprinkle fish food into the water and take notes in her logbook. She ended up winning second place at the regional science fair.

His eyes were bright blue. She had never seen such blue eyes.

He stopped by her desk, the little smile still playing on his lips, and leaned toward her. Her heart skittered, and her mouth got very dry. She tried to wet her lips, but her tongue had gone numb and stupid, and she prayed that she would be able to speak back if he spoke to her, that she would say the right thing.

"Stop staring at me, creep," he whispered, but not so low that the students close by them failed to hear it. There was more muted laughter.

"What was that?" Mrs. Mitchell called from the front of the room.

"Nothing," Christopher said innocently.

The tears started to spill before she could stop them. She put her head down as Monty had before, wiping her eyes on her forearms. *Not real. This isn't happening.*

He plopped down in the desk behind her and shoved his feet roughly into the storage cubby under her seat.

"You can all use the rest of the class as a

study hall," Mrs. Mitchell said. "Anyone who makes a peep will be joining Christopher after class on a trip to Mr. Burton's office. Got it?"

A few heads nodded.

Mrs. Mitchell put a hand unconsciously to her cheek, which was still blotchy with color. "Pass in your papers."

Emily ripped the sheet with her response on it out of her notebook and held it out tentatively, so that it just grazed Missy Hildabrand's shoulder in front of her. Missy grabbed it, huffing as if Emily were always passing her papers, so many papers that she couldn't get a thing done.

Christopher murmured in the rustling, so softly that only Emily heard him this time: "Crybaby. Go home and cry some more, crybaby."

2.

That day — the day she would find the body — was October 28, 1993. It had long been Emily's habit to go on solitary walks in an undeveloped area near her family's subdivision; she thought of this area as the woods, but it was little more than a tangle of trees and construction runoff stretching like a cocked thumb between neighborhoods, a place where gravel roads started and mysteriously stopped and concrete slab foundations had lain dormant for coming up on a decade. A ghost town, but for a place that had never even come to exist. Emily couldn't remember it any other way, and she had rarely seen another soul on her walks, though the paths she followed were old and well worn.

After getting off the school bus, she went home only long enough to stow her backpack in her bedroom and greet her older brother, Billy, who rode the short bus and always arrived sooner than her. "Off to Tasha's," she called to her mother, the necessary lie, and managed to slip out the back door unseen. Otherwise, her mother would want to know why her eyes were so red and swollen. *You're not coming down sick, are you?*

On Washington Lane, Mr. Powell was changing the oil on his car. He had straddled the wheels across the ditch in his front yard so that he'd have more room to slide under, and he pulled himself to a stand as Emily passed, mopping his face with a dirty shop cloth and adjusting his ball cap. He worked at the electric motor factory with Emily's father.

"Hidey," he said. He waved.

Emily lifted her hand and hurried past.

Her journey always took her to the end of Washington Lane, which her mother called "the dead-end street" with such formality that Emily had thought this was its name until she'd learned to read. Where the road stopped she had to navigate a small runner of space between two chain-link fences, the one to her right penning in the Calahans' mutt, a big, bad-tempered dog that looked like some kind of pit bull mix and always charged her as soon as he caught her scent. Today as always, the dog followed the length of the fence, snarling until his mouth foamed, docked tail pulled down tightly and whipping back and forth with a deceptive cheeriness. Emily hated the animal. But the dead-end street was her closest path to the woods, and circumventing the dog struck her as an important part of the ritual, as though she were required to prove her worth each time she passed from the world she knew into the world she'd created for herself.

And the reward, always, was the immediate transition from frenzy to quiet. The dog was only interested in Emily as long as he could see her, so when she reached the trail opening and disappeared behind a row of trees, the barking stopped almost at once, leaving in its stead a silence so near perfect that Emily's eardrums hummed. Here she paused and closed her eyes, marveling at the unnatural warmth of the October day. She was searching for words, for an image so bright and true that she could build a story upon it. This was how her private games of make-believe began.

The subject of much of her make-believe was Christopher Shelton. In the woods, it was he she imagined by her side, holding her hand, steadying her when she walked across logs or rocks; Christopher who listened to her talk about her day and told her not to worry about Leanna Burke or Maggie Stevenson, those popular girls who knew only how to tease and shun; Christopher who leaned in sometimes to kiss her, the touch so real that she could feel the texture of his lips (they had looked a bit chapped at school that day) and the cool burn of his peppermint gum. The Christopher she brought with her down Washington Lane and past the Calahans' dog was more real to her than the boy who had teased her today in Mrs. Mitchell's English class, and it never once occurred to her to amend her make-believe, to find another object for her interest.

Despite the unseasonable heat, it was late enough in the year that the air didn't hum with cicadas and birdsong, and the trees were in their last stages of shedding the summer's leaves, a few bright stragglers fluttering in the breeze like pennants. Emily followed her familiar path, the one she had spent years rutting, feeling freer and more herself with every step. In the summer, when the temperature sometimes broke 100 degrees and the humidity settled like a damp, napping beast in the valley of town, Emily found her gaze drawn close and downward, to the strange little universes tucked under rocks or in puddles of rainwater. She had started a rock collection, though the pickings here were limited: shale, limestone, sandstone, the occasional chunk of flint. Once she had found a jagged piece of drywall, puzzled over it, then dropped it back into the creek bed. She was more likely to happen across a rusty nail in these woods than an arrowhead.

But autumn was a good time for exploring, the poison ivy and sumac and the clouds of midges dead and disappeared, the way ahead clearer, the sun bright and reassuring overhead, confirming for Emily that she was headed consistently eastward. She knew that the woods were narrowest to the east and west, and she could keep moving in a straight line and eventually resurface on Grant Road, where they were finishing work on the new rich-person development. *Bankers and doctors and lawyers, oh my,* her dad would chant, tediously, every time they drove past it. She had walked to the construction site a few times to pick through the detritus and gotten hollered at during her last visit, when someone saw her using a cast-off two-by-four as a tightrope between cinder blocks. She wasn't used to being noticed by adults, much less chastised, and so she had run off and not been back since.

To the south, the land climbed steeply toward Harper Hill and the site of the new town water tower. She hadn't gone there much — that way was longer and harder, crossing an invisible threshold from where she felt justified roaming. But now she halted, conjuring Christopher in her mind's eye, imagining the brush of his shoulder against hers. "What do you think?" she said aloud. Her words vibrated thrillingly in the silence. There were days when the sound of her voice, real and irrefutable, killed the delicate illusion. But on others, like today, when her spirits were at their lowest, it could provoke in her an almost physical pleasure, a kind of drowsy vibration. Her eyes blurred, so that the treetops looked painted against the sky, and she spoke again, enjoying the sound even more: "Which way?"

"Let's climb," Christopher said. "Maybe we'll see the sunset."

She turned right, southward, and started at a brisk pace toward town, already feeling the grade pressing up against the soles of her sneakers. Her rambling had not made her athletic — she was big enough now that last autumn's pants pulled painfully at her hips and crotch, pushing up the soft flesh between her waistband and bra band so that it stood out from her body, tubelike, visible beneath anything but the loosest-fitting T-shirts. Christopher's presence at her side was so real to her that she registered embarrassment at the visibility of her exertion, and she couldn't help calling up the look on his face when he had stopped by her desk that day at school: the disgust, so evident in the curl of his lip, and the spat word, *creep,* said as though he were ridding his mouth of a foul taste. She felt the press of fresh tears (*crybaby*) and pushed herself harder, wheezing as the grade steepened. She was climbing now, grabbing the long, tangled grass for purchase, and the light overhead was slightly less golden than before, the sun starting to bleed into the horizon on her right.

Then she fell, turning her ankle as she went and throwing up her left arm in time to shield her face from a jutting branch. The breath was knocked out of her. Stunned, she flopped onto her back, getting her first good look at how far she'd ascended. She'd nearly reached the top of the hill, so the land rolled away beneath her steeply, offering her an unimpressive view of the woods, her woods, and the homes infringing on them both ways. In the distance, Highway 68-80 wound past the rock quarry toward Bowling Green. Much closer, only a hundred feet or so away, was the outer perimeter of Sheila Friend's property; a ragged barbwire fence penned in a few goats, small enough to be mistaken for dogs at a distance. She sent her mental fingers out for Christopher, as though she could catch the shirttail of the illusion she'd constructed, but he was gone, winked out. All that remained was an emotional residue, like a bad taste. A kind of sneering, hateful feeling, a whispered word: *creep.*

"I'm not a creep," she said aloud, lonelier than ever before.

She pushed herself up to a stand, putting most of her weight on her good right ankle, and tried shifting to her left. A twinge of pain arced up her leg from the instep of her foot, unpleasant but not excruciating. She could get home on it, and more easily if she cut across Sheila Friend's land to the road, where the rest of the going would be easier. She started hobbling toward Sheila's fence line, but as she approached it, she doubted herself. The barbwire snarled thick and furred with rust in three layers separated by only eight or nine inches, the highest strand about three feet off the ground. As she tested the spring of the barbwire under her palm, she could see two or three of Sheila's goats watching her with their black little eyes, waiting. Her parents had taken her and Billy to a petting zoo when they were small — Emily four or five, Billy eight or nine — and Billy had ruined the day, as he so often did, with one of his tantrums. "No, no, no," he'd started in a low, steady voice when the first goat came toward him and sniveled in his pockets for the treats Billy had bought from the dispenser outside. When the second goat approached, he had shrieked, then screamed. Emily remembered terror, quick movement; she remembered the swelling power of her own voice joining Billy's in affront. And then, dimly, the car ride home, and her mother's tired voice: *He's turned us all into prisoners.*

Emily backed away from the fence, embarrassed by her fear. The sun was going down, the goats silently assessing her, and her ankle yammered with increasing insistence. She needed to get home.

She hobbled downhill parallel to the fence line, moving quickly, feeling chilled as the sweat from her climb started to evaporate. At the corner of the fence she turned, prepared to follow it to the road, but no, that wouldn't work: the land sloped down steeply here into a small ravine, the barbwire in one spot grown around and even into the trunk of a maple tree. The tree itself was long dead, its roots exposed and dangling into the opening, leaving an ominous-looking hollow of darkness behind them. The gully was carved sharply into the hillside, narrowing as it ran down the grade, looking like the remnants of a streambed, though Emily couldn't determine where a stream would have originated. Certainly it was a spot where things fetched up after hard rains: limestone, looking like bone in the low light; rotten logs; tangles of limbs and the soft down of dead leaves — a hundred dark crevices where a snake or a rat might sleep, a hundred dark crevices where a twisted ankle could turn into a broken one. Right now, the girls in her grade would be talking to one another on

the phone about boys, and the boys themselves would be playing Super Mario Bros.
or a game of HORSE out in the driveway.
And Christopher — what would he be up
to? He lived in one of the Civil War–era
mansions up on North Main, his (it was
rumored) three full stories tall with a
ballroom, a library, and a separate servants'
quarters out back, now converted into a
guesthouse where Christopher was sometimes allowed to host overnights with his
friends. She could imagine him out in the
little building she'd only seen from the road
— it was gray stone, with a copper roof —
bent over a pool table or playing foosball
with his friends, a lock of dark hair trembling over his right eye as he twisted his
wrist or thrust his hips to the left or right.
She could —

But that's when she smelled it.

She stopped, peering into the gulch. The
smell didn't hit her instantaneously — she'd
been sensing it for a while now on some
subconscious level and attributing it to the
nearby goats — but her realization of it was
instant, wrenching her from the safety of
Christopher's guesthouse and plunging her
back into this twilight wood, where the
shadows were starting to stretch and run
into one another. When she inhaled again,

more deeply this time, and tried to determine what it was, or identify its source, her stomach trembled. She knew this smell precisely because she did not know it, because it was too alien, too removed from her safe, familiar world to be anything but what it was. It was death. She was smelling death.

Her breaths had gotten rapid and shallow. She put her hand on her chest and forced herself to exhale slowly.

It was an animal, almost surely. A possum, a skunk. Maybe even a dog. She had seen such death before: shapeless bags of fur drawing flies to the shoulder of the road. She had once watched a dog get run over by a car, run home to tell her mother, and returned to find only an oblong streak of blood on the faded cement. The smell was new; the idea of it wasn't.

She hesitated, suppressing a tremor of unease, and then leaned back a little, palm behind her for balance, and started working her way down into the trench. She picked her footing as carefully as she could on her bad ankle but slid on a decomposing fall of leaves, and so finally she sat and simply pushed herself downhill, aware that getting back out, scaling the other side, would be harder.

In the end she very nearly stepped on it. She was inching along the floor of the gully, wobbling from one loose-fitting stone to the next and clinging to the nimble trunks of trash trees for balance, when she slid, then overcorrected, planting her left foot against a stone and finally stopping her forward motion. She trembled with relief, her heart racing, and then she looked down at the stone she'd shifted and froze. The light was already dimmer than it had been when she first approached the crevasse — a light so low and gray that Emily could see better with her peripheral vision than she could straight on. What she thought she'd seen she didn't quite believe; she focused her eyes to the left of it, squinting, and then, still uncertain, she crouched down, her left ankle squealing now — and yes, there it was, pale and threaded with fine lines, dimpled in the center with dark soil: a human palm.

She jerked back. Then, slowly, she leaned in again. She grasped the neck of her shirt and pulled it up over her nose, but it did little good. The death smell was here, sitting atop that palm as though being held aloft, and she knew that she ought to turn away and go for help, but she also knew that she wouldn't be able to stand it later on if she didn't get a look while she had the chance. There was, along with the mounting horror within her, a curiosity, too, almost scientific: the same curiosity that drove her each day to flip the switch on that UV lamp, not because she didn't think it would kill the tadpoles, but because she wanted to know *how* it would kill them. With her left hand still pinching her shirt tight over her nose, Emily used the right to grab a nearby stick. She poked the shifted rock; it wobbled, then fell back into place. She poked again. At last she had to hold her breath and use both hands, moving the stick like a golf club, dislodging the rock and revealing beneath it the underside of a puffed wrist, pale but bruised looking, the hollows between the prominent tendons purple as grape Kool-Aid.

She felt her neck and face break out with heat, the sensation so shocking and instant that the roots of her hair tightened. There was, in this pocket of soil below her, a hand and a wrist — and the sight of both together, joined as they should be, discolored but still recognizable as human, set her off balance in a way that the palm alone could not. Before she knew what she was doing, she started knocking other stones and leaves away with the stick, and then she tossed it to the side and pulled the leaves and soil off barehanded, and when she finished half a minute later she'd unearthed the rest of the arm, the shoulders, and the head.

The body rested loosely in the soil, as if it had been hastily covered before the rocks were set in place. There was a wrinkled elbow, grimed and whorled like a thumbprint, and a couple of inches of exposed upper arm, the flesh so bloated and tight that it strained against the sleeve of a thin white T-shirt. The shoulders and back were also swollen, the weave of the T-shirt puckered, and Emily thought of the Halloween dummies she and her mother used to construct each year, before the time some bullies from Billy's school had set one on fire as a prank. They would close the sleeves of one of her father's old flannel shirts with rubber bands and stuff so many leaves into the torso that you could see the points spilling out between buttons. This body, too, was overstuffed, the back humped, the neck bulging against the razored edge of short hair. A man, Emily thought at first — the body seemed both fat and muscular, the hair too short to be feminine — but there was some detail throwing off the image of maleness, a clue that she was grasping with the edges of her mind but not yet consciously. She crouched down and put out a trembling hand, a pointed finger, and touched one of the fingers of the exposed hand. The nails, she'd noticed from above, seemed longish — had she once heard that they continued to grow in death? When she pushed, something gave and came free, and Emily didn't even jump this time; she just squinted in the low light, the vein in her neck pulsing with her excitement, and came as close to the object as she could stand to. It was a press-on nail, painted peach with an even white tip. It lay bright against the dark ground, like an opal.

She stared silently at the perfect, whole press-on nail, imagining the woman who would have glued it to her finger, a woman with a man's short hair and a man's plain T-shirt but the vanity to want her hands to look nice. She sat back and lifted her head to inhale, like a diver surfacing for air: a crescent of moon was etched against the night sky, so bright that when she blinked she saw its afterglow.

It was getting too dark to linger. She could make out between the trees the distant twinkle of lights from Sheila Friend's house. Higher in the sky, and brighter, was a single security lamp, marking the roadway. She started moving in that direction. Her body throbbed with an electric charge, energy that might have spilled into a sprint or a scream, but it was lodged in her, stuck, and she couldn't run on her bad ankle anyway. When she emerged at the road, she paused, nonplussed by the orderly procession of telephone lines, the reasonable graveled shoulder. Sheila Friend's mailbox was visible from here — it was tan, painted with bright cardinals and curling ivy. Emily stared at the birds, dazed. A full minute passed. Then, as if in a dream, she started hobbling downhill.

If Mr. Powell had still been out in his front yard as she passed it, she might have gone to him, reassured by his authority as a neighbor, as an acquaintance of her father's. But the car was pulled back into his driveway and the front door was shut tight. The light of a television flicked against the blinds of an otherwise dark corner room — probably a bedroom. Emily kept moving.

In another few moments she was home, the night around her now absolute. Her house, the small pale rectangle of it, was illuminated: she could see the pulse and flash of their own television in the living room, her mother's shadow in the kitchen window. Her father's Ford pickup truck was parked in the gravel drive.

She went in through the back door, and as soon as she entered the kitchen and its familiar smells — the low smoke of the wall heater; the stench of stewed cabbage, fleetingly reminiscent of the horror Emily had left back in the woods — her mother tossed her dishrag on the stovetop, took a shaky breath, and said, "Where on earth have you been?" She stopped, looking over Emily from head to toe, frowning. "You're filthy. What happened?" Her hands were on Emily's face now, warm against Emily's cold skin. She put a palm to Emily's forehead, considering, and then switched to the back of her hand, and then she was turning Emily in place as though she were trying to see if her shirt and pants fit right, the way she did when Emily tried on school clothes at Sears and Roebuck. "What happened?" Hands running up and down her legs, as though she were being checked by the police for a gun. "What happened?"

Emily's father appeared in the doorway, the lines around his mouth pinched in a way that didn't yet commit to anger or concern. "Where've you been? Kelly, what's wrong with her?"

Emily said, "I tripped and twisted my ankle." It was out of her mouth before she realized she was going to say it. She hadn't decided on that walk home not to mention the body — it hadn't occurred to her that she could opt not to — but now she was being led to a kitchen chair and her father was rolling up her pant leg to examine the ankle ("It's a little swollen, but it don't look broke to me," he was saying, and her mother, breathlessly, "Are you sure?"), and her stomach was growling a little at the sight of a bag of Doritos, unopened, on the table to her left. She hadn't screamed. She hadn't sounded an alarm. She pulled the sack of chips closer and tweezed the top between her fingers, pulling, releasing the putrid-pleasant scent of corn and cheese into her face as her father quizzed her on where, and why, and how, and *What the heck are you thinking, rambling around by yourself at night?* Her mother brought her a Coca-Cola, opened, and Emily did what she loved: she put a chip into her mouth and crunched, and while the crumbs were still circling inside her mouth, getting milled by her teeth and tongue, she chased them with a long draft of the soda, the sweet and bubbles washing it all down the back of her throat. She wiped her right hand, the one she'd used to touch that press-on nail, absent-mindedly on the thigh of her jeans, then reached into the bag for another chip.

She didn't know how to begin to say what she knew, to explain what she had seen. Already her memory of the body felt unreal, like something she could not trust, and she put another chip on her tongue, considering.

"We should take her to the doctor tomorrow," her mother was saying.

"I'd have to use my sick leave. Or else get docked a point."

"I'm fine," Emily said. "I don't want to go to the doctor."

Billy came into the kitchen, arms crossed with paternal gruffness. "You were late," he said. "Dinner is at five. Mom was going to make me eat my dinner late."

Emily glared at him. Billy was tall and pear-shaped, with a doughy stomach and broad, almost womanly hips. His eyes were large and moist, with thick, long lashes, and his full lips were raw with painful-looking cracks, because he had a nervous habit of chewing, then pulling, the chapped skin. His sweetness, his simple good nature, was held in check by a strong sense of entitlement, which their parents generally obliged, and so Emily had long ago fallen into a habit of feeling irritated by him, then guilty for the irritation. She did not realize how alike they were.

"He was anxious for you," her mother said apologetically. "He just wants things to be normal."

"Normal," Emily echoed.

"Yeah, normal," Billy said with the bratty authority of a second grader.

Her parents drifted back to their familiar places — her mother to the stove, her father to the living room, where he could watch TV — and Emily washed down another chip with a swallow of cola. Had she seen what she thought she saw? Maybe she should go back tomorrow, make sure. She was afraid — but there was also curiosity. Even possessiveness. If she told, she wouldn't be able to have another look at the body, and she realized that she wanted to. Just once more. Just to make sure.

CHAPTER TWO

1.

Susanna Mitchell was late again picking up her daughter from the KiddieKare. *There aren't enough hours in the day;* this is what she'd say to her sister whenever they both managed to carve out an hour of time for each other, on the phone or over thin, greasy cheeseburgers at the K-Grill. A cliché, but Susanna hadn't happened upon a truer way of putting it.

It was a quarter past five. Stuck at her third red light in a row, she slapped the steering wheel of her car a few times with the meaty heel of her palm, then back-handed tears from her eyes with a mascara-stained knuckle. "Damn it," she whispered. Then, because there was no one around to hear her: "Fuck."

Hound's Liquors was up ahead, just before the turn to the day care and her daughter, and Susanna popped her turn signal to the right. She was already late: in for a penny, in for a pound. It was Friday, and normally her husband, Dale, would give the marching band the night off from practice, or they'd be playing the halftime show at the football game, but tomorrow was state quarterfinals, and Susanna knew from experience that he'd be working them to exhaustion, letting them out no earlier than nine or ten o'clock tonight when the first parents started making threatening noises to pull their children off the field by force. She and Abby would be alone this evening, and Abby would probably be tired — it had been unusually warm for late October, in the midsixties, and she would have been out on the playground most of the day — so maybe Susanna could have some wine and a slow bath and a good cry without worrying about answering to anybody. Was that too much to ask?

She passed her gaze over the bright bottles, the fancy fruit-infused liqueurs with French and Italian names, the whiskeys that glowed amber with backlighting. Finally she purchased her usual seven-dollar bottle of pinot grigio, which was already chilled in the front cooler. Dale barely tolerated her wine drinking and groused on the rare occasions she brought liquor into the house.

Did she want to end up like her father? Like her no-account sister?

"Are you ready for the weekend?" the clerk asked, smiling as he punched the price into the cash register. He was a man Susanna knew by reputation, an Indian who owned both Hound's and the town's two newest hotels, a Comfort Inn and a Best Western, and he was probably a millionaire, or close. But he was always here, always dressed in a polo shirt and loose-fitting khakis that had the ragged look of a Goodwill purchase. His one show of wealth was a bracelet of near-orange gold, dense and glittery against the brown skin of his forearm.

"As I'll ever be," Susanna said tiredly. She always felt like a single mother during band season; she couldn't remember the last time she'd been able to go for a long walk, or out shopping with a friend, or even to bed early with a good book. Abby wanted not just company but constant attention, and Susanna, who'd had an uneasy childhood, was loath to deny her.

The clerk handed her the brown bag he'd packed. "Drive safely," he told her.

Back in the car she sat, engine idling, and looked at the bottle for a moment, thinking about her sister, Ronnie. They rarely drank together, she and Ronnie — Ronnie, like their father had, drank to get wasted and loud, and Susanna drank to get sedated. She wished that they could drink together tonight, though. She imagined it for a moment: Abby tucked in, out cold, and she and Ronnie downing vodka tonics and watching a movie that they both liked and having some laughs before falling asleep in their armchairs. Susanna could vent about work, and Ronnie could say something like, "Forget that little brat, and forget that rich bitch with the stick up her ass. She's a bored housewife with nothing better to do than get in your face," and Susanna would, temporarily at least, believe her. Susanna believed Ronnie about these things better than she did Dale. She knew that Ronnie wouldn't bullshit her.

Dale didn't like Ronnie. He didn't like her drinking or her swearing or the way she dressed — reasons enough, he said, to keep her away from Abby. Dale could always tell when Ronnie had come over to the house, because Ronnie couldn't go an hour without a smoke and Susanna wasn't going to make her sister sit outside every time she had one. He'd walk through the door, sniff, and frown. He'd check the trash can for ashes, the sink for a lipstick-stained glass, making a big show to prove a point, as though he were looking for the signs of a lover instead of his own sister-in-law.

It had been — Susanna racked her brain and did the math, putting her car into gear — about two weeks since she'd heard from Ronnie. Could that be right? She'd called Susanna on a Thursday night, when she knew Dale would be at band practice, and yes, it must have been two weeks (and a day) because Susanna had been complaining about having to do chaperon's duty at the high school's homecoming dance. "Why should middle school faculty get roped into that?" she'd asked. "I don't see high school faculty coming down here to run the concession stands at our football games." Grousing to Dale never did her any good. Dale taught music and band at both schools and thought that he had insights into the administrative realities that Susanna couldn't grasp.

But in fact, she was late picking up Abby because of one of those "administrative realities." Christopher Shelton's mother had wandered in after school let out, demanding to know why her son had been given detention. Principal Wally Burton, in typical Wally Burton fashion, had immediately ushered the parent to Susanna's classroom — God forbid he should have to put in an extra fifteen minutes after final bell — and left her in the doorway, smiling his slippery smile and saying, "Mrs. Mitchell will explain everything, don't you worry, ma'am," before disappearing.

Susanna had stood and extended a hand, already wary. She usually ran into two kinds of parents at Roma Middle School: the very poor and the very well-to-do. The poor parents Susanna could manage; they reminded her of her own folks, or at least her mother. The woman in Susanna's classroom today was one of the well-to-do parents, and not just manager-at-the-factory money, either, which was the kind of slightly above-average salary that could sometimes pass for wealth in Roma. Real money. *Executive* factory money. Unlike the lawyers' wives or the doctors' wives in town, this woman made no special effort to garishly display her wealth. No big rocks, except the stunner on her left-hand ring finger; no thick cloud of pricey perfume. She was dressed in simple clothes — a black blouse and slacks and riding boots, with a cropped red sweater as accent — and these items, though not ostentatious, struck Susanna as well cut, as suited to the woman's figure in a way that Susanna, armed with this same woman's credit card, could never have been able to approximate. The woman's dark blond hair, too, was very well cut, worn in a slightly angled bob — not so angled that it seemed unfeminine — and tucked behind an equally well-shaped ear.

"It's nice to meet you, ma'am," Susanna had said, all at once certain that the woman would spurn her extended hand. But Christopher's mother shook it firmly, smiling, so Susanna had cleared her throat a little and smoothed her wrinkled paisley skirt and motioned to a pair of school desks. "Would you like to sit down?"

"Thank you," the woman said, somehow managing to slide elegantly into one of the desks. Her voice fit the rest of her: sophisticated, pleasant, no trace of an accent. "Mr. Burton told me that you'd be the person who could explain why my son got detention today over some kind of a writing exercise."

Susanna, still smarting over this morning's humiliation, took a deep breath. Christopher — she had to admit this to herself — was a very, very bright boy, probably categorically "gifted." One of the best in his grade, and one of the best to pass through Susanna's classroom, too. His paper on *Bridge to Terabithia* had been a marvel, as well constructed and elegant as his mother's hairdo, and he could be earnest and insightful in class discussions. But he was also arrogant, dismissive of any activity he deemed beneath him, and this arrogance had been revealing itself lately in more frequent acts of defiance, today's by far the worst.

"Mrs. —" Susanna hesitated. "Shelton?"

"Yes. Nita Shelton."

"Mrs. Shelton, Christopher volunteered to read out loud a response he had written to a sample test question on John Knowles's *A Separate Peace*. It was a joke. A very offensive joke, in my opinion. He flat-out defied the assignment and me."

"Do you have a copy of it?"

"I certainly do," Susanna said, rising to retrieve it from a stack of papers on her desk. Her hands were shaking, and she felt a blush — that stupid goddamn blush, bane of her teaching career — creep across her cheeks and down her neck. She laid the paper down quickly in front of Nita Shelton, before its quivering could reveal her nervousness.

Mrs. Shelton scanned the paragraph with pursed lips.

"I think you see the problem," Susanna said. "If I'm going to be frank here, I'd say that it's tantamount to an act of aggression, and the punishment would have been greater than detention if I'd had my way. As it is, he'll get a zero for the assignment."

"Well," Mrs. Shelton said, "this is certainly very silly. I'm sorry to hear that he read it out loud. But I know Christopher well enough to understand what he's doing."

"And what's that?"

"He's countering absurdity with absurdity," she said. "Christopher gave you an answer that equaled the intelligence of the question."

"I'm sorry," Susanna said, face so warm now that she was nearly light-headed, "to hear that you'd advocate your son's disrespect of a teacher. Christopher is quite smart, but he doesn't have the right or the ability to question the intelligence of the question. It's his job to fulfill the assignment."

"These open-response questions," Mrs. Shelton said. "This is some kind of standardized testing thing?"

"That's right. The superintendent is trying to raise spring scores by two percentage points so that we can avoid state-imposed penalties, such as funding audits. I've been directed to devote one class period a week between now and January to test-taking strategies, specifically open-response questions. That prompt" — she pointed to the sheet Mrs. Shelton had placed on the desktop — "was my attempt to make the prep session relevant to our current course content."

"You're telling me," Mrs. Shelton said, "that my son is losing an hour of regular class time every week to these test-training sessions?"

"Yes," Susanna said tiredly. *Do you think I like this?* she wanted to shout into that smug face, so like the son's. *That this is what I went to college for? That I'd do it if I didn't have the administration's foot on my neck?*

Mrs. Shelton tilted her head prettily, scanning the sheet of paper again. "There's something I still don't understand. Can you explain to me how my son can score A's on each of the papers and reading quizzes and projects you assign but still get an 89 for his average in English?"

There it was. The bottom line. Christopher Shelton had brought a B home to Mother, and Mother was not pleased. "Christopher scored a B in English because he's performing far below average on his open-response questions," Susanna said. "The questions account for fifteen percent of his total grade for the class."

"I want you to imagine for a moment how this sounds from my perspective," Mrs.

45

Shelton said. "It sounds like you and your colleagues are in the business these days of protecting yourselves, and children like mine are paying the price. I'm not worried about the fact that my son made a B. But you've shaken his confidence. He tells me that he doesn't know the terms for getting an A in your course."

Susanna's heart was beating so quickly now that her eye seemed to be twitching along in time. "Your son knows fully well what he has to do to get an A in my class," she said. "And he chooses not to do it. If you reinforce for Christopher at home that he should take these open-response questions as seriously as his other assignments, I don't doubt that he can raise his grade to an A by the time report cards go out."

"I plan to do no such thing," Mrs. Shelton said. Close up, her face revealed the felt-like texture of translucent powder. Susanna could see the path of a delicate blue vein curving between her ear and the corner of her mouth, making her jaw look hinged-on. "It's the role of some teachers to reinforce the status quo among their students. It's the easier path, and I don't hold that against you. You're trying to teach eighty or ninety students at a time, but I'm raising one, and the way I see it, my role as a parent is to tell him to resist those things in the world that seem foolish or beneath him. These open-response questions are beneath him."

"I can see you're used to a certain level of privilege," Susanna said, a little voice in the back of her brain screeching, *Shut up! Shut up!* even as her anger made her articulate, "but this is a public school system, and nothing that I assign is beneath any of these students. That includes Christopher."

Mrs. Shelton pursed her lips. "You and I agree on one point. Christopher is no different than his peers. He's been raised to understand that. These open-response questions are beneath every boy and girl you force them upon, and the sad part is that most of the other children's parents won't have the nerve or the ability to tell you as much."

Susanna felt tears threaten and swallowed them back. This was, she'd think later, a version of the arguments she'd had when *she* had been in eighth grade with the richer and prettier and more popular girls in school. She felt the same crippling insecurity, the same despair, and the hardest thing was realizing that nothing much changed between the ages of thirteen and twenty-eight. "My hands are tied," she managed to say. "If I don't assign a grade to the open-response questions, there isn't any student accountability."

"Then perhaps my son has more integrity than you do," Mrs. Shelton said pleasantly. She paused, waiting to see if Susanna would attempt a rebuttal, but Susanna had nothing.

"Okay, then," Mrs. Shelton murmured, and she walked out.

2.

As Susanna drove the last leg between Hound's and the day care, she found that her passing concern about Ronnie had solidified into actual anxiety. Perhaps the stress of the day had made her more on edge than usual. Perhaps some instinct had kicked in. She and Ronnie weren't close the way a lot of sisters she knew were — their history was too fraught, their personalities too different — but every now and then they ended up on the same wavelength. Susanna would fight with Dale, and Ronnie would call, a welcome interruption. Once they'd run into each other at the grocery, glanced at each other's shopping carts, and laughed to discover that they'd both picked up Cheerios, Colonial bread, orange juice (extra pulp), and Neapolitan ice cream, which had been their father's favorite.

So there was a bond, if you want to call it that, however tenuous. But there was also Ronnie's history of personal screwups, colorful enough that Susanna would have been a fool not to feel a twinge of worry at her sister's recent silence. There was the time when Ronnie drank a fifth of Wild Turkey and woke up in the hospital with alcohol poisoning, and the day, five or so years ago, when Ronnie had mouthed off to a guy in a bar and gotten her nose broken. The earliest memory of this kind still frightened Susanna; she had never been able to shake it. She was twelve, Ronnie sixteen, and Ronnie was climbing into a conversion van with four or five guys — men, really — and Susanna could see that they were all drinking and smoking, and there were no other girls around, not one, and Ronnie was trying to get Susanna to come with them. *Are you a dyke?* she'd taunted, the look on her face a mixture of meanness and desperation that Susanna hadn't understood. The men had laughed. Susanna had backed away. In those days she'd had to put energy, real effort, into rebuffing her sister's attempts to corrupt her. She'd spent her adolescence hating and fearing Ronnie and her young adulthood forgiving her and worrying about her, and Ronnie, to her credit, had tried in the last few years to be a better sister. She'd given Abby a $500 savings bond on each of her birthdays and she'd never complained about the fact that Susanna didn't trust her to babysit or even take Abby alone for an ice cream or hamburger at the Dairy Dip down the street. Ronnie knew all the things she'd done, the reputation she'd earned, and she didn't feign self-righteousness. She was a realist.

At the KiddieKare, Susanna opened the door to see her daughter already launching herself across the room in excitement to greet her, midair before Susanna could get her arms outstretched, and then the child was clinging like a monkey to her middle, all clutching legs and arms, smelling of salty sweat and orange-scented tearless shampoo. Susanna kissed her neck, which was warm and a little sticky, then her forehead. There was a spider painted on her plump pale cheek; it was already threaded with cracks.

"Mama-mama-mama," she said, and Susanna said back, "Abby-Abby-Abby," because that was their routine. Susanna hugged her again, feeling her stomach flutter in the way it had when she'd first started falling for Dale. Abby was her sweetheart now, her one true love, and that excitement hadn't waned in the four years that the two of them had spent getting to know each other, as hard as mothering could sometimes be for Susanna. She'd taken to it like she'd taken to cooking: with intelligence and determination but no confidence, consulting books and her own mother's counsel the way she checked, every time she made a white sauce for macaroni and cheese, to make sure that the recipe called for two tablespoons of flour and not three. She wasn't the kind of woman who could throw three or four ingredients into a pot, willy-nilly, and create a meal. She wasn't the kind of woman who could give discipline or life instruction or even an allowance, willy-nilly, and create a daughter.

Cindy's smile was polite but strained. "Mrs. Mitchell" — she pronounced "Mrs." the way Susanna's mother did, emphasizing the "r," *mizz-rizz* — "we're supposed to shut up here by five on Fridays."

"I'm so sorry," Susanna said, emptying her wallet of its contents. She handed the bills, a ten and a five, to the young woman, who stared at them for a moment before folding them into thirds and slipping the wad into the watch pocket on her light-washed blue jeans. "I was held up at school."

"If you could just get here by five from now on," Cindy repeated, her expression flat, "we'd appreciate it."

"Can do," Susanna said. She took Abby by the hand and left.

At home, Abby was up another four and a half hours, until the Nashville news came on. Susanna grilled her a cheese sandwich with Velveeta, Abby's preference, and ketchup — a combination that still made Susanna nauseous, even as she served this feast to her child for the hundredth or more time — then she bathed her, taking care not to rinse off the spider face-painting, which Abby was on the verge of getting screechy about. "Don't clean it," she'd whined, lip fat, and so Susanna had worked around the grubby little black spot with her washrag-sheaved forefinger, getting Abby behind her ears and rubbing at the dirt ring on her neck until she whimpered dramatically, falsely, that Susanna was hurting her. Then, freshly done up in her Flintstones footed pajamas, an artifact from Susanna's own toddler-hood, Abby requested her mother's assistance on a handful of projects: reading *Lottie's Halloween Adventure* again before it was due back at the library, Susanna prevailed upon to make distinctions between the high-pitched voice of Lottie, girl investi-gator, and Max, her talking cocker spaniel; and then, after that fifteen minutes had been successfully killed, playing Duplo blocks in front of the television while Susanna watched a rerun of *Family Matters*. By the time Abby passed out, spread-eagle, in front of the television, and the dishwasher was unloaded, loaded again with the plates and glasses that had accumulated over the last few days, and set to run, Susanna was tired enough to just turn in and give up — but she'd promised herself the wine and the bath, and she hadn't swallowed down more than the messy sandwich rinds, those that hadn't touched the pool of ketchup, of her daughter's grilled cheese sandwich. She thought for a second and decided that yes, she was probably hungry. It had been a long time since her lunch of microwave lasagna.

She'd downed half a glass of her cheap wine, which was teeth-rattlingly cold and yet still sour, and was investigating a carton of ice cream, which was furred with freezer burn, when she thought about Ronnie again. It was after ten on a Friday, so calling was silly, but Susanna resolved to try her anyway.

She got the machine, as she'd known she would. "Ronnie, it's Sister," she said. That's how Ronnie knew her: Sister. That had been what Susanna's father always called her, solidifying her place as the younger and secondary of his children, but Susanna had never minded. "I realized tonight that we haven't talked in a while, so I thought I'd check in. Will you call me back?" She glanced at the clock above the microwave: ten thirty. Dale would be home soon, and he'd have to go to sleep immediately if he wanted even a few hours before embarking on his big day tomorrow. The students were due at the band room by six A.M., and Dale would get there by no later than five thirty to warm up the school buses and triple-check the equipment list. Nonetheless, she finished the message by saying, "You can call me when you get back tonight, no matter how late. Or early. Love you, bye."

This done, she topped off her glass of wine. It really was a glass, a regular drinking glass, because when she'd married at twenty-two she'd seen no reason to register for any stemware but water goblets — what was she, a dignitary? Queen of England? But, sour or not, the wine was doing its work now, and she went into the living room and curled up, feet tucked under her hip to warm them, in Dale's recliner. Abby's blocks and dolls were still, were eternally, scattered across the swath of pilled carpet in front of the TV. The TV was eternally on.

Susanna had met Dale at Murray State

University, at band camp the summer before her freshman year of college — his senior year — and they were a couple by the time the week was out. He was her first real boyfriend. Her first kiss.

Now, almost ten years later, she looked around Dale's living room. *Their* living room, she amended, swallowing more wine. This was still Dale's house more than hers; he'd purchased it, with help from his parents, the year he got the job at RHS. The only newish piece of furniture was the couch. Dale had allowed her to pick it out as a wedding present, and her twenty-two-year-old self had fixated on the kind of sofa her mother would have chosen: a floral brocade, overstuffed, in greens and reds and threaded with metallic gold. Hideous. She hated it now. The TV, a thirty-two-inch that perpetually transmitted through a layer of dust, was stored in a pressboard entertainment unit from Wal-Mart. The coffee table and end tables, hand-me-downs from Dale's parents, were varnished a dark and sludgy color, wet looking, like Karo syrup, and the glass tops were always smudged with Abby's fingerprints and rings of condensation. The only artwork on the wall was a framed print of a barn and a silo, the kind of thing you could find at a garage sale for seventy-five cents. Susanna didn't know where it came from, what had drawn Dale to it. She'd never thought to ask. It was as much an institution in this house as the grand-father clock that had been his granny's, ancient and unmoving, significant merely because it, like most everything else here, predated her.

The lock turned and Dale entered, already sliding out of his "RHS Marching Tigers" windbreaker. He squinted at her, furrowing his brow at her glass of wine, then hung his jacket in the coat closet.

"And hello to you," Susanna said lightly.

"Wild night at the Mitchell house." He crossed the room and kissed the top of her head. "Does this mean I might get laid?" He squeezed — honked — her right breast. It was his way of trying to make fun of himself.

Susanna took another swallow. "Well heck, if you keep sweet-talking me like that, who knows."

"I'm beat, baby," he said. "Set the alarm, will you?"

"For five?"

"Yeah."

She went to the bedroom to set the digital alarm clock while Dale looked in on Abby. She turned down the bedspread and top sheet, then removed the sham-covered pillows that she tried to keep nice, free of coarse hairs and drool stains. In a few moments she could hear him in the bathroom urinating — he always left the door wide open — and then he entered their bedroom stripped down to his boxers. He was a man of good but not exceptional height, and lean — a leanness that had seemed athletic nine years ago, when Dale was still the hotshot new teacher straight out of college, but now registered as . . . well, not as delicacy, exactly, but as cerebral and prematurely middle-aged, the figure of a man who could be coerced into no greater physical activity than the occasional brisk walk around the subdivision. But he had a good, thick head of dark brown hair, and his blue eyes, veiled by fashionable wire lenses, were wide-set and strikingly lashed. He was still attractive to Susanna. She registered this fact some days the way she always had, as a sensation of pleasure in her middle, but more often as an act of intellect — when she'd see a man, a man in worn jeans instead of pressed khakis, maybe, or a man who could sit in a restaurant and laugh loudly and openly, the way Dale never would, and she'd think, *Perhaps it would have been him.* And then, because she needed such touches with reality, she'd imagine the inevitable trajectory from excitement and thrill to predictability, the heartfelt whispers of love becoming empty, automatic recitations as they parted for work in the mornings, and she'd think, *Dale looks as good as he does,* and most days that sufficed.

They slid under the covers next to one another, and Susanna sidled into the space between Dale's side and his arm, letting him pull her close. She could hear, from the right side of Dale's chest, the distant echo of his heartbeat.

"Don't guess you'd want to go with us tomorrow," Dale said.

Susanna tried to make a face that suggested she was entertaining the notion. She'd gone to so many band competitions now that she could no longer distinguish the memory of one from another, and making the haul with Abby — rousing her at five A.M. and dressing her for the cold bus, trying to keep her entertained on the two-hour drive to Owensboro, appeasing her at the football field with nachos and hot dogs only to throw away most of the food uneaten, the endless ride back, the inopportune demands for bathroom breaks — would be a nightmare. Dale didn't want to deal with that either, she knew, but he always felt obligated to make the offer. To remind her that she was wanted.

"Guess not," she said. "I'm pretty wiped out."

"Tell me about it." He adjusted. "I got into it tonight with a parent. Corey Kirchner's dad. Goddamn redneck. He started in about how he couldn't arrange his whole life around picking his boy up and dropping him off at band practice, went on and on about how he has to work midnights at the plant and this and that. And you know me, Suze, I'm sympathetic. I really am. But nobody's making Corey take band, and I told this guy as much."

"You don't want him pulling Corey out of band, though."

"Well, no," Dale said, his voice going up an octave the way it always did when he was defensive. "He's a good drummer. He's a good kid. But I can't teach and chauffeur and fund-raise and do everything else these people want from me. The kids have got to practice. There isn't any getting around that."

He went on that way for another few minutes, and Susanna, listening, felt herself reliving her discussion with Nita Shelton, its insult and her own quiet fury, and she thought about sharing this incident with

Dale, as a way of supporting him, but she found that she couldn't bring herself to talk about it. Instead, she said, "I realized today that I haven't heard from Ronnie in two weeks," and she must have interrupted a point Dale was making, because he looked confused, then irritated.

"What?" he said. "You what?"

"Ronnie," she said. "I haven't heard from her in two weeks. I tried calling her tonight and she wasn't there."

He adjusted again, this time pulling his arm out from under Susanna's neck so that she had to lean back on her own pillow. He made an exaggerated display of flexing his bicep, as if in explanation. "Well, don't take this the wrong way," he said. "But that doesn't seem all that unusual to me."

"It is, though," Susanna said. "She usually checks in at least once or twice a week. I've just been so busy lately that I hadn't noticed."

Dale rolled to his side, placing his back to her, and pulled the bedspread up around his shoulders. He yawned. "I'm sure she's fine," he said. "Probably off shacking up with some loser. She'll be back in no time, asking for money."

"She's never asked me for money."

"She'll show," he said.

Susanna turned off her lamp and rolled over, too, wanting to place the cold bottoms of her feet against Dale's calves but reluctant to favor him with the intimacy. She both hoped Dale was right and resented him for being flippant; she thought, drifting toward an uneasy sleep and bracing herself for the ring of the phone, that she'd suffer a thousand embarrassments at the hands of Nita Shelton if Ronnie would show up at her door tomorrow morning, hungover and hoping for a free meal. She slept through Dale's alarm and his departure. The phone never rang.

CHAPTER THREE

1.

The next morning, as Abby lay on her belly in front of the TV watching *Garfield* and Susanna blew the steam off of her second cup of coffee, Susanna decided: she would go by Ronnie's today, take a look around. She'd have to bring Abby, and Dale wouldn't like that, but Dale be damned. Ronnie was her sister. Susanna didn't need her husband's permission to do right by her.

Ronnie lived across town, in a rental house near the sewing factory where she worked. It was, like so many neighborhoods in Roma, neither a bad place nor a nice place. On a street filled with working-class families and retirees, Ronnie herself was probably the most unsavory element. This was a street where the old women spent their springs coaxing lilies and rosebushes, hydrangeas and peonies, into short bursts of colorful glory. With the maples fully green and the dogwoods raining petals into a satin snow on the trimmed grass, a passerby might be charmed, even delighted. By October, though, the street had taken on a shabbier, more somber look. Hanging baskets of ferns no longer distracted from the faded wood siding on the old widows' houses. Bird feeders dangled empty, the hydrangeas shriveled back into skeletal gray spikes, and the little iron benches and chairs that had seemed so charming flocked with greenery sat useless on the small lawns, artifacts from a more abundant time.

Ronnie's house was a 1940s shotgun, its siding not merely faded but almost stripped, the gravel driveway so worn down that weeds were springing up in the hollow spot between tire tracks. The car — a maroon '89 Camaro, Ronnie's baby — was parked in the drive, and Susanna's stomach flip-flopped instantly with relief and annoyance. Ronnie must have pulled an all-nighter, or something close to one. And Susanna would bet good money that she was still asleep inside, probably sprawled atop her bed-clothes in the blouse and jeans she'd worn to the bars, snoring and mumbling and drooling on her pillow. Or perhaps there was a man beside her. In any case, it wouldn't be a scene Susanna could expose her daughter to in good conscience.

Yet she pulled her car, which she'd let idle on the street in front of the house, into the drive behind the Camaro and shut off the engine.

"We're going to see Aunt Ronnie?" Abby said in that strange little voice she got sometimes, the one of almost adult formality.

"I don't know," Susanna said. "What do you think?"

Abby shrugged, again with a kind of ironic exasperation that seemed much older than she was. "We're here, aren't we?" she said, and Susanna laughed out loud, running a thumb along her daughter's satin cheek.

"You're right." She pulled the keys from the ignition and stuffed them in her purse. "You sit here, though. I need to make sure Aunt Ronnie's up for company."

"Okay."

"You'll hold tight?"

Abby nodded.

Susanna crossed the yard to the front porch — there wasn't a sidewalk — and adjusted her purse strap on her shoulder. At the door she stopped, swallowed, and rapped as loudly as she could, using the side of her hand instead of her knuckles and bracing herself for the reappearance of Old

Ronnie, the Ronnie who'd tried to coax twelve-year-old Susanna into a van with a bunch of older guys, the sister who sometimes emerged when Ronnie was hungover or working overtime at the factory or having money troubles. *Stop the goddamn knocking!* that Ronnie would say. *Can't a woman get some fucking sleep?*

Susanna waited. It was a chilly morning, the first that really smelled like the promise of winter. Wearing only her belted cardigan, she shivered and pounded on the door again. "Ronnie!" she said. "Open up. I've got Abby out here. We want to see you."

A full minute passed — Susanna counted it on her wristwatch — and nothing. She looked back at her car and waved at Abby, who was watching all of this banging and shouting with interest. Abby waved back.

There was a window on the front porch to the right of the door, and Susanna cupped her hands and peered inside. Through the thin cotton sheers she could make out only shapes and shadows: the round hump of the sofa, the triangle of a lampshade, the furnishings of a home all simplified to their basic forms. There was a light on in the kitchen — the bedroom lay beyond it — but no movement. The light bothered her. The house seemed dormant, disused, and the light in the kitchen reinforced Susanna's vague but growing unease instead of lessening it.

She knew that Ronnie kept a spare key hidden under a rock beside the porch, so she retrieved it and unlocked the door but stopped shy of turning the knob. She was afraid, she realized. And the fear was irrational, of course, but it was real, just as it had been all of the times when she had to check on her sleeping daughter to make sure she was breathing or when Dale was late getting home and her mind went to *car accident* before any of the logical explanations took hold. But fears weren't always groundless, and Susanna knew that, too. She had dreamed about her father's death the night before her mother called to confirm it — but they hadn't been speaking then, she and her father, and so she'd dismissed the dream as rubbish. "He's dead to me anyway," she'd told Dale flippantly. She had been twenty-three years old.

Now she turned the knob and rushed inside all at once. "Ronnie!" she yelled again, getting ready to stride over to the bedroom door and fling it open, as though by being loud, by barreling pell-mell into her sister's silent house, she could will Ronnie into getting up and yelling back at her. Because Susanna was already half of the way to certain that she was going to find Ronnie dead or comatose. Maybe it was alcohol poisoning again. Maybe she'd OD'd. Susanna was willfully ignorant about her sister's drug use, thought that Ronnie just smoked pot occasionally but couldn't be sure.

She and Ronnie got by as much through what they suppressed as what they shared. Ronnie resented Susanna when she spoke like a schoolteacher, when she brought up politics or mentioned a book. Ronnie would get stubborn and obtuse; she'd pretend to understand less than Susanna suspected she did. In turn, Susanna knew that the Ronnie she saw these days was simplified and sanitized, her recklessness and darkness — the mean streak, the bouts of depression — tamped down. Maybe Ronnie only did smoke pot. Or maybe she did coke or pills as she had in the old days. Susanna didn't want to know, and Ronnie accommodated her by staying mum about it.

"Ronnie," Susanna said now, the word more a sigh than a call. Her voice fell flat, her greeting answered not by a sister but by a smell: powerful, nauseating, enough of a contrast to the cold, slightly smoky air outside that Susanna instantly felt ill. The house seemed shuttered and abandoned. The blinds were drawn, all the lights off except the one in the kitchen. The smell was a combination of mustiness and sweet rot, and before Susanna could make the leap from worry to panic she saw on the kitchen table the remains of a meal. She got closer, grimacing, and leaned over for a better look. There were white plastic bags, plastic forks and napkins wrapped in cellophane, red plaid paper baskets with grease dotting the sides. It looked — she turned away, gagged a little, then turned back — like chicken livers and gizzards, some remnant potato wedges, two Styrofoam cups half-full of coleslaw. The table was also strewn with an ashtray, a few cigarettes ground into corkscrews, and empty Miller High Life bottles, half a dozen of them. Ronnie's favorite denim jacket, the one with the tacky pattern of brass studs on the back, was draped over the back of one of the chairs.

Two cups of coleslaw, two baskets, two pouches for potato wedges. Six beers. Susanna looked up at the bedroom door. Her stomach did a lazy somersault.

She was sweating, despite the chill. And that, how about *that*: Why was it so cold in here? Why wouldn't the heat be on? She went to the bedroom door, thought about

68

knocking again, knew that doing so would be futile. So she grasped the knob and pushed into her sister's bedroom, and she was so convinced of what she'd find that the heap of pillows and blankets on the bed at first looked to her like a body, and she nearly screamed. But the illusion lasted only a second. The room was empty, the bed unmade but also unoccupied. Again, Susanna was struck by the sense of abandonment, of dormancy, but she'd have taken any of those oddities, those unknowns, over the sight of her sister lying glassy-eyed in a pool of vomit. That was, she admitted to herself, what she'd expected.

So it wasn't the worst thing. But what was it?

She looked around the bedroom, rolling her feet so that they wouldn't sound on the hardwood floor, hating the empty echo. Unmade bed, sheets in need of a wash. No surprise there. Drawer on the dresser half-open, peach-colored T-shirt hanging down like a flap of skin. Shades drawn. Lights off. She snapped on the bedside lamp and looked at the items on Ronnie's nightstand: face cream, alarm clock, a pot of lip balm. A book.

A book? She picked it up and felt her sinuses ache with the sudden press of tears.

It was *A Separate Peace*. A Wal-Mart receipt was tucked in between chapters 11 and 12. Ronnie had almost finished it.

There was one more item on the table: Ronnie's birth control pills. Susanna opened the compact and looked at the rows of depressed bubbles. The first two weeks were emptied, Sunday through Saturday. Saturday was the last day. Today was Saturday. Ronnie must have been home today to take her pill. Right?

Or else she'd taken it a week ago. Or two.

Susanna returned to the kitchen, checked the fridge: condiments; a paper Chinese food container, the rice inside shriveled to a hard, gray crust; a half-empty two-liter of Coke that didn't make so much as a sigh when Susanna unscrewed the cap; the rest of the case of Miller High Life; and a carton of eggs, three missing. In the freezer was a bottle of Gordon's Vodka, the big size.

She went to the table, to the litter of food and wrappers and bottles on its surface. A large paper sack was serving as a coaster for a few of the bottles; Susanna moved the bottles to the side carefully, retrieved the bag, spread it smooth. THE FILL-UP, the logo read. A local gas station chain. There was a receipt in the bottom of the bag:

```
           THE FILL-UP
         FUEL FOR THE ROAD
             ROMA, KY
      10/23/1993 11:50PM 01
      000000#0753 CLERK08


   MILL HIGH   $6.29
   LIV/GIZ     $1.29 × 2
   TATER       $1.09 × 2
   SLAW        $0.75 × 2
   SUBTOTAL    $12.55
   TAX (@.06)  $0.75
   TOTAL       $13.30

   CASH        $20.00
   CHANGE      $6.70
         THANK YOU
```

October 23. She counted back. That was last Saturday. Ronnie had bought this meal a week ago and left it unfinished on her kitchen table. She'd taken her last birth control pill on a Saturday. And her car was sitting in the driveway. Susanna looked at all of those times-twos on the receipt, at the emptied beer bottles standing like chess pieces on the table. Someone else had been here. Someone had been here, and now Ronnie was gone.

"Mama?"

Susanna jumped, put her hand to her chest. "Jesus, baby," she said. "You scared me."

Abby ran to her and grabbed her leg playfully. She was overdressed, as usual, in the red jumper, white tights, and patent leather Mary Janes that she insisted upon, no matter Susanna's protests. Ronnie had bought the shoes, Susanna remembered. Ronnie had called it a "no particular reason" present.

"Where's Aunt Ronnie?" Abby said, now hooking her legs around Susanna's leg, dropping her bottom on top of Susanna's foot.

"Don't know, baby," she said, lifting her leg and swinging it a little, bracing herself on the kitchen counter for balance. Abby giggled, the cheerfulness of that sound and that bright red dress ill fitted to this stinking home. Susanna trudged toward the door, dragging Abby like a ball and chain, trying to make a plan. Should she call her mother first? No, foolish to worry her before she had solid information. She'd try Ronnie's supervisor at the plant, find out if she'd shown up for work this week. Then Mother. Then the police.

Susanna was light-headed. She stopped at the door, rubbing her tongue against the roof of her mouth and patting her warm cheeks with her cool palms. She was still holding the receipt, she realized, so she tucked it into her purse, then fumbled for her keys. Abby clung to her leg. Susanna reached down, pulled her daughter up by the armpits and rested her on her hip, then shut Ronnie's house up behind her.

2.

Back at home she called the sewing factory only to learn — and she hadn't convinced herself to hope otherwise — that Ronnie had indeed missed the last week of work. No notice. No explanation. "And didn't you think that was strange?" Susanna asked the shift supervisor, unable to keep the edge out of her voice, and the woman's response was equally flinty: "Not really. She already had twelve points against her for the year. Clocked in late couple of times a week, claimed sick at least one Monday a month. I put a pink slip in the mail to her just yesterday."

"Well, I have real cause to be concerned about her," Susanna had said.

The supervisor huffed. "I'll bet she's just fine. I hope she is. But tell her when you see her that she isn't getting back on out here. I've had my fill."

So Susanna shouldn't have been surprised by the reaction she got an hour later from the on-duty cop at the local station. "I'm here to report a missing person," she said, shaking so much with nervousness that she could barely hold Abby up on her hip — Abby was too big for such nonsense, but she cried when Susanna put her down — and the officer, rather than dashing to his CB and calling an all-points bulletin, leaned back lazily in his chair, arms propped behind his head as though sunbathing, and frowned at her.

"How old?"

"Thirty-two," she said.

"Man? Woman?"

"Woman. She's my sister." He wasn't writing anything down.

"What's her name?"

"Veronica Eastman."

The desk cop smiled. "Ronnie? You're Ronnie's sister?" He shook his head, still grinning. "Ronnie Eastman. You're trying to tell me Ronnie Eastman's gone missing?"

Susanna shifted Abby to her other hip. "This isn't a joke," she said, blinking against tears. "I'm really worried about her."

The cop waved her to the empty chair across from him, conciliatory, and did Susanna the favor of at least lowering his arms from behind his head and mugging serious-ness. "All right," he said, reaching for a pen. He yanked a sheet of paper out of the pile beside an electric typewriter and paused in what Susanna recognized was an exagger-ated imitation of professionalism, as though he'd gotten his cop cues from the movies. "Tell me what's worrying you." The smirk, restrained but not hidden, twitched at the corners of his mouth.

"I went to her place today to check on her, because I hadn't heard from her in a while. She usually calls at least once a week. So I went over there, and nobody answered the door." Susanna pressed Abby's ear to her chest, covered the other ear with her hand. She lowered her voice. "I used her spare key to let myself in, and you — you could just tell, you know — the place was abandoned. There was food rotting on the kitchen table."

"Maybe she went on a trip," the cop said. SERGEANT PENDLETON, his badge read. He could have been thirty or fifty, too unlined to seem properly middle-aged, too much gray in his hair to look young. Everything about him drooped: the corners of his mustache, his eyelids — saggy, even sickly — the fold of loose skin under his chin. As though he'd been expanded, then deflated.

Maybe he was one of those morbidly obese men who went on a low-fat diet or bought a treadmill. Susanna had seen them on TV, newly svelte and active but suddenly older, as though they'd endured famine rather than *Sweatin' to the Oldies.*

"No," Susanna said. "She didn't go on a —" Abby put her hand on her mouth before she could say anything further, tweezing her lips together.

"Mommy, I'm hungry."

Susanna brushed her hand away. "Hold on, baby. Mommy's doing something important."

Abby grunted, went limp, slid onto the floor. She started to whine. "Anyway," Susanna said, trying to ignore the feather touch of her daughter's fingers on her calves, then the squeezing, the outright yanking. "Wait," she said breathlessly. "What was I saying?"

"Something about how your sister couldn't have been on a trip?"

"Right." She paused, ordering her thoughts. Abby's whining, high and nasal, had given way to a lower, more experimental sound. She was playing now. It was an odd, tinny popping, emerging from deep within her throat like a cricket's chirp. "Hush," Susanna hissed down toward her feet. She felt hot and stupid, incapable of saying what she meant. "For — for one thing, she doesn't have the money," she said finally. "And nothing was packed up. Her car was in the driveway. Her medicine — her birth control — was still beside the bed. And she wouldn't have gone off and left the food out that way. It smelled awful."

"People do strange things in a hurry," Pendleton said.

Susanna slapped her palm on the officer's desk, making Abby jump and Pendleton scowl. "You're not hearing me," she said hotly. "What's going on here? I'm telling you that something is wrong. Ronnie hasn't shown up to work this whole last week. She isn't on a goddamned vacation."

Pendleton stabbed a finger toward her. "That's enough of that," he said, scolding her with the same tone of voice that Susanna used on her disruptive students. "I'm doing my job here, and I expect you to speak to me respectfully." His mustache quivered. "And you ought to be more careful about what kind of language you use in front of your little girl."

She bit her lips shut, burning with anger. Her right leg started jogging, hard enough that the lamp on Pendleton's desk rattled. She crossed the out-of-control leg over the other, pinning both tightly against the leg of her seat, her whole body clenched and throbbing.

"I can see you're upset," Pendleton continued. "And maybe you've got a right to be. We'll do what we can here, but your sister's an adult, and there's no real evidence to suggest that she didn't just take off for a few days." Susanna started to argue then, but he shushed her. "I heard you before: car in the driveway, old food on the table. I've got it. But that's not enough."

"What would be enough?"

"Blood, for one thing," he said. "Or signs that her house had got broke into."

Susanna stared at him, mute. Abby had wandered over to Pendleton's bookshelf, which, Susanna noted with an automatic smugness, was mostly bookless: one *Webster's Collegiate Dictionary,* one copy of *The Kentucky Criminal Code.* Otherwise, there was evenly spaced junk: a model police car, which Abby was now halfheartedly wheeling back and forth; a figurine of a police officer leaning over to help a boy and his dog, rendered with the blandness and sincerity of a Norman Rockwell illustration; a stuffed Smokey the Bear; and what looked to be a framed wedding portrait, depicting — Susanna had been right — a heavier

Pendleton and an equally chubby bride with bangs sprayed several inches high. She realized, now fighting despair, that she was at the mercy of this man, of all people. That this man controlled her sister's fate.

"Okay," Susanna said. "What can we do?"

"There's a missing-persons database run by the state police that I can put her name into, but you'll need to bring me a current photo and fill out a form. I can do that today if you'll get me the picture right away." He leaned back in his chair again and lifted the page on a wall calendar. "It looks like Tony won't be back in town until Wednesday."

"Who's Tony?"

"The detective." Pendleton pulled a memo pad out from a desk drawer and wrote a few lines. "And what's your name and number?"

Susanna gave them to him.

"All right," he said, punctuating the note he'd written and tearing the sheet off with a flourish. "This'll be on Tony's desk when he gets back. You should get a call on Wednesday or Thursday."

"Wednesday or Thursday? Can't he come in sooner if it's an emergency?"

Pendleton was looking sour again. "He's at EKU right now finishing up an accident reconstruction course. We can't just pull him out of that early." He frowned a little at Abby, who was now rolling the toy police cruiser around on the carpet, imitating the rev of a car engine. "And at the risk of speaking out of turn, I'm not so sure this is an emergency, Mrs. Mitchell. I know Ronnie from way back. She was a freshman when I was a senior in high school." He shrugged. "She got around. She got around then, and all I've heard tells me she gets around these days, too. She's been busted twice on DUI since I've worked here, and that don't count all the times me or some other guy let her off easy with a warning."

"So you're saying someone like Ronnie doesn't deserve the help of the police," Susanna said. She was leaking tears now, and she tried to wipe her face dry before Abby could see. Pendleton seemed to soften a little, which only made Susanna madder. What a typical man he was. What a typical woman she probably seemed to him.

"I'm not saying that at all," he told her. "I wouldn't have let Ronnie slide all those times if I didn't like her. So I'll do what I can for her. But really, Mrs. Mitchell —" He stopped.

"Well, what is it?" she said.

"It's only been a week. She's probably just

off somewhere. Wouldn't that be like her?"

Susanna opened her mouth to protest but stopped short. Was it possible that she was overreacting? She'd been so keyed up lately, so vulnerable, so spiritually wrung out. That discussion yesterday with Christopher Shelton's mother had been only the latest sore spot in, well, weeks. Weeks and weeks of sore spots. Fighting with Dale. Shouldering most of the parenting burden while Dale, as he always did between the months of July and October, spent every free moment practicing with the marching band. Dealing with bullshit handed down by the state, worrying that she'd lose her job if she didn't get her students' test scores higher.

And there was Ronnie herself. Of course there was. Susanna twisted her hands together, popped a knuckle, aware that Pendleton was watching her, assessing her. She wanted to tell him about the four $500 savings bonds Ronnie had bought for Abby, about the patent leather Mary Janes. She wanted to tell him about her and Ronnie's father, the kind of drunk he'd been, and how Ronnie had found it in her heart to forgive him while Susanna, embittered and superior, had fled to Dale's house and never had another thing to do with him, and now never could have anything to do with him.

She wanted to tell him about the copy of *A Separate Peace* on Ronnie's bedside table, how she'd been only a chapter away from finishing it. But he wouldn't understand that, would he? Pendleton, with his dictionary and his book of criminal codes and his shelf full of stupid knickknacks: How could he understand that love, that faith, was sometimes present in an act as simple as placing a receipt between two chapters?

That was her sister. But there was also the Ronnie from that day so many years ago, the Ronnie who'd tried to coax Susanna, browbeat her, into that van with those men. She'd looked then much like she looked now: dark blond hair worn cropped, almost like a man's; shorts and T-shirt cinched tight around her narrow middle and her large chest, the legs emerging from her cutoffs muscled but thick, almost stocky. She hadn't been much on makeup in those days: just mascara, and perhaps too much of it, making her appear elfin, with that short hair and the short legs and those wide, startled eyes. Childlike. She'd always smelled of cigarettes and Red perfume, her splurge, that and her French-manicured press-on nails her only shows of uninhibited femininity. It was ironic, that question she'd posed: *Are you a dyke?* The way she'd taunted Susanna, the hoarse laugh, the way the men had echoed her laughter. Looking back, Susanna knew that Ronnie had needed her, or thought she did; and Susanna knew, too, what would have happened to her — what Ronnie would have let happen — if she'd gone along on that ride. *Are you a dyke?* Ronnie had asked, looking herself like Peter Pan hitchhiking with the Lost Boys, and Susanna had backed away and turned tail and run home hard as she could, betrayed and betrayer, choosing herself just as Ronnie would have.

"I'll go get that photograph," Susanna said finally. She couldn't meet Pendleton's gaze.

"All right then." He was almost kind. "I'll be here till five."

She reached down for Abby, the both of them grunting as she pulled to a stand — Susanna with the effort, Abby at the indignity of Susanna's hard fingers in her armpits — and they were most of the way to the car when Susanna realized that her daughter was still clutching Pendleton's toy cruiser. "Keep it," she muttered, fumbling one-handed in her purse for her keys.

CHAPTER FOUR

1.

Wyatt Powell's morning routine had been more or less the same for thirty-two years, since the day when he took a promotion — he guessed you could call it that, though there hadn't been an accompanying bump in pay — and moved from seconds at the factory to first shift:

Awaken at five A.M. He'd needed an alarm the first several months, especially while he was still retraining his body for the new schedule, but never again since then; he couldn't sleep past five A.M. now even if he wanted to, even if he went to bed after midnight.

Coffee. Back then his mother had used an old aluminum kettle, brewing it stovetop, but now he owned a Mr. Coffee automatic drip with a digital clock and a timer: he needed only to scoop out his Folgers before bed and pour in a pot of water, and the coffee would be brewed and steaming at 5:10, which was always just enough time for Wyatt to rise, urinate, and let Boss out back for his own pee. Of course there'd been no Boss in those early days, but there'd always been some dog to tend to, though not always an inside dog. Wyatt hadn't started sharing his house with an animal until it had become clear, sometime in his forties, that he was never going to find the right woman for the job.

Breakfast. For himself and for the dog. Today, as on most Mondays, Wyatt opened a new package of sausage from the groceries he'd purchased yesterday, peeling back the plastic sleeve and slicing off three thick pieces smelling of cold fat and sage. These he plopped into his cast-iron skillet, which was still sitting out, wiped but unwashed, from yesterday's use. As the sausages were cooking, the air redolent with smoke and the tang of red pepper, Wyatt spread margarine on two slices of white bread, popped them into the toaster, and poured his first cup of coffee. Here, too, his habit was many years fixed: one spoon of sugar and one spoon of powdered creamer, the sugar and creamer stored in little containers made of amber carnival glass, each with a divot between the lip and the lid where the stem of a spoon could extend. The set had been his mother's. It had been on the kitchen table all through his growing up.

He crumbled a sausage into Boss's food bowl, stirred in a cup of Ol' Roy kibble, and poured off the rendered fat from his cast-iron skillet. Boss, old enough now that he sometimes couldn't even bring himself to eat standing up — he'd sit and lean into the bowl, only getting his hind legs into the motion when he needed to stretch for some last bits in the back — was already grinding away before Wyatt could seat himself. They were a couple of old boys, old bachelors, and Wyatt had examined his face in the bathroom mirror enough times to reach the conclusion that there was more than a little bloodhound in his own features these days: the rheumy, sagging eyes and loose jowls; his hair graying just as quickly as the fur on Boss's muzzle was going to white. Boss paused, as he often did, and looked over his shoulder at Wyatt. "Go on, boy," Wyatt said, tucking into his own breakfast, smearing blackberry jam on one of the pieces of toast and folding the other one around the first sausage. He sipped coffee between bites, wiped crumbs off the paunch of his stomach before they could grease-stain his undershirt. All of these acts were familiar and comforting.

He dressed after breakfast, buttoning the collar on his work shirt to hide a scratch on his neck and examining his reflection carefully in the harsh fluorescent light framing his bathroom mirror. Then he slipped into his quilted flannel jacket and called for Boss, accompanying the dog outside this time for round two. He had to watch, confirm, or else Boss would get indoors and have an accident while Wyatt was at work. Sometimes it happened anyway. The dog wandered around the yard, sniffing well-known landmarks like the picnic table and an ancient garden gnome, probably picking up on the scent of the neighbor's cat. At last his steps became shorter and faster, and then he was walking his back legs forward and hiking up his bottom end, watching Wyatt over his shoulder again suspiciously — the look had always struck Wyatt as suspicious, anyway, and made him laugh, but not lately, not since last week — and then the dog was finished, coming back to the house without being called and giving Wyatt a wide berth as he entered.

The dog was balled up on the couch, chin resting on a pillow, when Wyatt came through the living room with his travel mug of coffee and sweet roll, fuel for the ten-minute drive. This was when he'd usually sit and rest a moment, catch a few minutes of the Channel 5 news out of Nashville, give Boss a good scratch behind the ears, a good belly rub to hold him over until nighttime. But Boss wasn't having it: not sleeping at the foot of Wyatt's bed, not greeting Wyatt at the door with his tail wagging, not taking treats directly from his master's hand. If Wyatt were to sit at his usual place on the couch now, Boss would hop down heavily, cross to the opposite side of the room, and lie with his back against the wall, chin on his forepaws.

"Don't move on my account," Wyatt said to the dog. He sipped his coffee, checked the clock: 6:20, too early to be heading out unless he felt like sitting for half an hour in the break room, waiting to punch in. He didn't know what would be worse: biding time in his own home under Boss's wary eye or trying to hide from the young guys at the plant, the eighteen- and nineteen-year-olds who called him Tubs and then tried to play it off like they were joking, laughing with him instead of at him. *Aw, Tubs, stop pouting. You know we love you, man. When're you gonna come out for a beer with us? When you gonna let us get you drunk?*

He rubbed a tight spot in his chest, the

place where his breakfast crumbs always landed, where the hollow between his pecs surged out into the hard, round curve of his stomach. He carried his fat high and close to his heart.

"I'll see you, then," he said to Boss.

The dog stared at him with his tired, milky eyes, and Wyatt went on and left.

He took the long way to the plant, cutting through town instead of using the bypass, even circling the square so that he could drive by Citizens Deposit and see the temperature. Fifty degrees. It was supposed to be warm again after the weekend's cold snap, maybe even up to the seventies, and Wyatt was of two minds about it. At fifty-five he felt the cold a lot more than he had at eighteen, when he first started at Price Electric, and so the short, halfhearted winters of recent years were in some respects a blessing. Saved him on electricity bills, too. But it didn't seem right that you could walk around outdoors in almost-November in nothing but your shirtsleeves. A lot of things didn't seem right about the world today, a lot had changed without Wyatt's say-so, but what could a guy like him do about it? Price had been talking for years now about shutting down the Kentucky factory and moving to Mexico. They'd already closed a plant in St. Louis, and these had been some strange years lately, foreigners coming in and local guys, folks Wyatt had worked with since his mother was still alive, getting laid off or retiring early, tired of switching from one job to the next and fighting tooth and nail for the sections of the plant with the better pay grades.

Wyatt held on, took whatever the higher-ups were willing to give him. He'd gone from the winding room to the die cast to the repair shop, and now they had him out in packaging, one of the lowest pay grades a man of his seniority could get, working alongside Bosnians with dark circles under their eyes and knobs of muscle under their T-shirts, guys who could load and seal a crate of motors before Wyatt could get the packing materials printed. And that was part of the problem right there: all these computers you had to use now, computers controlling the machines and computers to replace what had always been done with triplicate forms and an ink pen just years before, a system that had seemed fast and fine to Wyatt. Lord's sake, who couldn't operate a damn ink pen? Who in the hell had decided that wasn't good enough anymore?

He was ten minutes early at the plant and decided to go in, get on with it. The usual bunch of guys was stationed beside the Coke machines, smoking and sipping sodas. The cafeteria had been shut down two years ago, after the corporate office started making cutbacks. No coffee these days unless you brought your own. You got a frozen turkey at Thanksgiving, a ham loaf for Christmas, and there was a company picnic once a year with a free meal, rides for the kids, and a prize drawing. That was the extent of the freebies. Wyatt had won, in various years, an eighteen-inch color television — that had been the best luck of his life, and he still marveled at it — an off-brand clock radio, and something called a Whopper Chopper that he'd immediately traded in at Wal-Mart for store credit.

"Hey," Sam Austen said, tipping his Mr. Pibb can toward Wyatt. He was a good-looking kid, tall and blue-eyed with longish sandy-colored hair and a brand-new Dodge Ram that his pop had gotten him as a graduation present. He'd started at Price in May, right after school let out, telling everybody who'd listen that he was just earning gas-and-girl money through the summer until he went to WKU in the fall. Here he was, though, still at Price, working as a temp but hoping to get on full-time as soon as there was an opening. He grinned, swigged from his soda, and put the can high in the air as if he were making a toast. "Tubs! There you are, you silly bastard. So you heard from that woman you hooked up with yet? Man, she was a dog."

He was talking about the woman from the dance hall. Wyatt had been getting grief about her — about the shots he'd drunk in front of the guys, the fact that three alone had been all it had taken to get him to sing along with "Wichita Lineman" on the jukebox — all last week.

"I didn't do anything with that woman," Wyatt said, knowing it was stupid to get drawn into this but feeling trembly and flushed, mouth running on before his better instincts could check him.

"There's no shame in it," Gene Lawson said. "She wasn't that fat. She had a decent face."

Wyatt was red now, he knew, scarlet probably, and everybody was going to start laughing soon, egging him on, saying *Way to go, Tubs* and *No shame in Tubs's game* and *More cushion for the pushin'*. He hadn't taken the fat woman from the dance hall home. He hadn't.

"Leave him alone," Morris Houchens said. Wyatt hadn't seen him. He'd been in the back of the room, sitting and reading a section from a *Courier-Journal,* and the other men had blocked him from view. "Don't know why y'all care so much about another man's love life anyhow."

"Love life," Sam snorted. "We're just having him on a little, man. It's all in fun."

"I know your brand of fun," Morris said. They stared at each other for a moment, silent, and then the shift bell sounded. The men lined up at the time clock.

Wyatt hung back intentionally, waiting to go through after Morris. "Thank you," he said, embarrassed. He was too old to be bullied. Too old to need a rescuer.

Morris, hands plunged in his pockets, shrugged in an exaggerated way. He wasn't quite Wyatt's age — Wyatt had ten years on him, probably — but he wasn't one of the young turks, either, and he'd been around long enough that they had one of those pleasant but limited acquaintanceships, the kind that had weathered nothing more serious than an argument about who should take the last Nip Chee bag from the vending machine. "That son of a bitch Sam gave my boy trouble the whole time they were in school together," Morris said. "Him and a pack of his buddies came and set fire to a Halloween dummy we had in our yard, probably would've caught the whole house on fire if I hadn't seen it in time. I knew it was him, but I couldn't prove it. Nobody did a thing to him."

"That's how it goes around here," Wyatt said.

Morris punched his card. "You got that right." He paused before crossing into the factory. "No offense, but you're asking for this kind of thing, going out with those guys. They're not your friends. They're not good people."

Wyatt remembered Glen Campbell on the loudspeakers and his own earnest, drunken crooning, the guys all laughing so hard they had tears in their eyes, wiping them away and patting their knees and saying, "Woo! Shit!" before erupting all over again. *I am a lineman for the county . . ."*

"I know," he said. "I made a mistake. I thought it would be better if I gave in and went along one time." His hand was shaking so badly that it took him two tries to punch his own card.

"It's never better," Morris said. They were in the factory now, at the point where Morris would split left toward die cast and Wyatt straight ahead to packaging, and Wyatt dreaded the day so badly that he felt almost paralyzed. Despair was what it was. The despair of living a life that you didn't understand and hadn't bargained for, hadn't deserved, could only wish upon your worst enemy.

"I'd lay low if you could," Morris said, barely audible over the clank of machinery. "Don't give them ammunition, don't egg them on. Having them ride you is bad enough, but you don't want this guy and his buddies jumping you in the parking lot."

"You think he'd do that?"

"I wouldn't put anything past him."

Wyatt sighed. He couldn't figure out how he'd made such a mess of things.

They parted, Morris lifting his hand a bit in good-bye before striding over to his station. Wyatt continued on, unsurprised to see that Jusef was already in motion, pulling motors off one of Saturday's pallets and loading them, lickety-split, into rows in the first crate. "You move slow today," he said in that strange accent of his, the way he seemed to force each word off the thick mass of his tongue, his heavy fringe of eyebrows punctuating the syllables, making all of his pronouncements seem ill spirited whether he intended them that way or not. "You put me behind."

Wyatt went to the computer and jabbed the space bar with his thick, clumsy forefinger, interrupting the screen saver's neon-on-black pattern of spinning spirals and pinwheels. The program loaded, yellow text on a black background, little boxes in which he was supposed to type addresses, product ID numbers, quantities. "Do you hear me?" Jusef was saying behind him, and Wyatt was trying, he really was, but his finger was quivering, and the screen seemed to be quivering, and it occurred to him that it was absurd, going through the regular motions of a day and plugging numbers into a machine when nothing else in his life was regular. Morris's kindness had taken him by surprise. What he felt now, contemplating it, was not gratitude but despair.

He was warm, sick to his stomach, and he leaned against the table to steady himself.

"You put me behind," Jusef repeated. "Do you hear me?"

2.

Roma was what the locals liked to call a damp town in a dry county: you could purchase alcohol legally from a liquor store and beer from the grocery store but nothing by the drink and nothing at all on Sundays. If you wanted a bar or a dance hall you had to drive twelve miles south to Tennessee, to a strip of highway that had long ago been dubbed "the Tobacco Patch," where you could find enough 101-proof liquor and legal adult entertainment to keep you satiated until the next trip to Nashville. Just over the state line there was a decent barbecue joint with an attached grocery store, which was stocked floor to ceiling with cases of Coors and Natural Light and a shelf of nothing but Boone's Farm, the bottles gleaming under the fluorescents like quartz. POKE'S, the sign out front read, and the shack's other features included a half dozen picnic tables, good for the congregating smokers, and a large blue Port-o-San positioned maybe a dozen steps away from the restaurant's entrance. Down the road a bit from Poke's was the Patch's first real bar, the Salamander, a one-room lean-to that was always getting shut down by the fire marshal. The clientele there were locals, regulars, full-blown alcoholics. The Salamander opened at four and closed at one A.M., when its regular stable of old drunks was either unconscious or wandering down the highway toward Nancy's, where the luck of meeting up with a woman was better, though the drinks were much pricier.

Nancy's was a dance hall. It was a Quonset hut the size of a roller rink and similar to a roller rink in design: The dance floor was a broad oblong of polished oak with a

DJ's station positioned right in the center. To the right of the dance floor was a long bar and two levels of seating, floor and deck, and this was where you could usually find a decent crowd of drinkers on Fridays and Saturdays, sometimes hundreds of them, their cigarette smoke curling toward the ceiling where it hung, trapped, like a storm cloud. Nancy's had a live act and a cover charge on Saturday nights, the bands always country or rockabilly, their playlists never more daring or obscure than the tracks you could choose on the jukebox any evening of the week. But you paid for the thump of bass through the floorboards and the high screech of electric guitar vibrating off the metal walls, the three-dimensionality of the music when it was live and sweating and right in front of you. This was the appeal of Nancy's. This was why, two Saturday nights ago, a group of coworkers from Price Electric had journeyed southward in three different pickup trucks, Sam Austen's Dodge Ram leading the way, swerving left and right over the double yellow line because its driver was already halfway to sodden, a flask of something raw and almost chemical-smelling tucked between his legs and up next to his groin.

Wyatt, who was balanced in the backseat

of the king cab between a Styrofoam cooler full of beer and what appeared to be the remains of the truck's factory stereo system, thought the brew smelled more like kerosene than any drink he knew, and so he turned it down, politely as he could, when Sam offered him a pull on it. Already he felt foolish. Here he was, fifty-five years old, riding in the backseat of a drunk teenager's truck — he'd be in jail by the end of the night. But the boys had asked him, no, begged him, to come, and they'd been almost kind about it, and Wyatt couldn't rightly tell them that he had anything better going on. Most Saturday nights he and Boss sat on the couch and watched a movie Wyatt had rented for free from the public library. Sometimes, when the newspaper ran a coupon, he'd order a pizza for carryout, seeing no reason why he should pay a delivery charge and tip when he could drive the five minutes and get it himself. More often he would pick up a pound of ground chuck from Piggly Wiggly and fry burgers and onions in the same skillet he'd used in the morning to cook his sausage. Every now and then he'd purchase a six-pack along with his groceries, but he never had more than two beers in a night, and these he spread out over hours, savoring them. Wyatt was no great drinker.

Sam was singing along to an Alan Jackson song playing loud through his new compact disc player, a marvel of electronics so complicated looking, so full of buttons and blinking neon lights, that Wyatt thought it looked more like the panel on a spaceship than something you could purchase for two hundred bucks at the nearest Circuit City. Gene Lawson, riding shotgun, tipped back his can of beer, swallowed the dregs, and pitched the empty out the window, nailing a stop sign. "Bull's-eye," he said, putting his left hand up, palm open, as though requesting a high five. Wyatt, now well trained, opened the cooler and fished a can from the bottom, where the ice was packed. He put it in Gene's hand.

"Appreciate it," Gene said.

Sam gunned it through a yellow light, the truck's transmission squealing before he could jam the gearshift into fourth. The kid didn't know what he had, didn't know how easily he could lose it all, daddy or no daddy. Wyatt couldn't remember a time when he'd ever been that foolish, but maybe that was his problem. His own father had died of a heart attack when Wyatt was seventeen and a senior in high school. Wyatt hadn't been a good enough student to set his sights on college, so he probably would have ended up in one of the local factories anyway, but he'd missed out on those Sam-style years of partying and blowing his money and trolling the honky-tonks for pretty girls.

"State line," Sam called, and he and Gene touched the roof of the cab with their right hands, a gesture Wyatt didn't understand and cared too little about to bother questioning. The thought of his couch, of Boss's warmth under his left hand and the TV's remote control in his right, had never been more appealing.

"That's our little ritual," Gene said in the silence that followed. Gene was a few years older than Sam, old enough to drink legally, but he had a chubby boy's face that he attempted to hide, or age, with coarse whiskers. "Say a little prayer to your angel when you get to Tennessee, 'cause you'll probably need it. And thank the Lord for Kentucky when you drive back over."

Sam took another swig from his flask. "Praise the Lord!" he said stupidly.

The boys clinked their drinks together.

They passed Poke's and the Salamander, and then Nancy's was visible just around a bend in the road, glimmering in the moonlight like a half-buried relic. There was something kind of mystical about it, the metal structure pulsing like the mother ship, the security lights outside all haloed in clouds of limestone dust from the gravel parking lot. And of course Wyatt's presence here, riding backseat with a couple of manboys, smelling of the English Leather cologne that he usually only broke out for funerals and occasionally church, was surreal; the night had the texture of a dream. He would wonder, hoping, the next day: *Was it?*

"All right, Tubs," Sam said once they parked and shut off the car, cutting off Alan Jackson before he could finish his plea to not rock the jukebox. "We're parked. We're going to a bar. Might as well have you a beer while it's free."

"I don't mind waiting till we're indoors," Wyatt said.

Sam leaned around the seat and popped the lid off the cooler, making the Styrofoam squeal. "Get your ass a beer, man," Sam said. "We're not going in until you drink one. I'm determined to see you have a good time tonight."

Wyatt thought about saying that he didn't need beer to have a good time but knew how square that would be. And it wasn't the beer he had a problem with, anyhow.

But how could he tell these boys that? *I'm too grown-up for all of this. I was always too grown-up for all of this.* He'd come, hadn't he? He was in it for the night, like it or not.

"All right, Christ," he said, pressing the tab on a Coors Light. He took a long swallow, appreciating its chill, and then followed with another draft.

"Chug that sonofabitch," Gene said, and Wyatt thought, *What the hell.* He finished the beer a moment later, belched loudly, and leaned forward to pitch the can out of Gene's window. The boys laughed and clapped Wyatt on the shoulder, and then they were all climbing out of Sam's truck, Wyatt a little flushed but otherwise fine. All of this was silly, yes, but not the end of the world. He would convince Sam to let him drive home once the guys had gotten their partying over with, and if Sam refused, he'd slip out and call a cab. Nobody would notice, anyhow. In the meantime, he'd have a couple of beers, listen to the band, and watch the rest of the bunch get shitfaced. They were gathering together now, seven men from three different trucks, none of them except for Wyatt a year older than thirty: Sam the best looking of the bunch (and knowing it, too) with his blond hair and blue eyes and his slim waist, cinched in even tighter by a set of light-washed Levi's; Daniel Stone nearly as pretty with his black hair and suntan, but lacking the charisma to make the sale the way Sam could. The rest were passably attractive in the way that men who could attach themselves to more attractive men sometimes were. Wyatt hadn't even been that lucky. At Sam's age he'd been five foot ten, his current height, and about twenty pounds overweight (lean years compared to now); he'd worn his hair, already thinning, long in the front to hide his white bulb of a forehead. And what few friends he'd made in high school he lost upon dropping out, because he was too busy, always too busy, for anything but work and his mother, and when she died he was thirty-eight and already past the point, he'd believed, of being anyone different than he was already.

Wyatt watched, silent, as the other men chided one another, finished beers, checked their reflections in the windows of their vehicles and patted flyaway hairs into place. Vain as women.

"All right, fellas," Sam said, clapping his hands at the group as though they were a pack of rowdy dogs. "Let's get in there."

The bouncer at the door was checking IDs. Wyatt, at the back of the group, watched as Sam pulled his wallet smoothly from his back pants pocket, flipping the ID sleeve over with the conviction of a clergyman, and the guy barely glanced at it before giving Sam a nod and stamping his hand. Wyatt wondered if the fake had just been that good or if Sam had just been that good. Probably the latter. When Wyatt's turn came, the bouncer wanted to see nothing from him except his five dollars.

He smelled Nancy's before he could see it well enough to move forward. Cigarette smoke hung thickly in the doorway, and a set of multicolored lights behind the band flashed red and blue against the fog, turning it into something that seemed almost solid in the otherwise dim room. Behind the smoke he could sense the heavy, sticky edge of old frying grease; beneath that, the tang of body odor. It was almost hot despite the building's size and the time of year, and as Wyatt pressed ahead through the crowd, following the white glow of Daniel Stone's polo shirt, he could see an oily sheen on most of the bodies around him. He tripped a little and found himself almost kissing-distance to the face of a woman about his own age. The too-pale powder on her upper lip bubbled with hot sweat, reminding Wyatt unpleasantly of the sight of flour and sausage fat in his cast-iron skillet on the mornings when he took the time to make a little milk gravy.

"Excuse me," he said, backing up, but she seemed not to notice.

The men from work had gathered against the corner of the bar, each trying to claim the nearest bartender's attention, and so Wyatt looked around for an empty table, a place to sit and observe. At first there was nothing. The stools at the bar were all occupied, the tables laden with empty glasses and beer bottles and shoulder-to-shoulder with people, but then the band's leader announced a slow song, told the men to "grab the nearest looker," and some of the tables cleared out then. Wyatt seated himself at one immediately.

He'd been there for only a moment, peering through the bad lighting at the shift and spin of the dance floor, when he heard a soft "Oh" to his side, and he turned in time to see a woman backing away, a foamy pint of beer in each hand.

Wyatt jumped up immediately. "Did I take your table?"

She shook her head like a child would, making her hair, which was glossy blond and clipped unflatteringly in a bob that hit her cheekbones, whip back and forth. Some of the fine strands stuck to the sweat on her nose, and she tried awkwardly to push them to the side, lifting her right hand, beer and all, and backhanding them free. "I guess I just got confused," she said. "I mean, I must have. Someone was supposed to be waiting for me."

"Think you just got turned around in here? Easy to do in this light."

"I thought . . ." She trailed off. "Oh," she repeated then, tone of voice flatter than before, and Wyatt followed her gaze down to the edge of the dance floor, where a man and a woman were standing together, not even pretending to affect a twist or a sway. The man had the woman by her belt loops and was pulling her backward and forward, bumping her hips in a playful way against his. The woman, holding a cigarette next to her head as though she could lean a little to the right and puff through her ear, was laughing. As Wyatt and his new companion watched, the man reached out, grabbed the woman's bottom with both hands, and kissed her sloppily. As a final flourish on this bit of grotesquery, he pulled the woman's cigarette to his mouth, inhaled, and breathed a dirty cloud of smoke into her face, making her laugh again.

Wyatt didn't know what to say.

"That," the woman with the beers told him, "is my date." She set the beers on Wyatt's table with a thud — not a slam so much as a drop, as though her arms could no longer support the weight of them — and wiped the beer that had sloshed across her hands on the hips of her blue jeans.

"You should sit," Wyatt said, pulling out the chair next to his. She nodded absently, still watching the couple, and pushed the second beer to the space in front of Wyatt.

"Please take that," she said, and Wyatt nodded. So they both sat, and they both sipped, Wyatt dutifully, the woman forlornly, holding her glass steady with both hands and leaning down to slurp over the rim, again with a quality so childlike that Wyatt felt almost sick with pity for her. She might have been forty or forty-five, and she was, he supposed, categorically fat — big enough, at any rate, to do her shopping at the plus-size end of the clothes aisle, though not so big that her face seemed anything but full and, perhaps because of the fullness, youthful. It was a pleasant face, smooth and unblemished, her features proportioned much more elegantly than the rest of her: the attractive, normal face and slender neck sitting atop slumped, dimpled shoulders, heavy breasts, a swell of stomach that pushed past the breasts. She had on a sleeveless red top in a light, feminine material; the contours of her nipples and belly button were visible, and Wyatt could even, without trying, make out the lace pattern on her bra. He cleared his throat and sipped again, wondering if she could see his red cheeks. But her gaze was fixed on the sight of her date and his dance partner, and her fingers, strangely slender, tightened around her pint glass.

"Do you know who she is?" Wyatt asked.

The dimpled shoulders lifted and dropped. "I barely know who he is. But they seem awfully familiar with each other." She looked back at Wyatt and smiled crookedly, her lips pressed together. "This was our first time out. We found each other in the *Peddler.*"

"The *Peddler?*"

"You know, *The Olde-Tyme Peddler,*" she said in a stagy whisper, as though afraid of being overheard. "The personals section. I put an ad in there on a lark."

Wyatt felt a surge of admiration for her. He'd contemplated the personals a few times over the years but never had the courage to place an ad or respond to one.

"I didn't lie," she said. "I put it all out there. I said what I looked like and what I weighed. I've been down that road before. I got set up on a blind date once by a work buddy of mine, and the guy barely made it through the appetizer before bugging out. He told me he'd forgotten a doctor's appointment."

"I'm sorry," Wyatt said.

She waved irritably. "I've got thick skin. But this time seemed different. He knew what he was getting into. I thought he might be pleasantly surprised, if anything."

Wyatt wondered what he'd have done if this was the woman on the other end of a blind setup or a personals ad. Beggars couldn't be choosers, his mother would have told him, but the recollection made him feel small and unkind. This woman *was* sort of a pleasant surprise. Her lips were a pretty bow shape, and her voice was husky and confident, a strange but interesting contrast to the physical girlishness. He liked the way she gestured as she talked: she had this way of throwing her hand open, as though she were tossing rice at a wedding.

"And what about him? Look at him. He's no prize," she said. Wyatt looked. The man was tall and almost frightfully skinny except for a small mound of beer belly, which seemed alien yoked to the rest of him. His dark hair flowed like a grease stain around his neck and shoulders. "Me, I'm a nurse. I probably make twice as much a year as he does. I own my house." She downed a third of her beer in a swallow.

Wyatt matched her. "Sounds like you win," he said. "The guy's just a fool."

"But here I was, ready to buy him beers and dance the night away." She sighed. "What does that make me?"

The song the band had been playing ended with a two-note flourish on the lead's electric guitar, and the slow-dancers started making their way back to the upper deck. The woman's date was leading his new girl directly toward their table, holding her by the elbow as though this were a goddamn supper club and he a certified gentleman, and Wyatt wondered, suddenly furious, if the guy even remembered the date he'd arrived with.

"Let's dance this one," he said, grabbing those oddly slender fingers and pulling the woman up to a stand before she could argue. They took the long way down to the floor, avoiding the approaching couple, and it wasn't until they were standing on the slick hardwood, facing but not yet touching, that Wyatt felt struck by the absurdity of what he'd gotten them into. The song was fast-paced rockabilly, the bodies around them kicking and twirling, and the woman — he didn't even know her name yet — had an inch on him. She tucked the flaps of that too-short bob behind her ears, held her right hand up and to the side expectantly, and so Wyatt closed the gap between them, grasping her open hand with his sweaty left one and putting his arm around her waist, nervous at the sensation of heat and softness so poorly shielded by the barrier of that thin wisp of shirt. They started rocking slowly side to side, ignoring the steady thump of bass that urged them to lift their feet and really move, and the woman didn't lean her head down to Wyatt's shoulder — she would have been too tall to pull that off gracefully — or make eye contact with him. She smelled like vanilla and the metallic edge of strong deodorant, and Wyatt wondered if she, like him, had gone on too long in loneliness, too long in disappointment, to let a night like this one get to her. Perhaps that was the saddest thing: not that the disaster date had hurt her irrevocably or that Wyatt's pitiful act of compassion had redeemed the night somehow, but that neither would ultimately matter, the cruelty or the kindness. If she was like Wyatt, she'd accept the cruelty as the way of the world, the kindness as an anomaly.

And what of her kindness to him? Wyatt realized, holding her, that he hadn't touched a woman in a year or more, hadn't shared a touch this intimate in — good Lord — too long. He remembered the handshakes, the hugs, the kisses, rare as diamonds, that a regular person would have forgotten, wouldn't have taken strong note of in the first place. When his Aunt Sheila died three years ago, her daughter, his cousin, had clung to him so long and so desperately, clutching him, dampening his neck with her tears, that he'd found himself aroused — and she had known, had wrenched herself suddenly from his arms, and the look on her face had been worse than disgust. It had been more like horror.

He pushed the memory away now.

"What's your name, mister?" the woman in his arms said. The *mister* was intoned with humor.

"Wyatt."

"Wyatt," she echoed, her beery breath tickling his mustache. "I've always liked that name. Makes you sound like a cowboy."

He laughed. "I'm no cowboy."

"Sure you are." Her arms had relaxed in his, and so had the sway between them. Wyatt had a natural sense of rhythm, though never having an occasion to use it had made him forget.

"What about you?" he said.

"What about me?"

Wyatt, feeling a surge of confidence, dipped her a little. "What do you think? Your name."

"Sarah," she said, and there was another surprise. He'd expected Joyce or Wanda or Tammy, one of those country names, trendy in the fifties and sixties, that had nothing to do with the Bible. The kind of name you saw on the badge of your checkout girl at Wal-Mart or the woman frying your fish at Captain D's. He'd grown up with Peggys who weren't Margarets and Bobbys who weren't Roberts, diminutives that had forgotten the original. Sarah was a good name, a classic.

"Sarah," he echoed, testing the word's texture on his tongue. "Sarah, it's been awful nice meeting you."

"Likewise," she said.

And now her head did drop down to his shoulder, not as awkward a negotiation as Wyatt had expected. He pulled their extended hands in so that he was cradling her elbow rather than using it to lead her anywhere. The music galloped along ahead of them. Wyatt could feel Sarah's heartbeat through her thick pillow of breasts, though maybe it was his own heart reflecting back at him.

"Tubs!" someone called, and Wyatt winced, afraid to look up, to acknowledge the speaker. He'd forgotten Sam and the rest of those guys for a moment — he'd forgotten himself — and he knew from the way Sarah flinched that she'd assumed the call was directed at her, that she was the kind of woman who accepted ownership of every insult.

"Tubby Powell, you dog!" Sam was beside him, dancing with a woman who could have been his sister: blond, smirking, blue eyed. Just as skinny as Sam but augmented up top with a set of fake breasts, which she displayed like the trophies they were on the shelf of a corseted lingerie-style blouse. "Aren't you going to introduce me to your lady friend? Swear to God, Tubs, I knew you'd move in faster than any of the rest of us. Told Gene you'd be a regular poon hound, and look at you."

The girl with Sam blinked her eyelashes, which were furred with too many layers of mascara, and tweezed the fabric of Sarah's shirt between her thumb and forefinger. "Isn't this pretty," she said, giggling. "You'll have to tell me where you got it."

Sarah stopped dancing and put a hand on

115

her hip. "Wal-Mart," she said. "They don't carry my size at Strippers-R-Us."

"You got that right, you fat bitch," the girl said. She let go of Sam and crossed her arms. "I was trying to be nice."

"Like hell you were," Sarah said, and Wyatt waited nervously for Sam to hit the roof. He'd seen Sam throw tantrums twice before at work: once when the shift manager chewed his ass for failing to make quota, once when his buddies, not seeming to realize that Sam could dish it out a whole lot better than he could take it, teased him too hard about a new pair of prissy cowboy boots he'd worn. These tantrums were fascinating and frightening to behold, because Sam could somehow behave like a child — the screaming, the crimson face, even the stomping — and instead of losing the respect of his friends, even his boss, he somehow solidified it. It was as though these men, these grown men, were afraid of a person who was strong enough in his convictions to be a brat about them.

Sam didn't scream, though. He laughed. He threw his blond head back so far that his Adam's apple bobbed, howling, and he finished with a weird little double stomp and hand clap, calling, "Whew!" as though the hilarity were just too much for him.

116

"Gonna have a catfight on our hands. And, Missy-girl, I'd back the hell off if I were you. I don't think you got a chance against Roseanne Barr over here."

"I don't think either one of you would," Sarah said, and Wyatt could only stand there, silent, wishing that she wouldn't seem so damned bent on making it worse. You just didn't fight the Sams of the world, didn't she know that?

Sam stopped laughing then and grabbed Wyatt's arm above the elbow, leaning into his ear. "I don't want to mess this up for you, but you better shut her fat yap up." He backed away, lifting his hands, surrender-style, and smiling. "We're gonna go do our own thing now, miss. And do my boy a favor, won't you, and suck his cock tonight? I think it's been a while." The girl, his date, was smiling again, and she leaped on his back, hooking her bony arms around his neck. Sam reached back and patted her bottom. "Happy trails," he said. He carried the girl back to the bar, stumbling a little on the steps up to the deck level. The girl was kicking her platform heel into his thigh playfully.

"He's real drunk," Wyatt said apologetically. He couldn't bring himself to look Sarah in the eye. He was embarrassed, but not just of Sam's behavior. He was embarrassed that Sam had caught them cozying up together. He tried to imagine the picture they'd made, their big bellies pressed up to one another, Sarah's head on his shoulder when she could have been the one leading him, their slow sashay when everyone else was spinning and boogying around them. They *had* been laughable. Fat, sad, lonely. A joke.

"You were right," Sarah said. "You're no cowboy."

Wyatt flushed with shame. "I've got to work with that man. He's my ride home."

"You might have had another ride home if you'd give a damn." She took a shaky breath, and Wyatt glanced furtively at her face. Her eyes were damp. She had bright spots of red on each cheek, like Raggedy Ann, and Wyatt again thought of her girlishness, how oddly that fit with the big body and the coarse voice, and he wished that he were a good enough man to appreciate her. *She would have come home with me,* he thought, stunned. He might have touched those heavy breasts, put his lips on the pink bow of her mouth.

"I'm so sorry," he told her, and she did that little throwing gesture at him.

"Oh, heavens. I'm being silly. Haven't

even known you an hour and I'm ready to get all tore up about it." She patted his shoulder. "Thanks for the dance, cowboy. I'll see you around."

She started toward the door, moving her bulk carefully between dancers. Wyatt didn't know her last name, where she lived, whether or not she was truly okay. Had it all happened in the space of a bad song? It occurred to him, watching her go, that he would regret not following her. But he wouldn't know until the next day just how much.

A hand grasped the place where his neck curved into the shoulder and squeezed. Gene's.

"Nice work," he said. "It takes a real hero to push a woman like that away."

"Just shut up," Wyatt said, snapping before he could stop himself. "We just danced. She had to get home."

Gene laughed. "It's almost midnight. Coach is about to turn into a pumpkin." There was a silence, and Wyatt could almost hear the gears in Gene's brain turning. "Big old pumpkin pie."

He'd let her go for this. For *them.* He was a fool.

"Let me buy you a whiskey, Tubs," Gene said. "Least I can do."

"I don't know." Wyatt thought about a cab again, his familiar house, Boss sleeping heavily down next to his feet. He'd led such a small life, and he wondered why he was so desperate to get back to it.

"You're here, buddy. You're one of us tonight. Have a damn drink and lighten the fuck up."

Wyatt turned toward the bar, where the rest of the guys from work were gathered, laughing and tipping back longnecks. His home, his bed, his dog — they'd all be waiting for him. For the rest of his life, they'd be waiting. And it seemed to Wyatt that he could, at the least, finish the night he'd started. He'd share a drink with these young men. He'd do his best to part ways amicably. That would be it.

"One drink," he told Gene.

"That's my man," Gene said. He shook Wyatt's hand, a warm, genuine gesture, and clapped him on the shoulder.

Wyatt followed him to the bar, to the sweaty tumbler of Jim Beam they'd ordered for him. In another hour he was drunk.

3.

He stayed a few minutes past the three-thirty whistle to finish labeling the pallets Jusef had loaded, lingering over the work, and the second-shifters were taking to their stations by the time he sealed the last box. He hurried past a few familiar faces, waving absently, and ducked into the men's restroom. It was empty. He had broken out in a peppery sweat, but his arms were spiked with goose bumps, his bowels heavy and loose. He had been feeling worse and worse since lunch, and he'd barely made it to the end of his shift without collapsing. He splashed some water on his face, then grasped the wet porcelain and hung over the sink, nauseous. The fist was back in his chest, its mate running sharp little fingers along his bicep, and at the moment when Wyatt was certain he was going to collapse everything eased a little, and he breathed deeply in and out, and it seemed that he was passing some of the sickness out of him with each exhalation. He looked at his reflection. He was sweaty and ashen. But he was fine.

It was overcast when he emerged from the plant, a rain falling so lightly that it felt more like a mist, barely enough to dampen his clothes. He blinked as he always did, wearing the stunned expression of a person emerging from a Saturday matinee in the middle of summer. Each finish to a workday came as a surprise to him. He'd wished a third of his life away between the hours of seven and three thirty, and he'd used the rest of the time to sleep and watch television and eat the same succession of skillet-fried meals. A small life, a sad life, but look what happened when you tried to be a person you weren't. Look what happened when you started to think you could have more.

In a few moments he was topping Harper Hill and winding down the north end of Hill Street, riding the brake as he passed Sheila Friend's place, letting gravity carry him slowly down the road. He hadn't meant to come by here again. Sheila knew him, was probably as familiar with his Chevy S-10 as he was her Jeep, the two of them having shared a parking lot for better than ten years. Sheila was divorced, had gotten on at Price after finishing her twenty years for the city, working dispatch at the police department. Wyatt knew her the way he knew Morris Houchens, comfortably but not intimately, and she'd find it odd if she spotted him making regular slow-motion drive-bys. But he couldn't help himself.

He was descending past a sharp turn in the road, Sheila's house now out of sight behind him, when the little fingers clutched his left upper arm again, and his mouth flooded with bitter liquid. He braked, struggled with the gears, and managed to get his truck onto the gravel shoulder. Then he rolled down the window, bracing himself against the cool drizzle. The air smelled moldy, like piles of leaves gone slick and black. His lips were numb.

There was a flicker of movement ahead, along the tree line, and his heart set off again immediately, *wham-WHAM! wham-WHAM!,* the fist not knocking but beating, as though there were some guy inside him, some watchman, and he was saying, *Do you see this, Wyatt? Do you see this? Put the truck in gear. Drive. Get out of here.*

He couldn't, though. He stared, paralyzed, as a figure climbed the hill toward him, the shape slumped but vaguely human, pale, blurred in the drizzle on his windshield. It moved in an awkward but oddly quick shuffle, and when he opened his mouth wide to choke down a breath, nothing came. It was as if his body was tightening all over, fingers around his arm and his heart, fingers clamping his throat until he could only wheeze with the whistling uncertainty of an asthmatic.

"Scott!" someone shouted. "Scott, I told you to wait for me!"

The pale figure stopped.

"If you take another step, I swear to God

we're going home!"

A woman rounded the turn, run-walking, pausing to put her hands on her knees and slumping over to catch her breath. Wyatt lifted his hand, feeling the last of his energy burn away with the motion, and let it drop on the toggle that triggered his windshield wipers, increasing their speed. The pale figure was a child, he could see now — he could see it plain as day — with a white sheet draped over its head, the material dangling almost to the ground, and a plastic jack-o'-lantern clutched in one hand. A little ghost. A trick-or-treater. Yesterday was Halloween, Wyatt remembered, and the boy must have insisted on wearing his costume a second time.

The woman and boy were walking uphill, coming straight toward him, and he tried to turn the key in the ignition three times before realizing that the engine was already running, the truck in neutral. The tightening in his chest hadn't dissipated. He took the knuckle of his thumb and kneaded it into his sternum, circling the spot he called his crumb catcher. He put his right hand on the gearshift and grimaced around a fresh spike of pain. He'd seen that child and thought — Lord, he didn't want to admit what he thought. He needed to go, to not be seen here, but he couldn't even get the emergency brake released. He was stuck.

"Mister?" the mother was saying, peering cautiously into his window. "Sir, you all right?"

Wyatt managed to nod. "Okay. I'm okay."

She grasped the child's hand and looked up and down the road. "You don't look okay," she said. The child, the little ghost, was tugging on her arm, making an *ennnh* sound, and she grabbed his chin through the costume. The ghost face was exaggerated and mournful: a warbled O of a mouth, long black eyes, the boy's whites glinting in the slits his mother had cut. "Knock it off," the mother said. "Or we turn around and go home."

"I'm fine," Wyatt gasped, gripping the steering wheel against another knife of pain, and the woman said, "I'm going for help. I'll be right back."

No, he tried calling, realizing he hadn't spoken aloud. There wasn't any breath left. There was only the metal ping of rain on the roof of the truck cab, the cold mist blowing into his window, the intermittent squeal of his windshield wipers, and the agony in his chest.

CHAPTER FIVE

1.

"Hey, cowboy," a voice was saying. "Snap to, cowboy. I need to roll you over."

Wyatt lifted an arm to rub his eyes, grunting when its progress was stopped by a cord or cuff or something. He felt nauseous. There was a spike of pain in the center of his forehead.

"Sick," he muttered, rocking side to side, trying to lift himself. He grasped at air, sensed something hard being tucked into the space beside his shoulder and a firm hand pulling him toward whatever it was. The pressure made him gag, and he vomited hot, metal-tasting water.

"Is that better?"

Wyatt groaned over the bedpan.

Something was pulled out from beneath him, and he heard the crisp snap of the bedding being patted smooth. "Lean you back now?"

He nodded.

He was lowered gently to his pillow. His chest, which had been pinched as he'd lain on his side, opened up, the ache over his left breast suddenly apparent. It was bearable — he could vaguely recall when it hadn't been — but there was a dull throb emanating from a knot of muscle, as though he'd exercised vigorously or gotten punched.

He lifted his hand to rub the knot, felt the pull of the cord or cuff again. He sobbed before he could stop himself.

"There, now." A cool hand was on his forehead. He caught a whiff of vanilla. "It's hard right now. The worst is over." A pause. "You can move your left hand, you know."

He lifted it to his face, embarrassed, and wiped his eyes.

"So here we are again."

He blinked, confused. The light in the room was so bright it was bluish, but he could make out the IV in his forearm, the bed rails, the thin, rough top sheet and woven thermal blanket. He could see his sock-clad feet sticking out at the end of the bed, startled looking, and on the sink across the room a vase of yellow carnations with a white bow tied around the rim, like a delivery to the funeral parlor. He was in the hospital; that was evident. But leaned over him was the woman from the other night at Nancy's, he realized with a start, and his addled mind tried in vain to account for her. Had she found him on the road near Sheila's house? Did she have a little boy?

"Sarah?"

"You remembered," she said. She smiled in a sweet but reserved way. "I'm flattered."

He felt exposed and ashamed, lying on his back with his feet jutting from beneath the bedclothes, gown shifted around so that his pale, freckled shoulder was showing. He hadn't wiped his mouth since vomiting. "What are you —" He stopped, worried he was being rude. "How did you know I was here?"

She stepped back and swept her arms down with a flourish, indicating her outfit: pink hospital scrubs, an ID tag clamped on the breast pocket of the top. "I work here," she said.

"Oh," Wyatt said, remembering. "That's right."

"It's Tuesday morning." She reached up, checked the level of fluid in whatever was draining into his arm. "You've been in and out. You had a heart attack."

Wyatt had figured as much. He nodded a little.

"The paramedics got a clot blocker into you at the scene, so it wasn't as bad as it might have been. You're lucky that woman found you and acted as quickly as she did."

He turned his face into the pillow, aware that he was leaking tears again. "She should have left me."

"That's the medication talking," Sarah said briskly. Her warm hand, those oddly slender fingers, grasped his. "You've got to trust me on this one, Wyatt. Tomorrow you're going to remember why living's so good, even when it's so bad."

He felt himself shaking his head, denying her. She had no idea what she was talking about.

"You think of one thing you love, Wyatt — just one thing's all it takes — and hold that thought for a while. There'll be a doctor coming in soon with the bottom line, and you're going to hear some stuff you won't like much, but I can promise you that you'll be able to go home in a few days. You're going to be alive to do it. That's something." Her fingers tightened. "What's waiting for you out there?"

The question threatened to sink him further, because the first thought that sprang to mind was, *Nothing. Nobody.* Mother and father both dead. No brothers or sisters. No friends. He mentally walked the rooms of his lonely house, wondering how he'd lived among them so peacefully, even contentedly, for all these years, what delusion he'd been nurturing. The full-size bed with the depression in the center of the mattress. The cast-iron skillet, yesterday's sausage fat congealed to a waxy sheen. His neat line of baseball caps on the shelf in his closet. Boss no longer waiting for him at the back door when his truck rolled into the driveway every evening, tires throwing gravel —

Boss.

"My dog," he said, trying to sit up again. "What time is it?"

"Whoa, there." She blocked him from rising with the back of her arm. "Lie back, now. Calm down."

"My dog's been cooped up at my place since yesterday morning," Wyatt said. His chest throbbed. "No one's fed him or let him out. Somebody's got to get out to my house."

"OK," Sarah said. Her face was strong and purposeful. "Wyatt, hon, I hear you. I'm not going to let anything happen to your dog. Do you know someone who can go over there?"

He thought hard: someone, *anyone.* The

despair was suffocating him.

"A relative? Do you have family in town?"

"No."

"What about a friend? One of the guys you were with the other night? Would one of them go over there?"

Wyatt imagined Sam Austen in his home: finding the leash to hook onto Boss's collar, pouring a cup of Ol' Roy into the dog bowl. "God, no," he said.

Sarah bit her lip, gaze unfocused. "I'm stuck here until midnight, or I'd do it." She looked at him again. "Someone at work?"

Again Wyatt thought of Sam, then Sam's work gang: Gene Lawson, Daniel Stone, all those guys. He was ready to say no again when Morris Houchens came to mind. He was still ashamed of needing Morris's help yesterday morning and bristled at the thought of calling him, disturbing him at work — but it was Boss. His heart ached anew at the thought of the old dog pacing the house, trembling on weak legs, going back again and again to empty food and water bowls. Holding it until he couldn't any longer, then hiding under the bed in shame. So he gave Sarah the name.

"He'll be on shift at Price," Wyatt said. "You'll have to call the main line and ask for him."

"I'll call now." She patted his knee. "Don't you worry."

He did worry, though. Boss was an old dog, in worse shape physically than Wyatt. If his stupidity and weakness — his mistake — had caused something to happen to that dog, he wouldn't be able to live with himself.

Are you living with yourself now?

He put his left hand over his heart out of habit, massaging, and waited for Sarah to return.

CHAPTER SIX

1.

Christopher Shelton and Leanna Burke were an inevitable coupling, one that the eighth-grade class at Roma Middle School had been anticipating ever since Christopher moved to town the previous year. Christopher's father was a chemical engineer at Spector Plastics and Die Cast. The transfer to Roma had been accompanied by a moving stipend and a modest pay bump, but the real advantage, he'd explained again and again to Christopher in the weeks preceding the family's relocation, was in cost of living: they could live like royalty on a salary that would barely get them into a country club in Ann Arbor. Christopher had been doubtful, then morose, and his first weeks at the middle school were a misery. He'd hated the stupid, syrupy accents, the way that even the cooler kids still dressed themselves proudly in the silk shirts and

Eastlands that had been considered dated in Ann Arbor two years ago.

Then, inexplicably, Christopher wasn't unhappy anymore. He'd gone to a junior high of almost two thousand students before, a school where well-dressed children of relative privilege were the norm rather than the exception, and he'd drawn no special attention. In Roma, he was watched, emulated. When he wore K-Swiss sneakers to school in the fall, half a dozen of his classmates returned from Christmas break in a pair. When, on Friday nights, he put in a Pearl Jam CD instead of Sir Mix-A-Lot or Tim McGraw or Salt-N-Pepa, his friends came to school shortly after showing off their own finds from the Sam Goody: Nirvana, Alice in Chains, the Melvins. He cultivated a reputation for smarts and ironic detachment. He liked to recline in his chair in class, slip his feet into the book basket under the desk in front of him, and look out the window as though he were daydreaming, as though he were above it all — but it was an act. When a teacher snapped at him with a question, trying to trick him, to get him to jolt in his seat — "And what do *you* think about that, Christopher? We're all really keen to get your take" — he'd madden her by responding correctly and politely, barely shifting his eyes from the window. His classmates loved it. And his teachers hated it, or wanted to, but Christopher ultimately won most of them over, too, because he knew just how far to push them, knew when to let slip some hint at regret or gratitude. "Most people let me get away with murder," he'd told Mrs. Hardoby, the social studies teacher, when she kept him after class to lecture him about *the importance of at least appearing engaged.* "I respect you for calling me out on my BS. I really do," he'd said, and she'd beamed, perhaps even blushed a little, and Christopher had never had another moment's trouble from her.

On the surface, Leanna Burke was the ultimate local; she was a fourth-generation Roman, her father a prominent attorney in town, the kind of guy who'd gotten rich on other people's misfortunes, divorce and personal injury, mostly. He had an office on the square, and he dressed in the costume of a deeper southerner: seersucker and linen suits, bow ties, fine-woven straw Panamas — affectations he'd likely acquired during his undergraduate days at University of the South. There were two kinds of success stories in Roma: the ones who got away and the ones who stayed to exploit their own.

Johnny Burke was the latter, and Leanna was her father's daughter.

Christopher and Leanna had begun "going together" during Christmas break of seventh grade. Leanna's dad had allowed her to host a boy-girl party in the basement of their home, which he'd had built brandnew only a few years before: two and a half stories with an in-ground pool and tennis courts, three acres of land, a long, paved driveway lined in crepe myrtles. Where Christopher's house (his mother's full-time project) was antique, studied, and understated, Leanna's house was delightfully gaudy, everything oversized and overwrought, a mishmash of periods and aesthetics, high-end and low. The dining room featured a giant crystal chandelier that had been imported from France, but the table underneath it was a too-shiny veneered cherry, the eight chairs upholstered in a black-and-green diamond print that looked like it belonged on a bad sweater. The flooring was wall-to-wall beige carpeting, linoleum in the kitchen and baths, but the electronics were all state-of-the-art: there was a fifty-inch big-screen TV in the family room, another in the basement, and the basement also housed four La-Z-Boy recliners lined up side to side — one for each of the Burkes — plus a wet bar, a full-sized refrigerator, and a microwave oven.

Leanna's mother and father had agreed to stay upstairs until ten o'clock that night — rides home were expected by eleven — so time moved in that dark-paneled basement the way it does only for thirteen-year-olds. Relationships began and ended; alliances shifted; one girl spent the night in a corner alone, trying to hide the fact that she was crying. When the evening finally culminated in the obligatory game of spin-the-bottle — and already they were on the edge of being too old for it, of feeling embarrassed by the pretense — Christopher had known that somebody would contrive to pair him with Leanna, that the seventh grade wanted it as much as or more than the two of them did. And did he want it? He wasn't sure. She was pretty, she intrigued him, but he wasn't sure if he even liked her. She had this way of holding her face when someone like Emily Houchens walked by: lips drawn into a slight smirk, eyebrow tilted upward a trace, a look of amusement that hid something harder, like disgust, even anger.

But, drawn with her into the closet after her spin of the RC bottle had landed more or less in his direction, he didn't care. She smelled grown-up. Not like watermelon or cotton candy, the pink smells her girlfriends drowned themselves in, but spicy, like cinnamon and cloves. *Red* smells, he'd thought. She'd kissed him as if she'd kissed before, taking the lead, pulling his bottom lip between her teeth very delicately, letting him taste the tip of her tongue. When he hardened, she hadn't shifted or pulled away. She'd left her hips planted firmly against his. So that was his first night as Leanna's boyfriend, quivering in her heat and her smell, groin aching against her flat stomach, and he'd thought, that night, that it was probably only a matter of weeks before she'd let him do more. He wasn't thinking about sex, exactly — but he wasn't *not* thinking about sex.

That was almost a year ago now.

The compression of time that had allowed them to couple so quickly and easily that night in her basement was now agonizing, every week an eternity, every moment invested one that bound him that much more to her, even as he resented her for starting, stopping, giving, withholding. She strung him along with promises that almost always went unfulfilled — *give me another month, give me until eighth grade, wait until my parents are on vacation* — and with surprises that he hadn't anticipated: the night, for instance, when she'd shoved her hand down into the waistband of his shorts, gripping him, or when she'd let him, just the once, touch her bare breast. Dear God, it had made him crazy: the silk of her skin there, the Braille of nipple, the scolding press of underwire against the back of his hand. He wanted her, he resented her, he feared her — this last perhaps most. She was playing him brilliantly, and he wasn't even sure why. He thought that perhaps she just liked having control over him — that if they weren't a couple, *the* eighth-grade couple, then they were rivals, struggling forces of old and new. By kissing him, and occasionally — unpredictably — more, she kept him in her sights. By not having sex with him, she kept him in his place. He saw this, but he was helpless to do anything but surrender to it. This is what led up to the morning of the food war.

2.

Roma Middle School students didn't have a playground or a recess, exactly, but Coach Guthrie usually let them spend the last twenty minutes of PE in "free activity." This is when he'd open the equipment closet and the gym's outer door, instruct the class to keep the noise down, and then retire to his office with a can of Mr. Pibb and the latest *Sports Illustrated.* Some of the kids would play a quick game of HORSE in the gymnasium, some would find a quiet spot in the bleachers to nap. Others wandered out to the tennis courts and the football field, not to play, but to stroll and talk, sneak cigarettes. Christopher and Leanna spent this time as they spent all of the time they shared outside of the sharp gaze of an adult: tucked into some out-of-the-way corner, making out.

They were outside today because they thought everyone else was indoors. It was chilly, in the low fifties, and most people hadn't thought to bring their coats with them to PE. Neither had Christopher and Leanna, but that hardly mattered. She grabbed his hand the way she always did when Coach Guthrie disappeared into his office, gave him a Significant Look — she'd worn that look so many times now that it was practically a parody of such a look — and pulled him, casting glances back along the line of her extended arm as though she were guiding a pony, to the gym's outside entrance. He gave her no argument. They ended up at the tennis court because there was a green canvas windbreak woven into the chain link; from the outside you were obscured, but from inside, if close enough to the weaving of the fence, you could usually spot someone coming in plenty of time to jump to a stand and tame down your mussed hair. It was a good hideout, one they'd used several times.

"Tell me what you're thinking," Leanna murmured against his neck as they pressed themselves into the fence, huddling and groping now as much for warmth as for pleasure. She said things like that a lot. *Tell me what you're thinking.* Or, *Look at us right now.* Once, embarrassingly, *I'm aching for you.* She must have heard this stuff on television.

"I'm thinking that I'm freezing my ass off," Christopher said. He burrowed his fingers into the hem of Leanna's sweater until he reached bare flesh, satisfied when she winced and sucked in her stomach.

She pulled back and looked at him. God, she was pretty. She had dark eyes and brows, a faint dusting of freckles against her nose because her mother let her use the tanning bed once a week. Her pink lips were plump and flanked by dimples. He liked the way her wavy, dark blond hair was tucked behind her small ears, which stuck out, adorably, just a bit too much.

"You want to go back in?" Her voice, as

always, was double-edged: accommodating, flinty.

"Do you?"

When she responded by grabbing his belt buckle, harshly, his first instinct was to push her away, his first thought that she aimed to hurt him. That lasted just a second. Then he watched, heart suddenly jackhammering, as she pulled the tongue of his belt loose, worked the button of his jeans free of its loop, drew down his copper zipper — it rasped against his erection, making him shiver — and then crouched down, smiling up at him. Every action was achingly slow, deliberate.

"Leanna —"

Her hand, cold as his own must have been, slipped into the front flap of his boxers. He jerked against her, feeling the throb down there echoing across his body, and he clenched his eyes shut, gasping, only to jerk again as the cold turned all at once to wet heat. He felt as though he were being unraveled from the inside out and he threaded his fingers into the chain link behind him.

He was close when he chanced to open his eyes and thought he saw a pair staring back at him. He tried to make a sound of warning and felt Leanna nodding against him, her pace picking up, and he squinted, breath hitching, then felt himself start to convulse down there — he couldn't stop it — and he grabbed Leanna's hair and held her steady, needing to stop the ache, however good it was, and it was then, in the weakness of release, that he realized for sure who had caught them, who had seen it all. He jerked himself free and scrambled to zip his blue jeans closed again.

"Oh my God," Leanna said. She was wiping her mouth with the back of her hand, face thunderous. "What was *that* about?"

His hands were shaking too badly to work the tongue of his belt back through the buckle. His fingers were numb. "Someone saw," he whispered breathlessly.

She stood, liquid, cool as lemonade. "Where?"

He pointed. There was a rustling, a high-pitched sound that might have been a gasp. A shadow moved across the windbreak on the far end of the court.

Leanna sprinted after.

It happened very fast. Leanna, gazelle-like on those long, pretty legs, outpaced him, and when he caught up, shirttail finally tucked back into his trousers, he found exactly what he'd feared he would: Emily Houchens, jacketed arms clasped tightly across her chest, and Leanna blocking her entrance back to the gym.

"What the hell," Leanna said, not bothering with a mask of niceness. "What the hell, Emily."

Emily was looking off to the left and rocking nervously on her heels. It was — and Christopher felt guilty for thinking this — a stance he associated with her retarded brother, whom he'd seen a couple of times at the grocery store. *If she wasn't always on the honor roll,* Leanna had once told him, *I'd think she was retarded, too.*

"Well?" Leanna smiled in mock exasperation, turning to Christopher and fluttering her hands in a *Would you get a load of this?* kind of way. "What the hell? You like to spy on people?"

Emily shook her head emphatically.

"Because this is just weird," Leanna said. She was pacing now, her own arms crossed against the cold. Her short sweater had ridden up a bit in the back, exposing a mouth-shaped band of golden flesh and the scalloped edge of her underwear. She stopped. "Are you going to tell?"

Christopher looked at Emily carefully, but she didn't move. She didn't speak or nod. "Emily." He tried a voice that was gentler than Leanna's. He knew she liked him. He'd been good to her, in the past. And if he'd

144

called her a weirdo or a creep or something in class the other day, well, that couldn't be helped now. What was he supposed to have done? Her eyes had been on him, frank and adoring, her mouth drooping open a little — she was that unaware of herself, that spellbound. The whole class had been watching, waiting for him to react.

"Emily," Christopher said now, "are you going to tell? Please don't, OK?"

Her eyes met his. They were gray-green, kind of pretty. It rattled him, having those eyes on him again. He had recognized them immediately through the diamond of chain link.

Leanna followed his lead. "Please, Emily? You could sit with us at lunch today — or all week. Or whatever you want."

Christopher almost snorted. *That* was incentive?

"You could . . ." Leanna stopped, looking at him pleadingly.

Emily was waiting.

He went to her, touched her arm, left it there. "Remember Mr. Wireland's class? I helped you that semester, right? With your project."

She looked down at his hand on her arm, her upper lip twitching. He withdrew it. A cold wind whistled around the corner of the school building, rattling the pea gravel outside of the back entrance to the gym. It seemed to Christopher that they were all holding their breath.

And then the bell signaling the end of the period sounded. "Emily," Leanna said again, but Emily was leaving, bustling to the door with her arms still tight against her chest. She was limping a little, Christopher noticed, favoring the left ankle.

"Oh, no," Leanna said, her voice breaking. "She's telling. I know she is. Stop her, Chris, make her stop."

"What am I supposed to do?"

"Oh, no," Leanna repeated. They went inside.

3.

Emily hadn't blabbed between the gymnasium and the cafeteria. Christopher followed Leanna through the lunch line, holding his tray out for servings of food that he would have had trouble stomaching even had he been downright hungry. The salad was a few leaves of iceberg lettuce, carrot shreds, and exactly two radish slices, which were positioned side by side like blank eyes. The spaghetti was overcooked to stickiness, and a sheen of grease floated on the top of the meat sauce.

"I could kill her," Leanna was muttering ahead of him. "Where does she get off? And what now? She holds it over our heads?"

"Shh," Christopher hissed.

Leanna pushed her wavy hair out of her face with a puff, handing the lunch lady her ID card and two dollar bills. "What kind of person just — just *watches* like that?" Her voice had dropped into a hoarse whisper that was louder than her regular speaking voice. "She likes you, so she was probably into it —"

"Shut up! Jeez." His tray of food was rattling. He took a seat quickly at their regular table, dropping it with a clatter. He couldn't believe what they'd done, that it had happened less than a half hour ago. Half an hour ago, he'd gotten off at the tennis court. Leanna had gotten him off.

She was clammed up, red-faced with anger, when Craig Wilson slid into the bench across from them.

"What's up?" he said, jamming his fork into his pile of spaghetti. He pulled it straight to his mouth, leaning over to bite off the strands. His hair, which he wore gelled into spikes in the front, glinted under the cafeteria's fluorescents.

Then Maggie Stevenson came, sitting next to Leanna so that they could link arms.

They whispered to each other, giggled, and Maggie's wide-set eyes got wider. Christopher felt his neck flush with heat.

The rest of their group was joining them. Monty Higgins grabbed Christopher's shoulder for balance as he folded his long legs over the bench and under the table. Anita Page, Monty's girlfriend, was complaining loudly about the C she'd gotten in Mrs. Mitchell's class, as if hoping that Mrs. Mitchell, who was chaperoning lunch today, might overhear her. Under other circumstances Christopher might have joined her — Mrs. Mitchell was his least favorite teacher at RMS — but he could see that Emily had just approached the cash register, and Leanna was tensing up beside him. He could feel her arm harden against his.

"I swear to God —" she said, and he nudged her side with his elbow.

Emily was coming toward them now, her face unreadable. His heart resumed its jackhammering from the tennis courts, not only because Emily had seen him and could choose to tell on him, but simply because Emily had *seen* him, had seen that moment of his weakness and exposure, and what if Leanna was right? Was she into it? Was that why she'd watched? So she'd watched him, she'd seen him as she was never supposed to, but the thought he'd been trying to suppress ever since — the thought, true as it was, that he couldn't quite make sense of — was this: he'd watched her, too. He'd seen her eyes, recognized them, and finished anyway.

His stomach clenched around the two bites of spaghetti he'd managed to swallow.

Emily stopped in the aisle beside him. She was looking to the left away from them, and he could see the tremor in her hands supporting the tray.

"Your girlfriend's here, Chris," Craig said loudly. The table tittered.

Emily hesitated.

"Emily?" Leanna's voice was tight. "Are you sitting with us?"

Maggie Stevenson made a face of exaggerated disgust. "Is she sitting with us?" she said, eyebrows drawn into a peak. "God, I hope not."

Emily's eyes darted to Christopher's, then away again. She shifted her weight between her feet.

"I invited her to," Leanna said. She scooted away from Christopher, toward Maggie, clearing an empty space on the bench. "Here, Emily," she said, patting the seat. It was, Christopher thought, the way she called her dog when she was trying to get him to hop up beside her on the couch. "Sit here."

The table — their crowd — was very quiet now. And the quiet was spreading to the nearby tables as other students picked up on what was going on and turned to see, fascinated, what would have possessed Emily Houchens to approach the popular kids, to stand there until Leanna Burke invited her to join them. Emily: dressed today in her regular costume of ill-fitting stone-washed jeans; oversized flannel shirt; canvas Wal-Mart knockoff sneakers; brown, limp hair stopping at her shoulders as though it had gotten there and simply given up, lost steam. Was it an elaborate prank? Why else would golden Leanna Burke be shifting to accommodate Emily Houchens?

And why would Emily hesitate?

Christopher knew what he had to do. He had only to say, "Come on, Emily," and pat the seat as Leanna had done, and she'd accept the invitation. She'd slide into the gap they'd made for her, eat her lunch in nervous silence, and Leanna would keep inviting her back until enough time had passed to make moot the issue of what Emily had seen at the tennis court. With every silent day Emily would have less of a hold on them; every moment she kept her mouth shut made her a coconspirator. By next week, Leanna would be emboldened enough to tell Emily, politely or otherwise, to find another set of lunch companions, and she'd write the whole thing off to her friends as an experiment, an act of charity, a way to pass the time. Christopher knew all this. He knew how easy it could be, how necessary it was. He would be in huge trouble if this got to the principal, and Christopher didn't want to even guess how his parents would react.

Emily was watching him, waiting. The space between Leanna and himself felt cavernous, like something he could fall into.

Come on, Emily. Sit with us. That's all it would take.

He shifted, putting his leg into the space Leanna had cleared, pretending to stretch. "No room here," he said loudly, and Craig spat laughter.

"Christopher," Leanna was pleading, but he couldn't stop now.

Christopher turned. "Craig, you've got room over there. Can Emily sit with you?"

"Aw, no, man —" Craig was grinning, spreading his legs wide to take up more space. "Monty?"

"You can sit here," Monty said, patting his lap. "Don't know what these guys are so shy about. Come here, sexy."

Emily did an about-face, moving so quickly that Christopher barely registered her expression of dismay. She had made it to an almost empty nearby table — its occupants were pulling away from her as though she carried something contagious — when he called out, "Emily! Hey, Emily!"

She turned, not knowing that the spaghetti was already in his hand. That night, as Christopher tallied up the many ways he'd wronged Emily, he decided that this moment, more than the ones that preceded and followed it, was worst. She had turned, he knew now, with a look of relieved expectation on her face. She'd believed, after everything, that he might still do right by her, that he'd call out, *Just kidding, come back here.* And she would have come, too.

There was something in the lunchroom in that moment: a manic charge that Christopher was emitting and getting reflected back at him. He felt delight, horror, incredulity — he felt his peers feeling these things, and beaming at him, giving him the strength to do something that they could never have initiated themselves — and then his arm launched forward.

CHAPTER SEVEN

1.

Susanna was sipping a can of Slim-Fast and pretending to listen to her partner that day for cafeteria duty, Nathan Guthrie, who was on a tirade about state physical fitness mandates, when there was a scream and a crash over in the eighth-grade section. She was on her feet before Nathan could even furrow his forehead, and though the students had now erupted with shouting and laughter, some even standing on the benches to get a better look at the action, Susanna could spot the epicenter of the disturbance almost instantly: by the windows, where the popular crowd gathered. Here a knot of students had formed, and Susanna worked her way over, calling, "Knock it off! Take your seats!" and getting ignored by practically everyone.

She had to elbow her way through the circle of gathered students before she could see what had happened, and when she finally broke the barrier of bodies, pushing Monty Higgins to the side with a sharp exhalation of breath and getting ready to yell at the lot of them, she stopped in her tracks. Everyone fell quiet around her, and the quiet made its way to the back of the room as quickly as the shouting had, the quiet somehow worse than the noise had been. She'd expected to find a couple of boys hitting one another or wrestling on the floor, but there were no boys. There was only the figure of a girl, down on her knees with her hands covering her head as though the principal had called a tornado drill, battered with food from today's lunch line. It was all there: the soupy spaghetti with ground beef, the tossed salad and Thousand Island dressing, chocolate pudding. A piece of garlic bread clung to the filth on her back like a tick. "What is this?" Susanna said helplessly, and the girl lifted her head at the sound of her voice. It was Emily Houchens, her eyes huge and unblinking, and Susanna felt a chill race through her until the girl suddenly broke with sobbing, and then there was no chill, only heartbreak and horror.

"Who did this?" Susanna said, turning to each face in the circle, but it was obvious who had done it; they'd all done it. They'd picked this poor girl out for some reason and pelted her with their uneaten lunches, and those who hadn't done the throwing had stood on their seats and watched, screaming with laughter. She walked from student to student, forcing eye contact, jabbing the shoulders of the ones who were biting back smirks. She reached Christopher Shelton, finally, and he had the good sense to look at his feet in apparent remorse — but Susanna recognized the taunt in his arched eyebrow, noted how he crossed his arms behind his back and bobbed on his toes a little, as though he were holding back laughter. "Is this funny to you?" she said, and he shook his head vigorously left and right.

Nathan finally joined her, puffing up into coach mode and pointing his thick forefinger. "I want to know who started this," he yelled, and the students bristled more under his demand than they had Susanna's. They liked him. They feared him. The smirks slipped from their faces now, she noticed enviously, and a couple even flushed.

"Well?" He circled the students as Susanna had, and she yielded to him, ashamed of herself. Her role in this was painfully clear. She went to the nearest napkin dispenser and pulled out a thick wad, then approached Emily, trying not to let the disgust she felt show on her face. She placed her low-heeled dress shoes carefully between streaks of tomato sauce, gathered her skirt a bit with her free hand, and stooped next to Emily, who was still leaking tears but no longer sobbing.

"I'm just going to try to clean some of this off," she whispered. Emily didn't say anything or look at her. So Susanna took one of the napkins in her hand and started using it, awkwardly, to pull strands of spaghetti off of the girl's shoulders and hair, sick at the cheerfully bland smells of canned pasta and sweet instant pudding. She threw the first soiled napkin on the floor — she wasn't the janitor, she would *not* start sweeping this mess up — and then tried, best she could, to sop up the bigger smears of filth, feeling exposed, as though these students were witnessing her in an act of intimacy. There were other teachers on the scene now, and then Wally Burton with his shouted promises of detention and restricted cafeteria privileges, and Susanna thought she heard a few sobs that weren't Emily's, and that softened her a little, made her think of Abby. But these weren't children. They were eighth graders a semester away from high school. Teenagers.

"May I go to the bathroom?" Emily said hoarsely, startling Susanna.

"Of course you can," she said. She fished in her pocket for her keys, removing one from the ring. "Use the teachers' lounge. I'll come find you when I'm done here."

The students pulled away as Emily passed, their faces a mix of disgust and guilt and a dazed sort of confusion, as though they were under a spell.

Wally Burton waved over Susanna, Nathan, and the two other teachers who'd dropped in. "Rita" — he pointed to the middle-aged woman on Susanna's right — "get the seventh grade out of here and explain to their teachers why they're coming to class early. Tell them I'll make an announcement later on."

"Will do," she said.

"And send the janitors over!" Wally called after her as she left.

Nathan crossed his arms and huffed, the action almost feminine. "Damn," he muttered. "Great day in the morning."

"You see who started this?" Wally said. Behind him, the eighth graders were clustering in groups of three or four, holding their own whispered council. They should have been separated already, Susanna thought.

They should have been put at different tables and made silent, not given time to compare notes.

"It was a riot by the time I made it to this half of the room," she said. "But I'm sure it started at the table by the windows."

Wally turned to Nathan. "That sound right to you?"

"Susanna was the first one out here," he said. "You better take her word on it." She didn't know if he was standing up for her or covering his own ass, but Susanna felt a rare moment of gratitude to Nathan Guthrie.

"All right, then," Wally said. He walked back to the center of the room, holding up his hand for silence. The eighth graders, a group of about ninety, stared. "Which of you were sitting at that table?" He pointed.

No one moved.

Wally paced in front of the students, his shiny black loafers making intimidating clicks — or what Susanna supposed he hoped were intimidating clicks — on the asbestos tiles. "I'll punish every one of you if I have to. You all deserve it." He stopped in front of Sally McIntosh, who paled. Sally wasn't one of the popular girls in the grade. She was best known as the class's only diabetic, her silver bracelet with the red cross flashing on her wrist when she raised her hand, her ritual afternoon snack of Lance peanut-butter-and-cheese crackers so reliable that Susanna could have set her watch by the sound of tearing cellophane. Sally hadn't been anywhere near the window table.

"What about you?" Wally said, staring her down. "Did you start this?"

"No!" Sally said, trembling. Her eyes shifted involuntarily to where Christopher Shelton and his friends were gathered. "I wasn't even over there!"

Wally's expression was cunning. He was a short man with narrow shoulders and a slumped protrusion of stomach hanging over the waistband of his khakis. His button-down shirt was rolled up on the forearms and unbuttoned at the collar, his cheap-looking red tie yanked loose and dangling, and there was something simian about the odd crook of his arms and the way he put his knuckles rather than his palms on his hips as he talked.

"So did you try to help Emily?"

Sally's eyes were damp. She pinched her lips together and shook her head.

"How does suspension sound to you?" He was practically smiling. "A week, maybe? You and every person after you who plays dumb?"

She was crying now. She put her hands out in front of her, palms open, and waved them — Susanna thought at first she was pleading.

"I didn't do any of it!" she said. She shook her open hands again. "See?" She turned to Susanna and Nathan now, still holding out her hands. "See?"

And it hit Susanna like that, so quickly and obviously that she wanted to kick herself for her stupidity. "Their hands, Wally," she said. And then, because she knew it would take him another beat or two to catch up, she called "Show me your hands" to the group and made a beeline first to Christopher Shelton.

He'd wiped them, of course. But Susanna could make out the faint red of tomato sauce in the lines of his palm, and there were streaks of red and brown on the sides of his trousers. "Your mother didn't teach you not to wipe your hands on your pants?" she said, motioning. She couldn't help herself.

He shrugged.

Susanna leaned in, lowering her voice. "Don't you feel ashamed at all?"

He shrugged again, but Susanna thought she saw a shadow cross his features. His lips pulled at the corners, his eyebrows dipped down. He swallowed.

"Go over there," she said, motioning to a table in the corner. He did, not getting there in a hurry, and when he was seated he folded his hands on the tabletop as if he were about to deliver the State of the Union address. Susanna looked at the dozens of eighth graders left in the lunchroom: some wide-eyed, almost panicked, others scowling behind crossed arms, the rest keenly interested, confident enough in their relative innocence to watch with curiosity as the ones with stained hands were identified and sent to separate tables, to stew. The group of guilty students assembling by the windows was enough to make any small-town schoolteacher sick with dread. There was Leanna Burke, class valedictorian, whose father was one of the most prominent attorneys in town. She seemed the picture of nonchalance — her slim, tan legs were crossed prettily at the ankles — but her foot planted on the floor was twitching nervously, and she was tearing with relish into the cuticle on one of her thumbs. Maggie Stevenson's mother taught at the elementary school; Maggie stared straight ahead, eyes unfocused, and wrung her smeared hands in her lap. Craig Wilson, doodling on the sole of his high-top sneakers with a black pen, kept casting furtive glances Christopher's way. He was already starting for the high school baseball team, and Dale, who cared about such things, had told Susanna that he'd almost certainly get drafted to the majors, and maybe even right out of high school. He was the kind of kid that a whole community rode its dearest hopes upon, and Susanna took comfort in one small favor: at least it wasn't spring.

There they all were, a baker's dozen, trying to whisper — "Quiet," Susanna hissed — to wipe the drying food off their hands: RMS's best and brightest, the students who would pepper the "Superlatives" page of the yearbook when copies arrived next May. And poor, chubby, filthy Emily Houchens still awaited her in the faculty restroom.

2.

Emily was humming to herself when Susanna found her. It was an eerie sound: tuneless and phlegm choked, her breath hitching each time she tossed a wet, filthy wad of paper towels into the wastebasket. She had slipped out of the oversized flannel shirt she was wearing and now stood in front of the sink in a tank top and high-waisted blue jeans, which were buttoned so tightly around her midriff that Susanna wondered how she could sit comfortably. Her small breasts, which would have been hidden by the flannel, now puckered, child-like, through the thin cotton of her tank, and her stomach, rounded with fat like a toddler's, gave her the paradoxical illusion of age, as though she were an old man slumped in front of a shaving mirror, hot towel around his neck. What a sad figure she cut with her stout little body and cheap clothes, her grimed hair, which, at its best, was a brown so lusterless that it could seem almost gray in some light. There was a latent prettiness in Emily, though. She had pale, baby-fine skin, a straight nose with a delicate upturn, grayish-green eyes, and naturally long lashes. She'd never be a beautiful woman, but she might one day be a woman whose inner light — the sensitivity and intellect — would animate these better features. Susanna hoped that with all her heart.

Emily cranked out a couple of feet of brown paper from the dispenser, folded it methodically, dampened it under the tap. She started wiping the hairs at her temple, facing the mirror but not appearing to actually see herself. The broken humming continued.

"How are you feeling?" Susanna said.

Emily shrugged, working the towel across her hairline.

Susanna went to her and took the towel, turning Emily away from the mirror. She held Emily's chin firm, the way she would have held Abby's, and started blotting the towel, working fast, thinking that only a shower would help at this point but wanting to startle the girl out of the creepy trance she'd worked herself into. A tear leaked out of the corner of Emily's eye and rolled back toward her earlobe; Susanna blotted it, too.

"Will you tell me what happened?" Susanna whispered.

Emily's throat worked. She nodded her chin against Susanna's hand.

"Who started it?"

She pinched off another flow of tears. "Christopher," she said.

Susanna nodded. "Do you know what set him off?"

Emily's eyes shot to the left and back. "No," she said.

Susanna let go of her face. "You sure?"

Emily nodded, eyes on the ground, and Susanna knew that she was being lied to.

"Okay, then," she said. She wouldn't push her. "Is there someone who can pick you up from school? Mr. Burton's given you permission to go home for the day."

"No. My dad's at work and my mom can't drive."

"He couldn't take off work for a few minutes?"

She shook her head. "They'll dock him points."

"We'll get you a cab," Susanna said. "Is that better than waiting here until the buses run? You could stay in my class all afternoon if you want."

"The cab's all right," Emily said. "I don't want to see anyone."

They parted ways fifteen minutes later. Susanna had given her fifth period a practice open-response question so that she could wait with Emily on the school's front steps, and she knew that they were probably all just talking in her absence about the scene at the cafeteria, but she didn't much care. She handed the cabdriver a five-dollar bill from her own purse. "Her mother's expecting her," she told him.

Emily had slid into the car's backseat, windbreaker hiding her stained shirt, unraveling rayon backpack resting on her knees. Her eyes were damp and swollen. She looked as though she had blood under her fingernails.

"You come to me if you ever need me," Susanna said, hunching to see through the rolled-down window. "If you need a break or quiet time or whatever, just come to my classroom. I'll excuse it with Mr. Burton."

"OK," Emily repeated. And, huskily: "Thank you, Mrs. Mitchell."

Susanna swallowed hard. "Anytime, sweetheart." She wasn't usually like this with students. She didn't talk about her own life, she didn't make jokes, she didn't give hugs. It was getting to where those things could land her in trouble, anyhow. But she reached through the window and squeezed Emily's hand, and when the cab pulled off she had to turn and wipe a tear of her own quickly away.

3.

The school day passed slowly. Susanna was finally slipping into her light coat and heading for the door when Wally Burton blocked her path, his tie now loose, his thin hair wagging sadly from where he'd raked his fingers through it. "Damn Burke girl's dad is raising hell," he said. "I hadn't even gotten out all of what she'd done before he started hollering lawsuit."

Susanna huffed, exasperated. "Of all the nerve."

"I'm going to give them all a day's suspension and a week in ALC," Wally said, stiffening his back and lifting his chin, as if he were prepared to brook no argument. ALC, the "Alternative Learning Center," was a trailer on the school's campus where punished students were kept in isolation from their peers. "I think that's fair."

"One day? Come on, you're not serious."

He had the decency to look sheepish. "Burke was demanding only a week in ALC, so this is a compromise."

"It's not even meeting halfway!" Her voice cracked.

"He said that ALC's more punishment to them, and I think that's right. I mean, it's not high school. Their GPAs don't mean anything here. They stay at home and they're just going to think they got rewarded with a vacation."

"Wally." Susanna stopped, took a deep breath. She put out a hand, a "stop" gesture. "You saw what they did to Emily. It was, it was like" — she waved helplessly — "like a lynch mob or something."

"Now come on, that's over the top."

"Well, tell me this. Just tell me this. If ALC's more punishment to these kids, and if their GPAs don't matter, why is this Burke guy pushing so hard for it?"

"On principle," Wally said without a second's hesitation. "He just wants his way.

He thinks a long suspension would be embarrassing for the kids."

"God forbid," she said bitterly.

"I know it's no fun seeing him get his way on this one. And am I protecting my hind end? Absolutely."

Susanna fought rolling her eyes.

"But he's right about the ALC thing and he doesn't even know it. We can make it hard on them here. You can assign them whatever you want. I'll back you up. They get to do no extracurriculars this week, they can't ride the bus, they can't go to any athletic events."

"They can't go to a middle school football game? They can't ride the damn bus, Wally? These kids don't use the bus." She laughed, sharp and humorless. "I wash my hands of this. I dealt with Christopher's mother last week, if you recall. She didn't like her son's punishment then, and I didn't get a whole lot of backing up from you."

"This is different," he said.

"No, it's worse." She glanced around to see if they were being watched, then lowered her voice. "If this had been Thad Morrow and some of his friends, you'd have suspended them for at least a week, and you might have even expelled them. You and I both know it."

The redness, his blush of awkwardness, drained from Wally's face. The set of his mouth hardened. "I don't appreciate what you're implying. It isn't fair."

"None of this is fair," Susanna said. She turned sharply and headed for the door, her pace brisk, and he called out to her before she could get to the lobby.

"Two days' suspension." His shoulders were slumped. "A week in ALC. Could you live with that?"

Susanna nodded tiredly. "I guess I have to. I'm just about to the point of not caring."

"Better watch that," he said. "You'll end up like me." He was trying for affable, self-deprecating. She didn't have the energy to play along.

"I've got to go, Wally. It's been a long day."

"Oh!" he said, putting a finger in the air. "Wait just a minute. I meant to bring you this earlier but forgot in all the excitement." He trotted forward, pulling a pink slip of paper from his back pocket. "Lacey took a message for you."

Susanna accepted the note eagerly. The secretary had scribbled, "Detective called about your sister. Said he would be at station until 6:00 today, call at home if later." There were office and home numbers listed, and for the first time Susanna felt as if Ronnie's disappearance were being taken seriously.

Then she noticed the name at the top of the slip: *Tony Joyce.* Could it be *that* Tony Joyce? She hadn't heard he was living in Roma again.

Wally must have seen something in her face. "Susanna? Is everything all right?"

She nodded, swallowing against a lump. "Yes. I'm fine. But I've got to go."

CHAPTER EIGHT

1.

Susanna had a secret, which she'd never shared with anyone — not Dale, not her sister, and not even her college roommate, Anne Marie, though she'd come close on some of those nights they spent drinking at the Apple, when she found herself admitting to Anne Marie doubts about her engagement to Dale, how she wondered if there could be some other, better life for her. The sad thing about her secret was that it wasn't even a particularly good one. Dale, had he heard it, would have shrugged it off. Ronnie might have laughed. But the memory of it was one of her most shameful, and Tony Joyce was its subject, and so she drove to the police station in a double bind of fear for her sister and anxiety for herself.

Her father had been a racist. That was the first thing. Not that racism was uncommon around here, and Susanna had grown up with friends among whom whispered distinctions between black people and white were not just tolerated but passé, but her father's racism was a quality that complemented a host of other prejudices and superstitions and outright cruelties, and so the thrill she'd felt the first time she spoke to Tony Joyce — this had been her second day at Roma High School, when they'd bumped shoulders in the hallway between the arts wing and sciences — startled her. "Excuse me," he'd said, stopping to steady her. He, a junior, tall, glorious, and popular; she, a freshman, sadly hopeful in one of the two new outfits her mother had purchased for her at Sears and Roebuck. It was 1979, and she was fourteen years old. She'd put new pennies, heads up, into her loafers.

"Okay," she'd said, and he smiled, and that was it. It wasn't a crush yet, because crushes come with leveling expectations; this was so pure and surprising that she felt herself opening up, reaching toward him like a flower. It seemed to Susanna later that the miracle of his reciprocated affection must have also been rooted in this moment. She had been shocked into showing him, unguarded, her sudden delight in him.

Tony was already something of a local

celebrity. He'd started playing for the high school baseball team in seventh grade after years of Little League infamy, and he'd led the Cats to three consecutive state championships since then, mostly on the strength of his powerful left-handed swing. He was talented and polite, a black kid on an otherwise all-white team. People like Susanna's father would say, "There are black people and there are niggers, and he's just black." It was the highest compliment they could muster.

For a year she admired him at a distance, blushing when he deigned to speak to her, staying after school on Thursdays, when the Cats had home games, to watch him play. It wasn't even suspicious; everyone did it, everyone wanted to see if Tony Joyce would knock the ball out of the park. Then, her sophomore year, they ended up in Art 1 together, assigned by the teacher to share a table, and they talked often and easily. He was, she discovered quickly, a natural artist — with the drawing board propped against the table and resting on his thighs, his left hand flew over the page, confidently putting down light pencil strokes, then, when the curve was right, darkening them into certainty. Susanna's first still life was flat and static, her glass milk bottle just an outline, the flower petals all facing stolidly forward; Tony's bottle gleamed and refracted, the raised lettering on the outside, SCHEFF BROS, making just the tiniest hint of shadow on the opposing facet, the petals dewy and more vibrant than they were in life.

In spring they were assigned a portrait, and the week Susanna spent working on hers was blissful. For fifty minutes each day, she had permission — an obligation — to look at Tony, to scrutinize him. She was nervous at first about his skin color; her initial attempt, like the milk bottle, was flat, his features a coloring-book outline, his skin an even charcoal gray. He insisted on peeking, and she went crimson revealing it to him.

"It's actually pretty good," he'd said. "You've got the proportions right. But look at me." She darted her eyes to his face, then just as quickly away. "Do I have a hard line around my chin?"

"Not really," she said.

"What about my eyes?"

"No."

"Look for the light spots in my face and shade around them. Start with the faint strokes and then darken into the shadows. Like this." He erased a heavy line she'd drawn, then took her pencil and laid it on an angle, whiskering, the sound scratchily pleasant. He smudged with his middle finger, put down some darker shading, smudged a bit more. A fleshy cheek appeared on Susanna's page, an illusion of soft light, and he was close enough that Susanna could breathe in, unnoticed, what she'd started over the last weeks to think of as *him,* his essence: some kind of minty cologne, the sweet spice of his skin. At home one night, blushing in the darkness of her bedroom, she'd imagined nuzzling his neck, moving her lips against the teardrop of skin above his collarbone, swallowing whole the mint and spice of him. "Do you see?"

"Yeah," she murmured. She worked on the opposite cheek, clumsily mimicking him, having to erase a few times but finally getting something that looked a bit like what he'd done and, at the least, was a whole lot better than her first attempt. She smiled at the page. "Thanks, Tony."

"No problem."

"What about mine?"

He grinned. "What about it?"

"Let's see. C'mon, show me." Emboldened, she pushed his shoulder the way she'd seen Ronnie do with guys, teasing and playful.

"All right." He turned his own drawing

board toward her, and Susanna drew in breath — she really did — and put a hand out hesitantly to touch the image. It was like the still life, true but better than true: he'd accentuated her best feature, her dark eyes and long lashes; and her chin, miserably small and drawn like Ronnie's and their father's, had been sharpened ever so slightly, so that she looked cutely elfin. Her hair, an everyday, limp brown, pulled lightly from her temples and fell in waves around her shoulders. But more than these improvements — and Susanna might have been insulted by them, had not this other been true — he'd somehow put her spirit into the page. There was a light in her eyes, a slight sarcastic upturn to the corner of her mouth. There was a suggestion of the chicken pox scar beside her right eyebrow. It was beautiful and it was *her*, truly her, and it seemed to Susanna that he could only see her like this if he liked her. That he'd only have shown her the drawing if he wanted her to know he did.

"Oh, Tony," she said. It was the most romantic moment of her life. Almost fourteen years later, she still thought so. "Oh."

"Thanks." He said it sincerely, with feeling. He shifted nervously on his stool, then leaned toward her. "Suze. You want to go out sometime?" He added, as though it helped his case: "I've seen you at my games."

Her neck prickled. She ran a finger over his portrait of her, feeling the grooves in the paper, the places where Tony had made his mark hard enough to leave an indentation. It would one day occur to Susanna that she hadn't told anyone about this moment because she had never had the language for telling; she could never explain the bloom of joy and fear within her, the fierce pride, the physical hunger. If he'd asked her outside after school, it all might have ended differently. Alone, he might have kissed her — for so long she'd wanted him to — and if he'd kissed her she wouldn't have been able to say no to him. But they weren't alone. They were in a room full of their classmates, and the art teacher was moving among the tables, making suggestions, and Susanna had time, seconds, to think of her father. It wouldn't matter to him that Tony was a baseball star, a local hero; it wouldn't matter to him that Tony had gotten a full ride to the University of Kentucky, that everyone believed he'd be signed to the major leagues before he was twenty. Her father wouldn't let Tony into their house, and if Susanna tried to leave with him, there'd be hell to pay.

This next was the part of the memory Susanna always skipped over: she said no. She had, she seemed to remember, made some excuse, lame to her own ears, impossible to believe. Tony had been kind, quiet — he hadn't pressed her. He had, she would later realize, understood the truth of their lives in Roma better than she ever could. In the weeks left in the semester he spoke to her pleasantly enough but infrequently, and Susanna heard in April that he'd asked Sheralyn Hill to prom with him, and Sheralyn — a senior, black — said yes.

On the last day of school, Susanna went to her locker between periods and saw that something had been slid part of the way into the gap where her door failed to latch tight. It was the portrait of her, of course, an "A" penned onto the lower back corner, Tony's signature scribbled messily on the front. Years later Dale would find it, going through old papers, and he'd ask her in a rare moment of sentimentality if she would mind if he framed it and placed it in his office on campus. Surprised and moved, she would say yes. So that's where it now hung: on a cinder-block wall in Roma High School, perhaps fifty feet from the table where an eighteen-year-old had drawn it — a token, though Dale didn't know it, of the day when Susanna first set foot on the path to becoming his.

2.

She made it to the police station by four o'clock. She checked her reflection in the rearview mirror, embarrassed by the gesture even as she made it, but she couldn't bear the thought of Tony seeing her as plain, as lesser. Her hair, still long and brown, was drawn from her face with a fabric headband. Her makeup routine for anything but the rare special occasion was minimal: a dab of mascara and some tinted lip gloss, which she reapplied now. She didn't think much about her looks these days; married, a mother, she accepted as fact that she was a person defined more by these roles than any essential core, her job robbing her of what little she had left. Creativity. Intellectual curiosity. Eighth graders were the most self-absorbed kids in the world, and they didn't notice Susanna, didn't distinguish the days when she'd curled her hair from the days when she'd pulled it, unwashed, into a limp ponytail. Dale, slightly better, took pains to compliment her on Sunday mornings before they went to church and before the faculty Christmas party — any situation calling for

179

her to don a dress and pantyhose. But the clothes were mostly the same ones from five years ago, and so were his mild expressions of appreciation. She wanted, just once, for him to see her in a regular moment — cradling Abby before bedtime, chopping a carrot for dinner, tying her shoelaces before a walk — and to say, in that voice of pleased surprise she'd heard on TV and in movies, "Wow, you look beautiful."

When she bothered, she bothered for Abby. Abby appreciated her. "Mommy's pretty," she said once, running a paddle brush through Susanna's hair. That's why she'd never had the heart to cut it shorter, though she was, in her late twenties, starting to feel pressure from her mother to go with a more sensible style, to have it clipped close to her head and feathered, the way many of the women at church wore it. Of course, Abby, who so loved her long hair, was also the child who'd said "Aunt Ronnie's a princess" the time Ronnie came over in her trashiest club-crawling wear and dark purple eye shadow, hair sprayed to the rafters. Susanna laughed at the memory, then swallowed against tears. How she wanted her sister right now.

In the station, a receptionist directed her down the same hallway as before but to a different office number. The door was open, a triangle of bright fluorescent light carved into the pilled carpet. From inside there was a low hum and the staccato report of electric typewriter keys. Susanna stepped into the doorway, rapping softly against the frame.

"Come in," Tony said, waving her forward. He moved some papers to the side and flipped a switch on the typewriter, leaving the room in sudden quiet. "Well," he said, getting a look at her. He was smiling faintly. "I knew that I knew you. Suzy Eastman."

Susanna flushed, looked down at her hands. "I can't believe you remember me."

"You know better than that." He reached across the table, took her hand, squeezed it. He was more handsome to Susanna than he'd been in high school, when she'd so clumsily drawn him — his gangly limbs now even and strong, his hair clipped close to his well-shaped head. He had a goatee — it might have been hiding the slightest plumpness under his chin — and he was wearing an outfit that would have made Susanna smile if she'd been here under lighter pretense: a collared white shirt and blue tie, an argyle sweater-vest, pleated corduroy trousers. He looked like a college professor.

"You look great," she said before she could stop herself.

He shrugged, embarrassed, and released her hand. "Trying to stay respectable. Now, look at you. All grown-up."

"And feeling every bit of it," she said.

"Kids?"

"One. You?"

He shook his head, and Susanna was ashamed and amused at her relief.

"Haven't had time to settle down," he said, taking his seat again. Susanna followed his lead, perching nervously on an old wooden swivel chair that wanted to recline too far. It creaked beneath her weight.

"So tell me about Ronnie," Tony said. "You say she's been missing a little over a week?"

"It looks that way," Susanna said. She was reassured by his seriousness and professionalism, especially after her conversation with Sergeant What's-His-Name. "I haven't heard from her in two weeks — well, almost three now — and they told me at the sewing factory that she hasn't clocked in since Friday the twenty-first. I —"

"So she did report to work on the twenty-first?"

Susanna nodded.

He jotted down some notes. "OK, go ahead."

"I went to her house on —" She had to

think. "Saturday. Just this past Saturday, to check on her. I let myself in with her spare key. It smelled so bad that I thought at first —" She stopped herself again. "Well, I don't want to tell you what I thought. But it was food, a bunch of food that had obviously been sitting out for a while. Gas station food: livers, fried potatoes, stuff like that. And a lot of empty beers. Oh!" She grabbed her purse and unzipped it, fumbling around inside for the Fill-Up receipt, then smoothed it on the desk in front of him. "I found this."

He scanned it. "Looks like food for two," he said.

"I thought the same thing."

He jotted some more notes. "And Buddy Pendleton said there was something about a prescription?"

Susanna nodded. "Her birth control. The last pill she'd taken was on a Saturday. I don't know if you know how those work" — she was blushing — "but it's set up like a calendar, but without dates. I don't think it's possible that she took it this past Saturday. If she'd been in the house that day she would have called me, and I don't think she'd have left things the way I found them."

"So we're looking at the twenty-third. Or more likely, early on the twenty-fourth. It was almost midnight when she bought the food."

"Yes." His certainty had disarmed her for a second, but then it occurred to her what he was suggesting, what his notes were funneling down toward. "You think something happened to her."

His gaze was level. "You don't?"

She burst into tears.

A tissue was pressed into her hand. "Hang tight, Suzy. We don't know a thing. We're just going over every little bit we've got." He had moved around the desk to stand beside her, the spice of his skin familiar, the cologne bright and expensive smelling instead of minty. He touched her shoulder lightly. "We've got to keep a level head. You, too. I need your help."

Susanna wiped her eyes and nodded hard, like a child. "OK."

"I should go over to the house, take a look at things for myself." He hesitated. "Can you let me in over there now? Walk me through, show me what you found?"

She looked at her watch — it was a quarter after four, and Abby's day care closed at five thirty. She'd promised not to be late again. And Dale, who was demanding nightly practices in anticipation of this weekend's state semifinals, couldn't be roused to action on his daughter's behalf until seven or eight o'clock tonight. *Shacking up with some guy,* he'd said. She didn't know why her husband had brought her back to a town she hated, near a family he himself disdained, if he didn't want Susanna to have a relationship with Ronnie. It seemed to her now, for the first time, like an act of deliberate cruelty, like something her father, had he been smarter and cooler headed, would have done.

"Could I meet you there?" she said finally. "Around five o'clock? I know that you're supposed to be off duty soon. I don't want to keep you."

"It's no problem. This is my job."

"Five, then," she said. She rose, shook his hand again. "I'll be there. Thank you, Tony."

He waved dismissively. "It's my job."

3.

She could hear the band from the parking lot, even feel them — a vibration, rattling the rearview mirror of her car as she bent into the backseat to extract Abby. They were on the second movement of their show, *The Scores of John Williams,* and the song, the Yoda melody from *Star Wars,* was a soft transition between showstoppers.

Abby had only been to the high school a

few times, and she took in the sights and sounds of adolescence with bright interest: the beaten-up cars of band kids, some football players stripped to their T-shirts and pads even in the cold, a couple of pretty girls — drama kids, Susanna guessed — smoking cigarettes behind the auditorium, their nails painted blue and green and their hair tied back with patterned silk scarves. Costume or affectation, Susanna wasn't sure. Older girls fascinated Abby, and she was drawn to them like a sad puppy, pleased and beseeching, grateful for any show of attention. When one of the smoking girls smiled at her, she beamed.

"How's it going, half pint?" the girl said.

Abby grinned and didn't reply.

Susanna stopped Abby before turning the corner to the practice field and hunched over her. "It's cold out, duckie," she said, retying Abby's coat hood so that only a saucer's worth of pale face showed. She adjusted her daughter's gloves, tucking them into the elastic bands of her sleeves, then tapped her playfully on her nose, which was pink with chill.

"I can hear Daddy's music," Abby said.

Susanna took her small hand, feeling a hitch in her chest at the little fingers, thick and clumsy in their knit gloves. "I know you can." She started across the lawn briskly, while her courage and ire were up, Abby trotting a little to keep pace. Dale was up in the Box, which was really just a rickety wooden scaffolding, two stories high with a platform at the top and a relatively new set of handrails, which Dale himself had installed last year. As always, a long cord trailed from this perch down to a set of speakers on the ground, and Abby jolted, her hand clutching harder at Susanna's, as Dale's voice suddenly blasted from them, the music on the field disintegrating in little squawks and stutters before coming to a stop:

"No, no, no. You're falling apart again in the fifth set. Take it back to three. Mack, you're always about two big steps out of formation whenever the percussion backs into the circle. Your steps are too big. Smaller steps, OK? Color guard, what in God's name are you doing back there?"

"It's the wind," a girl shouted. "These flags are too light."

"Then put weights on them. But not until we manage to finish the show without stopping. This is ridiculous."

The students were groaning and shifting from foot to foot. It was a strange thing, how much power Dale had over the fifty or so teenagers standing in a November chill, their breath painting the air, fingertips torn from gloves so that every note of John Williams could be played to perfection. Susanna could see a resignation in them, even now, that was rarely present in her eighth graders. They were defeated but respectful. Dale had cultivated a reputation for paternal gruffness and heart — "your chewy center," Susanna said sometimes, playfully, to irritate him — and the students wanted mostly to please him, to see his mild smirk, to hear him say, in his unimpressed way, "Not bad." Daddy Dale, they'd call him when spirits were high: these teenagers, some almost to college, who wouldn't have been caught dead calling their own fathers anything but Dad. When Susanna was pregnant with Abby four years ago, the band kids all started calling her Mama Suzy, and more than one girl reached out and put her hand right on Susanna's belly, as though it were fine, as though they didn't need to ask. It was one of the reasons Susanna had started accompanying Dale to fewer competitions: not the distaste of being fussed over by teenage girls (though she was, a bit shamefully, uncomfortable with it, with them) so much as the distaste of being called Mama — as though, still then in her early twenties, she were not just Abby's mother but some band mother, a mother de facto, a mascot. As though her life, too, revolved around these kids and their practices and their small weekend triumphs.

"I want bigger punch from the brass, too." Dale sang some bars now in his pleasant tenor, calling the notes *dee*s and *dum*s and *dah*s. This had always embarrassed Susanna. "Like that: *dah* dee dah dah. OK, get into position. Let's see if we can make it through the song without stopping." The kids straightened their backs, lifted instruments into place. In the back of the field, the color guard held their flags, which were made with some kind of greenish, gauzy cloth, above their heads. Loyal. Determined. Dale would have been a great preacher, Susanna sometimes thought wryly. Or drill sergeant. Or cult leader. He was the kind of man with the public charisma to lead people to water or to Jesus or off the edge of a cliff.

"One, two, three," he chanted.

The music swelled again. Susanna looked up at the Box and thought Dale spotted her, so she waved. But he continued to hunch over the railing, one hand on his headset, and she supposed that he'd only glanced her way to check out the clarinets. This close, she could make out their low, woody hum above the sunny brass, the glassy flutes. Susanna had once played clarinet. It was a dull instrument, she thought — the instrument of dowdy brown-haired girls with heavy thighs.

It was a quarter till by her watch. She guessed that there were at least another eight minutes to the show from this point, if the kids made it to the end, and she shifted restlessly back and forth between her feet, Abby's hand still grasped tightly in her own. The students near her were squinting into the wind; at the back of the field, a tossed flag flew out of formation, and the girl who'd lost it went scrambling to retrieve it and return to her spot. Susanna couldn't watch them without feeling their stress, without worrying, as they did, that Dale would erupt into a rant of disappointment. But still — and worse for her today — they pressed forward uninterrupted, and Dale, his back to the brisk wind, was unconsciously conducting, his left palm bobbing, a motion that always reminded Susanna of putting her hand outside of a car window on a warm day, skipping it on a current of air, letting her fingertips jump driveways and mailboxes and walked dogs. She and Ronnie had made a game of it as girls, Susanna always in the seat behind their father,

Ronnie on the passenger side where there was more legroom, their arms extended out on both sides of the car like flapping wings.

She led Abby over to the scaffolding and put the gloved hand she was holding on a wooden beam. "Mommy's going to go up to tell Daddy something," she said. "You keep your hand here and don't move it, OK?"

"What happens if I move it?" Abby's expression might have been mischievous or it might have been wary.

"You lose the game," Susanna said.

Abby stood very still, her feet neatly side by side, back straight. Her arm was raised to almost shoulder level to grasp the beam, and the set of her mouth was serious.

"It'll just be a minute," Susanna said.

The stairs, she noted with unease, groaned as she scaled the scaffolding, and the wind up here was worse, whistling from behind her against the metal roof of the high school. Her sister was missing — she could be anywhere, anything might have happened to her — and here Dale was, riding this band tower like the captain of a ship, as though what he was doing really mattered. He was glancing over his shoulder as she surfaced, expression unsurprised, though this was the first time in their marriage that

191

Susanna had joined him up here, the first time she'd interrupted one of his practices. He might have felt the vibration of her ascent. But he had also seen her wave before. She was suddenly sure of it.

There was a lull as the Yoda theme ended, a hiccup of silence before the first startling blast of "The Olympic Fanfare," and Susanna said, stealing the seconds, "I need you to keep Abby."

He switched a button on his headset and moved the microphone down beneath his chin. His face was pink with windburn, his lips chapped, and he looked vigorous and strong, like he'd been skiing or out for a run. The band continued to play from below.

"I'm meeting a detective about Ronnie," Susanna said as loudly as she could without shouting. "I'm going to let him into her house. He agrees with me that something seems off."

"Why didn't you leave Abby at the day care?" He had *the look* already, Susanna noted: eyes popped, brows knit with incredulity; his mouth was slightly open, his head cocked to the side. She had always hated *the look,* even as she knew that she had her own version of it, the one she wore when he came home an hour later than he'd promised, or when he told her only the night before that it was his turn to bring snacks to the teachers' lounge.

"They close at five thirty. You know that."

"And you can't bring her with you? To this —" He waved his hand, conducting again. "This whatever it is?"

"I wish you'd take this seriously for a moment," Susanna said. "My sister's been gone over a week. She hasn't been at work. She's not answering calls. I'm not bringing our daughter to meet this detective. I can't keep my mind on this and her all at once."

Dale lifted his glasses and pinched the skin between his eyes. "Saturday. I ask for a little consideration until Saturday. That's it." A drop of rain hit his shoulder and he wiped at it roughly. "This is my job. This is what I do for a living."

"Ronnie is my sister," Susanna said. "Do you not get that?" More drops were falling, stippling the plank floor, and she trembled in her thin coat. "I don't have a choice. Your daughter is at the bottom of this tower, and it's raining, and it's about time you stepped up and did your part. None of this is important like you think it is. None of this." She waved her own arms mockingly toward the field.

"I have practice." He turned and leaned

back over the railing, shoulders hunched against the rain. "It's over in an hour. I can watch Abby then."

"I'm not kidding with you, Dale."

"Neither am I." He switched his mike back on. *He's going to electrocute himself,* she thought.

Let him, a voice inside her whispered. It might have been Ronnie's.

Susanna stumbled on the stairs down, so angry that her legs were unsteady. This was his job, was it? Standing in the rain? Bossing around children? And he only asked for a *little* consideration, as though it wasn't Susanna always picking Abby up, as if it wouldn't be time soon enough for concert band, All-District and All-Region, more long Saturdays away, more long weeknight practices. He made only three thousand more a year than she did. He worked the same eight-hour school day. But these practices, these fucking band practices, had given him — he thought — the entitlement to do as little as he desired to in the rest of their married life. Susanna did the parenting, the cooking, the cleaning, the grocery shopping; she paid the bills and balanced the checkbook; she sent birthday cards to Dale's parents and sisters and nephews because she knew that Dale wouldn't remember to, or be bothered to. She was the manager and the secretary and the janitor of their marriage, Dale the CEO, and she was sick of it, she was *sick*. She came to the bottom of the steps and saw Abby still standing in her hooded coat, hand still on the tower's scaffolding, her body a hard right angle. She loved the child more than she loved Dale, more than she had ever loved him. She loved her more than Ronnie. It was, she figured, a given that she loved her more than herself. But that was the cruel punch line of motherhood, wasn't it? You loved more than yourself, you lost yourself, and your husband grew to depend upon it, to take advantage of it. You made a daughter and wanted more for her than that, but you lost the ability to show her the way. A way to be a woman who loves rather than a mere vessel of love.

Susanna lifted her coat over her head and ran.

Abby might have called after her. Susanna felt the call rather than heard it, the band too loud for a four-year-old's voice to penetrate, and she hadn't even made it to the parking lot before she hated herself, before she felt certain she'd done the wrong thing. Dale was there — Dale would go to their daughter — but this was the kind of moment that Abby would never forget, her mother running away from her, ignoring her. There would be years and years to make this up to her, years stacked one atop another like those mattresses in the fairy tale, and beneath it all the pea, the tiny bit that shouldn't matter but does, the princess tossing and turning above it. Had Susanna ever forgotten the day at the van with Ronnie? Or the time she'd seen her drunken father, naked as Noah, passed out on the living room sofa? *He's dead to me anyway,* she'd said to Dale, remembering the scroll-work of curly hairs on her father's soft inner thighs, the flaccid penis drooping, his scrotum bunched like moldy fruit.

She looked back once before rounding the corner and making the last dash to her car. Abby hadn't moved. Her hand was still in place against the tower, the other lifted in good-bye, and Susanna was too ashamed to wave in reply, to let her daughter know she'd seen her.

CHAPTER NINE

1.

It was a cold night, the first of the season, and Christopher's mother had insisted that they light the fireplace — the real one, not the gas logs in the recreation room that you could coax into flame with a switch — and drink hot cocoa. So he did as she asked, letting her fill his Telluride mug from the saucepan on the stove, letting her drop in a half dozen mini marshmallows, letting her steer him to the room in the house that he most hated, where he'd have to sit ramrod-straight on the sofa to balance his drink. This was the Sitting Room. He thought of it that way, as a formal destination, and it was: a place you planned to go to, or where your mother told you to go, and not a place where you happened to end up. He came into this room perhaps half a dozen times a year. It faced Main Street and the formal entryway, a pair of double doors so tall that

197

Christopher couldn't reach the lintel if he stood on tiptoe and stretched his middle finger as high as it would go. He didn't even have a key to that door. Most days he entered the house through the utility room, grabbed a soda from the kitchen, and then went back out immediately to the guesthouse, where he'd been allowed to sleep since his thirteenth birthday. He had a twenty-six-inch color TV and a VCR out there — his parents' hand-me-downs, but still — a Super Nintendo game station, a foosball table, and a new IBM computer with a dot-matrix printer. The walls were draped with banners that he'd printed out over summer break, when the novelty hadn't yet worn out. The one hanging over his bed was five sheets of paper long and read CHRISTOPHER'S PAD in block letters. He'd found pictures of Corvettes in the clip art folder and used these to flank the legend.

She wanted him to speak first. He would *not* speak first.

"Well," she said finally. She was sitting on the sofa opposite his, looking at the fire, legs pulled up catlike beneath her hip. The soft light of the flames made her face seem prettier than it really was. Younger. She was a fixture in his life, a neutral — at most, perhaps, a reflective surface. He checked her face to make sure that he was loved, forgiven, approved of, amusing; he checked to determine if he was in trouble. He paid attention only to the things she said that concerned him. He was the center of her life — he knew this, had not considered it could be otherwise — so most of what she said concerned him. And this was true not because he was a bad child or an unusually spoiled child, but because he was a child still.

"We could watch TV if we were in the rec room," he said, filling the silence.

"Mmm." She still looked at the fire, not at him. Her dark blond hair, smoothed behind an ear, glinted. "That's true. And yet, here we are."

He looked around as if to confirm the fact, miming surprise, thinking she might laugh.

"They're going to suspend you, Chris," she said. "What on earth do you have to say for yourself?"

He choked a little on the cocoa he'd just sipped, surprised that she'd unleashed on him so quickly.

"Well?"

"Nothing," he said. "I guess I don't have anything to say."

Her face sagged into distress. "Why did you do that to that girl? Was it —" She ran her thumb along the lip of her mug. "Did it go how the principal told me it did?"

Christopher remembered the instant when he'd looked down, as if from a distance, and watched his hand take up a wet, sloppy handful of his pasta. Then the memory shifted to sensation — the hard fling forward, the pull in his shoulder. Finally, a snapshot: the ropes of spaghetti spattering Emily's shocked face. The act was in motion before Christopher could decide to do it. Which was not to say that he'd been possessed or out of control, that he hadn't wanted to hurt Emily in that moment, because he had, and he'd felt good — damn good — when he did. For the instant. By the time Leanna had lobbed her chunk of garlic bread and Craig his chocolate pudding, and the cafeteria had erupted around them all in gleeful, frantic confusion, Christopher was already wishing that he hadn't done it. He wished this as he threw the rest of his spaghetti, his own pudding and bread, his paper basket of iceberg lettuce and pink dressing — as he yelled "You freak!" and heard the word echoed by the kids around him. What power he had! He hadn't known how much until that moment.

"I'm sorry, Mom," he said, and he meant it.

She exhaled. "Jesus. What a cruel thing. To think that I was just at school the other day defending you, saying how mature you are."

He blew on his cocoa though it had already gotten cool.

"I mean it. I called your father at work this afternoon —"

Christopher gulped.

"— and told him everything. He didn't care like I did. He said boys will be boys. And I can see you wanting to smirk over there —"

He shook his head emphatically.

"— but I'd save it if I were you, because he's steamed about this suspension stuff. If it goes through, that's just the beginning of what you're going to suffer. Don't think it's going to be a week home playing video games and foosball." She rubbed her eyes. "But he has Johnny Burke on it, so we'll see. Though I'm not convinced that you should get off the hook for this one."

He shifted. The wooden couch frame dug into his neck.

"I'd punish you myself if I thought it'd make a difference. But is that going to teach you to feel bad in your heart? Taking away your Nintendo? Moving you back in the house? You've made me sick with this,

Christopher. I don't know if I'm ever going to see you the same again."

"Mom —" he started, but she made a curt gesture with her chin and he knew to close his mouth.

"Please go to your room and think about what you've done. I'm not coming in to take your computer. I'm not telling you what to do or not to do out there. But spare a thought for that girl you were mean to. Ask yourself how it felt to be her today. Will you do that?"

"Yes," he said.

She made a shooing motion. "Go on, then."

He did as she asked. He didn't turn on the computer or the TV; he didn't idly spin the knobs on his foosball table, as he sometimes did when he was daydreaming or thinking through one of his English papers. He lay on his bed, pushed his tennis shoes off, and stared at the ceiling.

Freak!

He remembered helping Emily in seventh grade with that stupid tadpole project. They had come in one morning to find them all dead, charred black by the UV lamp and floating, and she had started sniffling. "You didn't do anything wrong," he'd told her, resting his hand briefly and unthinkingly on her shoulder. It was nothing — empty comfort — but he had set something into motion that day.

Freak!

The diamond of pale skin through the chain link, the gray-green eyes wide, the way she'd suddenly jerked back and run as if to go tell.

Freak!

Leanna, still crouched in front of him: *Oh my God, what was* that *about?*

His eyes burned with sudden, hot tears, and though there was no one around to see him, he rolled over, hiding his face in a pillow.

2.

Sometime later, there was a knock at the door of his room.

"Come in," he called, still lying down, expecting his mother. When his father entered heavily, stomping on the front mat as he slid out of his suit coat, Christopher scrambled to wipe his face and right himself, jumping to a stand at the foot of his bed. His father hardly ever came out here. He worked long days, usually a few hours throughout the weekend, too, and he spent a lot of his time at home holed up in what he called his "office," though there wasn't much official about it by Christopher's estimation: a worn-in leather recliner, a small television, his books — he liked true crime stories, Tom Clancy, John Grisham — a dartboard. It was the only room in the house where he smoked, so it smelled of sweet tobacco, perhaps also a little of body odor, or laundry that needed washing. Dad's Pad. It occurred to Christopher, watching his father survey this room as though he'd never been inside it before (he was rubbing his thumb over a medal, hanging from a thumbtack on the bulletin board, that Christopher had received for placing second in last year's regional science fair), that he and his parents were like planets orbiting the sun: they were pulled toward the same center, but they lived in isolation from one another, their paths hardly crossing.

"I won't stay long," his father said. He sat at the computer desk, spinning in the chair and crossing his arms. Christopher could tell that he wasn't angry — and that he wanted Christopher to know that he wasn't. He was doing that jovial "dad" thing: shifting around, picking random stuff up, lifting his eyebrows occasionally with interest. He did a quick *ba dum dum* on the tops of his thighs.

"So," he continued, "Mom's pissed. You'll have to work that out between the two of you. I'm just worried about this suspension business."

"I'm sorry, Dad."

"Eh. Lot of good that does me. You didn't throw your fucking green beans in *my* face, did you?"

Christopher shook his head.

"I'm not saying it was a good thing to do, mind you. It wasn't. I never did stuff like that to little girls when I was your age. But, you know, I get it. Peer pressure, your friends gang up on you, everyone's working everybody else up. And it washes off, that's the thing. It's not like you hurt her."

"I think I hurt her," Christopher said hoarsely.

"Physically, son. This isn't Phil Donahue. This isn't about what the girl's going to tell her shrink in ten years. It's about whether or not a group of kids, really good kids, ought to get their records fucked up for doing one shitty prank. I say no. Leanna's dad says no. We'll see what happens."

They were silent for a moment, his father still spinning back and forth in the chair, Christopher leaning slightly against his bed frame.

"You can't go back tomorrow — the

principal's put his foot down on that. Maybe a second day, too. But two days won't mean much, and it's not like this is high school, at least, thank God. That's when you have to worry about your GPA."

His father was already thinking about college, making plans, getting all jacked up when Christopher didn't score high enough on the PSATs to qualify for the National Merit program. Christopher suppressed the urge to roll his eyes.

"We're fighting for you guys to spend the rest of next week in ALC instead of getting suspended. That's more punishment to kids your age, anyway. You'd just be watching TV if you were home, and at least this way you can keep your mouth shut for a few days and really think about what you've done. And it'll give that girl some time to readjust, too. And everybody can keep up with their studies, and nobody's education suffers. That's what Johnny's working on."

Christopher picked at a fingernail and nodded. He wasn't sure how to feel. This was all good news, right? And no one from school had called about anything that happened at the tennis court, so Emily hadn't even tattled. He didn't know why she'd keep her mouth shut after what he and Leanna had done to her this afternoon, but she had. So far.

"Well? What do you have to say?"

"Thanks," Christopher said. And, again, "I'm sorry."

"Yeah." His father stood, leaned over to squeeze his shoulder. "Lesson learned. OK, get some sleep. I think Mom has a bunch of chores planned for you tomorrow."

"All right," he said.

"We'll work it out." He stopped at the door. "You and Leanna still a thing?"

Christopher shrugged, embarrassed. Then he nodded.

"She's pretty, huh?"

"Yeah."

His father cleared his throat. "You're young to have a girlfriend. You don't even have a car. You still get an allowance, for God's sake."

"We just hang out," Christopher said.

"Yeah, I bet that's all." He put his coat over his arm. "Well, you be smart. And stick close to her until this blows over. Her dad's the last person you want to piss off right now."

"OK."

"Night, Chris."

"Night." The door snicked closed softly.

It was cold in the room, so Christopher

switched on the heater, almost enjoying the musty smell as the summer's dust started to burn away. It was a winter smell, a Thanksgiving smell. The end of the year would be here in no time. He slid out of his clothes, considered brushing his teeth — shrugged, for no one's benefit but his own, and decided not to — then slid between the cool bedclothes, shivering pleasantly. He was glad that his father wasn't pissed, glad to not be going to school tomorrow. Glad, he had to admit to himself, for the promise of a day away from Leanna.

Still, he couldn't help but drift to sleep remembering the tennis court, Leanna's hot mouth on him, the thrill and shame of it. He moved his feet out of the pocket of sheet he'd warmed, flipped his pillow. The smooth cotton felt good against his neck. He was hard again, and then he was thinking about Emily's face in the lunchroom, and he swallowed against a sudden rise of nausea. *Tennis court,* he willed. The slow pull of the zipper, the grasp of cold fingers, Leanna's hot mouth on him. The pull, the sense that he was being unraveled.

Freak! Freak! Freak! Emily's shocked face. Her tears after.

Leanna was unbuckling his belt, her hot mouth was on him.

He drifted off, caught for half the night in that restless place between dreaming and wakefulness, caught between his memories of the pleasure of the day and the horror, building toward a climax that ebbed, always, into snapshots from the cafeteria — Emily's tears, Mrs. Mitchell's anger — and then, when he felt his conscious self finally intervening, dragging him back to the room, where his groin felt bruised against the faint pressure of the sheet, he thought at last of Emily's eyes through the chain link, their bright shock, and he tightened his fingers into Leanna's wavy hair, found his breath again, and slept.

CHAPTER TEN

1.

It was after ten when Susanna got back from her meeting with Tony Joyce. She came in, dropped her shoulder bag by the coat hook, and observed Dale sitting stiff and neat in his recliner with a glass of milk in his hand. She could see on his face that he had noticed the irony of their reversed roles, that he had tried an evening of being the one waiting, left behind, and hadn't liked it.

"I've already gotten a phone call," Dale said. "Michael Sheffield, from the bank. Said he saw a flyer with my sister-in-law's picture on it. He offered his condolences."

Word had traveled fast. She and Tony had gone to the house first, where he listened seriously to her and took copious notes, and then they had gone back to the police department, sat down together at the office's one shared computer, and designed a

MISSING flyer. It had been . . . well, nice. He had shown her how to use CorelDRAW, and it was amazing, this computer world that had not yet interested her or touched her much, aside from the couple of hours a week at school that she had the students spend word-processing some of their writing assignments. She and Tony played with fonts and clip art, settled on bold text only, the oversized word MISSING like a siren call at the top of the page, the other pertinent info also in all caps and centered below a space where they would tape the photograph before making copies. They used the one good recent photo Susanna had been able to find of Ronnie. She had taken it herself the previous Thanksgiving (could that be almost a year ago now?), and Ronnie was not, for once, making a face at the camera or hiding behind her hand. She was smirking, still — *Get it over with,* Susanna remembered her saying when she brought out the camera — but smirking was a recognizably Ronnie expression. Most anyone who had seen her would have seen her making this look.

It had been like college again. Not just because Susanna was seated so close to a man who was not her husband, or because that man had once made her light up with joy, but because she was learning, doing something new; she was putting creative energy into something other than her classes and her daughter. That the object of her efforts was a poster advertising her missing sister did not rob the activity of all of its pleasure. She had felt more alive then, and later, driving around town with Tony to post the flyers, than she had in a long time.

"I guess that was nice of him," she said finally. "Premature, but nice."

"It's embarrassing." He crossed his legs. "Go ahead and make me the bad guy. It's fine. But I don't believe for a minute that Ronnie's missing, or no more missing than she wants to be."

Susanna threw up her hands. "What's with you, Dale? Seriously. Say she's off somewhere, like you believe she is. Say she just took off. What on earth harm is it doing for me to look for her?"

"The problem's drawing every person in town's attention to the fact that your sister's a cokehead. It wouldn't surprise me if she was selling herself, too."

"You should hear yourself," Susanna said. "That is beyond the pale."

"And now you've got the police drawn into it. You're not doing Ronnie any favors."

It hit her then. Standing in the doorway

still, not completely out of her coat, arguing with her husband about the value of her sister's life — she realized that he disgusted her. She had made this man the father of her daughter, and Abby would bind them to one another for the rest of their lives. On the heels of this revelation came another. She was startled by it, shocked that she hadn't recognized it sooner. She put her coat on the hook in a dazed way, the truth vibrating inside her, making her feel a little drunk.

"This isn't about Ronnie," she said. "It's about me. You're punishing me."

"Don't be stupid."

"See, there you go." She looked at their living room full of the things he had chosen and sat on the couch she had chosen. The couch was as good a reminder as any that she was responsible, too. That a woman who could hate a thing that had once, not that long ago, seemed so perfect for her was a woman who didn't know herself well enough. "If I don't agree with you I'm stupid."

He shook his head. "Don't be that way."

" 'Don't be that way,' " Susanna repeated. "That's our lives together in a nutshell. Don't be that way, be this other way."

"I'm not even going to speak again," Dale

said. "You're twisting everything I say into this — this feminist bullshit."

"Fair enough," Susanna murmured. And he was right, in a way; it wasn't fair to express her dismay in ready-made homilies, in someone else's generic terms for outrage. She wasn't his victim. She wasn't without blame. If he had been much older than she, maybe, or smarter — but he wasn't, and yet here they were, twenty-eight and thirty-one years old, and they were settling into a lifetime of unkindness toward one another. She knew that she would support Dale if his sister went missing, that she would, in some ways, express more care than he himself could muster — but wouldn't that, too, be a judgment of him, a subtle dig? She couldn't sit here and sort out the gradations of guilt, what separated good intentions from ill. There were more significant sensations, physical ones, like the fact that if he tried to kiss her cheek or put his hand on her thigh right now, she would shudder.

"I'm not a bad person," Dale said. "I'm not punishing you — what would I punish you for? I mean, sure, I don't like Ronnie. I don't like the choices she's made. And whether we want to think it or not, she reflects on us. You, too, Suze. And she reflects on Abby."

"Anybody who'd let a grown woman's actions inform their judgment of a four-year-old child is too foolish for me to give a good goddamn about." Susanna went to the kitchen, took out a glass, and hunted for the bottle of wine that she hadn't finished on Friday. Dale had pushed it to the back of the refrigerator, as though he wanted to make it disappear but didn't have the courage to just pour it out. She emptied it into her glass and sipped. It was still cheap, still sour. But what a delight to flaunt it in front of her husband, and of course there was the entirely singular delight of the drink itself, the ritual of rolling the liquid on her tongue, the little zing of pleasure when she'd consumed enough to feel her face warm. If she were another kind of woman, living a different sort of life, no one would begrudge her this. She would have real wineglasses and friends that she could go out with for drinks after work. She would have friends. She would still be living in her own apartment — she liked to imagine herself in a city — or maybe, by this time, she would have found a man who shared her interests, and perhaps they would not marry at all. How radical that would have seemed to her twenty-two-year-old self. How horrified her mother would have been.

"What have we here?" Dale said. He had followed her. "It's nice to see you bringing your argument to a conclusion in the honored Eastman tradition." He curled his hand around an imaginary glass and tipped it back and forth, wiggling his eyebrows like Groucho Marx.

Susanna smirked and shook her head. She leaned her hips against the kitchen counter and sipped.

Dale sighed loudly. "I'd thought we'd be thinking about a second baby by now," he said matter-of-factly. "Actually, I'd thought we might even have one. Four years apart is good. It makes sense."

"Not everything has to make sense."

"I realize that, believe it or not." He pulled a chair out from the dinette set and sat. "I never mentioned it. I never pushed you. I kept thinking you'd say something one day, or that it would just happen, like it did with Abby." He was looking at her intently, his face almost handsome with the scrutiny. "And then I just knew at some point that Abby was it. I realized that motherhood doesn't make you happy."

She blinked against the pressure in her sinuses. "I am a good mother. I am seventy-five percent or more of the parenting she gets."

"I didn't say you weren't good at it," Dale said. His voice was almost kind. "I said you didn't want to do it."

And because he was right — because he had seen the truth she could usually hide from herself, and because she resented that so much intimacy existed still between them, she finished the wine, snapped her bangs out of her eyes, and said, "Maybe I just don't want to be the mother to any more of *your* children, Dale. Did you think of that?"

His face tensed, and his jaw quivered. Otherwise, he was very still. "Do you love me?"

"Do you love me?" she said sharply.

"Yes," he said. Susanna could tell, despite everything, that he meant it. "Do you love me? I want to know."

Susanna held her empty glass tightly and broke eye contact.

"Well," he said. "Well, that's that, then." He rose, scratched the back of his head in a sheepish way. "I'm turning in. Good night."

"Dale," she called after him.

"Good night," he repeated. When she came to bed a few moments later, having crept into Abby's room long enough to plant a soft kiss on the top of her head, he was resting peacefully on his back, hands folded on his stomach, face smooth with calm. He was fully occupying his half of the bed, not hunched away from the center, and Susanna slid in hesitantly beside him.

"I wonder what's worse," he said, just as Susanna was relaxing into the certainty that he wouldn't speak again. "Being stuck in a marriage to someone you love, who doesn't love you back? Or being stuck with someone you don't love."

"Who says we're stuck?" Susanna said hoarsely.

He laughed and rolled heavily over onto his side, shifting so that the springs creaked.

"When you figure out how to get un-stuck," he said, "let me know."

CHAPTER ELEVEN

1.

The rest of Wyatt's week in the hospital passed strangely. It should have been bad, the worst week of his life. There was the endless procession of nurses, orderlies, and doctors, the instructions against all that he took pleasure in: fat, salt, sugar. On Wednesday there was the angioplasty, which he'd been painfully awake for, and then, afterward, a full day and night of having to lie flat on a single thin pillow, nourished only with fluids. The yellow carnations on the sink — a gift from Price Electric — stood alone, then wilted, flowers bent over the vase like bowed heads. His groin was sore from the catheter, and he kept thinking he could feel the stent now behind his breastbone, especially since they'd started lifting the head of the bed, making it possible for him to watch television. It was a tiny pressure, irritatingly foreign, and the impossibility of its placement — the fact that it existed inside him now, out of reach — made him nervous, almost claustrophobic. He continued to knead his chest, looking like he was about to recite the Pledge of Allegiance.

But Boss was OK — and, more than that, Morris Houchens had taken the dog in until Wyatt could return home. "He's a good old boy," Morris had said, standing awkwardly at the foot of Wyatt's bed on Thursday evening, hands plunged to the forearms in the pockets of his blue jeans. "Billy loves dogs. They're company to each other. And Emily's taking him for walks."

"I'm grateful to you," Wyatt kept saying, and Morris kept waving him off.

"Not a problem." Morris had shrugged sheepishly, looking down at Wyatt's bedcovers as though eye contact were too much for him. "When will you get out of here?"

"They're telling me Sunday."

Morris reached up to lift his baseball cap and scratch the back of his head. "I could come over here to give you a ride after I get home from church, if that's not too late."

Wyatt swallowed against a sudden ache in his sinuses. "You've already done too much. Don't you worry about it."

"No. I don't mind. I'll just take you home on Sunday, and then I'll do some grocery shopping for you if you need me to. Maybe you could make me a list between now and then." He said this all matter-of-factly, the issue already settled. "I've talked to HR. There's some forms for you to fill out when you're up to it."

Wyatt nodded, weighted with dread. He'd been worrying about work, about how quickly he'd be able to get back, about whether or not he'd be capable of doing the job once he did. *You move slow,* he could hear Jusef saying, his brows lowered. *You put me behind.*

"I could probably go over there on Monday for the forms," Wyatt said. "But I don't know if I can be at work just yet. I might need a few days."

Morris actually laughed out loud. "Heavens, they don't expect you back next week or the week after that. You can take a couple of months now that that act's passed, but you'll have to file for unemployment."

"Oh." This seemed too sensible, too easy. "Huh."

"I'll take you by that office, too. But it can all wait until next week. You just rest up now."

"I don't know what to say, Morris."

"Nothing's best. I don't like a lot of hoopla."

"All right, then."

"You sleep tight," Morris had said. "You've got a lot on your plate tomorrow."

And indeed, he had: the angioplasty early in the morning, the day flat on his back, needles, bitter pills, the sheets beneath him that were always too hot or too wrinkled, so that he could pass thirty minutes just thinking about the ridge of folded bedclothes passing horizontally under his back. Bland soups, sugarless Jell-O. Hobbling out of bed, rolling his IV stand with one hand and holding his gown closed behind him with the other, each creaking step to the bathroom a humiliation. Wyatt had plenty on his plate.

But he also had Sarah — and her presence in the days following was a surprise, a comfort, a wonder. She would come to him, even when she wasn't working, on official pretense: checking his chart; looking at fluid levels; asking him, as though she didn't trust her colleagues, if he were being attended to properly. Then, the ceremony complete, she'd take a seat beside his bed, grasp his hand, and smile her pretty smile. Its beauty, Wyatt thought, was in its layers of contradiction, for it was both brash and shy, confident and insecure, her straight white teeth so often flecked with a spot of her too-pink, waxy lipstick.

"I'm going to take you dancing someday," he said to her on Friday, so bold he shocked himself.

"I don't know if I've got another night at Nancy's in me," she said, but he could tell she was pleased.

"Not Nancy's. Somewhere good. We'll go to Nashville."

"Well," she said, "you better work on getting better quick."

He made a loose fist, mimed knocking on his heart. "I'm bionic now."

"Bionic, my ass," she snorted.

Her left hand was in his; he lifted it to kiss it. "You are keeping me alive," he said, and she said something smart-aleck in response, about drugs and orneriness keeping him alive — she could talk wise better than anyone Wyatt had ever met — but he knew what he said was true, and he could tell she believed him in the way she pressed her bright lips to his cheek. Wyatt touched the place her mouth had brushed.

"Nashville," she agreed finally, no longer chiding him. "I'll find something pretty to wear."

And Wyatt's old betrayer heart started thumping along joyfully as he imagined it. He was nearly delirious with excitement, with hope, and then he thought of how different everything would be if he'd just gone home with her that night at Nancy's. Sarah must have seen the look on his face change. She pulled away her hand.

"You okay?" she said, already steeling herself against him.

He nodded roughly, throat dry. "Just a pain."

Her expression shifted from wariness to alarm in a microsecond. "Wait, should I —" She was already leaning to hit the call button, but he put a hand out to block her, shaking his head.

"No," he said emphatically. "I'm fine."

She looked at the monitor, lay her palm against his cheeks and forehead. She checked his eyes, forefinger and thumb pressed efficiently against his brow and cheekbone. "You're warm," she said.

"I'm fine," he repeated. "It wasn't even a chest pain. Just a —" He waved helplessly.

"You sure?"

"Yeah."

She relaxed back in the seat. "Well, it's the damnedest thing," Sarah said.

"What?" Her hand was grasping his again.

"I seem to give a shit," she said.

2.

He had been about to fall out of his stool when he felt the pressure of strong hands against his shoulders, one shoving him upright, one steadying him from the other side, so that his head, bleary already, wagged back and forth on his neck like a puppet's. The light at the bar was whiskey colored. Wyatt rubbed his eyes, belched. He had been singing "Wichita Lineman" again but he'd lost his place. *"And I need you more than want you,"* he started again, because that was his favorite part, but then he lost himself, kneaded his crumb catcher against a flare of heartburn, and hesitated.

"And you want me for all time," a woman said from beside him, dryly. "Keep it up, you drunk dummy. I can't resist Glen Campbell."

"I'm gonna be sick," Wyatt muttered, and he felt a sharp jab in his side.

"Nuh-uh. I'm not watching that. Drink some water."

He shook his head like a child would, and a straw was pressed against his bottom lip.

"Drink this water or I'm calling the manager over here."

He felt the coolness spilling across his tongue before he'd even decided to pucker his lips. He had reached that state of drunkenness balanced wobblingly between despair and hilarity, nausea and manic energy. He wasn't sure if he wanted to crawl out to Sam's truck and go to sleep or pull this woman beside him onto the dance floor. He imagined twirling her to some kind of rockabilly song so that her skirt flared up, dipping her, letting his hand linger on the swell of her bottom.

"More. You can finish the glass."

He kept swallowing. He tasted the edge of lemon. His sinuses hurt.

"Better?"

He shrugged, stealing a look at her. She was wearing jeans, a T-shirt, a denim jacket with a different color of wash than the pants. No skirt.

"What about coffee? Could you hold that down?"

He frowned, a drunkard's frown: chin pulled in, mouth slightly ajar, eyebrows lowered in boorish affront. He swung his head to his left, blinked against a wave of seasickness, and peered into the crowd. He tried the other direction. Then, nearly falling again, he looked behind him.

"They're gone," she said sharply. "They split fifteen or twenty minutes ago. I think they left you with the tab."

"No," he said, trying to sober. "They

wouldn't do that."

"I'm telling you it's already been done."

The bartender placed a mug of coffee in front of him. The voice of the woman beside him softened. "How do you like it?"

It took him a moment to understand her, but then he did, and he muttered, "A sugar and cream, if there's any," and then he was slurping from the mug like it was soup. The coffee was sour, even with the milk in it, but he felt his head clear a little.

"Something tells me that this isn't you," the woman said. "You have kind eyes. You don't look like you belong with guys like that."

"I work with them."

"Don't mean you have to play with them."

He leaned on the bar, lifted his hip, pulled out his wallet. He unfolded it carefully (*Look how sober I am*) and checked its contents: two twenties, a single. He didn't carry credit cards or ATM cards. He didn't believe in them.

"Ma'am?" he said to the bartender. "What am I owing?"

She checked a notepad, punched numbers into an adding machine. Wyatt watched it burp paper.

"Seventy-five," she said.

"Bullshit," the woman beside him said.

"You know those guys walked out on him."

The bartender put her hands on her thin hips. "Somebody's paying this tab," she said. "If you want to chase down his friends and get them back here, go right to it."

"Bull. It's bull. What if they'd picked his pocket? Would you have stood by watching that, too?"

"I'll call the cops on you both," the bartender said. "He's drunk as a skunk and I've already heard about you." She put her hand on a cordless phone.

"You bitch," the woman said, then pulled out her own wallet — she carried a wallet, Wyatt noted with dull surprise — and threw down two twenties. She plucked Wyatt's forty dollars and added it to her own. "I want that five back."

The bartender thumbed the phone's "on" button. Wyatt could hear the faint *beep*! "I'm calling."

"Goddamn it," the woman said. "Come on." She started pulling Wyatt off of the stool. "Do you even remember where you live?"

"Roma," he said. He tried his feet, found them steady enough to hold him upright.

"Me too. It's your lucky night."

3.

In his dreams, it happened differently. It was worse than remembering the night as it had been. Worse, somehow, that his subconscious kept showing him different fates, all illogical, some downright silly: the version, for instance, in which he and Sarah decided to get married right there in Nancy's, on the dance floor, and Sam Austen agreed to be his best man. Or the other where he'd start to worry about the young, pretty woman, to wonder what had happened to her, and then she'd appear, laughing again, and in his sleep he'd feel a relief so profound that the heart-rate monitor beside his bed would record the slowing, and Wyatt would drift to deeper sleep on dark, gentle waves.

The previous recurring dream of Wyatt's adulthood had been one of violence. He would be beating a man, bludgeoning him, acting out of a vague notion of self-defense, and then there would always come a point when Wyatt realized, horrified, that he was beating not a person but Boss, that the dog was cowering under the blows, and it seemed to him in his waking hours that the dog was a kind of angel, the angel of his soul, saving him from any darkness within him, reminding him that it wasn't even right to kill in a dream. He'd thought, in the daylight hours, that he must truly be a good person. That only a good person would have a conscience, too, in his sleep, when no one was watching but God, and maybe not even Him.

The agony of these new dreams was in the waking, in discovering that there'd been no saving grace, no angel, that his life was exactly as he'd left it and the blessing of Sarah impossible, painful, too late, too late.

CHAPTER TWELVE

1.

She wasn't a kid anymore. She'd known this fact for years, of course, had believed it true before it was (*Stop treating me like a child!* she'd screamed at her mother, fifteen and full of hot blood), had registered it more deeply on her thirtieth birthday, though the day itself didn't upset her, didn't seem like a milestone excepting the fact that her friends told her, darkly joking, that it was. Her back and feet were strong, even after eight years at the sewing factory. She hardly ever got hangovers. She could throw back beers and rum-and-colas until the bars and dance halls she frequented closed, then sober on the return trip, taking the back roads between Tennessee and Roma too fast, singing along in her raspy but pleasant voice to Mary Chapin Carpenter and Bonnie Raitt and Loretta Lynn and veering when her headlights picked up the flash of a white deer belly. She had the kind of life that people like her sister frowned upon, but it was a good life — she believed this. She was always seeing the sunrise, always dancing and laughing. She could usually find a warm body when she needed one, and she had the confidence to enjoy it when she did, to not give much thought to the pucker of belly fat she'd never successfully worked off or to the cellulite marbling her thighs, which were otherwise muscular from regular step aerobics.

Thirty came and went, meaningless, and then one day she noticed in the mirror that lines etched her mouth even when she wasn't laughing, and the soft skin on her neck, when she caught her reflection in a certain angle of daylight, had the slightest silky looseness. She could see a faint outline of the little runway she'd traced on her granny's neck as a very small girl, that plane of flesh from chin to collarbone, the one that had made her jaw seem hinged-on, puppetlike.

Ronnie had never been vain about her looks. She had kept her hair short since her teens, when she started sneaking out to meet friends and boys. She'd not understood the girls she ran around with who had their hair feathered and long, a style that required an hour of daily preparation; Ronnie's heart was always racing with impatience, her hands not steady enough for curlers and sprays, and she couldn't stand those moments spent getting ready with friends, the careful application of eyeliner and shadow, the piles of discarded outfits. She and men, she had discovered, wanted the same thing from life: fun. She'd been just as successful at finding it in jeans and sneakers as other girls were in skirts and clumsy wedge sandals, so why bother? Why waste life on anything but living?

But she was not, it seemed, immune to these new changes in herself. She tried not to dwell on it, but she could see how her face had lost its freshness — the alcohol didn't help there, probably, and the coke in her mid- and late twenties certainly hadn't — and there had been a moment in Nancy's not too long ago, when she'd caught the reflection of a good-looking, blond-haired young guy in the mirror behind the bar and smiled flirtatiously, and it wasn't that he'd rejected her or insulted her; she'd been insulted plenty of times in her life, and the guy who broke her nose five years ago had called her a troll, a *dyke* troll. It was that this young guy had not seen her. Or rather, he'd seen her, he'd registered the fact of her, but he'd dismissed her. It was instant and impersonal, and Ronnie had realized, with the kind of eerily accurate insight that occasionally dawns upon the drunken, that she seemed old to him. She could have been one of the middle-aged waitresses with tops cut to reveal their papery, overtanned chests and crinkled cleavage. She could have been his mother. She wasn't old enough to be his mother, not by a long shot, but she'd passed for this guy into the realm of irrelevance, and to him it was all the same.

That was when she had started spraying her hair, putting on eye shadow, glossing her lips, running powder over her face to hide her pores and dull the shine between her eyebrows, where her face, always so full of expression, had worn itself into grooves. But something had changed, not just in her face but in her heart, and her nights at the Tobacco Patch weren't as fun as they once were, and the only man she'd brought to her bed in the last six months was Sonny, her friend from way back, a forty-year-old career military man who drove in from Fort Campbell every few weekends. She'd met him before he did his first tour to the Middle East with the 101st Airborne Division, written to him throughout his deployment, asked nothing of him, expected nothing. They enjoyed going to bed together, they enjoyed drinking, they enjoyed violent action movies. He wasn't a talker. They'd never joked about marrying. Ronnie had thought of the subject only to note, with interest, that she hadn't thought about it. She assumed she'd never be a wife or a mother. And that was OK, too, except for the fact that sometimes she looked at her sister's kid, Abby, and she could see those elfin Eastman features that were as much Ronnie's as Susanna's — the drawn chin; the large, wide-set eyes — and in another universe perhaps Abby would have been hers.

She had begun the evening of October 23 at the Salamander with shamefaced hope; the crowd there was old enough, usually, to make Ronnie feel like the belle of the ball, and she had plenty of friends among the regular set that she could count on for some good-natured flirtation. She was setting herself up for happiness. She arrived just after nine o'clock, when she knew the early drinkers would have settled already into an easy groove of big laughs and steel guitars on the juke. The bar, built in the sixties originally as a hunting cabin, had an old-fashioned tang of wood smoke and mold; lichen grew on the damp stones of the fireplace, which had been sealed since before Ronnie started frequenting the joint. There wasn't a dance floor; folks looking to dance went down the road. There were only a half dozen tables and a smattering of stools whose vinyl seats had been worn into scabs, unpleasant against the backs of the thighs if you wore a short enough skirt. On the busiest nights there were sometimes fifty people crammed into the building's one room, burnishing the wood floors with their work boots, their sweat and beer breath and pheromones creating a kind of bar smog, rich enough by the A.M. to get you light-headed. The Salamander was Ronnie's kind of place: loose, low-key, intimate. She felt more like herself there than she did at Nancy's, or at her sister's, or even in her own rental house, where she could feel not just alone but lonely, the lace curtains on the windows and the few knickknacks on the end tables like the punch line to a joke she'd missed the setup for.

She wore her favorite outfit, the one that featured the jacket Sonny had bought for her on one of their rare evenings out that hadn't been built around drinking and sex. They'd gone to the Governor's Square Mall in Clarksville, Tennessee. An odd thing — they must have been really hungover that day, or it was one of those times, infrequent but not wholly rare, when Sonny had told her that he didn't have the heart for dealing with a crowd. When Sonny felt like that — and it was always he who begged off the Tobacco Patch, never Ronnie — they'd eat out somewhere like Olive Garden, or they'd see a movie, or they'd just drive around the countryside, where Sonny would talk about his teens, the places that had been his regular haunts. And then there was this one time at the mall, so strange for them, especially for Sonny, who was not the kind of man you pictured strolling hand in hand with a woman past the Orange Julius and the J. C. Penney. Not this serious-faced man who wore long-sleeved shirts, even in the middle of summer, to cover the gasoline burns on his forearms and neck that he'd gotten in Kuwait. And yet he'd gone, it had been his idea, and he'd picked out the denim jacket with the brass detailing, told Ronnie to try it on, admired aloud the way the cut of it emphasized her nice breasts and small waist. He'd paid for it, too: sixty-five dollars.

She wasn't too coy to admit to herself that it was Sonny she most hoped to see that night at the Salamander. She could have called him — she had his number — but that wasn't how they worked, usually. It wasn't how she wanted them to work. Part of the pleasure of seeing him was the uncertainty of it, the surprise: the moment when she looked up over the shoulder of some regular like Danny Munford, who'd buy her drinks only if she'd listen to him tell the same story about meeting Elvis that he always told, and saw Sonny, her friend, the person who understood better than anyone else what gave her pleasure. It only occasionally dismayed her that Sonny, this man that she couldn't even pick up the telephone to call, was that person to her. And the dismay, she told herself, had less to do with him than with herself. She thought sometimes that she'd been built wrong, that a normal woman, like her sister, was supposed to desire stability and commitment. A normal woman would have asked for a ring by now, maybe. But normality had never really meant much to Ronnie. And what had it gotten her sister? A house that she lived in like a guest — *Use a coaster, Don't smoke inside, Maybe you should leave before Dale gets home, you know how he is* — a husband who treated her like a child, and a child of unusual solemnity, a little girl who seemed to register the gulf between her parents and had already learned to shoulder that burden as her own. Susanna was the unhappiest person Ronnie knew, and maybe unhappiness was normal, maybe it was what the rest of the world had settled for. Ronnie wanted more.

And what she wanted that Friday was Sonny. She wanted him so badly, she realized, that she could barely concentrate on what Sal Lochman and his wife, Annette, were saying to her. They were complaining about neighbors, some kind of dispute over their dogs crossing the property line — or was it the neighbor's dogs crossing their line? Ronnie was only halfway tuned in. She liked the Lochmans with amusement and a bit of disdain, the way she liked most everyone at the Salamander, though she wouldn't quite admit that even to herself.

"Well, I told him if the toe of his boot so much as scrapes our yard I'm coming out with the shotgun." Sal looked to his wife for approval, which she gave him with an emphatic nod. "I've had it with that shit."

Ronnie, feeling called upon to offer something, nodded, too. "Sounds to me like you handled it the only way the bastard would understand." She was doing math in her head: the number of weeks since she'd seen Sonny, the average number of times he hit the Tobacco Patch a month, the likelihood that he'd make it down tonight. She'd done this math already, decided that tonight was the night — it's why she wore the jacket he gave her, why she started the evening at the Salamander instead of going straight to Nancy's or taking her work buddies up on an offer to barhop on Second Avenue in Nashville. She hadn't had sex in at least a month. And though there had been a time, a swath of years, when extricating herself from that dry spell would have been easy as pie — if, indeed, she'd ever lapsed accidentally into a dry spell — things now were more complex. She wasn't confident any longer in her power to bring home the kind of man she wanted, the guy whose belt cinched a slim waist and washboard abs, the guy who could dance well, who had a good laugh and bright, straight teeth. She no longer knew if she could bring that man home, and she no longer knew if she wanted to, if the novelty of strangeness meant as much to her now as the comfort of familiarity. And not just comfort — because who was she to settle for such paltry compensation? Sonny was good in bed. She didn't have to tell him that her right breast was more sensitive to touch than the left; that she liked starting on the bottom and finishing on top; that she wasn't into sex talk, which could embarrass her so much that she had to laugh out loud, or the really rough stuff, which some men assumed a woman like her would enjoy. In turn, she knew Sonny's likes and dislikes: she knew that he liked having sex on his couch because he could watch their reflection in the glass door of his entertainment center, and she knew, too, that he didn't want her to know that he watched their reflection, that if she watched him watching he would look away or close his eyes. It only endeared him to her more, that primness. That and his desire, usually, to cradle her after, to not see her dress and rush off back to her own place. She knew to rise before him to start coffee; he always made it too weak. She knew that he kept the can of grounds in his freezer and that the filters were on the top shelf of the pantry, and she knew that his favorite mug was a twenty-ouncer with the 101st emblem on the side.

It was then, with the fortuitousness of a dream, that she saw him, spotting him this time over Sal's shoulder. She lifted her hand in hello, noticing that he had on his favorite green-plaid button-down shirt, that his hair had been recently cut — he always cut it so short, even where his cap would cover it, that he looked vulnerable and pink-scalped, like a little boy. She lifted her hand and grinned, not thinking to check herself, to hold something back, and so it was all the worse when she saw the woman he was pulling in behind him. There was a split second of mutual seeing — Sonny registering her grin and naked pleasure, Ronnie watching his face cloud with sudden memory — and that dawning recognition was the worst, because it meant that he'd brought the woman unthinkingly. He wasn't trying to make her jealous. He hadn't taken a chance on Ronnie's being absent this night. He'd simply, somehow, forgotten her.

"I don't know what the world's come to," Annette said. "I guess we'll have to teach them to use the can, next."

Sal barked laughter. "And wipe their asses."

Ronnie dropped her hand and flushed, the embarrassment so powerful that she felt an electric charge in the roots of her hair. This was déjà vu: her smile, her outsized confidence, the casual dismissal. Did she even exist anymore? Sal and Annette, still chattering, didn't seem to notice her change in expression — just kept going on and on about their stupid dogs and their stupid sense of entitlement about them, and Ronnie wanted to say, "I wouldn't want your fucking pit bulls on my property, either," but would they even hear her? What would it take to make people notice her again?

"Excuse me," Ronnie said hoarsely. "I need to get something."

She pushed between Sal and Annette — they'd backed her into a corner, she didn't have a choice — and took a ragged breath, trying to make a fast plan. Her thinking was already whiskey edged, her heart tapping nervously, and she wasn't sure what she wanted more: to escape the Salamander without dealing with Sonny or to run up to him and make him see her. She wasn't being sensible, she knew. They weren't exclusive, never had been. In the years since she started sleeping with Sonny she'd brought several other men to her bed, some of whom Sonny vaguely knew, and in turn she'd heard rumors about Sonny and a regular thing back in Fort Campbell, an ex with benefits. It had never bothered her. She wasn't the kind of woman who checked for signs of a lover any more than she was the kind of woman who expected, or wanted, a ring. But the Salamander was *their* place, she'd thought — it was where they went in search of one another. In a life she had built around superficial friendships and fleeting commitment, it was the one thing that she thought she could depend upon.

The anger surged in her, hot and certain. Her father's temper — he'd claimed it. "You got that from me," he had always said, almost proudly, and it was no wonder that she had been more his, Susanna more their mother's: Ronnie had clipped her hair, but her father had clipped her name, and she was the son he wouldn't have — strong, decisive, brash, foolhardy.

She crossed the Salamander in a dozen short, fast strides. Her hand never clenched into a fist — she knew that she was too petite to fight a man's fight, to make weapons of the slim knuckles in her small hands — but it hardened, the fingers lengthening into a plane, flexing back from the hard meat of her palm. She threw her arm back like a pitcher, moving with fluid instinct, and rocketed off the toes of her sneakers, planting her left foot in front of Sonny in time to steady herself before landing the slap, the more-than-slap — it began behind her, arced the hemisphere of her right side, and exploded against his ear with a clap loud enough to silence the bar's patrons, if not its background music of old country. Sonny sank a little, cupping his ear, and the woman to his side shrieked, and Ronnie vibrated for a second with triumphant adrenaline, her palm tingling, an echo climbing almost to her elbow. She gasped for good air.

2.

"She must've been done up on something," Sal said later to Detective Tony Joyce. "Didn't seem right all night. She was glassy-eyed when we tried to talk to her, then she just stalked off while I was in the middle of a sentence."

"Pushed us right out of the way," Annette added.

"And Sonny didn't do nothing to her. Walked in, is all."

"Everybody knew they ran around." Annette lifted her eyebrows suggestively. "But they weren't a couple. Never had been. And Ronnie's took a turn with half the men in the bar."

"Can you give me some names?" the detective asked.

"You'd have to ask them." Annette looked at this black cop with his notepad out — how strange that he was in the Salamander, how strange to see her husband speak to him politely and even reverently.

She'd thought for a while that Ronnie was after Sal. This was years ago — before Annette had gotten him to go to the courthouse and make things official with her, before she'd gotten her name on the deed to his property — and she could see with the eyes God gave her that Ronnie flashed her tail feathers whenever he came near, that she hovered and preened and all but sounded a mating call. On a night when everyone had gotten so drunk at the Salamander that Annette had started to urinate on herself in the line to the women's bathroom, she had stumbled outside to the darkest corner of the gravel parking lot to find Sal and Ronnie pressed together against her own car, the one that she was always giving Sal rides in, and Annette, even in the throes of intoxication, had not made a scene or announced herself. She'd hung back, waited in the shadows. She'd watched as Sal unzipped, took himself in hand, as Ronnie wriggled the skirt she was wearing up around her hips. She waited for them to start moving against one another, for their heavy breaths to stitch a binding line, for the betrayal to complete itself — but Sal kept faltering, cursing. The gold watch on his wrist flickered as he grasped himself, and Ronnie had finally said, "Go back to your old lady, Sal," and the car had groaned in its springs as she lifted her weight off it. And when Annette had gone to him a few moments later, had silently drawn the zipper to her damp jeans down and leaned in front of him and felt Sal harden against her, she knew that he was hers, that his body would not let him cheat on her. And she'd looked at Ronnie almost kindly after that, because it must be an awful thing to open your legs to another woman's man in a parking lot, to be the kind of person who'd do a thing like that, and to not even get any satisfaction out of it.

"Did Ronnie and Sonny say anything to each other?" Tony Joyce asked. "Before or after she hit him?"

"Yeah," Sal said. "It was, 'You won't forget me now, will you, asshole?' Something like that."

"She called him a son of a bitch," Annette said. "But Sal's got the first part right."

" 'You won't forget me now, you son of a bitch'?" Tony said. "Does that sound right?"

"That's it," Annette said, grabbing Sal's hand, letting him know, without even realizing she was doing it, that her memory of the night superseded his, was more real than his. It was one of those privileges she had gained that night in the parking lot. They never spoke of it, and she had never told him how much she saw, but the near miss with Ronnie had won Annette her husband, half of his property, and a lifetime of veto power. "That's what we remember," she said, and in the end that's what Tony Joyce wrote down.

3.

Ronnie had been at Nancy's only an hour when she warmed to what was going on with the pack of young men and their older companion. It was enough to break your heart, to make you forget briefly about your own humiliation. This older fellow, old enough to know better but transmitting to as far as Ronnie's end of the bar an air of innocence and desperate loneliness, was wincing through shots that the guys appeared to be concocting on cruel whim: hot sauce and Jäger, tequila and Kahlúa ("It's called a Tahlula," one guy said with straight-faced authority), grape-infused vodka and tomato juice, a few drops of cream. "Tubs, Tubs, Tubs," they'd chant as he regarded each shot, tweezing it between forefinger and thumb before choking it down all at once, and then they would cheer and start clapping him on the back, hard enough, Ronnie thought, that they must have been trying to trigger his gag reflex. "Add it to the tab," they all kept saying, for both the disgusting shots and their own beers and highballs, and Ronnie could see from a mile off how this night was going to end for the older man, even if she hadn't overheard one of the young ones say to another, "One more drink, and then I'll pull the truck around."

And still she might have done nothing, if it hadn't turned out that the young man at their helm was the good-looking blond who'd ignored her smile in the mirror over the bar all those weeks before. She spotted him not long after the older man started singing along to "Wichita Lineman" on the juke, because the blond was the loudest and rowdiest in the group, the kind of person who laughs not just because it's funny but because he wants to be noticed laughing. "Woo!" he kept yelling, playing patty-cake on his thighs and stomping his feet, once turning the two gestures into a quick little dance that culminated with his slapping the soles of his cowboy boots in a nifty rhythm that ought to have had fiddle music accompanying it. Oh, he was a charmer, she saw, and without a doubt a grade-A asshole, too. She'd known his type. She'd bedded his type. And she'd enjoyed it, because Ronnie had her own capacity for cruelty, her own occasional whim to hurt. It was how she'd gotten her nose broken all those years ago: she'd hooked up with a guy like this one, she'd given him as good as she got from him, and in the end he'd settled the matter with his fists, his only advantage.

She walked over to the group, buzzing on the two rum-and-colas she'd downed at the bar, unable to stop herself. "Hey," she said. "You can't just leave him like this. How's he going to get home?"

"Magic carpet ride," said the black-haired one, snorting laughter. "Right, Sam?"

Sam — that was the blond one — swallowed the last inch of beer in his glass and slammed it on the bar. The older man didn't even jerk; he was crooning along with the house band now, slurring and getting most of the words wrong, and two of the other guys in the group were laughing so hard that tears were streaming down their faces. "Mind your own damn business," Sam said, smiling broadly, but there was something in that smile that chilled Ronnie. The eyes behind it were utterly humorless.

"You fucking assholes," Ronnie said. Her anger now was mixed up, despairing. She had dulled her humiliation at the Salamander with liquor, but it was nagging at her now, worming its way back into her conscious mind. "You're a bunch of fucking pricks. Someone ought to call the cops on you."

Sam grabbed her elbow and shoved her away from the group. Later, when his gang had left the bar and abandoned the older drunk man, she'd find the crescent-shaped imprint of his thumbnail on the soft flesh of her inner arm. "You say another word," he whispered hotly into her ear, "and you're going to get a surprise. Do you hear me, you ugly skank?"

Ronnie swallowed against a sob, and he shook her.

"I said, do you hear me?"

She nodded.

He let go and stepped back, grin back on his face. "I'll be seeing you," he said. In another few moments, he and his group had slipped out the door. The older man didn't even seem to notice.

4.

Chris, the manager at the Salamander, had threatened to call the sheriff on her. "Don't, man," Sonny had said, hand still covering his ear, the scar on his arm just visible where the cuff of his shirt tugged down. "Don't, this is all me."

"You're damn right it is," Ronnie said, but she was losing her sense of righteousness,

251

faltering under the stares of the people she'd called friends for the last five years of her life. She could see in their eyes that they'd chosen Sonny, that they would have always chosen Sonny, that maybe none of them had ever even liked her. Annette Lochman was smirking a little, and Ronnie wondered if Sal had told her about them, those four times they'd slept together — five, it would have been, if he'd not been too drunk one night to get it up. Nearby, Danny Munford had his arms crossed, and the lights overhead were glinting off his glasses in a way that turned his eyes into silver coins. He'd given her a copy once of a story he'd written — a novel, he'd called it, though it only seemed about thirty or forty pages long, printed and bound with brass brads, so that you could flip the pages like a book — and Ronnie had unthinkingly tossed it into the backseat of her car. She hadn't found it again until months later, running the quarter vacuum at Kip's, and she'd trashed it along with the empty fast food containers and tattered sales bulletins, hardly registering the difference.

"You should let him call them," the woman with Sonny said. She was pretty in a sullen way, close to Ronnie's age or a bit older. The regular thing in Fort Campbell,

252

maybe — it suddenly seemed unimportant. "I can't believe she fucking did that."

"Maybe I had it coming," Sonny said, and Ronnie felt the needle of hot tears.

"The hell you did!" the woman said.

"Hush, now," he said. "She's on her way out. I'm going to show her ass to the door."

A few people clapped. It was a short, even halfhearted display, but Ronnie knew she'd be hearing it for a long time.

They were out on the front steps before Ronnie registered the pressure of his hand on her elbow, and she noted dully that it would probably be the last time he ever touched her.

"Goddamn, woman," Sonny said. "I ain't never."

"You got a lot of nerve bringing her here. I thought we had a truce about this place."

He barked a laugh. "Truce? Is that what you call getting drilled in the parking lot by Sal Lochman?"

"That was years ago. You were in Kuwait."

"Well, that other guy. The one from your town, that you work with."

Ronnie had to think a minute. "You weren't even here that night."

"I could have been."

"I knew that was your weekend on base."

"Thoughtful."

"At least I thought of you."

He laughed again and gave her a little push. "Drive home safe, girl. It's been fun."

"Fuck you, Sonny."

"I always liked you in that jacket." The set of his mouth was soft.

She speared a tear with her knuckle before it could roll down her cheek. "Why did you bring her? Seriously, Sonny. Did I piss you off? Didn't you want to see me tonight?"

He looked like he was at a loss. "Shit, honey, I just did," he said. "I didn't mean nothing by it. She wanted to go out for a drink and here seemed as good as anywhere." He pulled his hand from his ear and looked at it thoughtfully. "I'm bleeding," he said. "You made me bleed."

"Ain't that a bitch," Ronnie said.

"No, you are." He was still smiling, but Ronnie could tell that there was an edge of something else to his voice. "You're the meanest woman I've ever known. Mean as an old bear."

Ronnie snagged her keys out of her front pocket, started across the lot to the Camaro. She stuck her middle finger up in good-bye as she went.

"Been nice knowing you," Sonny called after her.

■ ■ ■ ■

PART TWO

■ ■ ■ ■

CHAPTER THIRTEEN

1.

On Friday, Mr. Wieland, Emily's science teacher from seventh grade, approached Emily in the hall during class change. "How're you feeling, kid?"

She looked around automatically for Christopher or Leanna, anyone from their group, and remembered that they were all still home today. Because of her. She'd been bumping up against that realization all morning, and it provoked in her a mix of relief and dread. Relief because she was free of them all for now. Dread because she knew that she wouldn't be for long.

"I'm OK," she said. She couldn't believe he'd asked her that, right out in the hall where anybody could hear him. She hugged her books more tightly to her chest.

"Has Ms. Nicholas talked to you yet about entering the science fair this year? You took that tadpole project pretty far, and you know they have a cash prize if you place at regionals."

Emily shifted her gaze between Mr. Wieland's shoes, a scuffed pair of leather hiking boots, and the middle button of his plaid shirt. His shirt cuffs were rolled up on his forearms, his hands thrust deep into the loose hip pockets of his khakis. Her eyes darted for just a second to his face — he was appraising her, friendly and paternal, and she felt a flicker of irritation. "Not yet," she said.

"She will," he said, "and you should. It's a great opportunity, a great confidence builder. And money doesn't hurt, does it? If you need any help, let me know. I've got a couple of new books that might give you some ideas."

"Oh. OK," Emily said.

Mr. Wieland looked at his watch. "Bell's going to ring in another minute, so I ought to let you on your way. Don't forget that Ms. Nicholas and I are both here to help. And there's a little extra money in the budget this year for materials, so we could do some neat things."

Emily nodded, adjusted her books from the left arm to the right, and started toward class. Mr. Wieland watched her go.

She was a strange, sad little thing. And as

sorry as he felt for her, as wrong as it was for those kids to target her — those powerful and handsome kids with their rich parents and their easy lives — Ed Wieland couldn't help but understand the reason, to feel, when Emily was around, something that pretended to be a small emotion, like distaste or amusement, but was actually more profound, too profound to name. Fear? It was *like* fear, a dark, slick thing in the pit of his stomach, a thing that muscled its way around on a silken underbelly, slow, deliberate. But *fear* wasn't the right word, either. And when Ed sensed that crawling inside of him, when he registered in Emily's presence how fully he wished to be somewhere else, he felt like a jerk. She was a girl, a smart, troubled girl, and he didn't like to think that had he been Emily's peer rather than her teacher, he'd have been one of the students pelting her with his lunch. But he wondered.

The bell rang, and he retreated to his classroom. He was liked at Roma Middle School. The students called him Mr. Wee, and the girls sometimes whispered to each other about how he was kind of cute for an old guy.

Emily, following Boss into the woods, thought about Mr. Wieland's suggestion. Tadpoles — what a joke. What a joke that she had cried over them. If he knew her current, secret project, he wouldn't be trying to distract her with kid stuff. What had once been so important to her — decorating the project board with construction paper, making frames for the Polaroid pictures she took, neatly lettering headings such as "HYPOTHESIS" and "RESULTS" — seemed trivial now, even pathetic in the wake of the discoveries she was making in the woods.

Mr. Powell's dog, Boss, wasn't used to going for long walks on a leash, and he was big and gangly, at least eighty or ninety pounds. Emily didn't walk him so much as let him walk her. They were a subject of recent amusement in the neighborhood: the girl and the dog, the dog almost as big as she was, stumbling around the streets and then disappearing, who knows where. Boss scampered with his head close to the ground and his silken ears waving around his snout, and the clumsy bones of his haunches angled up and down, machinelike, and his splayed paws landed heavily in the mud. He smelled pungent and alive, and his jowls were dripping in excitement: so much ground, so many scents, a world entire outside his master's property. He didn't move like an old dog anymore.

Emily, feet landing in hard stops to keep her from tipping over onto her face, grunted, "Boss, whoa," and yanked on the leash. He held back a bit and she caught her breath. Her ankle, still a little tender from last week's fall, hummed with a distant ache.

A week — she could hardly register that so much time had passed. On Saturday she had gone back to the woods, convinced after a restless night that the body wouldn't be there — that it had never existed or (worse) that someone else had found it. But there it was, now in broad daylight, now partly exposed, and the exposed parts already looked different than they had the previous night. Darker. She had thought about her science project then, "the effects of ultraviolet light," and had carefully pulled another rock away from the body, exposing a portion of the upper left arm. Yes, she thought, heart trembling. It was different.

With the tadpole project, she'd kept a little spiral-bound notebook to record her findings. It was still in her room, tucked into the drawer of her bedside table: a log patterned with her neat print, observations such as "Beginning to sprout legs" under the heading "Control Group" and "Darker color, growth stunted" under "UV Group." In two places, on a day when Emily had missed school because of a stomach bug, Christopher Shelton had tended the log for her. It was early in the project, and he'd marked "Swimming, no sign of change" under both headings. When Emily returned to school, she had run her fingers over Christopher's notations, thrilled at the intimacy of it: his words in her notebook. The ballpoint pen he'd used left an impression on the paper.

She wasn't writing her findings down in a notebook, but she began on Saturday to keep a mental log of what she was seeing, the subtle and not-so-subtle changes, and the control group was her own body, the taut, strong flesh she had always taken for granted. It seemed miraculous to her now: her plump forearm, its peach-hued ivory, the blond, fine hairs and tiny freckles. In class, while the teacher was lecturing or playing a video, she would put her arm on her desktop, delicate inside facing up, and she'd flex the tendons, observe the way a blue vein pulsed in the hollow of her inner elbow. Think, flex. Think, flex. The body, helpless to her will. But her awe had given way to something else, a sense of hopelessness. She wouldn't call it depression. But she couldn't look at her own arm now without imagining the arm of the body, the body that had been a person but was now an object of as much spirit as those UV-cooked tadpoles. What, she wondered for the first time, did it mean to live? What was she? An encasement of flesh and hot blood, a puppet, a collection of cells, an accident. Each day she promised herself that this was the last visit, the last time she'd "make sure" before going to her parents. Each day she stayed silent, easing her conscience with another promise.

After what had happened on Wednesday, she gave up on even the pretense of the promise. Watching Christopher and Leanna at the tennis courts — that thing he had let her do to him — disturbed and frightened her, and it hit her harder, in a way, than what happened moments later in the cafeteria, because she still wasn't really letting herself think about that. She had to look at the memory in the way she'd looked at the body that first night in the woods; some instinctive order of her mind had cast a protective darkness over those events, making it easier to examine them with her peripheral vision than straight on. In her nightmares, she relived it all: the cruel glee on Christopher's face, the chorus of shouts all around her, the dull impact of all that greasy, gelatinous food and the nauseating processed smells of it. In the waking day, it was something she brushed up against accidentally: when she saw a certain malicious humor in the eyes of a classmate and knew what the person was thinking, or at lunch, when she found herself reaching for a paper tray of salad or a margarine-soaked slice of garlic toast.

Yet she still couldn't think about Christopher without feeling the same tender ache as before, and perhaps that was one of the reasons she had succeeded so well in protecting herself from the horror of what had happened in the cafeteria on Wednesday. She believed, perhaps now more than ever, that the Christopher of the tennis courts, the Christopher who had started that assault on her in the cafeteria, was not the real Christopher — the one who had helped her with her science project, the one who had joined her on so many of these walks in the woods. In a way, his suspension had only aided her in this delusion; not confronted each day with the boy who had given her every possible reason to hate and fear him, she was left with the boy her imagination had carefully constructed.

She was passing the Calahans' mutt now, and it and Boss were snapping at each other through the fence, a new part of the ritual that Emily had still not gotten used to. She tugged and tugged on the leash and finally shifted Boss's course, tipping him back toward the trail, which recaptured his interest. He knew where their journeys always led, and he was as curious now as she was, though the first time she brought Boss to the body, Tuesday evening, he'd howled and rocked back on his haunches, and then he'd started stalking back and forth beside it, coming forward for a sniff and just as quickly jumping back, as though he believed that the body might roll over and grab at him. The smell had been very bad that day, which was in the fifties after a weekend of steady drizzle, but now the temperatures had dropped into the high thirties, and Emily didn't think yesterday that the smell was as pronounced as it was before. Or maybe she had just gotten used to it.

"Good Lord," her mother said one night after she came home from a walk. "Did you step in something?"

"I don't think so," Emily said, but her mother made her go back outside and check her sneakers anyhow. And though Emily hadn't seen anything, she could tell, putting her nose close to the shoe's rubber tread, that she'd carried home the stench of death. She had raked the shoes across the damp grass, and then she went inside and retrieved the Lysol from under the kitchen sink. She sprayed the soles and left the shoes sitting out on the back step to air, and she thought for the first time, hard, about what she was doing — what she'd done by staying silent. The stench had followed her home like a ghost. Perhaps it had followed her to school. She had noticed how the other kids — even some of the teachers, like Mr. Wieland — recoiled from her. Had it always been like this? She was, she thought, a good person. She hadn't hurt anyone. She hadn't hurt the woman. She had only watched her and stayed quiet about her, and in all of these days someone else could have discovered her. It wasn't Emily's fault that no one had.

It was cold, cold enough that her breath clouded, and she'd worn a pair of cheap red knit gloves, the stretchy kind that looked as if they'd only fit the hands of a small child. She and Boss made a noisy procession, snapping branches underfoot, Emily's exerted respiration mimicking, in a way, Boss's urgent sniffs. She smelled it at almost the same time the dog did — or perhaps that was wrong. Perhaps she just knew now the way the tension in the leash changed the moment he caught his first whiff. They both slowed, and Boss leaned even closer to the ground, zigzagging, halting, jumping back. A fast spring forward. And, despite herself, her heart lifted a little. It was the pleasure of visiting with a friend, a good friend that you hadn't seen in a while, though Emily knew neither of those pleasures: the pleasure of real friendship or the tender ache of temporarily doing without it.

She and Boss slid down into the ravine and stopped. Emily looped the dog's leash around the trunk of a sapling, as she always did, so that his span of reach fell short of the remains. She approached the body and stood beside it, head dropped in what might have appeared to be mourning — but she was staring, calculating, making notations in her mental log. Her pulse had picked up, and her skin warmed with a flush of excitement. It was only here, after what had happened in the cafeteria on Wednesday, that she felt fully alive, and safe; here, measuring the resilience of her own smooth flesh against the body's. Each day it was different — scary, yes, but there was a comfort to the body's decimation, too, for she could see now how the earth seemed to be reaching around it to reabsorb it, and she could believe, only here, only momentarily, that there *was* a greater power dictating these things.

"Or who even needs God?" Christopher said. His fingers were twined in hers. His smell obscured the low, lingering stench of the body; his cologne was always strong and grown-up smelling, as if he borrowed his father's.

"Sometimes I do," Emily said. She could never remember Christopher's face out here exactly as it was. He wasn't an image but an idea, more vapor than person.

"The need is what makes it bullshit," Christopher said. Emily remembered his complaints about Mrs. Mitchell's test-preparation sessions, and she'd liked the coarse edge to his voice, could conjure the sound of it now more easily than she could conjure the shape of his face. "He would only exist if we didn't need him to."

Emily closed her eyes and squeezed her right hand. "You would hate me even more if you knew about this," she said.

"I don't hate you, Emily. I really like you."

"You called me a freak. You embarrassed me in front of everybody." This was the hardest part to explain to herself.

"I can't be myself at school. You know how much pressure there is."

"And that's why you're Leanna's boyfriend?"

Silence.

She imagined Leanna Burke finding the body, Leanna Burke calling the police, Leanna Burke being celebrated in town as a hero, everyone asking her what the body had been like or if she'd been frightened. Leanna would not, Emily knew, have the strength to stay quiet as she had. She would have exposed the body, exploited it; it would have been a gross thing to her, a thing to seal up in a box and forget about.

"Leanna wouldn't understand what this means," Emily said. The Christopher of the woods could follow her thoughts, fill in the gaps.

"Of course she wouldn't," he said. "But I would."

"Really?"

"I'm more like you than I let on at school. I would understand. I would respect you for waiting for the right moment to tell."

"Who do I tell?"

"Who do you think?"

She looked at the disarray on the ground. "What if someone finds it before I can tell?"

"You know what to do about that, too,"

Christopher said.

Emily dropped down to her knees and started scooping up handfuls of dirt and leaves, covering what she'd uncovered, doing a better job than the person who had originally buried it had. Boss pulled on his leash, whimpered, keeled back on his haunches. She ignored him. Her gloves were filthy and damp, and Emily couldn't bear to wear them home. She peeled them off, dropped them onto the ground beside the body, and kicked some dirt over them with the toe of her tennis shoe. "Let's go, Boss," she said, untying his leash from the sapling. She left Christopher behind at the gully to keep watch over the dead.

3.

"Don't you have that Mitchell teacher at the school?"

Emily, watching television, hadn't been listening to her mother. Boss was stretched out on the carpet beside her — "He smells like he ain't had a bath in ages," her mother had groused when Emily's father brought him home on Tuesday — and she let her hand rest on the warm swell of his stomach. She'd been feeling a surprising kinship with the dog. He was the only one who knew her secret, and he hadn't spurned her for it; if anything, he'd adopted her as his favorite in the Houchens household, sleeping at night on the rug beside her bed and following her from room to room, even if she was just getting up to use the toilet.

"Emily."

"Huh?"

"That Mitchell woman. Is she your teacher? The one who called the other day? The day —" Her mother waved a hand, hesitant. "The day you took the cab home," she finished lamely.

"Uh — yeah," Emily said. "English class."

"It's a sad thing," her father said.

Emily roused a little, frowned. She had been watching an *Andy Griffith* rerun. "What's a sad thing?"

Her mother huffed. "I wish y'all would turn the TV off every now and then. We're raising a couple of space cadets."

"Your teacher's sister is missing," her father said. "I saw the posters up around town today."

Emily sat up so quickly that Boss, startled, ambled awkwardly to his feet. "What posters? What did they say?"

"That she was missing," her dad said, throwing up his hands, feigning exasperation. He hadn't showered yet since work, so he was on the couch next to Emily's mother in his oil-stained khaki shirt and pants, sock feet slim and almost fragile looking. His boots, she knew, would be sitting on a rug in the utility room. "Said she went by the name Ronnie and that she'd been gone since weekend before last. There was a photo."

"What did she look like?" Emily's mother asked.

"I don't know." His brows drew. "She had short hair and a lot of makeup on. Kind of tan, sort of."

Emily ventured hesitantly, "Pretty?"

"Heck, I don't know," her father repeated. "I guess so. In a funny way." He smiled at Emily's mother, teasing again. "Not my taste, of course."

"Well it's scary," her mother said, not returning the smile. "There could be some crazy person out there. I don't like you wandering off out of sight with that dog, Emily."

"I don't go out of sight," she lied.

"My foot." Her mother jabbed a finger toward the backyard. "I tell you, Morris, she's gone from the time she gets home from school until right before you come through the door. I look out and there's no sign of her. Where do you and that dog go off to?"

"God, Mom, not that far." Emily felt her face burning. "Sometimes to Tasha's."

It was a mistake, she realized. Her mother, with her daffiness and her soap operas and her stories about the good old days, was easy to underestimate — but she'd seen through Emily's lie, and they exchanged a glimpse of recognition.

Her mother cleared her throat a little. "Tasha's."

Emily nodded wordlessly. Her father's gaze was back on the television.

"I think it's time to give Tasha's folks a rest," she said. "She can come over here sometimes. If y'all are just so set on spending every minute together."

Emily frowned down at her hands, which were knotted together on her lap.

"Or maybe you want me to call Tasha's mom and tell her so."

"No, Mom, God," Emily said. "I'll stay closer to home. It's not a big deal."

"We're going to have to set some ground rules around here," her mother said.

Emily's father stretched his arm across the back of the couch and kneaded her mother's neck, conciliatory. He had been putting out fires between them for thirteen years. "That sounds good to me, honey. And Em oughta be doing homework after school anyhow."

"I agree," her mother said.

"We'll be taking the dog back to Wyatt's soon enough." He rose, put his hands on his lower back, and leaned against them, wincing. "He'll want the company. And it's getting too cold to be outside all the time."

"I need the exercise, Dad," Emily said. She felt her flush deepening. "I'm trying to lose weight."

"Lay off the Debbie cakes if you want to lose weight," he said.

"Morris," her mother hissed.

"What?" He started toward the bathroom, paused to ruffle Emily's hair along the way. "She's the one talking about losing weight."

"Just leave her be," Emily's mother said.

He shrugged a little and left the room. The bathroom door closed, and the faucet on the bathtub creaked, the echo rattling through the plumbing all over the house. Seeming to sense that some tension had exited the room along with Emily's father, Boss backed slowly down and flopped onto his side with a sigh.

Emily, pretending to watch television again, felt the soft press of her mother's hands on her shoulders. "I worry about you," she said tenderly. Emily waited for the follow-up, the offers of fun: *Why don't you*

have a sleepover? We could order a pizza, or
*Do you think one of your friends would want
to go to the mall with us on Saturday?* Perhaps
she would start touching Emily's limp hair,
combing her fingers gently through it and
lightly scratching the scalp (a move that
had, in Emily's earlier childhood, always
provoked in her a sleepy bliss), offering to
use the curling iron or pull it into a French
braid. "You always hide your beautiful
eyes," was her refrain. "Just once I'd like to
see you keep your hair out of your eyes."

But she did none of these things, made no
offers.

"I wish I could tell you to just be yourself.
I like you, Daddy likes you, and that ought
to be the end of it. If you're happy." She
hunched down, trying awkwardly to cradle
Emily, and Emily could smell her sour coffee breath. "But you don't seem happy. You
don't even seem yourself to me."

Emily stiffened against her mother's
touch, felt both relieved and guilty when
the hands pulled away and her mom rose.

"It's becoming a teenager, I guess," her
mother said. On TV, Barney Fife was gesturing theatrically, eyes bulging. His gun fired
by accident. "You're getting farther and
farther away from me. I don't know how to
help you."

"I don't want help," Emily said. "I just want you to leave me alone."

There was a pregnant silence, long enough that Emily, still facing the television, thought that her mother had perhaps left the room. She cast a quick glance over her shoulder and saw that her mother was standing and crying a little, clamping her hand over her nose and mouth as if she could hold it in that way.

"Do you want to have friends, Emily?" Her voice was hoarse, high-pitched.

Emily shrugged.

"I think you do," her mother said. "I think you do and don't know how. Maybe it's my fault. Maybe I — I don't know. Playacted with you too much."

"Oh, *Mom,*" she said miserably.

"What I'm saying is that if you want people to care about you, you have to meet them halfway. I wish that being yourself was the answer, but, honey, it's not. I'm sorry. It's the truth. You have to act interested in other people, and you have to ask them questions about themselves, and" — she was weeping openly now — "you've got to be normal sometimes."

"I'm not normal," Emily said. She looked up finally, taking in her mother's damp, magnified eyes and sun-spotted neck. Her skin, Emily noticed for the first time, was loose and slightly crinkled. Overripe.

"Baby, normal's not who you are or how you're born." Her mother was smiling a little, calm again, as if Emily had made the only statement that she could have formulated a response to. "It's how you act. It's something you do on purpose."

CHAPTER FOURTEEN

1.

The alarm sounded at four thirty A.M., and Dale, as he always did, snapped his bedside lamp on. Susanna stiffened, heart racing, and remembered her anger at him. Remembering was satisfying. The worst mornings were the ones when she softened, allowed him to kiss her, and then realized that they had fallen asleep arguing, nothing resolved, her acceptance of his kiss an absolution that she hadn't intended to offer. On this morning she rolled away from the light and folded the end of the pillow over her eyes. She heard, muffled, the closet door rattle and slide on its track, the opening and closing of a dresser drawer. He left the light on when he went down the hall to the bathroom, and Susanna, muttering, rolled back over and fumbled, eyes pinched shut, to find the knob to turn it off.

She was wide-awake now, bladder tight,

back cramped. She wouldn't relieve herself until Dale finished his shower and went to the kitchen in his robe and slippers to pour a cup of coffee. There would be a minute or two, while he poured and stirred in half-and-half, when she could slip into the bathroom and out unseen, then crawl back under the covers as if she'd never awakened. Then Dale would return with his mug to the bathroom, wipe steam from the mirror, shave. He would dress in his best band director's attire — the dark gray wool suit, the white shirt, the black-and-gold silk tie that the students had presented him at the band banquet two years ago. He would move his coffee mug well out of the way before dousing himself with the strong cologne he favored on field days, the kind that smelled to Susanna like grass clippings and lemon. He would gel his short, dark hair so that the bangs lifted a little and a stiff part coursed left of center.

Their arguments had never been like this. They had, since Wednesday evening, been for the most part mutually silent — easy enough to maintain since Dale kept the band practicing late again both Thursday and Friday, coming in at night in time to kiss Abby while she slept, change into his pajamas, and fall immediately into a snoring deep sleep. They hadn't shared a meal, a conversation. Abby had told Susanna with exaggerated, confused delight about the other evening with Daddy, how he'd let her come to the top of the band tower and watch the performance, how she said "Good job, team!" into his microphone and the big kids cheered, how he took her to Mc-Donald's for a Happy Meal on the way home. She kept playing with the prize from the Happy Meal, a wind-up character from a Saturday-morning cartoon that she wasn't old enough to enjoy. "I didn't like the rain," she said a few times, as though her conscience were tugging at her for painting too rosy a picture. "I didn't like the rain, but Daddy said that I wouldn't melt."

"And you didn't," Susanna told her.

"Little girls can't melt," Abby said.

Now he was standing in the doorway. Susanna, back in bed with her eyes still closed, felt him rather than saw him. His cologne tickled her sinuses.

"I'm leaving," he said.

She groaned a little and propped herself up on her elbows, blinking in a sleepy way. She could tell by how he was looking at her that he knew she was putting on, and it embarrassed her. "Okay," she said. "Be careful." Then, an afterthought: "Good luck."

He nodded. "We won't be back tonight. We're going to stay to watch the finals no matter what. I went ahead and booked a block of rooms on Thursday."

"Better not to be on the road late," Susanna said. "It makes sense."

He rubbed his mouth suddenly, a quick, brisk side-to-side, and Susanna noticed for the first time how tired he looked. "You could come with us. You don't have to bring Abby. I called your mom last night, and she said she'd take her. I mean, it's not a real trip away, I know, but we'd have some time alone, at least. I'm following the buses in the Blazer."

"Dale —"

"Hear me out," he said. He had a hand up, as if he were stopping traffic. "I know that you don't love sitting in the bleachers all day. I know you've got work to do. But we could get lunch in Louisville tomorrow, go to that bookstore you like, go to a museum. We could go to that movie you were wanting to see — *The Piano*? Was that it? They'll have it in Louisville."

Susanna sat up in the bed. Her chest felt constricted with something, a guilty, tender ache. He was right about the movie she'd mentioned, had remembered her muttering over the preview when it had shown on TV, her remark that the Blockbuster in town would probably not ever even get it on video. He was wrong about the bleachers, because there had been a time, before Abby, when she *had* loved hanging out in the bleachers all day — when, almost as much a kid as her husband's students, she had sat wrapped in a blanket, blowing into a paper cup of hot chocolate, and felt goose bumps at the sight of her husband on the sidelines in his sharp dark suit. She had known the shows then almost as well as Dale did, remembered the melodies, the formations, each toss of a flag, how the drum line did that little spin of their sticks between numbers, always to a round of game applause from the audience. Even now, she could imagine the pleasure of a late-autumn marching band competition, the awe of watching a 4A band take to the field in hundreds, the theater of richer schools who had smoke machines and set pieces and elaborate costuming. She'd not grown immune to all of those charms — just too tired, now, to appreciate them.

"I'm meeting the detective about Ronnie again today," she said. "I was going to get Mom or Denise to take Abby. We're going back to the gas station to talk to the person who was working the night Ronnie would've come. She's been out of town the last few days."

"All right," Dale said evenly.

"It would go a long way toward" — Susanna waved her hands between them — "this. Making this better. If you were to support me a little." She picked at a thread on the quilt. "I appreciate your invitation. But I need your support more."

He walked over to the bed and sat, and she moved out of the way, trying not to jerk, to seem as if she were avoiding his touch. His hip was next to her calf and he propped his arm on the other side of her legs, leaning forward a little, trying for intimacy, she knew, but instead making her suddenly claustrophobic, her feet pinned beneath the covers, her body forced to dip toward his.

"I don't want you to be stuck with me," he said. "I love you. I want you here. But I don't want you stuck here."

She looked at his earlobe and cleared her throat. "I'm not stuck," she said quietly, and she couldn't tell if it was a lie or not.

"It isn't always easy for me, either," he said. "There are nights when I think that we could have had more than this."

"More than this house and these jobs and our child."

"Yes," he said again, forcefully, as if he

expected an argument.

Susanna swallowed against a sharp pain. "I wonder what it would have been like," she said.

"So do I." He turned and looked at the alarm clock on his bedside table. "I've got to go. I'll be late." He rose and let his fingertips graze the bedspread over her thigh. She could see him wanting to say that he loved her again but worrying that she wouldn't say it back to him.

"Be careful," she said firmly and, she hoped, with finality.

"Yes," he said. He adjusted his trousers and tucked his dress shirt back into place. "Thanks. I will."

He brought Abby to her before leaving, an old, indulgent ritual they had lately abandoned. He tucked her, still sleeping, into Susanna's open arms, so that Susanna could rest her chin on Abby's head and Abby's feet could rest on the tops of Susanna's thighs. She reached down and held the little feet in her hands, delighting, as she always did, in their plump smoothness. They were the part of her daughter that still felt and looked more a baby's than a child's, the bones hidden in layers of flesh, the soles unblemished. Abby's hands were already slimmer. Susanna had looked one day and realized that where the knuckles had once been dimples in the flesh — concavities — there was now the slightest angle of bone. The visible skeleton, memento mori.

Dale kissed their cheeks. "Bye, girls," he said. The floor creaked, the outer door closed. Outside, the Blazer roared to life.

Abby shifted around and scrambled up Susanna, papery toenails catching purchase. She put her arms around Susanna's neck, tangling her fingers in her long hair, and she drew her legs up so that her knees pressed into Susanna's stomach. Abby was warm; she always felt hot to Susanna, even when her temperature — she so often checked — was normal. Pink-faced and sweaty, breath moist and sour with last night's glass of milk. What was this creature they'd created? This living, growing thing, more animal at times like this than human? What if they had dared to have a life without her?

These thoughts inevitably led her to Tony Joyce, and just letting her mind slide along the syllables of his name sent — she could not help it — a thrill of excitement through her. Today she would see him again. Today, they would continue their search. Her heart, which Abby's forehead was pressed against, thumped harder for a few beats as she imagined it: dropping Abby at her mother's, meeting Tony at the station, accompanying him back to the Fill-Up. They would learn something, she just knew it. Maybe they would even track Ronnie down. At that last thought her stomach knotted with vague dread, a sensation that Susanna made an effort not to settle upon. She thought instead about how it had felt to be near Tony, at the computer and in his police cruiser, and how she would get to repeat that pleasure today. And, for the first time, she thought about the fact that her husband would be gone overnight, hundreds of miles away.

CHAPTER FIFTEEN

1.

The stupidest thing Tony Joyce had ever said to another person also happened to be the truest thing: "You don't understand the life of an athlete."

It was a stupid thing to say because he had offered it, self-pityingly, as explanation for an action for which there was no real justification. He was twenty years old, nine months into his first real relationship with a woman, and that woman, Stefany, had discovered he had cheated. The time she knew about was not the only time, but it was the time he was trying to answer for, and it — the betrayal — had happened while he was on the road with the Bluefield Orioles, just as all of the other unacknowledged betrayals had.

"I don't. Understand. The life. Of an athlete." Stefany had repeated it back to him like that, slow and pissed off, eyes cut in a way that made Tony a trifle fearful that she would try to hit him. "Oh, poor you. Poor Tony with his great job and his girlfriend and his trips all over the country. Poor Tony with dinner fucking waiting for him every time his bus pulls into town from a game. Poor Tony, who gets to do exactly what he loves while the rest of us are just struggling for a paycheck." She was standing, he remembered, across the kitchen peninsula from him, hands on her hips, head cocked sharply to the side. "No, how on earth could I understand that? Of course you had to get some bitch on your jock the minute you got out of Bluefield."

He had felt bad. He had. But the explanation, as inadequate and audacious as it sounded, was real. She didn't understand the life of an athlete. She didn't understand what it was to be him. And though Tony didn't grasp it all himself — his was a life, up to this point, mostly unexamined — he knew intuitively that there was no life of the mind and heart for him that wasn't intimately connected to his physical self. His joys, his sorrows, his sexuality, his cobbled-together spirituality: he experienced these sensations through his long, strong, talented limbs. Later, when Tony was no longer at the mercy, in all of those bad ways and glorious ways, of his physical self, he would realize that he had possessed, at his peak, a kind of genius. The occasional pains he'd known — a sprained wrist, bruising, one slash along his shin deep enough to require stitches — were specific and ephemeral and only made him appreciate more his body's default status: its utter painlessness, its ease. At bat, he saw a ball coming and his body knew the stance to adopt, the way to hold the bat, the degree to which he needed to shift his weight to his left leg. He could, machinelike, compute from the moment of contact whether the hit was good or not, if his intention had been made manifest or if some uncalculated factor — a gust of wind, a movement in the grit under his cleat, an uncaught trickle of sweat loosening his grip on the bat — had subverted him.

So this, the unearthly physical genius, was part of it. But the life of an athlete, for a young man of his gifts, extended beyond the field. Sure, some of it was power, the power of living in a culture that valued his talents as much as he personally valued them — and this wasn't true, certainly, of his artistic abilities. That power, though Stefany would deny it, was what had helped him land her. Oh, she could (and did) say that she loved him for him, that she would want him no matter what, but she, like most of the girlfriends among his teammates, had started as an Annie, a groupie — a Bluefield townie who knew that the minor leaguers always turned up by the end of the night at Ramsey's, where the owner fronted them free pitchers and pool after a game. She, like most of the girlfriends, had enough knowledge of the sport to spot the potential shining stars; Stefany had even, he later learned, started reading the industry rags, so that she could follow firsthand the statistics and rumors, the bold claims such as the one by a journalist who wrote in a minor-league seasonal roundup that "Tony Joyce may well prove to be the Orioles' next Cal Ripken Jr." The players went through the groupies like they did pitchers of beer and treated them poorly, swapping one woman for the next, breaking promises, throwing punches, taking cruel advantage — Tony had once seen Kyle Barberie, who ascended the next season to the majors, throw an unconscious woman over his shoulder and carry her to a bedroom — but they knew that they, too, were being used, being sized up as some woman's ticket out of the backwater, and even a relationship like Tony and Stefany's, long by anyone's standards, couldn't emerge from the shadow of its beginnings.

What Stefany could perhaps grasp least about the life of an athlete was how important that fraternity became to you. Tony had grown up an outsider — black in a white town and a white sport — and though he had been popular at RHS, it was a popularity that did not always hold up out of school or off the field. Tony could feel comfortable around his white teammates and their white girlfriends, but the minute he showed up at one of their houses, sat down at the dinner table with their white mothers and fathers, he could sense a static charge in the air between them. It wasn't always rudeness, though sometimes it was; and once, unforgettably, a father had instructed him in a low, steady voice, "Get the fuck off of my property." But in some instances, Tony sensed, if anything, that his white hosts were treating him with more care than they did the other young men at the table — passing him food first, agreeing too emphatically with his opinions. And while this was certainly preferable to the rudeness or the outright menace of those other situations, he could not escape the belief that what he was witnessing was a careful staging, after which, in his absence, his hosts' real selves would emerge. Why else would Jake, whose

mother had insisted so enthusiastically that
Tony "come back soon, dear," never invite
Tony over again?

The team was different. He was one of
only two black men playing that season, but
Tony felt he had more in common with the
lot of them, black and white, than he'd ever
had with anyone back home — even his own
family. How could his father, with his stoop
and his soft middle and his job as a custodian at the nursing home, ever know what
Tony knew? Who but Tony's teammates
would understand, not laugh, if Tony admitted that he sometimes felt a spiritual connection with the ball? They played together
— not always harmoniously, often in the
face of petty jealousies, but even those
jealousies were welcome to Tony. It seemed
to him only natural that a man could resent
his swing, though he still could not fathom
why a man would resent his skin color.

A lot of them were poor kids from nowhere, like Tony. Like Tony, they had their
heads filled up with major league dreams of
money and fame and women (though there
was never, even in the minors, any shortage
of those). Was it a wonder that they were all
bad boyfriends and husbands? They gave
their best, truest selves to the game and to
each other, and so the women, in the wake

of that, were interchangeable: objects toward which to direct their pent-up sexual energy, the occasional reminder of softer domestic pleasures. And though Tony had tried hard with Stefany, had stayed with her long after one of his teammates would have moved on to the next girl, he had to admit to himself, watching her cry and rage that day in the kitchen, that his only true allegiance was to his team, and what he was getting from Stefany he could get, and had gotten, from a dozen other girls. He could see in her face that she knew it. This was the irony: she was angry, and she wanted to go through the motions of punishing him, but she needed him more than he needed her. She would not be the one to leave, Tony realized, and so she could mock him all she wanted for saying that thing about the life of an athlete, but her every action only proved him right.

"I need to know that this won't happen again," she said finally, breathless. She had halted her zigzagging progression behind the kitchen peninsula, and she uncrossed her arms and put the palms flat on the countertop. "Tell me this won't happen again, Tony."

"It won't," he said. The necessary lie. He wasn't even sure why he said it, since he found that it didn't matter much to him if his relationship with Stefany continued. But she was a habit, effortless, and it was better to tell her what she wanted to hear than to force her to acknowledge the obvious: that this thing between them was temporary, that she would not be following him to the majors, that he wouldn't be her ticket out of Bluefield. As it turned out, he wasn't even his own ticket — he blew out his back moving a big-screen television, his first major adult purchase. It had taken him another two years to pay off that TV, time enough to weather two surgeries, a year of physical therapy, and the realization that he'd never be well enough, or young enough, to play again. The TV still sat in his living room. The picture hadn't been right since he dropped it that fateful day ten years ago, but he'd be damned if he didn't get his money's worth out of it.

2.

Now, here he was: Tony Joyce, detective in a town of ten thousand people. He was thirty years old and renting a one-bedroom apartment in a complex on the edge of town. He thought occasionally about buying a nice little house — he could afford a ranch in one of the town's middle-grade subdivisions, or he could get an older home near the library and start putting some work and money into it — but buying here in Roma would be the final admission of defeat, the final acknowledgment that he'd given up not only on all of those major league dreams but on the minor league ones, too: the dream of living somewhere other than this town, of making a name among people who didn't know his previous glory and couldn't measure him by it. In towns like Lexington or Louisville or Nashville, he knew he could ascend quickly among the ranks. He was educated — one thing he did do right was return to college part-time to finish his degree — and capable, articulate. His two years in Bluefield would be interesting trivia, the kind you wanted your low-level politicians and car salesmen and fast-food franchise owners to have. Here, if he were to run for sheriff — and he thought about it a lot; Timothy Coe had all but promised to step down after finishing out his current term — he would be fighting a battle against his blackness as much as any opponent, and it would be high school all over again, the smiling, tense faces and worried murmuring the minute his back was turned. He didn't know if he could do it. If it could be done.

But there were certain inescapable facts to consider, like his mother and father, who still lived in Roma and who were both in poor health and who would, he suspected, live with gaping holes in the walls of their house if he didn't happen to see and fix them. It wasn't as if his brother and sister were any help. Or perhaps it was just the fact of his own cowardly heart — for he'd once felt certain of his prospects, had seen them as his due, and what he had learned was that nothing was his due.

He was on his second cup of coffee and his fourth ibuprofen, trying to watch a Saturday-morning cartoon (something jerky and neon-colored with screechy, obnoxious characters — this is what kids liked?), when he realized that it was going to be a Darvocet day, after all. He tried to lay off it, especially when he had real detective's work to do, and he usually succeeded. But the pain, which never receded entirely, liked to step forward occasionally and announce itself. *Tony! Here I am! Did you think you were rid of me finally?* Yes, the pain had become sentient: it was a character, an arch-nemesis, with a voice not unlike that of the characters on this cartoon he was trying to watch on his damaged big-screen TV. Yes, he thought, just like that fellow with the huge pink eyes and ears and the mouthful of jagged teeth; the pain was *gnawing,* that was the right word for it. On the good days, it annoyed him — made it hard for him to find a comfortable position in bed, protested when he leaned over to pick something up. On the Darvocet days, it would not be ignored; it put sharp fingers into his lower back, sent tremors even into his hips and shoulders. The scar from his surgery felt as if it were glowing with heat, and indeed, each time Tony checked it in the mirror, he was surprised anew by the shiny vein of it: a darker black on the normal days, an itchy red on the ones like this. He downed one pill, thought about it, and swallowed another.

They were starting to take hold a half hour later, as he was pulling his unmarked cruiser in at the Fill-Up and scanning the lot for Susanna's car. The pain was calling at him from such a distance now as to not even be audible, and a beautiful calm had settled over everything. It was like wading hip-deep through clear, still water. He backed into a parking spot — a habit so ingrained that he never even registered doing it anymore, or remembered the reason he started — and felt a tremor, a ripple in the calm, as he realized that Susanna was there already, standing in front of the gas station and waving to him. He lifted a hand back. She was wearing jeans today, and her long hair, not held in place with a band or barrettes, was lifted in a gust of cold wind. She kept trying to comb it into place with her fingers, and he could see through the windshield and even through the fog of his medication that she was nervous, a nervousness that had as much to do with him, he knew, as with the information they hoped to gather today. He grabbed his satchel from the passenger floorboard and started across the parking lot.

"Good morning," she said. Her smile was broad despite the nature of their outing, her cheeks bright with cold.

"Hi there. Ready for this?"

"As I'm going to be."

"OK," Tony said. He unzipped his satchel and removed a notebook and pencil. "Having you here with me isn't quite protocol, so hang back and let me do the talking, even if there's something you really want to say. Just save it up and tell me later."

"Got it," Susanna said. She was close enough to him that he could smell her clean scent: not perfume, nothing strong, but soap, maybe shampoo. Her dark hair was tucked behind a small, round ear. He could remember the day he'd drawn that ear, the feel of the rough paper beneath his fingertip as he had smudged a shadow, softening the curve. It had occurred to him over the years, when he chanced to think about that semester and his misguided, misplaced affections, that he had thought it love because he had drawn her, and to draw a person that way was intimate, almost a transgression.

The convenience mart inside was like most of them, smelling of burned coffee and old frying grease, the fluorescent lights overhead harsh and unforgiving. He approached a woman at the food counter and put on the serious but reassuring expression that he'd found was most effective in these situations, especially with potential witnesses. People could be guarded around cops — suspicious. They thought that you were out to get them. At least this woman wasn't white; Tony hated trying to win over the old, poor white folks.

"Ma'am, I'm Tony Joyce, with the police department. I let your manager know I'd be coming by."

"That's right," she said. She glanced between him and Susanna, who was waiting by a rack of snack crackers, and transferred a handful of fried chicken from a stainless steel pan to a warming tray. She was a very small woman with her graying hair in a net, and she looked like she was probably in her late sixties — an age when a woman ought to be able to retire, Tony thought, not work the night shift at a gas station.

"You're Patricia Williams? You were here on late evening of October twenty-third, morning of the twenty-fourth?"

"That's what Mr. Highland say. What the timesheets say, he tells me." She turned the pan over and dumped the crumbs on top of the pile of chicken.

Well, this was off to a promising start. "Do you have any recollection of that night at all? Anything that would set it apart from another?"

"I guess it was the evening I worked midnights. I only work midnights when Lana has her grandbabies for the weekend."

"OK, great," Tony said. He flipped the cover on his notebook over. "I'm going to show you a photograph. What I want you to do is think about whether or not you recognize the person, that's all. And if you do, tell me how you think you know her." He slipped Ronnie's photo out of the pocket on his notebook cover and handed it across the counter. Mrs. Williams took her plastic glove off and pinched the photo by the very corner, as if she was afraid of smudging it.

"Yeah, I saw them that night."

Tony sensed Susanna stiffening behind him. "Now, take your time," he said, pencil poised. "What do you remember?"

"I'd seen her before. I think she works at the sewing factory — they come over here at shift changes."

"But you said 'them'?"

The old woman nodded. "She had some man with her. Some older white man. They bought food and beer."

Tony scribbled all of this down. "This man. What can you tell me about him?"

Mrs. Williams shrugged. "I hardly looked at him."

"But you could see he was older. How much older?"

"His fifties, maybe," she said. "He kind of hung back, like she's doing." She nodded toward Susanna. "I didn't get a good look at him."

"What kind of build did he have?" Susanna blurted out. She glanced apologetically at Tony, then bulldozed forward. "Thin, fat? Tall or short?"

Tony had to restrain himself from hissing at her. He waved Susanna back and patted the counter, trying to get the old woman's eyes on him. "Mrs. Williams," he said. "Back to me, ma'am. We're not trying to rush you.

I just want you to take your time. Don't push yourself to remember something you don't."

"He was overweight," she said decisively. "I remember that much. And taller than the woman by a good bit. She was a little-bitty thing."

Tony glanced at Susanna. "Ronnie's two inches shorter than I am," she said sheepishly. "Five foot."

"When you say overweight, what do you mean? Can you be a bit more specific?"

The woman put her hands out in front of her, as though she were pregnant, or Santa Claus. "He was pudgy but not great big. Had a stomach on him and a round face."

"OK, great." Tony wrote some more down. Then he stopped and thought. He wasn't sure if the idea he had was a good one or a bad, but he paged forward in his notebook to a clean sheet. "Susanna," he said. "Grab me a couple of magazines from off the rack there, would you please?"

She seemed eager to fulfill the request, as though it might make up for the fact that she had spoken after he asked her not to. "Here you go," she said, putting a *People,* a *Newsweek,* and a *National Enquirer* on the countertop. Tony set the *National Enquirer* to the side right away, then paged through the others. He found two photographs, one in each magazine, and put them side by side. The first was of a sitcom star, a big, heavy man with a face that had probably once been handsome before all of his high school muscle had turned to fat. The second photograph was of a British politician whom Tony had never heard of, a man with sagging, doughy skin and a ruddy bulb of nose. His hair, blondish and thin, was brushed raggedly across his forehead. Tony, operating from instinct, had chosen the men not for their features so much as their feel. One seemed vigorous and confident in his weight, the other defeated — pathetic, even.

"If you had to say which of these men the fellow you saw was more like," Tony said, "which would it be?"

"Neither, really." She looked skeptical.

Tony cleared his throat. "Don't overthink it, ma'am. Just go with your gut."

"Well, if you held a gun to my head" — she tapped the photograph of the politician — "his face shape was more like that. But the man who came in that night had a mustache."

"Good, good," Tony said. His heartbeat had picked up, and his back twinged. He took his pencil and drew a mustache on the image of the politician. "Is that closer?"

"You're going to have to pay for that magazine," Mrs. Williams said. "Or Mr. Highland going to take it out of my check."

"Yes, yes, that's fine," Tony said. "What I want to know is if the image looks closer to what you remember, or what's still wrong about it."

She closed her eyes for a second. "His nose wasn't big and red like that," she said finally. "And his hair was dark and slicked over so it looked wet."

Tony started sketching on the clean sheet of paper. He referred once or twice to the magazine, just as a way to give the face structure, to remind himself of the protrusions and hollows, and made adjustments based on the woman's description. He kept the notebook on the countertop as he drew, so that she could watch his progress, and he was satisfied when she stopped his hand to say "No, his chin was softer than that" and "I don't think he had as dark a eyebrows as you drawing."

At last he stopped his pencil, and Mrs. Williams didn't say anything. It was, he knew, a quiet borne of helplessness rather than satisfaction; he had gotten the drawing as right as he could get it, but that didn't mean it was right. The old woman had simply run out of words for explaining to him how he could make it better.

"It's a good drawing," she said. "To be honest, I'm not sure I remember what the man even looked like anymore. I'm getting it mixed up with those." She pointed at the magazines.

"That's all right," Tony said. "That's how it goes. You lose the real memory when you try to make it concrete. But I think we're farther along than we would have been otherwise."

"It's a good drawing," she repeated. "You got talent, young man. You ought to be an artist."

He laughed. "I'll think about it." He took the pencil and shaved a line down with the eraser, so that the eyes looked more even. "Can I ask you one more thing, Mrs. Williams? It's kind of a funny question."

Her eyebrows drew together. "All right, then."

"How did the guy seem to you? I don't mean his looks. I mean —" Tony waved his hand as though he were reaching for the words. "I mean, what kind of vibe did you get?"

"A vibe."

"Yes, ma'am."

"Lord, I don't know. He seemed like a sad case, I guess. Like he was happier being with the woman than she was with him. I don't know what gave me that idea, so don't quote me on it."

"I won't," Tony said. "You've been a real help to us, Mrs. Williams."

"You sure have," Susanna said. Tony could see her gaze fixed on the sketch, the fear and hope in her eyes, and he almost wished he had never drawn it.

"That's fine," the old woman said. "Now, I'm going to have to ring you up for that magazine, mister. I hate to, but I'm going to have to."

3.

They were sitting in Gary's Pit Barbecue together over lunch, and Susanna couldn't stop looking at the sketch Tony had drawn. He had fussed with it a bit in his car outside of the gas station, putting in a few lines between the eyebrows and at the corners of the eyes, shading the irises and whitening a spot of light with his eraser. It was guesswork, or perhaps just outright fabrication, but what Mrs. Williams had said about his sadness struck him, and it bothered him that the image didn't communicate it.

"It gives me the willies," Susanna said. She was only picking at her sandwich. "It scares me to death to imagine that she was with this man."

"That's just made-up." He forked some pork and corn bread, then dribbled hot sauce on top. His own appetite was, it seemed, just fine. "I did it mostly to get her to tell me what I was missing, like the mustache. The memory's a funny thing. Sometimes you can't say what you saw unless you do it in the context of what you didn't see."

"I have a feeling about this." She tapped the page. "I think we should put up new flyers with the sketch on it. We might get some leads."

"Leads." He huffed. "If I put that drawing up around here I'll be asking for trouble. Do you know how many fat white men with mustaches there are in this town?" He turned in his shoulder and thumbed surreptitiously to the left. "That guy over there could be him, if this is all we've got to go on."

Susanna frowned. "That man looks nothing like this."

"I'm willing to bet that he bears as close a resemblance to this drawing as the person with your sister that night does."

"Well what do you suggest then, Tony?" She was, he noticed for the first time, pale and stiff, and her eyelashes were damp.

"This is my sister. What do you suggest?"

He used a paper napkin to wipe his goatee, then his fingers. "Tell me more about Ronnie. Where would she go on a Saturday night? Where were her haunts?"

"I don't know a lot about that part of her life. She went to Nashville sometimes." She sipped her tea, brow furrowed. "Oh! And I think she liked going to that crappy little town across the Tennessee line — the one with the line-dancing club."

"The Tobacco Patch?" The town's real name was Sylvan, but no one ever called it that.

"That's right," she said.

"Was she big into dancing?"

"She was big into drinking," Susanna said dryly. "And picking up men. There was one guy she had kind of a regular thing with, I think, and they met up there at the small bar, the one that looks like a cabin. She didn't say much about him, but his name came up enough over the years that I put two and two together. A soldier from Fort Campbell."

Tony tilted the drawing back toward himself. "This doesn't look like a soldier."

"No, it doesn't."

The waitress came over to refill their drinks and lingered. "Miz Mitchell, right?"

"Oh," Susanna said. She seemed startled. "Yes?"

"I thought it was you. My son's in the band. I was surprised you weren't in Louisville with them today."

Susanna's cheeks pinkened. "I had some business to attend to in town."

The waitress looked at Tony. It was an expression he'd grown familiar with over the years, though never used to. "Well, holler if you need anything else," she said, tearing the check off a booklet and sitting it on the table before walking away. Tony watched as a spot of condensation soaked through and bloomed across it.

"What now?" Susanna said finally.

"I guess I go to the Tobacco Patch tonight."

"Just you?"

"I think that's best," Tony said. "I'll have to put a call in to the sheriff there and work with the local force."

She sighed. "I'd still like to put this drawing up around town. At least let me do that."

"Susanna."

"Please?" She wasn't even making eye contact with him now. Her brows were knit, her fingers curled so that the nails dug into the tabletop. "If there's something I might do to find her sooner, I want to do it. I'm not kidding myself here. I know this is a long shot. But I think it's better to try than not."

"This could get me flak in the department if people start pointing fingers in the wrong direction."

"Better than no direction at all."

"I'm not so sure of that." He dug through his wallet for a twenty and set it on top of the bill.

"Let me —" Susanna began.

"No," Tony said. "It's on me." He finished the last of his tea in a swallow. "Listen. I'll take the sketch to Sylvan with me, see what I hear. If I don't hear anything to contradict Mrs. Williams, I'll let you post the drawing up in town. I'll make the copies for you, and I'll help you do it."

"Okay." He could tell she wasn't satisfied.

"I'll call you when I'm back from Sylvan tonight, all right? I'll let you know what I hear, and I'll bring you the drawing. I won't make you wait another day for it."

Susanna nodded more enthusiastically. "All right. Thanks, Tony."

"You're welcome."

She took a scrap of paper and a pen out of her purse and scratched something down. "That's my address. I won't be able to sleep until I hear what happened, so just come by."

He took the scrap and looked at her. Her expression was frank, defiant even.

"However late," she said.

4.

"She must've been done up on something," Sal Lochman said over at the Salamander, and his wife, a sawed-off woman with freckles and orange hair, nodded her agreement with an unsettling zealousness. Later, driving the half mile between the Salamander and Nancy's, Tony's official escort for the evening, Sheriff Lyle Gatlin, had grunted. "Those two seemed done up on something themselves, far as I could tell."

"I thought so, too," Tony said. He liked Lyle so far — the man seemed smart and experienced but was content to mostly stand to the side and let Tony conduct his investigation.

"Still," Lyle said, "this Ronnie woman sure doesn't seem to be much on making friends." Tony had to agree with that, as well. On the night of her disappearance, she had publicly slapped a man whom she was dating, screamed at him, gotten rebuked, and stormed off. No one could say where for sure, but more than one person suggested that the next logical stop in the Patch, if Ronnie hadn't given up entirely on having a good time, would have been Nancy's. When asked about Ronnie, the patrons at the Salamander responded on a spectrum between aggravated amusement and outright hostility. If this was the place that Ronnie Eastman had seen fit to frequent, Tony wondered how out of place she must have felt everywhere else in the world.

"I guess I shouldn't complain about the Patch," Lyle continued, "because it keeps me working. I reckon that's one way to think of it. But I hate it. I mean, if someone had tried hard to think up a way to get the worst of everyone's leftovers into one place, they couldn't have come up with better than this. Old drunks, young punks, and sad-sack women."

"And line dancers," Tony said as Lyle pulled into a handicapped spot at the front of Nancy's gravel lot.

"Them too, for that matter." Lyle spat brown juice into the neck of a Mountain Dew bottle with something that almost resembled grace. "Have you ever seen those people? I think they bus them in from the loony bin."

The doorman waved them past. It was still fairly early in the evening — there was only one man drinking at the bar and a dozen or so people seated at tables. No one was on the dance floor yet, though something country was playing loudly through the juke; Tony didn't like that kind of music and wouldn't have been able to name the band if his life depended on it. A few heads lifted as he and Lyle, who was wearing his sheriff's khakis and wide-brimmed hat, strolled across the floor, toward the long plank bar that ran alongside the right-hand wall. Tony imagined that a black man was a rare sight here, rarer than the occasional lawman in uniform, and he wondered what the patrons would do if he kicked into a boot, scoot, and boogie, or however it went. He was relieved in a way to have Lyle with him, and he was ashamed to feel the relief. He had as much right to be in Nancy's as anyone.

"Tony, this is Ashley Justice," Lyle said when they reached the bar. The young woman he was gesturing toward looked barely drinking age herself. She had purple, sparkly eye shadow painted up to her eyebrows and silver rings on all of her fingers, even the thumbs. "Miss Justice, Tony is a detective out of Roma, Kentucky. He's going to have some questions for you. You just answer to the best of your recollection and be as honest as you can. All right?"

"Okay," she said. She took Tony's out-stretched hand with a measure of confusion, as if she'd never shaken hands before. The silver rings clanked together as he squeezed.

Tony showed her Ronnie's photograph. "Do you remember seeing this woman on October twenty-third? That would have been two Saturday nights ago."

She glanced at the photo, and Tony knew before she even spoke that she recognized the image. It was a narrowing in her eyes. "Yeah, I served her. Two weeks ago sounds about right. She tried to stiff me."

"Stiff you?"

"Yeah. This pack of guys'd come in together and run up a big tab, had me making all these disgusting shots for this old guy to drink, and then they all walked out on him. I mean, it was a shitty prank, but that's not my business. You're a grown man, you better know who you're drinking with." She pursed her lips, and Tony thought he caught a glimpse of what Miss Ashley Justice must have been like in her not-long-ago high school days. "Anyway, she thought I shouldn't charge him for the drinks, and then she tried to stiff me the tip, but I threatened to call the cops on the both of them." She looked at Lyle. "I'd heard what went down at the Salamander."

"So she paid their tab?" Lyle asked.

"Yeah. Well, the old guy might have had some money, but she paid the rest of it. Then she helped him outside, and that's the last I saw of them."

"You keep saying 'old guy,' " Tony said. "How old?"

She shrugged, pausing as she towel-dried a pint glass. "Older than my dad."

"Fifties? Sixties?"

"Probably," she said. "Not, like, ancient. But old." Lyle, perhaps sixty himself, threw Tony an amused look.

"What else do you remember about him?"

"He was fat. I think he had a mustache. He was really drunk, and he was just slobbering all over the bar by the time that woman came over. The whole thing was weird."

Tony drew his notebook out of his satchel and paged through to the sketch. "Was he anything like this?"

"Did you do that?" she asked, setting the glass on the counter. Lyle, too, was leaning in, curious; Tony hadn't yet shown him the drawing.

"Yeah. Talk to me, is this in the ballpark?"

She turned the drawing more fully toward

herself. "Yeah, it is." She bit her lower lip and waved her finger along the line of the sketched cheeks. "His face wasn't as fat as the rest of him. He had loose skin like this." She pinched her own cheeks along the jaw-line and made a pouty face. "And his eyes were droopier."

Tony erased and smudged, put down more lines. The young woman and Lyle watched with interest.

"Yeah, that's getting there. Fuck, that's freaky. Did he do something to her?"

"We don't know anything about him," Tony said. "We just want to find him and talk to him. Is he a regular here?"

"I've never seen him but the once."

"What about those guys you said he was with at first? The ones who pranked him?"

"Yeah, them I've seen." She tapped her index fingers together like drumsticks. "There's a blond guy, loud and good-looking. He seems to be the one the rest of them look up to. And there's another really good-looking one, but he's black haired and blue eyed."

"Do you know anything about them?"

"Not really," she said. "I think they all work together somewhere, but I don't know where."

"How likely is it that they'll come in to-night?"

She shrugged again. "I don't know. Fifty-fifty? They make it over here once or twice a month. They're not, like, every week or nothing."

Tony and Lyle stayed another two hours, but the pack of young men never showed. They talked to a second bartender, the manager, and a few regular patrons. None of them remembered the man in the sketch, the one who'd been left with the young guys' tab. A few of them knew Ronnie, had heard about the drama at the Salamander. The other bartender told Tony that he thought the ringleader of the young men, the good-looking blond guy, was named Sam. But he could be wrong about that.

"If I had to guess," he said, "I'd figure they come from one of the factories. They seem like the type."

"Which factories?" Tony stopped scribbling. "Wait. What type do you mean?"

"I don't know. Just out of high school, money in their pockets." The bartender himself could have been a haggard thirty or a well-preserved forty. "We don't get the college crowd much here."

Tony nodded. His lower back twinged, like a guitar string getting plucked. "What are the factories you have in mind?"

"Springfield has some. We get a bunch from the vacuum cleaner plant. We get them from Clarksville. Roma, too."

"Maybe they were from Fort Campbell," Lyle said. "Don't you get a lot of traffic from the base?"

"Yeah, but —" The bartender shrugged.

"Didn't seem the type?" Tony said.

The bartender nodded.

Tony and Lyle parted ways back at the sheriff's office at a little after eleven. Lyle promised that he would send a deputy by Nancy's and the Salamander on a regular basis to check for the persons of interest, and Tony told him that he'd bring a sheath of flyers over: both the MISSING poster he and Susanna had already distributed around town and a poster with the sketch of the man whom, far as Tony could tell, Ronnie had last been seen with.

"What are you thinking, Mr. Joyce?" Lyle said finally. He was standing behind the open door of his cruiser, getting ready to climb in and drive home for the night, and the security light shining from the front of the office made his head of thick white hair glow. "Are you hopeful?"

"I don't know," Tony said. "I think I have to be until I can't be any longer."

Lyle nodded and patted the roof of his car in a final way. "Well, let me know how I can help. I hope you got something you can use tonight."

"I did," Tony said. "I definitely did."

The night was clear and cold, invigorating, and the air tasted of car exhaust and gravel dust. The Darvocet had worn off long ago, and the pain in his back had returned, but it was a clarifying pain, the kind that brightened lights and darkened shadows and sharpened the edges of everything. Tony started back to Roma feeling the kind of excitement he remembered best from his walks to home plate, the bat a pleasant, swinging weight bumping against his calf. He imagined how he would explain to Susanna the information he had gathered and the next steps he would have to take with it, and it was as if he were digging his cleat into the dirt, eyeing the pitcher, calculating the release of the ball and the way he would have to adjust his stance to meet it. His detective's instincts weren't yet as honed as that, and perhaps they never would be, but he had the sense that he had gathered all of the information he needed to take the next step, and the next, and the answers now were not just close but inevitable.

Chapter Sixteen

1.

The address Susanna had given him was in Glendale, a subdivision on the west side of town. In Tony's childhood, it had been one of the newer, nicer developments, the kids who lived there all white and comfortably middle-class. Now, barely twenty years later, it was already on the decline. You could get more bedrooms and bigger garages out in the country, two-story family rooms with grand fireplaces, chandeliers. You could live on a cul-de-sac, on a "lane" or a "way" or a "boulevard" instead of a street. It was funny, driving now through Glendale, to imagine the time when this was close to the best Roma had to offer an average family. Tony remembered those rare days when he went home after school with a white friend, the little thrill of pride he'd felt at boarding Bus 10 instead of Bus 4, which went through the part of town that everyone thought of as the Black Bottoms. He remembered disembodied details from various visits, various houses: a basement rec room, a tree house with solid plank floors. Satellite television. A refrigerator stocked with Coca-Colas instead of a rinsed-out milk jug full of Kool-Aid. He remembered that Stephen Wilkerson had a color TV in his bedroom bigger and newer than the one that Tony and his family gathered around in their living room each night, and he remembered that Stephen's mother would bring them popcorn in individual bowls while they played Atari. It had been a strange and wonderful treat in those days before microwave ovens: his own little bowl, his own drizzle of melted butter in zigs and zags across the top, and a bottle of soda to wash it down.

Susanna's house might have been any one of those homes from his classmates' childhoods. It was a single-story, sturdy redbrick ranch, saved from utter plainness by a small front porch with wrought-iron supports and a wrought-iron railing. Shrubbery, shorn squat and fat, made a procession across the length of the house, and the window boxes still held the skeletal remains of fall mums. Tony turned off the engine and popped the glove box. His back was a misery again. He uncapped the bottle of Darvocet and dry-swallowed two. A light came on at the front porch and the door opened.

A shadow figure waved. He waved back.

He could almost feel angry, looking at this house, though it was a house he could himself afford now — he'd scanned the real estate listings in this neighborhood just a couple of weeks ago. He could feel angry about those nervous bus rides spent trying to hide his off-brand backpack between his legs, about his pathetic gratitude to have been invited, if only for a short time, into a white world. He could be angry at himself for his appreciation of Mrs. Wilkerson's beauty, of how nice she always was to him, and how he had believed then, without a trace of guilt, that his life would be so much better if only he had a slim, yellow-haired mother who would serve him popcorn in a bowl, on a tray. A mother who stayed home and kept the house tidy, a father who went to work in a button-down shirt and tie, a light-filled house with waxed hardwood and linoleum floors. He could feel angry, but the Darvocet was already leveling him, and when he emerged from the car and scaled the porch's front steps, the expression of pleasure on Susanna's face was so genuine that he forgot for a moment the reason for his visit, much less those long-ago grievances.

"Are you sure it isn't too late to stop by?" he asked. "I don't want to disturb your family."

"Of course not, come in," she said, waving him forward. The house was very warm, and he let her help him out of his coat. "Dale's in Louisville overnight for the state finals, and I went ahead and left Abby at my mother's because I wasn't sure when to expect you." She motioned for him to take a seat on the sofa. "Can I get you something to drink?" She blushed. "I'm going to have a glass of wine myself."

"Just water would be fine."

She nodded quickly and went to the kitchen. The house was smaller than he remembered these houses being. Shabbier. There was a toy trunk propped against the wall, filled so far past the brim that the lid wouldn't close. A doll wearing a shirt but no pants was lying on the floor by Tony's feet. Its skin was bright pink, blond hair cut unevenly into a bubble, and its eyes, the kind that were supposed to close when it was reclined, were half-open. Tony nudged it onto its stomach with his toe.

"Ice?" Susanna called from the kitchen. He could hear the refrigerator door opening and closing.

"No, thank you," he called back.

"Are you hungry? I was worried that you might just work through supper."

"No, thank you," he said again, though he thought about popcorn. "I managed to sneak in a bite at the dance hall."

She returned with two glasses — his filled to the brim with water, hers with white wine. She handed him his drink and settled back into a rocker-recliner, tucking her bare feet under her hip. The bare feet were a surprise. An intimacy. He saw that she was dressed comfortably but neatly in fitted blue jeans and a black long-sleeved T-shirt, her long hair carefully brushed and arranged around her shoulders. She had wanted to look nice for him, he realized. The hand bringing the glass of wine to her lips, which were shiny with gloss, was trembling slightly.

"What did you hear?" she said. Her voice was clear and just slightly too loud, the words carefully enunciated. She had, he suspected, started on her bottle of wine before his arrival.

Tony walked her through what his investigation had turned up that night — the fight at the Salamander, Ronnie's appearance later in the evening at Nancy's. He took out his notebook and showed Susanna the updated sketch of the man from the Fill-Up. "The bartender was more confident in her description than Mrs. Williams was, and they agreed on several of the particulars. So if you still want to post this drawing up around town tomorrow, I can do it. I'm not convinced it's the right thing to do, but I'm willing."

Susanna held the notebook and stared at the image for a long time. "I want to," she said softly.

"You need to remember that I'm not a trained sketch artist. This might turn out to be completely off base."

"I have a feeling about it," she said. She tapped the drawing with her fingernail. "This man is out there. He knows something."

"Then we'll use it," Tony said. He felt, despite himself, a nervous thrill at the thought. This was the boldest action that he had taken in his position as Roma's detective. He had not, so far, ever even unsheathed his weapon.

She closed the notebook and pressed her palm against the cover, as if keeping the man in it contained. "What happens next?"

"Tomorrow I start making some phone calls. I need to track down that Sonny guy from Fort Campbell, the one she smacked."

"Even though she was seen with this other guy after him?"

"Yes," Tony said. "She could have gone to Sonny sometime after that, or the witnesses might not have the timeline exactly right. It would be awfully coincidental if the fight at the Salamander had nothing to do with her disappearance."

"Maybe she was embarrassed," Susanna said. "She has a lot of pride. If she felt humiliated, she might have run off." She gulped her wine. "She has a melodramatic streak."

"All the more reason to find Sonny Ferrell. Maybe she's been in touch with him."

"Okay, then," she said. "What else?"

"Then I work on finding that guy." Tony pointed to the notebook. "I think I'll start by making a list of all of the factories in the area and cold-calling, see if I can't turn up some information on this Sam guy and the group he came with. It might be a dead end, but it's something to do."

"And can I help?"

"You can hang posters," he said. "I'll put them together first thing tomorrow and bring a stack by here."

"Tony, thank you." She handed the notebook back to him. "Thank you for taking this seriously."

"I don't know what kind of man I'd be if I didn't."

The corner of her mouth twisted. "I do."

Tony slurped back some of the water she'd brought him.

"Do you remember that drawing you made of me?"

He hesitated, then nodded.

"I still have it," she said. "Well, my husband does. He framed it and hung it in his office at the high school. I see it whenever I go by there."

"It seems like a long time ago," Tony said. It occurred to him that she had still been mostly a child then: narrow and petite with a round face, an almost birdlike quality to her wide-set eyes and heart-shaped face. Now she, like himself, was out of her brightest youth — face leaner, little creases around her eyes, thickness in the chest and hips where once there'd been none. The tiniest threads of gray in her dark hair. He had noticed them earlier in the bright sunlight, had thought to himself that another kind of woman would have plucked them. Maybe she believed, like Tony's mother, that two gray hairs would grow in their place.

"You asked me out," she said.

He smiled to mask his discomfort. "And

you shot me down."

She nodded hard, inhaling, and Tony wondered if she was on the edge of crying. "I was stupid," she said in a rush. "I was — well, you know how it was then. I was a coward, Tony, and I've always regretted it."

"It was a long time ago," he said carefully. He watched as she swallowed the last of her wine, as if for courage. His arms and thighs were prickling with something that was perhaps arousal, because he could feel where this was heading, could see what Susanna meant to do. But maybe it was also simply awareness: of the wine and her bare feet, the absent husband and daughter, the dreary comforts of her home. An awareness that Susanna could never share or even understand, of his blackness and her whiteness, his presence in another man's house with another man's wife, an offense that he could have been killed for in the not-so-distant past, that could hurt him in ways he couldn't quite calculate in the here and now. If he were to run for sheriff, say. Yet she was thinking only of herself, of her bad choices, of the roads that had led her back to Roma. He thought, perhaps cruelly, hardly consciously, that she was like this house — once so coveted, so beyond his reach, and now, in the earliest stages of her declination, on offer. Did he want her just because he could have her? Was that all it was?

If he had wanted to hurt her — or maybe himself — he would have asked her what became of that drawing she'd done of him. He wondered if she even knew. If she realized it mattered. But instead, when she leaned toward him, determined to take the chance she had once denied herself, he met her halfway and put his hands on her jaw the way that he knew women liked, the way that made a kiss seem like an act of love instead of lust. He didn't know what he felt. It might have been love or it might have been anger, and the Darvocet dulled him so that he couldn't track where one emotion left off and the other began. Her mouth tasted like the sour wine.

CHAPTER SEVENTEEN

1.

On Sunday morning, when she normally would have been driving with Dale and Abby to church, Susanna was heading to her mother's place to pick up Abby. It was cold but achingly bright, and the sunlight through the windshield was almost hot on Susanna's nose and cheeks. She felt energized, a little jittery, like she could lace up her old sneakers and sprint around the block a few times or jump double Dutch, which she'd never had the speed or grace for as a girl. An image popped into her mind, absurd: Abby at one end of the ropes' handles, Ronnie on the other, Susanna in the middle, legs pistoning, soles of her shoes smacking cement. All of the songs they had sung then were about babies. *Fudge, fudge, call the judge. Mama's gonna have a newborn baby. Wrap it up in tissue paper, send it down the elevator.* And then the chant, everyone's emotions intensifying as the stakes climbed: *boy, girl, twins, triplets.* Girl was better than boy, and triplets were best of all. Susanna had never gotten farther than "paper," but Ronnie, when she still deigned to do it (and by the age of ten, she no longer did), was a jump-roping whiz, and her friends' arms usually gave out before she did.

Susanna's mother still lived in the house where Susanna grew up, a subdivision over past Harper Hill. It was a ranch house with a gable roof and a picture window; a fine crack, running diagonally across the window, had been held together for years with three bands of electrical tape. The shell of the house was brick, a yellowish color that Susanna's father had called Piss Poor when he was still alive to complain. That was the home's most decadent touch. There was an oil-stained carport — empty now, because Susanna's mother didn't drive. This was the reason Susanna depended on her mother to keep Abby only when she was in a tight spot or in situations when Susanna knew she could come over at a moment's notice.

She pulled into the carport, turned off the engine. She looked at her reflection in the rearview mirror and put the backs of her hands up against her pink cheeks to cool them. She had been waiting all morning to feel guilty, to feel sad, to feel like a bad person, but there was only this energy, vibrating so strongly through her that her leg kept jogging. Sitting under the roof of her mother's carport, pulling her handbag out from the backseat, she thought suddenly of that first kiss of the previous night, Tony's hands on her jaw and his thumb grazing her pearl earring, the coarse brush of his goatee on her chin. There had been the slightest bitter edge to the taste of his tongue, as if he had swallowed an aspirin, but it wasn't unpleasant, exactly, and it was just the sort of detail that made the kiss real for her now, the kiss and what followed. Clutching her purse, she needled herself, put things in the worst possible light, allowed for no mercy: *I'm picking up my daughter and thinking about the man I cheated on her father with. I betrayed the father of my child. I betrayed Dale.* But she couldn't make herself feel sorry, truly sorry in her heart. At the very least, she needed to stay smart and stop getting lost in her thoughts like this, as her eighteen-year-old self, drunk on first love, had done. If she couldn't be sorry, she could be smart.

She went in through the side door without knocking. "I'm here," she called. She passed through the kitchen to the living room, where she found her mother and Abby in her mother's big recliner, a blanket spread across both their laps. Abby, watching some kind of Japanese cartoon, waved absently. She was still in her pajamas. Susanna's mother blinked as if she might have been sleeping.

"Morning, sweet pea," her mother said. Susanna bent down to kiss her cheek, then grasped Abby's chin and turned her daughter's face away from the screen. Abby's eyes pulled to the right, to the sight of some kind of warrior transforming into a dragon.

"I'm going to smooch on you," Susanna said, and Abby giggled in a polite but distracted way. Well, Susanna could understand distraction. This morning more than most.

"Thanks for keeping her all night," Susanna said. "It was a big help. We were able to get the drawing up all over town this morning."

"Did you bring one for me to see?"

"Yeah." Susanna pulled a folded-up sheet of paper from her purse and spread it smooth on the arm of the recliner. Her mother put on her glasses and peered at it around Abby's shoulder.

"He looks practically my age," she said. "Lord, Lord. I don't know about that girl."

Susanna, hunched down beside the chair,

shifted uncomfortably. "Tony turned up a lot of information last night. A bartender at Nancy's said that the guy" — she tapped her finger on the drawing — "was in really bad shape. Some people he came with pranked him and left the bill, and then they split on him. It sounds like Ronnie was trying to help him out." She didn't see any reason to mention the fight Ronnie got into at the Salamander.

"That was always Ronnie," her mother said. "Mean as a snake to anybody who tried to help her and sweet as pie to the no-accounts." She peered at the finer print on the page. "You put the part about the dance hall on here? Just what I need is people all over town knowing my daughter goes to that place."

"People all over town know she's done worse," Susanna said roughly.

Her mother pinched her lips and patted Abby on the thigh. "Pop up, hon. Get in the floor with your blocks or something. Mamaw's got to refill her coffee." Abby jumped down without a fuss and did as she was asked. Susanna's mother had that effect on people, though it was a side that emerged well after Susanna and Ronnie were grown. It happened, Susanna supposed, after her father died. Her mother just seemed to occupy more space in the world now.

They went to the kitchen, and her mother held up the coffee carafe with her eyebrows raised. Susanna nodded.

"I've got a dab of two percent left if you want milk," she said, spooning creamer into her own cup.

"Creamer's OK." Susanna borrowed her mother's spoon and then set it to drip on the plastic tablecloth. The food left over from the breakfast her mother had cooked sat on a plate in the middle of the table, as it always did: half a dozen canned biscuits, two strips of bacon, a link sausage, a spoonful of scrambled egg, all soaking into a paper towel. Her mother bought the link sausages because she knew Abby liked them. Susanna tore the fatty end off a piece of bacon and nibbled it.

"You hungry? I could heat you some toast. Or there's some sweet rolls in the bread box."

"I'm just munching," Susanna said.

Her mother set a biscuit on a plate and spooned some molasses and margarine on top of it. "I make too much, eat all day. I'm still cooking for four."

"You're scrawny. You could stand a few more biscuits."

Her mother grunted in a pleased way.

"Tony's sending word to some TV stations. He thinks that WBKO will run it tonight and at least one of the Nashville stations ought to pick it up. So that's good."

"Is it?"

"You want her found, don't you?"

"Of course I do," her mother said. She wiped at her eyes. "I love her. Always have. She hasn't made it easy, God knows." She shrugged. "I just don't like our business out for everyone to see. If she's gone on purpose, she's gone on purpose. She don't want us finding her. And if she's not —"

"If she's not, what?"

"Then it's all hopeless," her mother said hoarsely.

"You sound like Dale," Susanna said. "Nothing is hopeless. I'm her sister, Mama. I still feel her out there. She could be unconscious in a hospital or something. She could be hurt."

"She could be dead," her mother said.

"And what if she is?" Susanna was up now, pacing. The floor felt soft in spaces beneath the linoleum, and she remembered how Dale had promised years ago to come over here and put a new floor in, how he'd told her mother, *I've got nothing but time come summer.* "We don't try to find out what happened to her? We don't try to find this man and see what he had to do with it?"

"Stop fussing at me," her mother said. She had started to cry. "I guess you know the right way to act and I don't. You've always thought so. This is just moving fast, is all. Ronnie's been taking off on me all her life. She ran away for a week when she was a teenager till your father hunted her down and beat her black and blue. I guess you don't remember that. She might come by here to check on me once a month, and usually it's longer than that. So you tell me she's gone, but it don't feel any different to me. It feels like usual."

"It's not usual," Susanna said, more gently this time. "You're going to have to trust me when I tell you it isn't."

"All right." Her mother picked at her biscuit. "Now I want to ask you something. But I don't want you getting mad at me."

Susanna steeled herself. "OK."

"Shelby Wilhelm told me she saw you eating lunch at Gary's yesterday. With some colored fellow."

"Mom, he's black. Not colored. You can't go around saying that. He's black, and he's the detective. That was Tony Joyce."

"That's what I told her. I told her you stayed in town to look into what happened to Ronnie, and I told her that was the guy. I remembered him from the newspaper."

"What's the problem, then?"

"I told you not to get mad at me."

"Well, that's a hard thing to promise, Mama. That's just about out of my control."

Her mother pinched her lips again and shook her head.

"Say what's on your mind if you're going to say it. I know you mean to."

"It don't look right. You having lunch with some man not your husband, while your husband's out of town. Then you call me to keep Abby overnight even though you're going to be home. At first I didn't think too much about it, and then I did."

"And then you did. And what did you come up with, Mama?"

She averted her eyes. "That it didn't look right, is all. And I thought about how Dale's going to come back here today, and if Shelby can tell me then someone can tell him. I worry about you. I've seen Ronnie make enough mistakes to not want you going down the same path."

"Dale knows why I stayed home, and he knows who Tony is. Unlike the old hens around here, he realizes that a grown woman can have lunch with a man who isn't her husband and not have to sew a scarlet letter to her chest." Susanna's anger was genuine, as if she truly had nothing to hide. "God, I hate this town sometimes."

"There's no call for all that," her mother said. "And I don't appreciate you calling me an old hen."

"It burns me up," Susanna said. "It burns me to think that you're worried more about who I'm seen having lunch with than where Ronnie's gone to." She realized that she was still holding a piece of bacon and tossed it on the table. "If I up and left Dale tomorrow, told him I wanted a separation, that would be my own damn business and no one else's, and it wouldn't be the end of the world. It wouldn't be life or death."

"It would be Dale's business," her mother said. "And it sure as heck would be that child's business." She jerked her chin toward the living room.

"Oh, yeah," Susanna said sarcastically. "A girl needs a father. Just like Ronnie and I needed an old drunk to beat us black and blue."

"That old drunk kept a roof over your head."

Susanna laughed and looked around. "Yeah, a real palace."

"I'll tell you right now, little girl, there's worse. I've lived it."

"Well, guess what, Mama. I'm not you. I have a job of my own and a mind of my own, and I'll do what I know is right. For me and Abby, both."

"So you *are* leaving him," her mother said. She looked bitterly satisfied.

Susanna sat down heavily, feeling tricked. "What? No." She gulped her coffee, grimaced. Her mother always made it weak, and it had cooled quickly. "No one's leaving anybody. I'm just trying to make a point here. I'm speaking in the hypothetical."

"You're awfully riled up about a hypothetical."

"You get me that way."

"I reckon I always have."

They sat silently, long enough for Susanna to follow some of the dialogue in the cartoon in the next room, long enough for the house to shiver as a jet flew overhead.

"I'll be honest with you," her mother said. "I never cared much for Dale. I thought the first time you brought him home that he was full of himself. A snoot."

Susanna barked a laugh.

"He's still a snoot, far as that goes," her mother said. "But his heart is in the right place, and he loves that girl. And he's not a drinker."

"Which makes him Prince Charming

around here, I guess."

"Maybe you think I was too stupid to want better than your father, that I never thought about taking off with you girls. Well, you're wrong. I thought a lot about it."

"What stopped you?"

"This and that," she said. She was sixty and looked it, and her hair, which she dyed to a darker shade than her youth's brown, only exaggerated the toll of years. "Mostly, I figured out that nothing I could do would make my life easier or better than it was. I'd just be trading one kind of hurting for another. And I'd be better off with the hurt I knew than the hurt I didn't."

Susanna took a shaky breath, thinking of the hurts she'd known in this house. The screaming, the punishments. Her father, nude and unconscious on the living room sofa. Yet this was still, perversely, home to her, more a home than her place with Dale ever would be. She remembered the time her father came home with this very dining room table and chairs, scavenged from a dump site, none of them with seats, and how he'd spent a long Saturday in the kitchen, beer near at hand, braiding new seats patiently and neatly from a spool of jute. One good memory among a host of bad ones, but it was there, and the power of it made her momentarily weak.

"Is that supposed to be a pep talk?" Susanna said. " 'Stay with your man'? 'He could be worse'?"

Her mother shrugged. "Since you're such a modern woman, and since you already know more about the world than I ever did, let me put it another way: if you're going to leave what you've got, you better know what you're getting."

CHAPTER EIGHTEEN

1.

The hospital lobby was chilly from the opening and closing automatic doors, so Sarah brought Wyatt's wheelchair to a rest by the gift shop, where they still had a view of the front drive. Morris Houchens had gone to the parking lot to bring around his truck. Wyatt, to his surprise and deep embarrassment, was getting blubbery again.

"Oh, hush," Sarah said. Her hands left the handles of the wheelchair and rested on his shoulders. "You're supposed to be happy to leave the hospital. You're going to sleep in your own bed tonight. You're going to see your dog."

"I know," Wyatt said hoarsely.

"And you know I'm coming over to visit just as soon as my shift ends," she said more softly. "You know that, too, right?"

Wyatt nodded hard and with his mouth pinched closed, as a child would.

"It's the medication. It has your chemistry all out of whack."

And that was probably true. But what Wyatt was feeling, on this threshold between his hospital room and the waiting world, was the terror of exposure. In the bed, plugged into machines and drips and watched over by Sarah, he had been protected — hidden. This homecoming was too much, too quick.

A red Chevy pulled up and stopped. A few seconds later, Morris crossed in front of it and opened the passenger-side door.

"Here we go," Sarah said, rolling the wheelchair forward and out the hospital doors. Wyatt hastily wiped his eyes with his shirt cuff.

Wind was whipping hard through the cul-de-sac out front and whistling against the shelter roof above them as Sarah locked the wheels of the chair and gave him an encouraging, motherly thump on the back. "OK, do what God gave you legs for," she said, and Wyatt placed his palms against the wheelchair arms and his feet between the footholds, then trembled to a stand. Morris was holding out an uncertain arm.

"You got it?" Sarah said in her bright, no-nonsense nurse's voice.

Wyatt removed his steadying fingertips

from the arms of the chair and took a small step forward. "Yeah," he said.

He felt weak, and his joints ached from so many nights in that stiff bed, where the tubes and wires chained him from rolling over or making adjustments for comfort. But he was doing better now than he had expected to be. He had walked a few moments each day in the hospital, dragging the IV rack behind him, and now he was walking to Morris's truck, and the process was still just putting one foot in front of the other. No more and no less than that. He was even stepping up, climbing into Morris's elevated cab. Life went on.

Sarah leaned close to him as Morris was striding around to the driver's seat, and Wyatt inhaled, as if he wouldn't be able to again, her vanilla perfume. "I'll see you before you know it. Keep a light on for me."

"I will," he said.

She stepped back and closed the door, then wiggled her fingers in good-bye. The cab of the truck was toasty warm, and Wyatt put his hands out in front of the vents, sighing a little at the small pleasure. They were pale hands, almost translucent, with blue and yellow bruises from the IV needles.

"She seems nice," Morris said. "Seems

like y'all know each other from sometime before."

"A little bit," Wyatt said. He hesitated, not wanting to mention Nancy's Dance Hall.

"That's good," Morris said. "It's good to have people when you're going through a tough time."

Wyatt watched the town unfurl outside his window, marveling at how alien it all seemed, as if he had been shut away for months rather than a bit less than a week. They passed the country club's golf course, which was predictably empty on a day as cool and gray as this one, and the warehouse housing the aluminum recycling facility. A dump truck outside of it belched black smoke. They passed the town's main cemetery, which stretched a few acres back on both sides of the road. They passed the Roma Dairy Dip, where Wyatt sometimes picked up a sack of burgers after getting off of work. He could smell, even through the closed window, its distinct fragrance of frying grease and grilled meat, and his stomach rumbled in a way that might have been hunger or nausea.

"What I figured," Morris said, breaking the silence, "is that I could drop you off at home, then go back out to pick you up whatever groceries and things you think you need." He was restating the plan they had already made, just trying to fill up dead air. Wyatt opened his mouth to agree, then closed it again. Then he said, "Can we run back to the Dairy Dip for a minute? I have a hankering for a milkshake."

"Well, OK," Morris said. "You sure you ought to have anything like that right now?"

"It won't kill me," Wyatt said wryly. "And I guess I just want to stretch my legs and get some air before being shut up again." That much was true. He felt something like sorrow at the thought of handing Morris his shopping list with its doctor-approved choices of steel-cut oats and skinless chicken breasts and green vegetables that he wasn't even sure how to cook if they didn't go into a pot with a ham bone and a hunk of butter. He also felt a deep dread at the thought of his house and even of Boss. Of the prospect of hours alone.

Morris parked in a spot close to the order window. "You sure you don't want me to get it for you?"

"Nah," Wyatt said. "I'll be all right."

He climbed down carefully from the cab of the truck and walked to the order window, unfolding his wallet as he went. A teenage girl slid over a glass partition and spoke to him through the opening. "Help you?"

"Yes, please. I'd like a —" He scanned the menu. "A banana milkshake, please, miss. A small."

He put a dollar and a quarter through the opening, and she handed him a nickel's change. She turned her back to him and pressed a silver handle, measuring a ribbon of soft-serve ice cream, turning the RC Cup with brisk efficiency. Wyatt's gaze wandered to his left, where business cards and advertisements had been taped to the inside of the glass.

What he saw almost immediately was his own face. HAVE YOU SEEN THIS MAN? spanned the top of the sheet of paper in bold print, and below the image, in smaller letters, it read, "Person of interest in the disappearance of Veronica 'Ronnie' Eastman. Seen together at Nancy's Dance Hall in Sylvan and the Fill-Up gas station in Roma on October 23. Age: 50–60. Height: 5'8"–6'. Weight: 190–230 lbs. Wanted only for questioning." An officer's name and phone number followed.

Wyatt started shaking. The image — it wasn't exactly right; even in his panic he could admit that. The person who had drawn it had exaggerated his receding hairline and elongated his face. His mustache was thicker than he normally kept it.

But the artist had also captured something recognizable and true about Wyatt, and the sight of the face with its sad, haunted eyes and its pursed, self-pitying mouth made Wyatt want to rip the poster down, run, hide. The young woman came back with his milkshake and thrust it through the open partition at him. Her expression was blank, disinterested. When Wyatt did not at first take the cup, a flicker of irritation, evident in nothing more than a microsecond's tightening of the brows, flashed across her face.

"Sir?" she said, shaking the cup a little, and he took it from her. Then she slammed the partition closed.

2.

Think. Think.

He was home. Morris had already been to the store and back, and the groceries were stowed neatly in the cabinets and refrigerator. Boss was stretched out in the middle of the living room floor, napping, amiable enough — as if Wyatt were a roommate that he got along well with but wasn't all that close to. Sarah had promised to walk him when she came over later. The milkshake, still mostly full, was sweating beads onto a coaster near Wyatt's right hand. Any appetite he had was long gone.

Think, goddamn it.

But thinking was hard with the exhaustion and the meds. What he wanted to do was recline his chair, shut off the lamp, and nap until Sarah arrived. His brain was hostage to his body. What it registered was a panic that occasionally leveled into blurry anxiety as he momentarily forgot the source of his problem. Then the drawing of his face on that poster would come to him with full force, and he set back out on the same uncertain mental zigging and zagging, wondering if the time hadn't come for him to simply get in his truck and drive out of town. But Sarah — what about Sarah? Any life without her, he decided, was not a life worth preserving.

He rose, walked as quickly as he could to the kitchen, and bent over the sink. He splashed cold water on his face. Without bothering to towel himself dry, he pulled a glass from the cabinet and found, in the back of his refrigerator, a half-full two-liter of Coca-Cola, probably already flat. He poured a couple of inches into his glass and knocked it back like whiskey, grimacing at the sweet blandness. Then he went to the window and shoved it up a couple of inches, so that some cold air could leak in. At last

— perhaps as much for rousing himself with the motions as the actions themselves — Wyatt's mind cleared a little. He remained standing by the window, legs trembling, and thought.

It was three P.M. now. Sarah had told him that she would come by at ten P.M., as soon as her shift at the hospital ended. Seven hours. Plenty of time.

He began to assemble the things he would need. There was a strange pleasure in these preparations, in this discovery of his instinct to survive. He had always thought himself weak, but here he was, scheming to protect himself, proceeding despite the risks. There was something manly about it, and he thought that he was perhaps no longer the person who had submitted to so many indignities at the hands of Sam Austen and his gang. That if Sam were to call him Tubs now, he might be in for a surprise.

3.

That night at Nancy's, the woman who paid his tab had said, "Well, train's leaving the station. Come on if you're coming."

He followed her outside, knees quivering, trying to avoid the bodies swaying around him. He scanned the crowd for Sam and Gene, still not quite believing that they would have deserted him. OK, Sam would have, but *all* of the rest of the guys? Both trucks? And it was early yet; even Wyatt could make that out. Not even midnight. They'd all been dancing, talking to pretty women, ordering shots — having a good time. Why would they all have left? Without him?

A prank, he realized.

"I'm this way," the woman said. They were outside, and the cool air was clarifying. He felt now the suggestion of a headache, just a little twinge behind his eyes, and he focused on the wink of the woman's light-colored shoes in the darkness. His senses were heightened unpleasantly; he could feel in the cup of his ear the rasp of her sneakers against the gravel, could make out the trail of her perfume, which was muskier than that of the woman he'd danced with. Where Sarah's vanilla had suggested a kitchen table and oven-warm cookies, this woman's cologne was wilder, spicier. There was something in it that reminded him of the way Boss smelled when he came in from exercising — not sweaty, but like he'd carried in some of the outdoors, the smell of damp earth and tree sap, the spirit of his own exertion.

Wyatt bent over double, hand pressed

against a nearby truck for support, and vomited the hamburger he'd eaten earlier. Sweat popped against his neck and forehead, and his bowels felt loose.

The grind of gravel halted. "Better?"

He paused, assessing. His skin stopped prickling, and he took in a gulp of clean air. "Yeah." He nodded, too, for emphasis, then stood, wiping his mouth with the cuff of his shirt. It was his good shirt, bought at Dillard's for $25, marked down from $40. It was a deep blue, subtly pin-striped, with a nice, fine weave. He wore it tucked into a pair of khakis, with his old brown belt and his wingtip shoes, a pair he'd bought over thirty years ago for the high school graduation he would never attend and had carefully preserved with polish and a single resoling. He'd thought, assessing himself in the mirror earlier that night, that he looked good. He'd combed his thinning hair over, rubbed some pomade between his hands, patted the flyaways into place. He'd used a fresh Bic razor to carefully shave his cheeks and chin and neck, managing not to nick himself, and then he'd trimmed his mustache neatly with a little pair of scissors. He could still pluck the gray hairs from his mustache; the hair on his head he touched up every few weeks with a Just For Men kit.

"I ought to be ashamed," he said. He didn't want to make eye contact with the woman. But she came up to him, took his hand in hers, squeezed it, and he couldn't help looking up at her. He tried to smile, bashful, and he noted with surprise how young she was, despite the raspy voice and the bravado. Her hair, which seemed to be brownish or dark blond in the dim lights outside the bar, was clipped short, boyish, but ruffled up in the front and hair sprayed, lending her a touch of femininity. She had wide, startled-looking eyes, the effect heightened by heavily applied mascara, and her full, painted lips anchored an otherwise absent chin, giving her an aspect of almost homely cuteness. She was pretty, but in a way that defied the individual parts that comprised her.

"Now stop that," she said. "We're all entitled to a little embarrassment. I've had my share tonight and then some."

"You have?"

"Yeah." She dropped his hand. "Do you want this ride or not?"

"Please," Wyatt said.

"All right." She pointed to a dark-colored Camaro. "If you think you're going to puke again, though, you let me know in time to pull over. You puke in my car and I'll kick you out right there and then."

"OK."

She drove with her window rolled down, the air biting but fresh, and Wyatt noticed the way she flew her left hand along outside, letting it roll in waves. She was propped on an extra cushion for lift, but even so she had to perch at the end of her seat to reach the wheel and the pedals and the stick shift, and she seemed to be constantly in motion, switching off hands on the steering wheel every time she had to put the car into a different gear, hips flexing as she pumped the brake and the clutch, eyes on the road, then her rearview mirror, then on Wyatt. She made the process of driving seem difficult, her own efforts heroic. They might have been riding in a time machine to Roma instead of a Camaro.

"Have you had this car long?" Wyatt asked after several minutes of silence.

"Little over two years." She was pushing the car to seventy-five now, taking the little rises in the road too quickly for Wyatt's nervous stomach. Headlights appeared in the distance and she dimmed her own. "Finally decided, fuck it. I'm never going to be a millionaire. If I want something nice, I'm just going to have to get it and enjoy it while I can." She restored the brights. "It was used," she added, as though she had to justify herself.

"I wish I'd spent more time thinking that way," Wyatt said. He felt sweat popping on his forehead despite the cold. The security light on a distant farmhouse wavered in his vision like a shooting star. "You don't want to be pushing sixty and realize that you always played it safe, you always planned ahead. Thing is, you're just planning for some time that never comes. Or you're planning for a day when you'll be too old to enjoy it."

"Hell yeah. Live in the now, that's what I say."

Wyatt closed his eyes, nodded into the cold air whipping through the car. He didn't believe it for himself, but he believed it for this pretty young woman.

"I think about this stuff," she said. "I think about, OK, I spend forty hours a week at this shitty factory job —"

"Which factory?"

"The sewing plant."

"Huh," Wyatt said. "I'm at Price."

"You know what I mean, then." She was now motioning with her free right hand, adding a step to the already complex dance. "I sew pockets into blue jeans. That's all I do. This." She lifted both hands off the wheel now, miming: she lowered them, as though she were putting a tray on a table, and then she flattened her hands and moved them around like a planchette on a Ouija board. She finished with a sweeping yank — the thread getting cut, Wyatt recognized. "Ta-da. Multiply times fifty."

Wyatt was nodding.

"What's funny is, I can't really sew. My sister brought me a dress pattern for my niece one time, thinking I might be able to make it, and I just laughed. I can sew pockets into jeans. I can use that one sewing machine. I don't know the first thing about making a little girl a dress." She drove for a moment silently. "I heard one time that they used to have women making bombs in factories, and they gave each one a specific role so she wouldn't know how to put the whole bomb together. 'Cause then what would she do? God knows I'd like to bomb the hell out of Sew-Rite some days."

"I don't even make anything," Wyatt said. "I used to be in the winding room, and then I did die cast, but now I'm out in packaging. It's better, in a way. It's not as hot out there in the summer. But I can't seem to move fast enough anymore." He felt a little burn of anger at the thought. "I can't do what these Bosnian kids do. They're desperate. They come here and think it's the greatest thing ever since we don't have bombs going off outside. This Jusef guy —" He shook his head. He didn't have the heart — or maybe the clarity — to complete the thought.

"I don't know your name," the woman said.

"Wyatt," he told her. He held out his hand and she shook it briskly.

"Ronnie."

He mouthed it silently. A man's name.

"Wyatt," she said. "I don't think I'm in the mood to be alone yet. How're you feeling?"

"Better," he said truthfully. "The coffee helped."

"So did yakking, I bet. Could you eat something? I always get hungry like this when I drink. I have this strange hankering for chicken livers. Nasty, right?"

Wyatt's stomach, parted from its hamburger, actually rumbled. "Sounds good to me."

"My treat," Ronnie said. "Along with your drinks and half your buddies', the fuckers."

He flushed. He'd almost forgotten his humiliation. "I'll pay you back. I promise."

"It's the principle, Wyatt. You can't let people treat you like that. Get the money out of them or don't bother."

"I'll try to," he said.

She smirked, but she was kind enough not to say more on the subject. "The Fill-Up'll be open. We can get the food there and just take it back to my place, and I'll drive you home when you're wore out. Or you can crash on my couch." She added this last almost sheepishly, and Wyatt's heart started thumping. He couldn't read her. He couldn't make a guess at her intentions. Was she a lesbian? That would explain her name, her hair, her lack of unease around him: a man, a stranger. But he didn't think she was. Did she see him as a father type? He could be her father. He placed her at late twenties, early thirties. He would have already been working at Price when she was born.

"I feel like you get me," Ronnie said. She was pulling into the gas station, and the red neon lettering of the sign made her skin look pink and raw in the dark. She shoved the gearshift home to first with finality, shut off the engine, looked at him. "I've had a rough night. Hell, I've had a rough life."

"I'm sorry."

She shrugged. "I'm not some good Samaritan. But I saw what those guys were pulling on you, and I kept thinking that I should say something. No one else was going to do it. I watched them keep putting these shots in front of you, and you swallowing it like poison but like you wanted so bad to please them, and I thought, *That's a nice man over there. Too nice.*" She leaned across him to pull a pack of cigarettes out of the glove box, hitting him again with a whiff of that spicy-smelling cologne. She tucked one between her lips, then raised her eyebrows and pointed the mouth of the pack toward him. He shook his head. The cooling engine ticked.

"Anyway," she continued. "I could use a friend tonight."

"So could I," Wyatt said hoarsely.

She grinned. "Let's pick out some grease, then." Wyatt, a little drunk still, and dazed, followed. Was this happening to him? Was he about to go into this store with this young woman? *With* her?

He did. He watched her move: the purposeful stride, the muscular thighs, the fine, girlish hairs tickling the nape of her neck. The outline of her wallet against her swaying bottom. And he felt swell within him a desire so intense that he himself swayed a little, making Ronnie laugh and ask him if he needed to visit the bushes again.

There was an old black woman behind the

counter — she tiredly donned plastic gloves as Ronnie placed their order — and Wyatt registered a pang of regret that the cashier wasn't a man. He wanted a man to see him with Ronnie. At midnight, with their beer breath and their sudden, silly hunger and their exchanged looks of relief and hilarity, how else could a man see them as anything but a couple — as lovers? A man would notice, would be curious. This woman hardly saw him. She was tucking the wedges into a white paper sack, folding over the opening, reaching farther to her right to grasp a handful of livers, which would taste, Wyatt knew, of cooking fat and dirt. *Look at me,* he willed, moving in as close to Ronnie as he dared to, heart rat-a-tatting with the thrill. *Look at me.*

The black woman glanced up as if she'd heard him. Frowned. It was only a second, but Wyatt was satisfied, and he wandered to the front of the store to wait while Ronnie finished placing the order and ran quickly to the coolers to grab a twelve-pack for the road. He didn't know what would happen after tonight. He didn't know what Ronnie meant by "friend." But he'd been seen with her, and that made everything real for him in a way it wouldn't have been otherwise.

"Ready?" Ronnie said, handing Wyatt one

of the grocery sacks and the twelve-pack.

"You bet," he told her.

"Well, let's go," she said, and they went.

4.

Wyatt jolted awake with a gasp. His hands flew to his face, came away damp. He had been having a nightmare. It had started, like the bad dreams always did, with his beating a man, defending himself from some abstract harm; and, like usual, the man had turned into Boss, and it was the dog receiving his punches and his curses, and it was Boss howling with pain and confusion. But this time, his realization of the transformation hadn't stopped Wyatt's hand, the rain of rage-filled blows.

"Hello? Hello? Anyone home?"

"Here," Wyatt called hoarsely from his recliner. He struggled to shift up to more of a sitting position, feeling blanched and limp. He had never been so tired.

Sarah was still wearing her pink scrubs, and she smelled faintly and reassuringly not just of her vanilla perfume but of the hospital: the alcoholic whiff of antiseptic, that lemony hand wash that she had to use so many times a day. She dropped her purse on the couch and rubbed Boss briskly on his head, setting his tail to thumping. "My goodness, you're enormous," she said, hunching over to pet his side, easy with the dog in a way that pleased Wyatt even in the fog of his discomfort. "We'll go out in a minute, boy. Yes we will."

This done, she came to the recliner, set her hip on the arm of the chair, and leaned in for a kiss. There was awkwardness — this was their first night together outside of the hospital, unobserved by nosy others — and she smiled in her brash way, not wanting to acknowledge it. Then her lips touched his, and it was as nice as it had always been — nicer — and some veil of formality lifted.

"Miss me?" Her face was still close to his. Unlined, cheeks bright with life.

"More than you could know," Wyatt said.

Sarah frowned and put her hand on his cheeks, then his forehead. "You're clammy as hell, Wyatt." She felt his wrist. "Jeez, your heart's just racing. What on earth have you been doing?"

"Just a little tidying up," he said. "I didn't want you coming over to a mess."

"You must be looking to have another heart attack," she said. She retrieved her purse and pulled out a blood pressure cuff. "Roll up your shirtsleeve."

"I don't think that's necessary, now —"

"You roll up that sleeve before I roll it up

for you."

Wyatt did as he was told. Sarah pulled the Velcro closure apart and fastened it around his upper arm, then pressed the cold stethoscope inside his elbow. She tucked the earpieces in and started squeezing the pump.

"Sarah —"

"Shh," she hissed. And then the monitor hissed and the tension on his arm lessened. Sarah released some more air and looked at the dial. "One seventy-five over one hundred. That's not good, cowboy. I find that really troubling, actually."

"I just overexerted myself."

"I think you might need to go back to the hospital."

The idea wasn't entirely unpleasant: the safety of his room and bed, the certainty of Sarah's tender ministries. But he couldn't stay there forever, and besides, now that he was out, now that he knew exactly what was at risk, he didn't know if chaining himself to a bed again was a good idea.

"Let me stay the night here," Wyatt said. "You can check me in the morning. If it's no better then, I'll go."

She exhaled in an exasperated way. "Are you sure?"

He nodded and took her hand. "Will you stay with me? I could use the company."

"All right," she said with uncharacteristic softness.

So that was how, for the first time in his life, a woman slept the night next to him in his bed. He climbed under the covers in his drawstring pants and white undershirt; she borrowed one of his oversized flannel shirts and stripped otherwise to her underwear. Wyatt was too exhausted to be aroused but not so exhausted that he couldn't appreciate the flash he saw of her pale thighs as she scooted quickly under the sheet. She was a big woman, the kind of woman whose nakedness Sam Austen and his like would express disgust at the sight of, but Sam was wrong, he and his like. This was beauty: a smooth-fleshed woman, wise and funny, her eyes filled with love. It was beauty, more beauty than he deserved, and he pulled her close with a confidence he had never before possessed, and her warm cheek rested against his collarbone, and her cool legs tangled with his.

"If I had my way," Wyatt said, mouth against her hair, "this is what life would always be like."

"Me too," she said.

In few moments' time, Sarah was breathing deeply enough that Wyatt knew she was sleeping. Still, his thoughts stirred. He wondered what would happen if Sarah saw one of the posters around town, if she put the image and the date and Nancy's Dance Hall together and tried to make sense of it. He couldn't kid himself any longer: someone was going to come to him with questions. It was just a matter of when.

In the meantime, he held Sarah tighter.

CHAPTER NINETEEN

1.

Sarah was humming to herself when she checked into the nurses' station Monday morning. Most of the other women complained about the hours — it was a habit, a shtick, a way to pass the first dreary phase of the day, when eyes were still itchy with sleep and breath still sour with coffee — but Sarah liked the twelve-hour shifts, always had. She liked rising before the sun and driving to the hospital on silent, mostly empty roads. She liked the fact that the nurses' station was a lively oasis among dimmed hallways, the hospital still mostly a kingdom run by women before the first doctors started trickling in at eight or nine to make their rounds. She liked the conversation at six A.M., the good-natured grunts and groans, the dry humor, the way she and her colleagues moved around one another in an unconscious but graceful dance, reaching for clipboards and phones and doughnuts, leaning to the side so that someone else could pull a file drawer and tuck away papers.

Sarah liked her colleagues, too, and after twenty-one years she even loved some of them like sisters and mothers. Betty Shaw, who had trained her, still worked two days a week, coming in long enough to help the young ones who kept missing veins and to sass difficult patients into compliance. Sarah realized that she was practically the age Betty had been when she first started at Roma Memorial, that the new girls saw her as she had once seen Betty: caught in that no-man's-land between youth and old age. This wasn't a happy thought, especially since Sarah had neither a husband nor children to show for her early middle age, those all-important markers of womanly success — but it was accompanied by a second, kinder understanding, one that made the extra weight and the lines on her face worth it: that she was easier in her body now than she had been at twenty-two, that she could speak with confidence and listen with interest and generosity, not always comparing herself to someone else. Would she like sometimes to be thinner, or to live in a more exciting town, or to have made her career at a hospital where she might have eventually ascended to some kind of administrative position? Sure. Did she ever think about how she'd probably missed her childbearing years and so, without ever getting to consciously make a decision on the matter, she'd ended up, officially, childless? Yes, that too. But she was happy in her work, and she loved the pretty little house she owned two blocks from the public library, where she went weekly for a new stack of mystery novels. She liked coming and going as she pleased, stepping out after her shift for beers with Jan and Shurice and even Betty on those rare days they could talk her into it. If Sarah had married Jason Holmes at twenty-three as she had planned, and if they had started having babies, she'd have teenagers in the house right now. Teenagers! She felt not so much longing at the thought as a sense of having narrowly escaped an unsavory fate.

"Morning, Tilly," she said, checking the board. "I see you saved Mr. Anderson for me."

"Morning, sweetie." Tilly spun around in her chair and looked at the board, too, as if surprised by what she herself had written there. "So I did. Well, you know, it's probably because you have such a way with him."

"Way with him, my ass," Sarah said, but even the thought of drawing blood from a cranky seventy-five-year-old couldn't dampen her spirits this morning. "Coward."

"That's me," Tilly said. She rose and stretched her arms above her head, sighing deeply. "Whew. Long old boring night. I tell you."

"Wouldn've been so boring if you'd gone to Mr. Anderson's room in the middle of the night to stick him."

Tilly laughed. "That's not my kind of excitement." She stood and shouldered a leather handbag. "I'll see you on Thursday, hon. You be good."

"What fun is that?" Sarah asked, waving a little good-bye. She realized she was grinning to herself as she went to the supply closet to load her cart for morning rounds. The room smelled like rubber and the memory of alcohol. She sang under her breath as she gathered syringes, vials, probe covers for her new digital thermometer, making tick marks on an inventory sheet as she went. It was a Mariah Carey song that you couldn't turn the radio on without hearing — not normally her speed, but she found herself repeating the chorus softly under her breath, smirking a little around the silly words about a dream lover and getting rescued. Jan, if she saw her like this, would say, "Girl, you're *gone.*" Sarah reckoned she was. This thing with Wyatt had come as an utter surprise to her, especially after the way they'd left one another that night at Nancy's, and she hadn't felt this glad in a long while. Gladness, that's what it was. Because she hadn't been unhappy before, exactly, or even lonely; she had both her parents, still, and they were in good health; she had her brother, Daniel, his wife, and two sweet little nieces; she had several close friends. But romantic love was different, and she was remembering finally why it was different, why it was a thing worth craving. She thought about the warm pleasure of feeling Wyatt's legs tangled up in hers, her ear pressed to his chest. She thought about his kindness and seriousness, about his strange core of sadness, and how her presence seemed to turn on a light in him. Sarah had devoted her life to making people well, and she thought that she often succeeded, that she caused much more good than harm. But this was more than that. This was love as medicine, and she didn't think there was another person in the world that she could heal through loving. Not even her parents, whose devotion to one another had always, she suspected, transcended their devotion to her and Daniel.

"Sarah," a voice called from outside the supply room. Jan. "Are you back there?"

"Yeah," she called back.

"Get out here. You've got to see this."

Sarah finished stocking her cart and wheeled it out to the nurses' station, thinking, as she did every morning, that she really needed to get some WD-40 on that squeaky wheel. "Nice of you to show," she said to Jan, pushing the cart out of the way into a relatively uncluttered corner, and Jan waved her over impatiently.

"Yeah, yeah, yeah. Five minutes, sue me. Get your fanny over here."

"Jeez, Jan, what is it?"

She had a copy of the local biweekly newspaper, *The News Leader,* folded so that only the top half was displayed. "Special Early Edition," it read, followed by a headline in a large, blaring font: LOCAL WOMAN GOES MISSING, POLICE SEARCHING FOR SUSPECT. Beneath that, in italics and slightly smaller font: *Community Meeting to Be Held Tonight at First Baptist.*

Sarah scanned the first couple of paragraphs. "That's terrible. I hadn't heard."

"Yeah, it's terrible," Jan said.

Sarah read a bit farther and then handed the paper back to Jan, trying for an appropriate level of somberness. "Well, thanks for filling me in. I've got to hustle, or Jill White's IV is going to start beeping."

Jan clutched her arm. "Wait." She turned the paper over to the front page's lower half. "Look at that. Look at that and tell me what you think."

The bottom of the page was dominated by two images. The first was a photograph of a woman, the missing woman. Sarah didn't recognize her, and the name, Veronica Eastman, didn't ring any bells either. The second image was a drawing of a man's face, and she lost her breath for a moment, pulled the paper closer, and quickly read the caption underneath: "Police sketch of man last seen with Veronica Eastman. Detective Tony Joyce called him a 'person of interest' and hopes that he will come to the station voluntarily for questioning."

"You see it too, don't you?"

Sarah cleared her throat and dropped the paper on the desk. "What do you mean?"

"It looks like that man who was in here last week, doesn't it? The one who had the heart attack? Powell, right?" Jan pulled out a drawer and walked her fingers along the top of the hanging files; her right hand dipped down suddenly and emerged with a folder. "Yeah, Wyatt Powell. Dr. Patel performed an angioplasty on him last Wednesday."

Sarah forced herself to consider the sketch again. "I guess there's some similarities. It's a pretty generic picture, though."

Jan, paging quickly through the file, seemed almost giddy with excitement. "Generic! No way!" She waved her fingers around her face. "He had the eyes and the mouth and all that. You know what I mean. I think we should call the cops, maybe."

"Now, that's just silly," Sarah said. She went to her cart and grabbed the handle roughly, bearing down on it with both hands so that she wouldn't shake. "The man just had a heart attack. The last thing he needs is the cops beating down his door."

Jan's eyes bugged out. "He might be a murderer, Sarah. We might have had a murderer in this very hospital. We might have been treating him and making him better, for God's sake."

"Which is our job, as a matter of fact." Sarah pushed the cart and lifted her eyebrows when Jan wouldn't clear the path. "You mind? One of us is going to have to check on patients, Nancy Drew."

"You really don't think it could be him?"

"It could be him or a thousand other men. I don't feel qualified to say."

Jan slumped a little. "Huh. Maybe you're right. You spent a lot more time with him than I did. I guess you'd know."

Sarah made it to the hall, then stopped. She felt a sharp ache arcing from her throat down to her stomach, as if she'd swallowed an aspirin without water, and turned back toward the nurses' station. "I don't want to keep you from calling the police," she said in as natural a tone as she could manage. "I could be wrong. It wouldn't be the first time. So you should do whatever seems right to you."

Jan looked from the image to the folder, then back again. "I guess I won't. For now, anyway."

"OK," Sarah said. Her knees were so weak that she didn't know if she could stand on them. She was thinking about something she had noticed after Wyatt was transferred from the emergency room to her wing, when she and Shurice were attaching electrodes and hooking Wyatt up to an IV: how he'd had scratches on his forearms and neck, one long enough and nasty enough that she'd applied some antibiotic cream to it. *Cat get ahold of you?* she'd asked him at some point in the week, and he'd gotten a funny expression on his face, like he was embarrassed, and said, *I don't know where those came from. I must have done it in my sleep. It must've been a bad dream.*

CHAPTER TWENTY

1.

There wasn't room in the ALC trailer for all of the food-fight offenders, so Principal Burton placed the girls there, including Leanna, and spread the boys out in locations on opposite ends of the campus, as if they would otherwise try to climb through the air vents to get to one another and stage a coup. Christopher, branded the leader of the mob, had gotten the worst possible real estate: a supply closet in the back of Mrs. Mitchell's classroom. Christopher felt sure that he would have been able to charm his way into allowances from any of the other teachers, but Mrs. Mitchell had been holding a grudge against him from the start, and Christopher thought that she took no small amount of pleasure in showing him to the cramped desk, which was tucked between dusty boxes of old textbooks, and explaining to him that he was to complete a ten-page essay on *A Separate Peace* if he hoped to emerge from the supply closet before Christmas break — that on top of all of the assignments he was otherwise expected to complete for his other courses.

There was one dim overhead bulb, a reading lamp brought in from outside (the one show of something other than outright austerity), and a foot-by-foot window on the door with a grid-work of metal mesh across it. No clock. Barely room enough to stand and spread his arms out wide. Mrs. Mitchell had left him with a glass of water and instructions to hold his bladder until she came to fetch him: once in the morning, once at lunchtime, and once in the afternoon. A couple of hours into his internment, so bored that he couldn't even fix his eyes on his textbook, he started to feel the uncomfortable press of his bladder, and with nothing to do but think about it, the sensation intensified. He would have relieved himself in the corner, on a stack of copies of *Literary Journeys,* if he hadn't felt certain that his punishment would be an extra day or days trapped in Mrs. Mitchell's special hellhole. His father had been right about suspension — even with his mother's chores, it had been a vacation compared to this.

The doorknob rattled and turned, and Christopher blinked stupidly in the onslaught of bright daylight.

"It's ten o'clock," Mrs. Mitchell said. "I'm going to walk you to the boys' restroom. You aren't to talk to anyone we pass. If I see you even make a funny face I'm going to keep you in ALC for an extra day. Got it?"

Christopher nodded.

He followed her through her empty classroom, making an exaggerated, unseen grimace at the sight of her hips moving beneath the cloth of her shapeless khaki jumper. To think, he grumbled inwardly, that she was married — that a man did it with her! She even had a kid to prove it. Christopher had seen them together once at Wal-Mart: the little girl pretty much like any little girl, Mrs. Mitchell mortifyingly clad in blue jeans, sneakers, and a sweatshirt. His own mother wouldn't ever wear such garb; even to prune the roses she was pulled together and slim, made-up enough to face the world. Christopher had never been embarrassed by her.

He dragged his feet in the hallway, despite the throb in his groin. It felt good to stand and walk, to hear his footfalls on the shiny, speckled tiles in the hallway. The air, slightly ammoniac, was still fresher out here, and sun shone brightly through the skylights. He lifted his face to it. He had always liked being in the hall while class was in session, liked the hush, the neat line of closed lockers, the little glimpses he caught of his peers through the narrow windows on the classroom doors. If he were patrolling the halls alone, armed with Mrs. Hardoby's hall pass (a mini-chalkboard, its surface painted in white letters with exaggerated decorative serifs, like a vacation Bible school project), he would stop and hover near one of these windows, angling himself so that the teacher was out of view, and mug until one of his friends saw him. He could always get Monty Higgins to laugh out loud just by pulling up the hem of his shirt and rubbing his belly, and when he did, he would slip quickly down the way and around the bend, gone before the door opened behind him, before Mr. Grimly or Mrs. White could step out and crane their neck in search of a disturbance.

But Monty Higgins was tucked away in his own supply closet somewhere, and Mrs. Mitchell kept turning around to frown at Christopher, hoping, he bet, to catch him doing something she could punish him further for. She seemed to be in even worse a mood than usual — maybe because of her missing sister. Word had spread quickly over the weekend, and Christopher had heard his parents talking about the disappearance in hushed tones: *They're saying that she was completely wild,* his mother had whispered, and even Leanna had circumvented her punishment of a week of lost phone privileges long enough to get a call in to him: *Hear about Mrs. Mitchell's sister?* she had said almost gleefully.

"Pick up your speed, Christopher," Mrs. Mitchell said. "If you don't need to use the facilities we can go back to the classroom."

"I do need to go," he muttered.

"Move it along, then."

They reached the door to the boys' room, and she stood beside it like a guard.

"Don't dawdle, or I'll come in after you."

He huffed a loud sigh and went in, choosing a stall over a urinal in case she kept her promise.

The hours between that first break and lunch were just as slow and mind-numbingly dull as the previous couple had been, and the hours between lunch and late afternoon were worse. Christopher thought about just putting his head down to nap, but even napping felt like effort, hunched uncomfortably in the small desk, hearing the murmur of Mrs. Mitchell's fifth-period class outside, and he still had all of that work hanging over him — including the paper on *A Separate Peace.* Mrs. Mitchell had told him, with a meaningful look, that she wanted him to write about the theme of peer pressure and adolescent cruelty. "The book's defining action is when Gene jostles the tree branch and causes Finny's fall," she told him. "I want you to trace the causes of that action and the consequences of it, and I want you to think about what Knowles was trying to say about guilt and redemption."

Christopher thought, but wouldn't say, that Mrs. Mitchell was wrong about the book. He had read it, though he'd taken delight over the last couple of weeks in giving her every possible reason to suspect that he hadn't, and he'd even, begrudgingly, liked it — Finny's pink shirt and all. Actually, he was a lot like Finny: a leader and a trendsetter, the kind of guy who could get away with a pink shirt because he would know better than to doubt himself in it. He thought, too, that the book wasn't about adolescent cruelty or peer pressure or any of those stupid catchphrases from after-school specials. Gene hadn't jostled that branch because he hated Finny or merely because he was jealous, and he hadn't jostled it thinking that Finny would fall and become a broken version of his once glorious self. He had done it because there was something about Finny that made him ache, something that he desired, and the desire terrified him, made him weak. It was typical for Mrs. Mitchell to miss that, to see only the obvious.

For once, though, he would take the easy way out and just give her what she wanted. He opened the battered paperback copy of *A Separate Peace* he'd been issued in October, planning to comb through it for some quotes he could use to pad his essay, when a square of paper fell heavily to his desktop. It was a carefully folded note, he saw — the kind with the little corner piece tucked in to lock it closed. *Leanna,* he thought at first, but how the heck could she have gotten this to him from the ALC trailer? When would she have done it? Also, Leanna's notes were usually on pink or purple paper and decorated with her silver paint pen. She must have spent ten times the effort making the note look fancy than she did on its contents, which were hardly ever anything interesting, nothing she couldn't have told him in a few seconds during class change: *See u in gym class,*

XXXOOO, or *Mr. Grimly was stupid today right?* He always pitched them into the wastebasket right after glancing at them, though he knew that Leanna saved every scrap of paper Christopher had ever given to her, even the ticket stub from the time his dad had driven them to Bowling Green to see *Jurassic Park.* He knew because she had shown him where she stored them, in a cardboard cigar box that she had decorated with contact paper, ribbon, and Lisa Frank stickers. *Leanna + Christopher,* she had etched across its top in puff-paint script.

This note was on college-ruled paper, the cheap-looking kind with dark blue lines, and the only thing written on its outside, in carefully blocked pencil, was his first name. His heart suddenly beating hard, he pulled the paper open and spread it flat on his desktop to read it.

Christopher,
  I am sorry that you are in trouble. I didn't tell on you and I will not tell on you no matter what. I feel really bad about what happened and I hope your parents aren't too mad.
  I know you must hate me but I need to show you something. It is about Mrs. Mitchell. Can you meet me after school?

I will ride bus 5 and exit near the old hospital. You don't have to talk to me on the bus. I can explain when we're off the bus.

Sincerely,
Emily Louise Houchens

Christopher swallowed hard and looked around. She must have slipped in here during lunch, in the twenty minutes he was allowed to eat silently in the old smoking lounge with a few of the other ALC students, though they had been segregated to separate tables and positioned with their backs to one another.

He reread the note several times, flipped it over, read it again. What on earth did she want from him? What could Mrs. Mitchell have to do with it? He wondered if she was setting some kind of elaborate trap — trying to get him to confess to what had happened at the tennis courts. Maybe she was going to hide a tape recorder under her oversized flannel shirt, then go straight to Mrs. Mitchell with the evidence, get him kicked out of school for real.

That was probably stupid. But what else could it be?

If he went, he would get in trouble, even if it wasn't a trap. He had strict orders from his mother to walk straight home from school: no Leanna, no Monty or Craig. Homework, dinner, more homework, and bed. Lights out by nine P.M. If he hopped on Bus 5 and went all the way across town to Harper Hill, he'd need another half hour or more to walk back to his house on Main Street. He wouldn't finish being grounded in this lifetime.

I am sorry that you are in trouble. Did she really mean that? He wasn't sure if he should be grateful to her or angry. What kind of person went through what Christopher had put Emily through and apologized for it? What kind of person was he to have done what he did to her in the first place? He remembered what his mother had said about sparing a thought for the girl he was mean to, about feeling bad in his heart, and he did feel bad, he did. He felt like he deserved almost anything Emily wanted to put him through, even if it was a trap, even if he did get expelled. And if incurring more of his mother's wrath was the worst of it — well, he was still getting off easy.

He didn't want to go. But maybe he owed her that much.

Also, he was curious. *I need to show you something. It is about Mrs. Mitchell.* He couldn't imagine what Emily was going to show him, why it would be on Harper Hill, or what it had to do with Mrs. Mitchell, but he had another two hours to think about it, to imagine the craziest things. Like, it was sort of a rough neighborhood; maybe Mrs. Mitchell bought drugs over there, and they could report her and get her fired. Or maybe Mrs. Mitchell *lived* over there, and Emily was going to show him her shitty house, and he'd be able to come back and tell Leanna and Monty about how bad it was.

He tried going back to *A Separate Peace,* but he kept reading the same lines over and over again without being able to make sense of them. He could already feel the stares as he climbed up on the bus and hear the whispers as he exited after Emily. Maybe people would think that he was going to tease her, hurt her, make her pay for tattling on him. Maybe that was the explanation he would give to Leanna later, if circumstances unfolded in such a way as to make an explanation necessary.

And was it possible that a small, small part of him — a part he would never be able to acknowledge — *wanted* to see Emily?

Chapter Twenty-One

1.

Emily hadn't dared believe he would come, had spent the afternoon in an agony of dread and anticipation, but he was here, sitting several rows behind her — she dared not turn to look — and the bus was lumbering up Harper Hill, brakes whistling as it slowed to make the usual stop on Hyacinth, where a couple of siblings, fifth and sixth graders, always exited. Emily slid across the green vinyl seat, grasped the loop on top of her backpack, and rose, hoping that the shake in her legs wasn't obvious. The bus driver, Mr. Washington, was usually too disinterested to follow the students' comings and goings, though the middle schoolers were technically required to hand him a signed note from a parent if they planned to take something other than their usual bus, or get off at something other than their usual stop. But he had let Christopher board without even a question, and so she hoped that her good luck would hold out for a while yet.

It had been, in its way, a day of luck: lucky that she had managed to slip in and out of Mrs. Mitchell's storage closet unseen while Christopher was at the cafeteria, lucky that no one had missed her, lucky that Christopher had found the note (she hadn't dared leave it in the open), lucky that he had been moved to follow its instructions. She hadn't truly believed he'd come — well, not since last night, when she drafted the note and revised it. Then, the plan had seemed faintly possible. At three-thirty P.M. today, exiting her last class and waiting at the sidewalk for the buses to line up, it seemed hopeless. Worse than hopeless — foolish. More material for Christopher and Leanna to use against her.

She swayed in the aisle as the bus lurched to a stop. The doors squealed open.

Lining up behind Terry and Jeffrey Chappa, she pushed forward, hugging her backpack to her chest. "G'bye. Bye. Bye," Mr. Washington was saying without energy. "See you in the morning. See you in the morning." Her sneakers slapped cement, and the cold, damp air slapped her cheeks. She walked quickly toward the old hospital's loading bay, which was littered with broken glass, cigarette butts, and a single canvas sneaker grimed with dirt, its laces spread loose as if it had been blown open. Finally she stopped, caught her breath, and squeezed her eyes shut. The bus's doors squealed again, and the engine revved. She could hear its procession up the hill and the silence in its wake. She realized she was terrified. Her mouth was so dry that she couldn't even swallow at first; her tongue was like a chewed-up lump of biscuit at the back of her throat.

"Emily." There were footfalls behind her. A throat cleared. "Emily, I'm here."

She turned, caught his eyes briefly — just long enough to confirm she wasn't imagining things — and then dropped her chin to stare at his shoes, her cheeks and neck hot. She swallowed again, trying to wet her tongue, and forced herself to meet his gaze, but the best she could do was to dart her eyes vaguely in the direction of his face, knowing that she probably looked like her brother: unfocused, confused. Creepy. *Stop staring at me, creep,* Christopher had said to her, and yet he was here, and the expression on his face was — well, not friendly, but gentle. There wasn't the darkness in it she had seen on the day he caught her staring at him in class, or in those moments in the cafeteria just before he started pelting her with his food.

"Thanks for coming," she said. Her voice was low but steady, and her heart lifted a tiny bit. If she could say that much, she could say the rest.

Christopher tugged on the straps of his backpack as if he needed something to do with his hands. He looked around. "What's up," he said, making it sound less like a question than a statement. "I got your note."

"That's good," Emily said stupidly.

He looked around again, as if checking for signs of an ambush, and leaned in. "You said it was about Mrs. Mitchell," he whispered.

"Right. Right, it is."

Emily watched him take in the broken glass, the abandoned hospital, the slumped front porches where animals probably nested behind the torn lattice. A Trans Am up on cinder blocks in someone's side yard. "Does she *live* in this neighborhood? I mean, God. I've never even been over here."

Emily wasn't sure what emotion she felt more strongly, anger or mortification, but she found herself snapping, "No, *I* live in this neighborhood. My house is on the other side of the hill," and the sharpness of her tone surprised her. Even Christopher felt it; the smile dropped from his face, and now he was the one to look down at his shoes, to shuffle in place.

"I didn't mean anything by it," he said. "Is that where we're going?" His mouth seemed to curl slightly with distaste. "Your house?"

"No," Emily said. She turned and started walking uphill. "It's in the woods. We're going to have to walk a bit."

She pressed forward even though he wasn't following her, then finally stopped and turned. He was standing perhaps a dozen feet back, hands squeezed into the pockets on his jeans so that his wrists jutted out at an awkward angle. He looked nervous.

"Are you coming?"

"I think I need to know where we're going," he said. "I'm already going to be in trouble for not coming straight home. If I'm not back by the time it turns dark my mom'll have a fit."

Emily retraced her steps and stopped a few feet from him. "I found a body," she said. "In the woods." She paused to register his reaction, feeling a thrill of satisfaction at the way he paled and how his lips slightly parted. A vein in his neck pulsed. "I think it might be Mrs. Mitchell's missing sister."

She turned to walk again but he grabbed her shoulder. "Wait — wait," he said. He licked his chapped lips and pulled his other hand out of a pocket to run it through his hair. It was a desperate, almost grown-up gesture. "You found a body? A person's body?"

"Yes," Emily said.

"In the woods over here?"

"Yes."

"Emily, why didn't you tell your parents? Why didn't you get them to go to the police?"

She had known he would ask this. It was surreal, forming her mouth around the words she had planned in her head over the weekend, finally testing the Christopher Shelton of real life against what the Christopher of her heart had told her would be true. "I was scared," she said now, the words strong and clear because they were honest. But then she pressed on: "They're still mad at me about what happened at the cafeteria on Wednesday. I'm not supposed to go in the woods, and I didn't know how to say anything without making them madder at me."

"They're mad at you about the food fight?" Christopher's face twisted up with something like anguish, and Emily felt a bright trill of gratitude course through her. "But that . . . that wasn't your fault."

Emily thought about how her mother had cried when she first saw her emerge from the cab in her food-stained clothes, how she'd washed Emily's hair for her in the kitchen sink, prepared her favorite supper that night (fried chicken, mashed potatoes, corn on the cob), murmured reassurances to her throughout the evening ("Sweetheart, it won't always be this way, I promise"). Emily thought about her father's forced joviality. He had known that she wouldn't have been able to tolerate his pity, and so he withheld it, acted as if nothing happened, and offered to take her to the library, or out for ice cream, or to Wal-Mart to get a new set of sneakers. "Love you, kiddo," he'd said, kissing her good night. She could, even now, feel the press of his lips in the center of her forehead.

"They can be hard on me," she told Christopher vaguely. She averted her eyes, let him draw his own conclusions. It wasn't an outright lie. There were days when it seemed to her that her parents *were* very hard with their nosy questions, their helpful advice. *You've got to be normal sometimes,* she could still hear her mother chiding. And her

father, telling her to *lay off the Debbie cakes.*
But she could see in Christopher's eyes
what he assumed, which is what she had
hoped he would assume, and the flash of
shame that passed over her features was so
authentic — she didn't know this — that it
sold the lie, made it solid and irrefutable.
No matter what followed this moment,
Christopher believed her; he would remember bruises she had never borne, imagine
hurts she had never suffered. He would at-
tribute what happened in the coming hours
and days to what he imagined Emily had
suffered at the hands of a cruel mother and
father, and it would help him to understand
how she might be the way she was.

"Okay," he said. "I'll follow you."

She pinched her eyes tight in relief and
nodded.

They were close to the hill's apex, Emily
trying to mask her exertion by breathing
through her nose, when Christopher
touched her shoulder again. "Wait," he said.
"Wait."

"What?"

He licked his chapped lips again.

"Why me? Why tell me? Why am I the one
you're —" His eyes widened and he swallowed. "The one you're showing it to?"

She wondered what she should tell him,

how much she could admit to. *Because you belong to me. Because you know me.* "Because you owe me," she said, which was part of the truth — or just enough of it to leave him satisfied.

"Okay," Christopher said. "Lead the way."

2.

Christopher had never felt such a confusing and contradictory set of sensations as those he experienced on his walk into the woods with Emily. At the surface was a vibration, a kind of static charge — his pores had tightened, the little hairs all over his body had stiffened, and his jaws, while not chattering, exactly, were shivering against one another like plates in a dishwasher. Beneath that, it was harder to say. There was dread, a dread that made him want to turn tail and run — and fear, of both the body Emily had promised and Emily herself. Was he scared of her? Is that what all of his cruelty toward her — all of their cruelty — had amounted to? It was an easy answer, an answer that promised to release him from some of his guilt, but not good enough, he knew. He hadn't forgotten that moment at the tennis courts. And now, too, mixed up in his fear and dread and curiosity was something like the excitement of those moments: a heady, uncomfortable anticipation that promised relief. What was wrong with him? Was he as weird — as much of a freak — as she was? He felt guilty for using the word *freak* again, even in his own mind, but none of this was normal. She should have gone to the police. Christopher would have to make her.

"Are we getting close?" he asked. They had slid down from the roadway into a slimy pile of black leaves. The air was cold and damp and close; he wished he'd worn his knit cap and gloves. His nostrils filled with the musty scent of autumn decay and he sneezed into the crook of his elbow. He was, he'd said many times to his parents, allergic to Kentucky; last year he'd broken out in rashes in both fall and spring, and the fact that so far this year he'd only had watery eyes and heavy sinuses made him think, with some regret, that he must be acclimating. Or assimilating.

"Yeah," Emily said. Her cheeks were pink from the work of climbing the hill — pretty, almost. She pointed ahead at a dump site, where an old recliner and a dozen oozing bags of trash were huddled beneath a line of small trees, as if they'd been rolled downhill like bowling balls. Christopher's heart started pounding, but then Emily said, "We have to go around that and then over just one more hill," so it slowed again slightly. Emily knew this terrain, walked it like she owned it, and he thought he sensed some eagerness in her manner now, as if the thing she were about to show him were not a body but a stabled horse she loved, or the secret entrance to a private garden.

The only sounds were their breathing and the crackle of leaves and branches underfoot. The light of the day was already gray. In another hour the sun would set; its low rays honeyed the crown of Emily's head. The trees quivered in a slight chilling breeze, and a single red leaf spun down from above, landing neatly in his outstretched palm. There was a surreal quality to all of this, as if he'd entered Emily's dreams. The feeling was a bit like déjà vu: he had been here before, walked this path, felt this same fear and anticipation. Maybe it was Emily's manner, the way her self-consciousness had suddenly fallen away. She kept turning and catching his eye with a familiarity that assumed so much, too much — as if she knew him, as if he weren't just some kid who had been briefly nice to her at school, and then briefly mean to her. At the top of the second hill she reached back and grasped his hand, and he was so startled by the action that he didn't resist her, didn't know he had the right to. Her palm was warm against his icy one.

"It's just ahead," she said. There was a tone of reverence in her voice.

His heart had surpassed its previous rapid rhythm, and he flushed down to his fingertips. She was looking at another rise in the land, this one hollowed out from beneath by long-ago erosion. There was a large tree, black with death, its roots dangling down like talons, as if the tree were a giant claw poised to push off from the embankment and spring toward them. A barbwire fence made a ragged line just past the point where the land sloped away, circling the tree and turning at an angle to disappear from sight. Christopher could hear, faintly, the bleating or whinnying of some kind of animals, sheep or goats or mules. He'd grown up in the city and knew only as much about farm life as his childhood See 'n Say had taught him, and the alien sounds increased his sense of unreality.

Emily tugged his hand. "Come on," she said.

They covered another dozen steps, and Christopher felt a sudden tension in Emily's grasp — it tightened, and then she snatched her fingers away from his, making him feel a momentary sense of loss and helplessness. She hurried forward, stopped, head darting left and right. She made a sound, a sound almost like that of the unseen animals, a sob or a bleat, choked, primal. Before he could stop her she was on her knees and crawling through the leaves, pushing away stones and sticks, raking back dirt with her bare fingers. "It's gone," she said breathlessly, and when she turned, her eyes were wide and wild, and Christopher noticed for the first time how bluish the skin beneath them was, like dirty thumbprints. Tears started running down her cheeks, and her scurrying became more frantic, the sound of sorrow she emitted steadier and constant, just this creepy humming that he thought she must not have even known she was doing. He shuffled his feet and squeezed the handles of his backpack. His first thought was that she had gotten the place confused, and he started darting his own head around, casting his gaze, as though the body were something she had dropped and was in an obvious place she was just too hysterical to notice. His second thought, which intruded insidiously on the first, was that she was lying, putting on a show for attention. There was never a body. It was just something that Emily had come up with to get him out here, so that she could be alone with him, so that she could hold his hand. He wiped his fingers on his jeans and grimaced, backing away in quiet disbelief.

"Someone took it," she was saying. "I put the rock and the branch on top of it. I know I did. But now the rock is over there" — she pointed toward the hollow under the tree — "and I don't even see the branch."

"I've gotta go," Christopher muttered. He turned and started scurrying up the other side of the washout, heading back toward the dump site and the road, and he felt Emily's hands on him and almost screamed, which was stupid, because she was just a dumb girl with a crush on him, a weird girl who made up shit about dead bodies because she was that screwed up in the head about how to make a boy like her back, and what could *she* do to *him*? Hurt him? Outrun him? Even if she told people he'd come here with her, he'd lie and say he didn't, and that's what people would believe.

"Wait, Christopher," she said, blubbering like a baby, and he was sick at her touch. She even smelled bad, he realized — really bad — like she hadn't bathed in weeks. He hadn't noticed that about her before, but like her hint about her parents, how hard they were on her, he quickly incorporated that detail into his understanding of her, how Emily-like it would be for her to not take regular baths, being poor and weird and gross. "Christopher, you have to believe me, it was here. It was really here. Somebody must have moved it."

"I need to be back home," Christopher said. "I'm going to be in a crapload of trouble over nothing." He backed up again, pulling his arm away from her grasping hand. "I guess we're even now."

"It was here! Somebody moved it."

"Bullshit!" Christopher shouted, now near tears despite himself. She grabbed at him again and he didn't think — he just pushed as hard as he could, and she went flying and landed roughly on her backside, her sobs coming to a sudden stop as if the wind had been knocked out of her. He thought of how all of his friends would have laughed at the sight, how they would have cheered him on. "It's bullshit, Emily. You're lying and you know it. Just cut it out."

"I'm not lying," she said, so softly he barely heard her. She was a sight: hands grimed with dirt, the knees of her blue jeans brown and wet, eyes red from crying, and hair hanging in strings over her cheeks. "You have to believe me. I'm not lying to you."

"Then you're crazy," Christopher said.

"Either way, I don't want you to ever speak to me again. Leave me alone, and leave Leanna alone. Don't talk to us, and don't spy on us, and maybe I won't tell people that you're a nutcase ranting about made-up bodies in the woods."

It felt good to talk to her this way, to use his words like fists. He almost hoped she would keep arguing with him so he could say more. It was confusing, how much he felt pulled between pity and contempt, how one emotion flowed so easily into the other.

"All right?" he said.

She didn't speak, and she didn't nod. Her head dropped, and she covered her face with her hands, shoulders shaking silently.

"All right, then," he told her, and he scrambled up the embankment toward Hill Street.

CHAPTER TWENTY-TWO

1.

Sarah's day passed in a fog. She did her job. Mr. Anderson narrowed his brows at the needle as if preparing to give her grief, saw something in her face, and pinched his lips shut. She drew his blood without saying more than a perfunctory "Good morning" and "Thank you" to him, then moved on to the next room. At lunch she ate too much in the cafeteria, taking helpings of both the Salisbury steak and the lasagna, plus a banana pudding for dessert, then rushed to the bathroom half an hour later to vomit. It was stupid, she kept telling herself — stupid to be this upset, to succumb to this despair. She didn't know anything for certain yet. But she had by now read the article in its entirety, seen the fact that the man was spotted with the missing woman at Nancy's the same night Sarah had met Wyatt there. Between this detail and the similarities in the drawing, there was no disputing the fact that the image was of him — that Wyatt was the man the police were looking for. She couldn't kid herself; she wasn't the type. And so Wyatt must have also been the man at the gas station with Veronica Eastman, and what did *that* mean, exactly? If Sarah weren't the woman who had just spent the night in this man's bed, lacing her arms and legs with his — if she weren't the woman who had nursed him back to life, to the desire to live, and seen how sweetly sincere he was, how thoughtful, how tender — would she believe there was a chance he wasn't connected somehow to the woman's disappearance?

No. She wouldn't.

Back at the nurses' station she reread the article surreptitiously, not wanting Jan to notice her, hoping to find some detail that changed things, that made all of her darkest suspicions groundless. There was nothing. She thought back to that night at Nancy's, to the group of young men that Wyatt had accompanied there, and realized that any one of them could be making the same connection she was now making — or had perhaps made it already. She wondered if she should call Wyatt at home, to see if he was still there and how he sounded, but her hand kept faltering short of the telephone. What would be worse? Hearing the phone ring and ring and ring, or hearing his voice, trying to decide what she could say in response to it?

The patient call alert sounded loudly, but no more loudly than it always did, and yet Sarah jumped. The newspaper fell out of her hand and onto the floor.

"What's with you today?" Jan said. "You want me to get that?"

Sarah nodded silently.

"All right, then." Jan put down the fashion magazine she was reading and rose. "But if someone filled his britches, you're getting the next five."

"That's a deal," Sarah said softly.

By five o'clock she was a nervous wreck. She had told Wyatt she would come to his house as soon as her shift ended, to make him dinner but also to check his blood pressure, which had been better this morning but still not good. Even now, as torn up as she felt about what she had seen in the paper, she couldn't just shut off feeling concern about him. If he had not continued to show improvement over the course of today — and she had insisted that he stick to his bed and easy chair, not exerting himself — then her plan had been to insist he go back to the hospital immediately. But now, with Jan's curiosity piqued, could she? And more important: Did she want to?

She went to her car in a daze and sat behind the wheel for a while; when she finally turned her key in the ignition, the digital clock read 5:20. He would be wondering about her by now but not yet concerned. He would think she had swung by the grocery store on the way to his place, that she was picking up ingredients for dinner. That was, in fact, what she had intended to do. A heart-healthy romantic dinner: she'd originally planned, driving in to work, to buy fish, brown rice, salad greens. Wyatt had mentioned to her that he would miss the catfish at Gary's Pit Barbecue, and so she was going to whip up her almond-coated, oven-baked tilapia, a recipe she'd happened upon years ago in a *Ladies' Home Journal* and trotted out whenever she was making a new go at a diet. She had even thought that she might splurge on some candles. How absurd this all seemed now.

She started driving toward his place. It was cold out, but she rolled down her window halfway and hoped the brisk air would clear her head, would make her see the right course of action. She could confront him, demand an explanation. Perhaps she owed him that. Perhaps she owed herself that. She could go to the police. Her thumbs tapped out a beat on the steering wheel, her breath hitched. She imagined the conversation with him: *I saw you in the paper. I know it's you. What happened? Don't lie to me.* She tried to script for him a response that would explain everything, that would make it all right for her to love him. *She just gave me a ride home. I honestly don't know what happened to her after that.* Or maybe the man in the sketch wasn't him, it was all a ridiculous coincidence, and he had an alibi proving that he wasn't with Veronica Eastman at the gas station.

Her car wheezed as it climbed Hill Street. There was, she was realizing, another part of her operating, a more coldly logical part, and it was taking inventory. Who could connect her to Wyatt? How drawn into this situation was she? She had danced with him at the bar, but she left early, without him — even that blond-headed shit with the trashy girlfriend would have to acknowledge this was the case. She had tended to him at the hospital, but that was her job. Perhaps she had given something away on Sunday in front of Wyatt's work friend, the one who drove him home from the hospital — but it couldn't have been too much. They didn't kiss. She had been keenly aware, before she had an obvious reason to protect the secret of this new relationship, that it would not be wise for her to let her work life be too evidently influenced by her personal life. That was why she had not yet even spilled the beans to Jan and Shurice: she had wanted to make sure this thing was real first. A part of her had wondered if what was developing between them wasn't just some kind of Florence Nightingale thing; it was a cliché, but she had been hurt before, and so she had decided to tread quietly and cautiously.

She imagined how her parents would react if it got around that she was dating the man from the police sketch, the "person of interest." The police might say that Wyatt was just wanted for questioning, but the subtext was clear, and the newspaper had spelled it out in fifty-point font: SUSPECT. They would tell her she was being foolish, kidding herself; they would tell her that she was hurting the family, her brother and nieces, who didn't have a say in whether or not Sarah attached them to a killer. And they would be right, goddamn it — but did she really believe that Wyatt was capable of this? Wyatt, this good, gentle, loving man who answered her brash posturing with sweetness and patience, who kissed her as if *he* were the lucky one, as if she weren't the kind of woman that other men stood up or walked out on?

A kid ran across the street as she started her ascent of Harper Hill, and Sarah braked hard — too hard, really; he was a good twenty feet ahead — her face slick with sweat. "Get it together," she whispered to herself, easing the car forward and cutting the boy a hard look as he passed. He waved absently, backpack bouncing against his shoulder. Sarah wiped her forehead with the hem of her blouse.

The fact was that she couldn't conceive of Wyatt doing harm to another person. The idea was ridiculous. She might not have known him well yet — they hadn't even gone on a date — but every day she was forced by her work to see people at their most frightened and humbled, which meant that she saw people at their worst. She had treated abuse victims and spoken curtly to the men by their sides, the men whose heavy brows and set jaws implied a threat that they wouldn't come right out to her and say aloud. She had treated half a dozen people who were arrested in their beds for DUIs, one of whom awoke to the knowledge that she had hit and killed a ten-year-old boy riding his bicycle home from a friend's house. She had treated two participants in a fight, big men with lacerated lips and broken noses and shattered bones in their hands, one with a ruptured spleen, the other a punctured lung, and listened mildly as they cursed each other and the woman who'd driven them to it. She knew something about the darkness of human nature. She thought she could recognize it when she saw it, and she did not see it in Wyatt.

She pulled onto his street and slowed her car almost to a crawl. Wyatt's truck was in the driveway, and lights were on in the front room and kitchen. Nothing seemed unusual. Her yearning for him was a physical ache, as if the only thing she needed to do to fix her anxiety was to go inside that home and embrace him, to allow herself to love him and feel his love in return. She was forty-three years old. She had assumed for a long time that love would happen to her, then grown to assume it wouldn't, and now here she was, a little over a week into this brand-new gladness, in which the impossible had suddenly seemed not just within her reach but within her rights. She hadn't been unhappy before. She'd had her job, her family, her home, her good friends, and all of those people and things would still be waiting for her if she drove away right now, if she pretended these last two weeks of her life away. But it would never be the same, she knew. She exhaled, noting how her breath clouded, fogging the windshield. But her head was at last clear. The choice wasn't between staying or telling; it was between a sorrow she couldn't conceive of and a sorrow she could.

She rolled up her window and hit the gas.

CHAPTER TWENTY-THREE

1.

Christopher ran downhill most of the way to town and made it in half an hour, before full dark. Out of the woods, his thoughts had rebounded with a child's selfish flexibility to home, its comforts, and even what punishment he'd endure at the hands of his loving, indulgent mother. He started plotting excuses, then just explanations, anything that wouldn't get him into more trouble than he was already in: *Mrs. Mitchell kept me after school — she wouldn't even let me out of the closet until four o'clock today.* That was pretty good, blaming her, but what if his mother got mad and went to the school again? *I know I wasn't supposed to, but I stayed to watch the basketball team practice. I'm sorry.* His mother would buy that one, but maybe that was too safe a route; he'd almost certainly get another night's grounding, and maybe more. It was

413

like gambling, finding the right lie: risking just enough to minimize the extra punishment but not so much that he brought down on himself all of his mother's wrath.

He decided that the best bet would be a combination of things: *Mrs. Mitchell kept me a few minutes after to have me finish some work, and I walked home extra slow because I was so messed up after being in that closet all day. You wouldn't believe this room they put me in, Mom. It was like prison. It was prison, but it was worse than prison. I'm kind of claustrophobic. I couldn't breathe. I kept thinking I might get sick.* He nodded to himself, pleased, thinking that he could get his mother going on one of her rants about the local education system — how archaic it was to put a child in a storage closet! He was smiling a little coming into downtown, and he decided he'd made good enough time to walk the rest of the way, catch his breath. He stuffed his hands in his pockets and enjoyed the stroll, the way the trees on the square were still clinging to some red and gold, how you could see some straw littering the ground from the previous weekend's Tobacco Festival. He passed Leanna's dad's law office and rolled his eyes, because her dad was such a joke — "Atticus Finch for the ambulance-chasing set," his father had said a couple of times, and Christopher wasn't exactly sure what that meant, but he got the gist. "Hello there, young man," Johnny Burke would call out in his deep drawl when Christopher came over to Leanna's to hang out, eyeglasses pushed up on his head so that his gray hair stuck straight up, slurring a little over the drink in his hand. Or, if he were really sloshed, he'd say, "If it's not our enemy from the North, come to steal our daughters," and Christopher had learned to just bob his head sheepishly and grin in an aw-shucks, *You got me, Mr. Burke* kind of way. "Is your dad for real?" he always asked Leanna when they escaped to the basement rec room, and she always groaned dramatically. "God, Chris. Don't encourage him."

What a strange town this was, a strange place to end up.

He dragged his feet at the final approach to his house. The adrenaline from his run spent, he now felt heavy with dread, a dread that had nothing to do with the scolding he anticipated receiving from his mother. It was just sadness, a sadness like nothing he'd known yet in his life — abstract, physical. Like he was only getting most but not all of what he needed in a breath. Had he really been in the woods with Emily Houchens just moments ago?

He sat on the steps of the house's side entrance and crossed his arms against the cold. Both of the cars were gone. His dad would still be at work, but his mom? God, she was probably out patrolling the streets already, working herself into a tizzy. He thought that he ought to go inside to shed his coat and stow his backpack, make it look like he'd been there longer than he had, but he felt tired and numb; he couldn't rouse in himself the momentum to stand up and unlock the door.

Forty-five minutes later, he blinked against the approach of headlights. He was relieved, he realized. He hadn't wanted to be in the house alone. And if his mother would just give him a hug and stay close to him tonight — yes, he wanted his mother, what of it? — he thought that he could endure whatever she wanted to dish out.

The car stopped shy of the garage, and his mother emerged. "What are you doing outside? Did you forget your key?" She was wearing nice clothes, dress trousers and a suede jacket, and she had on the red lipstick she only wore for garden club meetings and dinner parties. There was something brisk and distracted about her manner that made Christopher hesitate.

"Um, yeah," he said finally.

"Honey, I'm so sorry. You must not have even gotten my note. How long have you been sitting here? Why didn't you walk to the library or something?"

Cheered that the exact right words were coming to him, he said, "I was afraid I'd get in trouble if I wasn't here when you got home."

"Oh, honey," she repeated. She put her hands on his cheeks. "You're freezing cold. Let's get you inside." She dug around in her purse for her keys. "I didn't know I'd be gone so long."

"Where were you?" He followed her into the kitchen. She flipped the lights and stowed her bag on the island, then scowled at a dirty coffee cup.

"I swear," she muttered. "Your father knows good and well how the dishwasher works." She turned to put the mug in the washer, then grabbed a towel to wipe the granite. "There was a meeting at First Baptist about Veronica Eastman — trying to organize some kind of volunteer search effort."

"Mrs. Mitchell's sister?"

She raised an eyebrow at him. "The one and only." She tied an apron around her waist and went to the refrigerator. "Cocoa?"

"I guess," he said.

"It was a mess, really," she said, putting the milk and cream out on the counter. "Completely unorganized. More symbolic than practical. I think people felt like something had to happen once it made the Bowling Green news, so they're going through the motions."

"Didn't you tell Dad she was wild?"

Her face reddened. "Well, you must have been eavesdropping. That's just something I heard. I don't know if there's any truth to it." She unhooked a saucepan from the rack and pointed a finger at him. "Not that it even matters, young man. Her personal life has no bearing on what's happened to her."

He shrugged and looked at his hands. "Was Mrs. Mitchell there?"

"Yes, she was. I said hello to her. I thought it might do you some good for her to know I made the effort."

Christopher scooted onto a bar stool. "Yeah, well, she hates me. So you shouldn't have even bothered."

"She's still young yet. She doesn't seem young to you, I'm sure, but I don't think she's even in her thirties. She's going to take everything personally. It wouldn't hurt for you to show her some respect."

He shrugged and grunted a little.

"At any rate, she's going through a hard time right now, so you'd be wise to pick your battles." She went to the pantry and came out with a foil-wrapped square of chocolate. He liked watching her carve the bar into shards with her big knife, then whisk the shards into the cream. She shook some sugar out of the bowl, not measuring, then a few drops of vanilla.

When the cocoa was finished, she poured some into a mug, dropped mini marshmallows on top, and scooted it across the counter at him. "Forgive me for getting home so late, sweetheart." She leaned across the island to kiss his forehead, then wrinkled her nose. "God, Chris. You smell awful. What on earth have you been doing?"

He lifted his arm and sniffed his sleeve, where Emily had grabbed him. There it was, that stench: she had marked him with it.

"I ran home from school," he said.

"Through a pigsty?"

He shook his head.

"Well, you need to hop in the shower after you finish that. And put those clothes in the washing machine right away."

"OK, OK," he said, embarrassed.

"I've got to go change before I make dinner. Do as I say with those clothes."

"God, Mom. I get it."

She left, perfume making a delicate trail behind her. Christopher tried sipping his cocoa, but now that Emily's smell was in his nose he couldn't enjoy it. The liquid was thick and overly sweet, his tongue fixing on some distant sour note in the milk, a precursor to rancidness.

Chapter Twenty-Four

1.

Tony wasn't enthusiastic about leading a community meeting on Ronnie's disappearance, but he'd been given little choice in the matter. Sunday evening, after the ABC affiliate in Bowling Green ran Ronnie's picture on the local news, he got a call at home from Reverend James Riley, head pastor at First Baptist. "Roma," Brother Jim had said, "is the kind of community that circles the wagons in times like these." Tony had promised to keep the suggestion in mind but told the reverend that organizing a search would be premature. Where would they begin? He wasn't even convinced yet that there was a body to look for.

Half an hour later, the police chief, Evan Harding, called.

"I've got the mayor in my ear," Evan said. "The mayor's got Brother Jim in his ear. Make this thing happen, will you? They just want to get on the Nashville news."

So Tony did as Evan asked and returned Brother Jim's call. Yes, he said — on second thought, a community meeting sounded like a fine idea. Yes, sir, it would make a world of sense for you to start by leading a prayer. Five o'clock tomorrow sounded just fine. Thank you for generously offering the use of your church.

The meeting was better attended than Tony had anticipated it would be on such short notice, but he guessed he had underestimated his neighbors' morbid curiosity. The Channel 5 news did come, and Tony heard Brother Jim offer the reporter his line about circling the wagons; he was dressed resplendently in a tweed suit with a bow tie, his shave so close that his jowls were faintly flecked with red. The crowd was a motley assortment, some dressed as if for Sunday service, some arriving in their work clothes: coveralls, heavy canvas button-downs and trousers, restaurant uniforms, hospital scrubs. Tony had not slept Sunday night, worrying that he might have a crazed mob on his hands — that folks would come ready to start pointing fingers at every balding, mustached man in the county, or that they'd cry and wring their hands about community safety — but the group gathering in the pews, even occupying the far left and right wings, seemed merely interested, even excited, like fans at a baseball game. They smiled and shook hands across the pews; every now and then a bark of laughter would rise above the regular din. Tony didn't know if he should be disturbed or relieved, but he leaned on the latter. If the worst he could expect was some crass rubbernecking, he'd take it.

Before the meeting started, Susanna came up to him with her husband. Their hands were linked, and her eyes were almost comically round, as if she were a hostage trying to silently send him a signal. They had spoken on the phone earlier that day, when Tony called to let her know about the meeting and about his conversation with Sonny Ferrell, who was looking like a dead end — he'd stayed until one A.M. at the Salamander, plenty of folks to vouch for him, and then he and his lady friend had driven together back to Fort Campbell, where she spent the night with him. Sonny had not heard from Ronnie and seemed genuinely upset to learn that she was missing. So Tony had filled Susanna in on all of this, businesslike, but they'd not seen each other since parting on Sunday morning, and now here she was with her husband: a very tall, lean man with glasses and a slight hunch to his shoulders, the kind of hunch that usually went with much greater age.

"Dale," she said, and Tony wondered at the fact that the man seemed to miss the tremble in her voice, "this is Tony Joyce, the detective looking for Ronnie. Tony, this is my husband, Dale."

They shook hands, and Dale smiled in a distant but pleasant way. He looked almost as uncomfortable as she did, and he kept darting his eyes back and forth at the crowd. "Quite a group you've got gathered here, Tony. It's a little overwhelming."

"Well," he said, proceeding as diplomatically as he could, "Brother Jim felt strongly that the community should be kept informed."

"These things take on a life of their own. That's what I tried telling Suze." He spoke with what seemed like forced cheer, and a shadow of irritation passed across Susanna's features — a drawing of the brows, easy to miss. Tony could see she was uncomfortable with the meeting, that she hadn't realized the implications of making her worries about her sister public.

"Maybe something will come of it," Tony said. He was talking to Susanna now — for her — and he hoped she realized it. "I have to say honestly that I don't know what searching would accomplish at this point. But getting the info out there's a good thing, and getting it on the news again is a very good thing."

"I hope so," she said softly.

Brother Jim had ascended to the pulpit and was tapping the microphone. "Folks, if y'all could settle down, we'll get started here. Bless you all for coming. We're going to start here in just about a minute."

The meeting proceeded without protest or disruption or accusations or unexpected grandstanding — and that was about the best Tony could say for it. The opening prayer was melodramatic and overlong, and Brother Jim kept saying things about Ronnie that made Tony think he knew nothing about her, such as, "Lord, please touch us with your light of knowing, so that we can be joined again with our sister Veronica, a fine Christian woman and beloved member of the Roma community." Tony was afraid to lift his head in case the camera was trained on him, but he sneaked a peek at Susanna, and he saw that her jaw was set, her expression closed and verging on angry. *Beloved member of the Roma community* — well, from all that Susanna had told him, that was certainly putting a bright polish on things.

Tony kept his own remarks short, not elaborating much beyond the information already on the flyers: her last known whereabouts, the man in the drawing. "He's just a person of interest at this point," he said. "We hope he'll hear word and come voluntarily to us, just so we can talk to him."

There were a few questions and comments during the Q & A, but nothing too contentious. Someone suggested a community curfew for children and teenagers, but others dismissed that quickly as a drastic measure, especially since — as one man tried to carefully put it — the disappearance seemed "personal, not random," and at any rate the missing woman was thirty-two years old. Another person asked about cadaver-sniffing dogs, and Tony told her, avoiding looking at Susanna, that it would be premature to draw on that resource until they had more information to go on. He invoked the phrase "needle in a haystack." At last he added, "The best you can do for now, I think, is to keep your eyes and ears open and to contact the police department if you have any information. There may come a time to search, but I don't think we're there yet."

The meeting broke up just shy of six o'clock, when Brother Jim rose from his seat onstage to invite people to the Fellowship Hall "for a bit of refreshment, courtesy of our Women's Auxiliary." Two currents formed, one to the parking lot and one to the deeper recesses of the church, where plates of cucumber sandwiches and bowls of potato salad awaited, and Tony took a spot out of the way of both, in case Susanna needed to exchange a fast private word with him. He wasn't sure how much he wanted to talk to her, especially here, especially with her husband so nearby — but he felt the duty of his position. He thought that he was a better person than the boy who had cheated on Stefany all those years ago, that he was, in fact, truly a man at last, a grown-up who could anticipate the fallout of his actions. Yet had he not, in a church, just mildly shaken the hand of his lover's husband? And what was his duty, really — his intentions? He had seen in Susanna's eyes love, or something that thought itself love, which was funny, because Susanna had only been back in his life for a week and the past they shared was so very distant: a high school art class, a missed date. That Susanna had fixated on it in the years since made him wonder how much this all had to do with him, really.

Wonder all you want, he thought. *You still slept with her.*

Susanna didn't come to him, though, and he didn't even see her leave. He knew that she would bypass the Fellowship Hall, would not be able to endure people's questions and awkward condolences, and so he guessed that she and Dale had slipped out the front door as soon as Brother Jim made his announcement. Tony wished he could have gotten away with doing the same.

The sanctuary had nearly emptied, and Tony was contemplating whether or not he had to stop in to the dinner when a young man approached him. He was white, tall, lean, with a head of thick blond hair that looked strategically shaggy, just as his blue jeans seemed purposefully ragged, as if they'd been bought new from the store already with the faded spots and worn-through knees.

"Hey, man," the guy said. "Talk for a minute?"

Tony nodded warily. "Sure. What's on your mind?"

The young man looked around and rubbed his chin, then leaned in. His blue eyes were very bright — Tony was almost taken aback by them. "What I need to know

— what I'm wondering, I guess — is if there's a reward for tips. I mean, if a person had information leading to an arrest, is there some money in it?"

Tony sighed and shook his head. "No reward. If you have information, it's your obligation as a citizen to provide it."

"I mean, I just ask because I know people have gotten rewards in similar situations. You see it all the time. It ain't exactly unusual."

"That would have to come from a private donation, and the family in this situation doesn't have the resources for that," Tony said. "Is there something you want to tell me?"

The young man shoved his hands in his pockets and appeared to be thinking. "Well, maybe so. I think I know who the guy in the picture is."

Tony shifted his weight from one foot to another, dubious. "Oh, really?"

"Yeah. I work at Price with him. We were at Nancy's the night you're talking about. It was just kind of a prank, we didn't mean anything by it."

"Wait," Tony said. His pulse had quickened, and he had to stop himself from reaching out to grab the man's arm. "Are you Sam?"

The young man backed up a step, alarmed. He put his palms up. "Whoa there, man. How do you know my name?"

Tony could not believe his luck. He had started calling factories today after striking out with Sonny Ferrell, but he hadn't made it very far down the list, and so far, no soap. For this Sam to come to him — for the drawing to have actually worked —

"You're just the man I was hoping to see," Tony said.

2.

Tubs, Sam Austen explained, was their nickname for the quiet older fellow who worked out in packaging — the guy who was always confusing orders and backing up the line.

"You know, 'cause he's fat," Sam said. He had agreed to follow Tony back to his office at the police station, where they could tape-record the conversation, and he rocked back comfortably in the rickety wooden guest chair that Tony kept meaning to replace. Sam was enjoying himself now, getting on like a natural raconteur. "But mostly, you know, we call him that to get a rise out of him. He's real tight-wound, always throwing me and the guys these pissed-off looks when we're goofing off. So that's why we pranked him."

"You left him with a large drink bill and no ride," Tony said flatly. They had gone over this before. "And you believe you took off at" — he consulted his notes — "between ten thirty and eleven P.M."

"That's right," Sam said. "We went over to this girl's house after the dance hall, and I distinctly remember seeing a clock in her kitchen that said eleven thirty. She lives in Roma, so we couldn've left much later than eleven."

"Did you see him talking to anyone outside of your group?"

Sam laughed. "Oh, yeah. He danced with a woman."

"Really," Tony said. "What did she look like?"

"Some big fat lady with blond hair. She and my girl got into it a little, but nothing serious. Then she left."

"What was the nature of the argument?"

Sam shifted, and the chair chirruped. "Like I said, it wasn't nothing big. We were just teasing a little, and she got offended."

"You and your buddies must really love to tease," Tony couldn't help saying. "That's the impression I'm starting to form."

"Man, you know how it is," Sam said. He might have been a little uneasy — uneasy in

431

the manner of a person who is wondering for the first time if his actions might have personal consequences — but his cockiness was irrepressible. He radiated it.

The sad thing was, Tony *did* know how it was. Once, in Bluefield, he and some of his teammates had slipped their first baseman, Teddy McCalister, a couple of Valiums with his vodka tonics. Then, when he'd passed out, they stripped him to his underwear and moved him, La-Z-Boy and all, to a median strip on a major four-lane highway, where he woke up the next day in a state of such utter confusion that he nearly got run over trying to make it back to his apartment. They'd chosen Teddy ostensibly because he'd played a series of bad games that season but really because they had determined, without coming out and taking a vote on the matter, that he was the weak man among them: the guy who got homesick, who complained about the length of practices, who would let you stick him with the pizza bill because he was too nervous to argue with you when the time came to split the check. That guy. Tony had never been one of the Sam Austens of the world, but he felt a grim sureness that he had plenty in common with the pack of guys Sam hung out with. Their names were in his notebook now: Daniel Stone, Gene Lawson, Roger McCreary, Chet Roth, a few others. He hoped he wouldn't end up having to call all of them.

"And you're sure that this woman he danced with left?"

"I didn't see her after that," Sam said. "Gene talked Wyatt into coming back to the bar, and we spent about an hour after that getting him to do shots. Then we split."

Tony scribbled a note to himself: *Mystery woman?* Aloud, he said, "What would you say was the state you left Wyatt in? How drunk was he?"

Sam laughed. "Pretty blitzed. Looked like he might put his head down on the bar and take a nap."

"Did you ever find out how he got home?"

Sam frowned. "Well, no. He was at work the next Monday, like always. We ribbed him some, but we didn't ask. I assumed he called a cab or something."

With friends like these . . . , Tony thought. "And what's he like in general? Nice guy? Easygoing?"

"Aw, he's a baby doll," Sam said. "He's a little strange, I guess, but he's basically just a wimp. I don't think he hurt nobody. Anyhow, he's been in the hospital for the past week, so he probably doesn't know anything about your drawing, or he'd have come to you himself."

"Hospital? What for?"

"Heart attack," Sam said. "A woman found him pulled off the side of the road on Hill Street."

Tony wrote furiously: *Heart attack, hospital. Parked off Hill Street.* "What day did this happen? Do you know if he's still in the hospital?"

Sam squinted as if he were thinking. "Happened a week or so ago. I think that's right. You know, the days all run together at the plant." Tony detected a note of genuine sadness in the young man's voice.

"And he's at the hospital?" Tony prodded.

"Maybe. I'm not sure. He's not back at work yet, at least."

"OK," Tony said in a soft, slow exhalation, speaking mostly to himself. He stared at his notebook and tapped his pen against the desk's surface, wondering if there was anything he hadn't yet considered. He was trying to connect the dots, but he didn't see the way to. Dancing with a "fat woman." An argument; she leaves. They get him stupid on shots. They abandon him. And at some point, for some reason, Ronnie enters the equation, and she and Wyatt end up together at the Fill-Up in Roma.

A week after that, Wyatt has a heart attack.

Sam cleared his throat. "We done here?"

Tony finally nodded and punched the stop button on the tape recorder. "Yeah. Well, wait. The missing woman, Ronnie Eastman. What do you know about her? Do you remember seeing her?"

There was a pause, long enough to notice. Then Sam shook his head no.

"You sure?" Tony asked, trying to catch his eyes. "You don't seem sure."

"I mean, I think I saw her around at Nancy's a few times. She was always trawling for fry."

"Trawling for —"

"Trying to move in on younger men," Sam said.

"And you didn't see her that night? For sure?"

"No," Sam said. "I didn't." He rose, the chair squealing one last time in good-bye, and paused when he reached the door. "Oh, and, Officer? If any reward money was to come along, remember who told you first about Wyatt Powell. All right?"

"All right," Tony said wearily. "I will."

CHAPTER TWENTY-FIVE

1.

Wyatt was dozing in his easy chair when a loud knocking awoke him, setting Boss to howling. He sat up suddenly, heart racing, and then exhaled, hand on his chest. He lingered a moment, catching his breath, and checked the time on the VCR above his television set: seven fifteen. Sarah should have been here almost two hours ago. He had drifted off waiting for her.

He pulled in the chair's footrest and hobbled to a stand. His blood pressure was better today, but he was feeling the full brunt of last night's exertions in the muscles of his biceps, calves, and lower back; his hands, which were arthritic, were so stiff he could barely squeeze them closed. He awkwardly patted his thin hair into place and ran both hands over his crumpled shirt, wondering why Sarah would knock now when she hadn't knocked last night. He'd left the back door unlocked for her, just like he had yesterday.

The knock sounded again, and Boss bayed again. "Damn it, Boss, shut up," Wyatt said. The knocks had been at the front door — that was why they seemed so loud. His sleepy brain stabbed once more at understanding *(Did I lock the door after all? How long has she been standing out there?)*, and then he widened his eyes, rubbed his face briskly, and was awake enough to realize that it wasn't Sarah knocking at his door, that Sarah hadn't shown. Which could mean anything, really — that she had been delayed on her shift, that something else came up — but his heart, stitched together as it was, told him that she had seen the sketch. She had seen it, and it frightened her away.

Did she call the number on it? Would he open the door to the police? He swallowed against a taste of bitter bile and turned the deadbolt.

Illuminated by the porch light, face calmly polite, was a man — a black man, tall, youngish. He was dressed in a way Wyatt couldn't quite make sense of. Not in the jeans and big sneakers he thought those guys all wore, or in the dark blue uniform of the local police force, but like — well, he didn't know — an English countryman or something: tweed sports coat, sweater, a red pop of tie at the collar, a leather satchel strapped across his chest and resting on his hip. Wyatt stood behind the storm door, trying to keep Boss back, and said, "Yes?"

"Wyatt Powell?"

"Yes?" Wyatt repeated.

The man pulled his wallet from his back pocket in a friendly, almost sheepish way, as if he were going to give Wyatt a business card, and folded it open. A brass badge glinted. "Good evening, sir. I'm Tony Joyce. I'm the detective for Roma's police department, and I was wondering if you had time to answer a few quick questions." He seemed to register Wyatt's uncertainty. "I promise it won't take more than five or ten minutes. I've heard you're recovering from a heart attack, and I'm sure you need your rest."

"Did Sarah tell you that?" It came out before he could stop himself.

"Sarah? Well, I can't exactly recall. Who's Sarah?"

Wyatt swallowed. "Nobody. A nurse."

Tony Joyce smiled in what felt to Wyatt like a patronizing way. "At the hospital? Someone who took care of you?"

"Yes."

"Actually, then, no. I haven't been in

contact with a nurse named Sarah." He was still wearing that pleasant expression on his face, but something steeled beneath it. It was a change Wyatt didn't see so much as sense — a quiver of the jawline, a vein in his temple becoming more pronounced. "Actually, it was your friend who told me. Sam Austen? From Price Electric?"

"I don't know if I'd call him a friend," Wyatt said as evenly as he could.

"Mind if I come in, Wyatt? Just for a bit? It's pretty chilly out here."

Wyatt hesitated, then nodded, stepping to the side so Tony could enter. Boss immediately set to prancing, plunging his snout into the detective's crotch, and Tony reached out to pet the dog's head, amiable enough.

Crossing the room back to his chair, Wyatt switched on a couple of lamps — his living room had been dim, illuminated only by a wedge of light coming in from the kitchen — and then cleared the couch of the pile of flyers and pamphlets he'd been sent home from the hospital with: *Life After a Heart Attack, Your Healthy Heart Diet, The Five Habits That Could Save Your Life,* a bunch of others just like them. He had paged through a few today, wanting to do something that would please Sarah, but they only depressed him. The injunctions to go walking or biking were accompanied by sun-filled photos of tan, silver-haired couples on the beach, the diet tips with equally light-filled images of glossy fruits and vegetables and amber-colored bottles of olive oil. A smiling woman took a big bite of an apple. A good-looking man in his sixties held a toddler, presumably his grandchild, laughingly above his head. The pamphlets told him to fix his life by entering a world he'd always been denied, a world of leisure and love and plenty. He had planned to tell Sarah this; he had wanted to hear her thoughts. He could imagine her getting fired up on his behalf just as easily as he could imagine her gently ribbing him for his sensitivity *(Jeez, Wyatt, they're telling you to eat an apple, not to remortgage your house and go to a resort),* and he had looked forward all day to the surprise of her reaction.

He wouldn't hear it tonight. He wondered if he ever would.

Tony sat on the couch, laughing a little when Boss jumped up to lie on a cushion beside him, and Wyatt dropped into his easy chair with a wheeze.

"You've got a good dog," Tony said. "Bloodhound?"

"Yeah," Wyatt said. "That's Boss. He's the

boss around here."

"Looks that way," the detective said, laughing again. "I bet he's good company to you right now. How's the recovery coming?"

Wyatt rocked a little and kneaded his crumb catcher. "Bit by bit, I reckon. It's not been easy."

"I'm sorry to hear that," Tony said. "My father had a heart attack four years ago. He had a rough couple of months, but his life got more or less back to normal."

"I've got to get back to work or I'll go broke on bills," Wyatt said. "I know that much."

"You got that right." Tony leaned back into the couch cushions and crossed one leg over the other. "Of course, when my dad had his heart attack they didn't require employers to give medical leave. He's a custodian at the nursing home. He took a week and a half of sick leave and another half week of vacation, then he was back to pushing a mop around. He told me he kept wanting to crawl into one of the empty beds and give up."

"I don't blame him."

"When was it you had your heart attack, Wyatt?"

"A week ago today," Wyatt said.

"Sam told me you were parked over on Hill Street."

Wyatt nodded. "That's what they tell me. I don't remember much about it, though."

"You pulled over because you were having pains?"

"I reckon that's what happened."

"Lucky that woman came when she did," Tony said.

"I reckon it was." Wyatt folded his hands in his lap to keep them from fidgeting. "Is a man having a heart attack normally police business? No offense intended, but I'm just wondering what it is we're discussing here."

Tony smiled gently. "No, I'm not here about your heart attack. I was just chitchatting to break the ice."

"I'd say it's broke. What's on your mind?"

Tony unzipped his satchel and removed a binder. He opened it, slid a piece of paper from a plastic sleeve, and did a quick hunching walk across the space that separated them to hand it to Wyatt. Then he backtracked to the couch. "Do you recognize the woman in that photograph?"

This was it — the moment Wyatt had known was coming.

"Yes," Wyatt said. He felt his armpits prickle with sudden sweat as he stopped himself just shy of using the past tense. "Her name's Ronnie. I can't remember her last name. I met her a couple of weeks ago."

"Can you tell me how you met her, Wyatt? As much as you can recall about the circumstances?" The detective's expression was alert and keenly interested. He had, Wyatt noticed, slipped a notepad out of the binder, and his pen was poised over the paper.

"Why?" Wyatt asked, handing back the photograph, which Tony stood up to receive. He hesitated, then added: "Did she do something?"

"You don't know?" Tony asked, sitting again. His eyes were steady and unblinking. Wyatt had never felt so studied.

"I guess I must not," Wyatt said. "I haven't been getting out. I've got a lot else to worry about right now."

"She's gone missing."

Wyatt thought that the detective had ceded something he had not planned to. "Really? I'm very sorry to hear that."

"Yeah," Tony said. "She hasn't been to work. She hasn't contacted her sister. The reason I'm curious about the circumstances of your meeting is that it appears that the last night anyone can account for her was Saturday, October twenty-third. And what I understand from your friend Sam Austen is that you and a group of men from Price

Electric were all at Nancy's Dance Hall in Sylvan, Tennessee, on that evening. Does that sound right?"

Wyatt squinted in thought. "I guess so. I'm a little shaky on dates since the heart attack, but that ought to be right."

"And you met Ronnie at Nancy's the night you were there with your friends?"

He wondered why Tony kept calling Sam and his gang "friends." He felt a burn of irritation every time he used the word. "Yes."

"So if you would, please, tell me about those circumstances."

"Well, let me see," Wyatt said. He folded out the footrest on his chair, aware that his rocking was starting to take on a frantic note. "I went over there with Sam and Gene. I didn't really want to, but they'd been working on me a few weeks, trying to goad me into it. At some point I figured why not. It turned out they were just playing a big joke on me. They got me drunk and took off, stuck me with the bill." He let some of his authentic anger show on his face here. "Which is why I said I wouldn't call Sam a friend. I think it was a real lousy thing for them to do to me."

"So do I," Tony said.

"Anyway, that woman in the photo, Ronnie, she saw what happened, and she offered me a ride home. It was real good of her to do. I don't know what I'd of done if she hadn't."

"And she drove you straight home?"

"No," he said. "She asked me if I was hungry, and for some reason I was. So we went to a gas station and got some food and beer. Then we went over to her house and ate it. Then she drove me home."

"OK," Tony said, writing in his notebook. "So the last you saw her was when she drove you to this house and then left."

"That's right," Wyatt said.

"About what time would that have been?"

Wyatt thought. "Late," he said. "One thirty or two in the morning."

"Did she tell you that she had any other plans for the night?"

"No," Wyatt said. "I assumed she was going to go home and go to bed."

"But you don't know for sure."

"No, I don't."

Tony scribbled something, then flipped back a page to look at his notes. "Wyatt, I'm going to ask you a personal question."

Wyatt squeezed his right hand, which was dangling on the far side of the rocker, out of sight. The pain was clarifying. "Yes?"

"Did you sleep with her?"

Wyatt felt his face bloom with heat — he

couldn't stop it from happening. "Wh—" His throat was dry, and he swallowed hard. "What?"

Tony dropped the notebook to his lap and leaned forward. "Did you and Ronnie have sex?"

"Of course not," Wyatt said harshly. "She was young enough to be my daughter."

"But you did drink with her at her house."

There was a high tone sounding in his left ear. He grabbed with a shaking hand at the glass of water on his end table and tried leaning back into his chair with it, managing to spill some in his lap. "I'm — I'm sorry," he stammered. "I'm having a spell."

"Are you all right?" Tony said. "Can I get you something?"

Wyatt held up the near-empty glass. "Refill this for me?"

While Tony was in the kitchen, Wyatt wiped his face with his shirtsleeve and worked on steadying his rapid breath. It was frustrating, infuriating, to be a slave to his body this way. When Tony came back with the glass of water, which was clinking with a few fresh ice cubes, Wyatt nodded gratefully and drank half away in a draft. At last his face cooled.

"Do you think you need a doctor?" Tony asked. His concern seemed genuine.

446

"Nah." Wyatt finished the water. "My blood pressure's been up and down all week. I haven't been drinking as much water as I'm supposed to."

"You sure?"

"I'm sure."

"I'll let you rest. I've already stayed longer than I intended to," Tony said. He put the photograph and the notebook away in his satchel and rose. "Thank you for your time, Mr. Powell." He removed his wallet again and this time did produce a business card. "I'd like you to give me a call if you remember anything else about the night you met Ronnie Eastman. It sounds as if she was a really nice woman, and I'm sure you'll want to do everything you can to get her reunited with her family."

Wyatt felt his sinuses swell with tears. "Of course," he said. "Of course I do."

The clock on the VCR read 7:43. When the engine on the detective's car had sounded and headlights cut across Wyatt's picture window, he put down his head and started sobbing.

2.

Tony had an idea.

He drove from Wyatt's house straight to Ronnie's. He had been over it twice already, shooting photographs, taking notes on the food, the arrangement of the furniture. He did these things mostly because he could, because the only resource getting used was his own time and some film; it wasn't, so far as he knew, a crime scene, and he couldn't yet justify to the police chief the expense of treating it like one. At any rate, though, Wyatt had owned up to coming to the house to eat. Fingerprinting would reveal what they already knew.

He let himself into the house using the spare key Susanna had given him and went to the kitchen. A rotten, shut-up smell lingered in the room despite the fact that Susanna had, with Tony's okay, come over yesterday to pitch the old food into the trash and to lay out some ant traps. "Don't spray down any surfaces," he'd told her, and it looked like she had followed his instructions, though his nostrils prickled at an odd floral note — some kind of air freshener, he suspected.

A wooden box labeled MAIL was mounted to the wall beside the refrigerator. Beneath slots labeled BILLS, COUPONS, and PERSONAL was a little shelf and a series of hooks; Ronnie's car keys dangled from one of them, as Tony had already noted in his inventory. He didn't know if this was a spare set or her primary set, and Susanna hadn't been sure, either — the difference might make for radically different scenarios for her disappearance. He slipped on plastic gloves, hooked a finger through the loop on the key ring, and went outside to the Camaro. The night had gotten bitter, and a light rain, almost a mist, drizzled down. Maybe it would become snow if it kept on, he mused. Uncommon this time of year, but the forecast called for freezing temperatures overnight.

He had pulled a flashlight from the glove box of his car, and he switched it on now, shining it with his left hand on the lock and using his right to turn the key, then pull the handle. The door sighed as it opened, and Tony was hit with the musk of worn-in leather. He got down on his haunches and let the light play over the inside: the driver's and passenger's bucket seats, the floorboards (clear of trash but grimed with dirt and bits of dried leaves), the narrow backseat. There was something back there — he leaned around the seat carefully and grasped it, pulling it forward to where he could get a better look. It was a pillow or a cushion of some kind: round, overstuffed, and tufted with a single button in the center, little ties trailing off where it would have been looped to a chair back. According to Susanna, Ronnie was a small woman, barely five feet tall; this looked like the kind of thing she might have used to give her a little extra lift behind the wheel.

But it wasn't in the driver's seat. It had been in the backseat, on the passenger's side of the car — as if the person behind the wheel had tossed it there.

Tony put it back where he had gotten it and slipped gingerly into the driver's seat. He was six foot two, and the windshield bore down on him oppressively, but his legs fit under the steering wheel pretty comfortably, and he could extend his arms in a natural way to mime moving the gearshift and hitting the turn signal. If he were going to start this car and drive off, he might move the seat back another couple of inches.

When Wyatt met him at the door, Tony had noticed that the man stood, in sock feet, perhaps three or four inches shorter than he, putting him at five foot ten or five foot eleven. A man of that height could sit in this seat and get to the gas and the clutch with no problem. A woman of no more than five feet would have to sit forward on the edge of the seat, and even then she might not have the reach to depress both pedals at once. To do so, he thought, would be an exercise in pointlessness, when that simple latch on the chair could move her into a more sensible position, lickety-split.

He locked the car, returned the car key to its hook inside the house, and shut off all the lights in the house before locking the house, too. When he opened the door to his cruiser, a message was crackling on his radio — he caught only the last words, "to the station, please copy."

He picked up his handset and depressed the button. "Dispatch, this is eight oh five, copy. Please repeat your message."

"Eight oh five, I thought you were off duty. I tried you at home."

Tony smirked into the microphone. "Nope. Still plugging away. What's going on?"

"We have a family at Two eleven Poplar reporting a missing child. Eight ten took the call. Can you come to the station?"

Tony looked back at the little shotgun house and the Camaro. "Copy," he said, wondering how he'd managed to get so busy in just a week's time. "I'll be there."

CHAPTER TWENTY-SIX

1.

While Pendleton took point with the parents and began with some other officers to make an initial sweep of the child's neighborhood — which happened to also be Wyatt Powell's neighborhood, Tony noted with unformed disquiet — Tony was conferring with the police chief and a state Search and Rescue official to plan a more organized, large-scale search effort. By nine thirty he was on the phone with a representative from a nonprofit out of Elizabethtown, the Commonwealth Bloodhound Search and Rescue, to find out when the nearest dog and handler could get to town. By eleven he was joining a search team in the housing projects just south of Emily Houchens's neighborhood. The temperatures dropped to the midthirties, and flurries, fine and dry as salt, started to drift down. There was no time to rest, no time to wait for better light. A thirteen-year-old girl was out in this, perhaps injured, unable to move. The parents had said she'd sprained her ankle a couple of weeks ago, and so it seemed to Tony that she might have been clumsier on that ankle than usual and had perhaps aggravated the injury.

"I asked them why they waited until after seven o'clock to call, and they told me that the girl had a habit of taking off on walks after school," Pendleton said when he and Tony touched base at midnight. They were standing in the station parking lot, collars on their light jackets raised against the cold, and Tony rubbed his bare hands briskly together. He hadn't brought gloves to work today. "She'd come in from the bus, yell hi, and take off again. They tried to put a stop to it last week, after word got around that Ronnie Eastman was missing, but they say she can be willful." He hunched his shoulders so that his ears got more cover. "Anyway, she was always home by dinner before, and tonight she missed dinner."

"Do they know where she went?"

"They didn't seem to have a clue. Nice, right? The mom told me that she claimed to be spending time with a friend in the neighborhood, but we asked the girl and she flat-out denied it. She said she hadn't even talked to Emily Houchens in the past year."

"That's strange," Tony said.

"Yeah, I know. Other than that, she'd been walking a dog for a neighbor, some guy who'd been sick. But that was only a few days last week, and now the dog's back with the owner."

"Huh," Tony said. "Well, she's thirteen. She's not exactly a little girl. Maybe she has a secret boyfriend or something."

"That's what I kind of figured at first. The parents — they're nice enough, I really don't get a bad vibe from them, but they're clueless. There's a retarded kid in the household, and I got the impression that he takes a lot of their energy. He was bawling and carrying on in just the time I was there."

"Did they let you look in her bedroom?"

"Yeah," Pendleton said. "They're being cooperative. I had Mrs. Houchens help me go through it — I was curious to see if anything surprised her. Anyway" — he lit a cigarette — "if the girl's got a secret life, nothing in that room pointed to it. It was all kid stuff, old dollies, rock collection and twigs, binders full of pressed leaves and shit. I didn't see anything like a real diary, just stuff about science experiments. It was a little bit odd, actually. When my stepdaughter was thirteen she had posters of boys up all over her room."

"She sounds a little sheltered," Tony said. He was thinking about the rocks and the twigs, the binders of pressed leaves.

"Sheltered," Pendleton said. "Yeah, that's the right word."

"All those rocks and things — she'd have to gather them up somewhere."

Pendleton nodded. "There's a group searching the woods between this subdivision and the Grant Road development. It's a lot of ground to cover — half a mile between the subdivisions, and then it extends all the way to the bypass on the north side. That's about a mile and a half. And then three-quarters of a mile toward town."

Tony exhaled tiredly. "What did the mother say about the room?"

"That it all looked right. That Emily's a good girl, smart and serious, kind of quiet. She told me she'd been having a hard time at school lately — some of the kids were bullying her. Apparently a pack of them got suspended for throwing food at her in the cafeteria. Guess who one of them was."

Tony shrugged.

"Johnny Burke's kid."

"Figures."

"Think we should ask around about that?

Maybe it's a stretch."

"I have a friend who works at the middle school," Tony said. "I'll say something about it to her tomorrow if we still haven't found the girl."

"All right," Pendleton said. "I'm going to try to catch some shuteye. When's the dog getting here?"

"I talked to the handler an hour ago, and she's on her way. She has a two-hour drive."

"Will she get started right away?"

"I don't know," Tony said. "I think it's supposed to be best if the dog works while the trail's still fresh, but we don't even know for sure where the trail starts."

"I'd like to see it in action," Pendleton said. "I sure love a good dog."

"I'll trade you," Tony said. "You meet the handler, and I'll go home and sleep."

Pendleton laughed shortly. "No, thanks. I'm older and fatter than you are. I can't go and go all night."

Tony put his hand on his scar unconsciously. "Go on," he said. "Leave this to the professionals."

When Pendleton had taken off, Tony pulled out his pills, thought for a moment, and broke one in half, swallowing it dry. He couldn't afford to get sleepy right now; he had a feeling he was going to be in for a long night.

2.

When the dog team first arrived at one o'clock, Tony experienced a surge of energy and even hopefulness. The dog, Maggie, was a beautiful creature, younger and leaner than Wyatt Powell's bloodhound, with a coat so lustrous that it shimmered under the security lights, and the dog's handler, Sharon, emanated confidence and good sense. She was petite, fortyish, and pleasant in a prematurely matronly way, with feathered dark blond hair that she'd sprayed into an unmoving helmet; a scrubbed-looking, unlined face; and the sturdy body of a mother. In fact, she referred several times to her children as Tony drove her to Emily's house to select a scent article from the things in Emily's bedroom, always calling them "my boys." "My boys are playing in a basketball game tomorrow night," "My boys would go crazy over that skate ramp," and, to Emily's parents, "Maggie and I are going to do everything we can to find your daughter. My boys are right around her age." Tony could tell that Emily's parents, too, were soothed by her manner — that she came across as the kind of person who simply wouldn't truck with failure on her watch.

Tony brought them first to Emily's regular bus stop, where she would have disembarked if she had, in fact, ridden it home. Sharon unzipped the plastic bag she'd placed some gauze and the scent article in — it was a dirty T-shirt of Emily's — and put the cloth under the dog's nose. "Maggie, ready," she said, and the dog's head bobbed, its ears shivering. "Find." Maggie put her nose close to the ground and stalked around in circles. For a second, it seemed as if she'd found a trail, but she led them directly back to Emily's house down the road. "Are you sure she didn't come home at all?" Sharon asked Tony. "Maybe she popped into the house without the parents noticing."

"Mrs. Houchens and Emily's brother both insist that they never saw her come in. And her habit was to leave her things in the bedroom before going out again, but they didn't find her backpack."

"No backpack," Sharon said, musing.

"No."

"Well, Maggie's probably just backtracking, then. She would have walked this way to catch the bus in the morning, too."

Tony sighed in frustration. "Let's go around the house."

They tried the road leading in the opposite direction from the bus stop without luck. Then they tried the Houchens's backyard, which abutted a vacant property and offered a path, if one didn't mind cutting through between fences, to another cross street. Nothing there, either.

"Could it be the snow interfering with the scent?" Tony asked as they made one last circuit of the yard. Sharon's brisk confidence was starting to annoy him, and the whole business of a trail-sniffing dog struck him suddenly as suspect, as if he'd contracted the services of a psychic or some other crackpot. "Maybe it washed it away?"

"No, sir, the wetter the better," Sharon said in a singsong way that suggested this was a catchphrase of hers. She had Maggie on a long lead, which she'd shortened by wrapping it around her arm several times, hooking it between her forefinger and thumb. She kept spooling to pick up slack on the leash and unspooling when Maggie fixed on something interesting. "Precipitation actually helps things." She finally stopped the dog and patted her hide. "We could both use a drink of water and a break. You said there was one more starting point you wanted to try?"

"The middle school," Tony said.

Twenty minutes later, they started Maggie

at the double doors exiting the seventh- and eighth-grade wings, and Sharon repeated her mantra: "Maggie, ready. Find." After some furious sniffing, the dog seemed to fix on something, and she took off eagerly down the steps and along the sidewalk. Tony's heart started to thump, and he thought very briefly of Pendleton, and his interest in the dog, because he couldn't deny that this was thrilling to watch. They made a hard right as they approached the street, walked another twenty feet, and Maggie halted, circling near the curb.

"This is where the buses line up," Tony said. "Does this mean she got on one?"

"Looks like that to me. It's possible she's picking up on an old scent, but she's reacting to it like it's fairly fresh."

Tony leaned over and caught his breath. "God," he muttered, lifting up and stretching to open his lower back. He huffed. "OK. I'm sorry, I'm just worn out. Can she follow a person's scent if they're in a vehicle? I mean, theoretically, could she follow the bus Emily took?"

"Theoretically, yes," Sharon said. "I haven't been able to do a lot of that kind of training with Maggie, though."

"I'd like to give it a shot," Tony said.

It was almost three in the morning, and

Sharon's eyes had bruise-colored shadows beneath them. Tony remembered that she'd driven in from Owensboro and felt a twinge of guilt.

"OK," Sharon said. "Let's try it."

For another half an hour, she brought Maggie out into the road, held the scent article under her nose, and chanted, "Find." The dog was worked up, jowls foamy, tongue lolling. They tried her at several points along the path of the bus — from the school until Sunset Street was one-way — but the dog just kept circling as if she were going after her own tail. Tony knew the feeling.

At three thirty he dropped Sharon and Maggie off at the Best Western Motor Inn on the bypass and thought, as he told the clerk the police department's tax-exempt code, of booking himself a room, too. He was too tired even to drive home. But he was also, he realized, too tired to sleep.

"Will you leave in the morning?" he asked Sharon.

"I don't know," she said. "Is there anything else we can do? Anywhere else to try?"

"There's the wooded area near Emily's house — we could go there depending on what the search team tells us. And we haven't talked to any of the girl's classmates

461

yet. At least one of them would have seen her on the bus, so maybe we can narrow down which she took and where it went."

"I'd like to make it home for my boys' game. So . . ." She counted under her breath. "Four o'clock. I need to be out of here by then."

"Thanks so much," Tony said. They were standing under an eave outside the woman's room, and he looked down at the dog, who was now sitting and panting, eyes drooped to slits. "Can I pet her?"

"Of course you can," Sharon said.

He hunched down to rub the dog's head and knead the base of her ears with his knuckles. "Good girl, good girl," he said. Her hot breath was an oddly pleasing combination of sweetness and stink, like a nursing baby's. Maybe it was the exhaustion, or maybe it was that half of a Darvocet he'd taken earlier, but he felt suddenly moved by this animal. What an amazing thing this creature was, how simple and wonderful. It was a kind of magic, wasn't it? A dog that could sniff out an hours-old path. They just needed to find the right starting point.

CHAPTER TWENTY-SEVEN

1.

Dale shook Susanna awake. She groaned, exhaled hard, and turned to check the digital clock: 5:30 A.M. When her eyes adjusted to the low light she noticed he was holding Abby, dressed, in his arms. She was slumped against him, head on his shoulder.

"Oh my God," Susanna said, tossing the covers aside and holding out her arms. "Is she sick? What's wrong?"

"No, nothing like that," Dale whispered. "I didn't mean to scare you. I'm sorry, I wasn't thinking."

Her heart was slow to resume its normal rhythm. "Are you sure?" She rubbed her eyes and swung her feet over the side of the bed; the nap of the carpet was reassuring against the soles of her feet. "God, Dale, what's going on?"

"We better go on and drop Abby at your mother's. Something's happened."

Susanna jumped to a stand. "Ronnie?" Her stomach lurched. "Did they find her?"

"No," Dale said. "Jesse Benton called about half an hour ago. A girl's gone missing — one of your students, an eighth grader."

She tried to process this. "Jesse Benton called here?"

"Yeah. I grabbed the phone before you woke up."

"And someone's missing? Who?"

"Emily Houchens."

"Emily," Susanna repeated.

"Isn't she the one you were saying got pummeled in that food fight?"

"Yeah," she said softly.

"She never made it home from school yesterday. The bus driver said he thought he'd seen her but couldn't be sure, so they're not even totally certain how she made it off school grounds."

"What's happening now?" She looked helplessly around the room, unsure of whether she should take Abby, get in the shower, or start throwing on clothes. "Are they having another meeting?"

Dale laid Abby on the bed and went to the closet; Susanna could see that he was wearing only his trousers and undershirt, and he was thumbing now through a rack of his button-downs. "You have time to clean up if you want," he said, pulling out his favorite plaid shirt and shrugging into it. "They've organized a search party. Some of them started last night, and they're continuing with a bigger group today at first light. But Jesse wants as many of the school system employees as he can gather to meet at the high school at six thirty so we have some kind of organized front on what to tell the students. It sounds like they're going to implement a bunch of new safety procedures, at least temporarily."

Abby got off the bed with a grunt and left the room. The television roared to life down the hall. "Has she had anything to eat?" Susanna asked.

"I got her to drink some juice. She said she wasn't hungry, so I didn't push it."

Susanna started laying out clothes on the bed: some khaki trousers, a turtleneck sweater, underwear, bra. "They don't think this is connected to Ronnie, do they?"

"I'm sure some people do." He wound a tie around his neck, and Susanna wondered if she should opt for a skirt instead — if the meeting called for a certain level of formality or if this was just one of those instances of Dale and his exaggerated sense of occasion. "This is a lot of excitement for a town of this size, so people will put the two together even if it doesn't make sense. I tend to think it doesn't."

Susanna yearned to talk to Tony, to hear what he knew. Whatever his instinct was, she would trust it. "Do people think she was abducted or something? Or that she ran away?"

"They really have no clue."

"She was having a bad time of it at school," Susanna said. "What those kids did to her was beyond cruel."

"That's what I told Jesse." He had on his field-day cologne, and he was checking his hair in the mirror. He seemed charged with purpose, the way he did before competitions, and for a mean moment Susanna thought that he was probably glad for this distraction. He always got distant and gloomy at the end of a marching band season; he didn't know what to do with the free evenings, the lack of an immediate goal. "I told him all about the food fight. He said the police might want to get some particulars from you."

She made a noise of unenthusiastic affirmation. It annoyed her that Dale had shared this information with the superintendent on her behalf, though she couldn't really pinpoint why, or how he might have better handled things. It just seemed like — well — sucking up. He liked being the person with the most information, the person whom the rest turned to when their own lines of gossip played out. Even last night, despite his discomfort at being tied publicly to Ronnie, Susanna had sensed his getting into the spirit of the community meeting, reveling a little in his position as the man by her side. "She's been having a hard time," she'd heard him saying softly to a work colleague of theirs, his tone of voice suggesting that he, too, had struggled heroically with the pressure of Ronnie's disappearance — that being a support system for Susanna had taken its toll.

Or maybe she was being unfair to him. The last two days had been like this: judging Dale bitterly for his wrongs, then feeling almost suffocated by her guilt, convinced that she'd villainized him only to justify her own terrible actions.

"I can drive Abby to your mother's while you're cleaning up, then swing back here to get you. Does that sound OK? It should save us some time."

"All right," Susanna said. "Just let me kiss her good-bye."

In the shower she cranked the heat until it was steaming, grateful for the rare few moments truly to herself. Ronnie. Emily. Even in a town this small, what were the chances that she would know them both? She thought about Emily in the bathroom after the incident in the cafeteria, how she was humming tunelessly and trying to wipe spaghetti sauce out of her hair with a brown paper towel. She thought about the way tears had magnified her big green eyes and how utterly lost and alone she seemed. Maybe she *had* run away. Maybe it had been too much for her to face coming back to school, knowing that her tormenters were there, even if they were — for now — hidden from sight. It made Susanna feel another wave of anger at Christopher Shelton, that little privileged shit, and she attacked herself with the washcloth, remembering how his mother had had the audacity to approach her last night, to express her sympathy. "Let me know if there's anything my husband and I can do," she had said, as if there were any way in the universe that Susanna would take *their* help — as if Nita Shelton truly had any help to offer. "I'll tell you what you can do," Susanna muttered now, putting her soapy head under the showerhead. "Keep your sociopathic asshole of a son in line, that's what you can do."

Then it happened, out of nowhere: She realized that she might not ever see her sister again. That Ronnie wasn't just making herself scarce for a couple of weeks, wasn't just a few clever steps from being found. How could she have known but not known? She couldn't breathe, couldn't hold her head so that the water didn't stream into her nostrils, and so she hunched, gasping, and finally the attack passed. The water flowing down her back was cool now. Dale would be home any minute, wondering what was keeping her.

2.

Eighth graders were old enough to appreciate drama, but most of them weren't yet old enough to truly fear for Emily Houchens, or to wonder if what had happened to her could happen to them. If they were wondering, it was in a thrilling way — the way they'd once wondered if the Bell Witch would get them if they said her name three times fast at the stroke of midnight, or if there really was the ghost of a dead girl in the window of the house by the old cemetery, as town legend claimed. In fact, Susanna could see that most of them were enjoying the day, the break in the routine. They didn't even mind the hassle of the new safety measures — signing in and out of the bus or getting checked out at the end of the day by a registered parent or guardian — though they might eventually grouse if the routine continued long enough to lose its novelty.

As they'd been instructed to do by the superintendent, the teachers all kept their homeroom students through first period, explaining to them the nature of the disappearance and the safety procedures, then allowing time for a brief discussion period, so that students could, as Jesse Benton put it, "work through the trauma together." Susanna had been given a handout titled "Methods for Helping Children Understand Crisis," which stated that children needed "a SAFE ENVIRONMENT in which to express themselves," "the SUPPORT of their peers," and "ACTIVE CHANNELS OF COMMUNICATION between parents and teachers." Most of the suggested tips and activities listed in it seemed geared to much younger children, Susanna thought, and so she spoke to her class plainly and simply, explaining what she had been told and admitting that she was worried about Emily but very hopeful. The students were solemn during this speech, unusually quiet, and they hung on her every word. She knew that they would spend the rest of the day heatedly comparing notes with their peers, flushed with pleasure at the new energy in the school, teachers whispering furiously to one another, Mr. Burton coming into classrooms to silently hand off papers to the teachers, as if he were a producer passing an update to the news anchor. Susanna found she couldn't blame them for it.

She had allowed Christopher Shelton to join the group for this special session, and it was he, surprisingly, who appeared to actually be troubled by the news. Where the other students' solemnity seemed put on, as if they were acting out behaviors they'd seen on television, Christopher was drawn, morose; his color was bad. He sat silently in the back of the room until she invited them to ask her questions or talk about their feelings, and then he tentatively raised his hand. Some eyes widened; the students were expecting, at the least, some of his patented irreverence.

"Where are they searching for her?" he asked.

It was an odd question, she thought — more like something an adult would ask. "Well," she said, "what I understand is that they're starting from two different center points and working out from them. One is

471

actually this school, because we haven't been able to confirm whether or not she rode the bus home." She swept her eyes across the larger group. "If any of you have information about that, please let me know. The other is her house."

He nodded and stuffed his hands into the pockets of his coat, which he was wearing inside despite the warmth of the classroom. It was a Starter jacket brandishing the Detroit Red Wings logo, and it was so puffy that he kind of sank down into it, only a pale bit of face emerging.

He still didn't seem himself when Susanna escorted him to the bathroom for his morning break. Where yesterday he had sauntered down the hall, eyes roving with interest from one classroom door to the next, today his head was down and his shoulders were slumped, and there was something faraway about his expression.

"Are you coming down with a cold, Christopher?" Susanna asked him on the walk back to her room. "It seems like you should be hot in that coat."

He looked at the jacket as if he'd forgotten he was wearing it. "I don't know. Maybe," he said. "I lost my house key yesterday and had to sit outside until Mom got home."

"Maybe you should go to a doctor," Susanna said gently.

He shrugged. "I'm all right."

She found herself worrying about him. Perhaps it was a mother's instinct, or perhaps Christopher's manner in sickness was just such a contrast to his usual cockiness that she felt confident for once in her power over him, and this confidence made her generous. Maybe she just needed the distraction from thinking about Ronnie and Emily. At lunch she opened the door to the supply closet to find him with his head down on the desktop, and he quickly sat bolt upright. His face was red and blotchy.

"Chris, I'm thinking I might need to call your mother to come get you," Susanna said. She put her hand on his forehead, then touched his cheeks with the backs of her fingers. He was clammy, his hair damp.

"I'm all right," he said again.

"You don't want to go home?"

He shook his head.

"If you're worried about finishing your punishment," Susanna said, "don't. I'll make sure you get credit with Mr. Burton for today even if you do leave for the doctor. OK?"

"I'm OK. I don't want to go home."

"Well, it's lunchtime. Are you ready to go

to the cafeteria?"

"I'm not hungry," he said. By the windows, the radiator clanked and hissed. The room was otherwise very quiet.

"If you're not sick enough to go home, you need something on your stomach," Susanna said. "What if I go and bring you something back here?"

He shrugged.

"Juice? Some fruit?"

"That's fine," he muttered.

She went to the cafeteria, surprised at what a difference a day made — that she would now trust Christopher alone in her classroom. The menu was boiled hot dogs and baked beans, and the smell was enough to turn a healthy stomach. She went through the line with a tray, taking just a paper container of fries for herself — she had planned to have her regular microwave lunch, but she didn't want to take the time to pop by the teachers' lounge. The only fresh fruit was a bowl of small, mushy-looking apples, so she grabbed one of those and also a container of fruit cocktail, the kind she hadn't eaten in years, with little cubes of peach and pear and maraschino cherries. The orange juice came in a plastic cup with a foil seal, and she took one of those, too.

Christopher picked at the food. She had insisted that he join her in the empty classroom, thinking that at least the light and fresh air would do him some good, but it was awkward between them, always awkward to be a teacher and a student out of a familiar context, away from the rituals that defined who and how they were supposed to be to each other. Susanna finally pulled out the novel she'd been reading off and on for the last two weeks, spreading it open between the thumb and pinky of her left hand so that she could lift French fries to her mouth with the right. It was a John Grisham thriller, the kind of thing she should have been able to finish in a day or two, but focusing was hard lately; planning her lessons each day was challenge enough. Still, it gave her something to fix her eyes upon, even if she did have to reread the same sentence several times, and she had gotten through most of her meal this way, hardly registering the taste of the mushy, undersalted fries, when Christopher said in a choked voice, "Mrs. Mitchell, there's something I think I need to tell you."

She laid the book on the desktop. His eyes were very red, as if he had allergies, and his fingers were woven together and clenched tightly. "Yes?" she asked. "What is it?"

"I know something about Emily Houchens. About where she went after school yesterday."

Susanna's temples prickled. She felt a sudden, horrible certainty that Christopher had hurt Emily — that perhaps he, in concert with some of the other punished students, had played another, more dangerous prank on her. "If you know something," she said, trying to keep her voice even, "you better say so immediately."

"Are you going to tell my mom?"

"I don't know what you're about to say, Christopher. There might be no way that I can't tell her."

She was shocked when tears started rolling down his face. "Emily gave me a note yesterday and told me to ride the bus with her after school. She said she had something to show me. She said it was about you." His hands were tucked into the sleeves of the puffy jacket, and he wiped his eyes on the crook of his shoulder.

"Slow down," Susanna said. "She told you to meet her? Not the other way around?"

"Yes," he said emphatically. "I came back to the closet after lunch and the note was in one of my books."

"And she said it was about me?"

"Yes," he said again.

Her mouth tasted dry and starchy from the fries, and she swallowed hard. "Go on."

"We rode Bus Five. We sat in separate seats. She told me to get off in front of the old hospital on Harper Hill, so that's what I did. I guess it's close to where she lives."

Susanna had heard Emily lived in Pratt's subdivision, near Susanna's mother. She nodded.

"I went because —" He stopped and sniffed back phlegm, like a child would. "Because I felt bad about last week. You probably don't think I do, but I did. It got out of control that day. So I thought if she wanted me to do this, I could do it, even if it meant I got in trouble with Mom for coming home late."

"What did she want from you?" Susanna said. "What did I have to do with it?"

His voice was so low she almost couldn't make it out. "She told me she found something. She wanted to show it to me."

"What?"

"A body." He was shaking all over now. "A dead body. She said it might be your sister's."

For a moment Susanna was in the shower again, the water running into her nose and mouth. She was drowning in this school desk. Her fingers scrabbled across the

477

groove where a pencil was supposed to rest.

"She told me she would show it to me. She told me she couldn't show her parents because they'd be mad at her. So I followed her into the woods at the top of the hill, and we went to the place where she said it was, but there wasn't anything there. She lied about it." He was rambling now, his words stumbling over one another. "I got mad and I told her to leave me alone, and I pushed her, but it wasn't that hard. She wasn't hurt or anything. Then I left her there and ran home. It was so weird. There's something wrong with her. She just lied about it. There wasn't a body."

"You're sure there wasn't," Susanna said. She had tears in her own eyes now, and she willed herself not to spill them. Not in front of Christopher. Not now.

"No. She freaked out and said somebody moved it."

Susanna pressed her fingertips against her eyelids. Her head was pounding.

"I think there's something wrong with her. I think her parents must beat her or something. She doesn't act right."

"And you didn't do anything to her . . . You and your friends? Play some kind of joke on her? If you did, you can tell me. We just want to find her."

"No!" He practically yelled it.

"Okay," she said. "Okay. I believe you, Chris. I believe you." She shifted out of the desk and stood. "I'm going to have to call a person at the police department about this. Can you show him how to get to where Emily took you?"

Christopher nodded.

CHAPTER TWENTY-EIGHT

1.

The boy sat beside him on the ride to Harper Hill, staring out the window and twisting his fingers in his lap. He wasn't a boy, really — Tony remembered too well the kinds of thoughts that had been on his own mind at thirteen, and they weren't innocent — but the situation had stripped Christopher of the teenager's bravado. His eyes were wide and round, the set of his mouth slack. At the middle school's principal's office he had answered Tony's questions in a rushed whisper, eyes darting to his mother's to check for anger, and the mother — Tony had to give her credit — had sat to the side quietly and calmly, not once interrupting. It would have been a mistake to pull Christopher from school without calling her, but Tony had been hesitant nonetheless. "She's very protective and entitled," Susanna had warned him in a stolen moment. "And

Christopher's playing boyfriend to Johnny Burke's daughter, so it wouldn't surprise me if she tries to bring Burke into things."

"He may end up needing a lawyer," Tony said. "Depending on what we find. Something about this story doesn't add up."

"Tell me about it," Susanna had muttered.

But they were being cooperative, mother and son, and Mrs. Shelton didn't call Johnny Burke or her husband. "My husband would complicate this," she'd told Tony, tucking a lock of blond hair behind her ear decisively. "He'd mean well, but he'd complicate it. I'm sure that time is of the essence."

"It is," Tony said.

"Let's go, then," she told him.

Pendleton met them on Hill Street with Sharon and the dog. Tony made hasty introductions, and Sharon shook hands with Christopher's mother.

"Sharon," Tony said, "this is Christopher. He's going to show us where he last saw Emily."

Sharon hunched down a bit, smiling warmly, and offered him her hand. He grasped it hesitantly. "Hi, Christopher," she said.

"Hey," he replied hoarsely.

"This is Maggie. Do you like dogs?"

481

He nodded.

"You can pet her," Sharon said.

He stroked the dog's glossy head, and a smile twitched at the corners of his mouth.

Sharon swapped the dog's leash for the long lead she'd used the previous night — or this morning, Tony thought, correcting himself. She looked nearly as tired as he felt, but at least she'd gotten a few hours' sleep and a decent breakfast. Tony had been up for almost thirty hours, and the only thing he'd put on his stomach since yesterday's lunch was a honey bun from the vending machine in the police station and lots and lots of coffee. He had not lain down, had barely sat — he worried that if he relaxed for even a few moments he'd lose whatever momentum was propelling him on and just fall over on the spot. Until Susanna's call forty-five minutes ago, he had been on the brink of despair. The overnight search parties had turned up nothing, and the bigger group that gathered at sunrise wasn't having better luck. With every passing moment it was less and less likely that they'd find the girl alive, and the weather last night had them all nervous. Though the bit of snow that fell was already melted from everything but the deepest recesses of shadow, a bone-chilling damp lingered.

"It's best if we keep the group small to keep Maggie focused," Sharon said. "Mom, you'll want to stay up here with one of the officers. Gentlemen" — she looked from Tony to Pendleton — "who wants to join me?"

Tony crooked an eyebrow at Pendleton. "You said you wanted to see Maggie do her thing."

He shook his head. "This is your lead, Tony. You better see it through."

There wasn't time for him to argue. "All right," he said. He had to admit to himself he was glad. He didn't think there was a connection between Emily's disappearance and Ronnie Eastman's, despite the fact that Emily lived in the same subdivision as Wyatt, but Christopher's story was enough to ignite his curiosity on that front. And Pendleton was right: he had to see it through.

He suddenly remembered something Pendleton had told him last night: *She'd been walking a dog for a neighbor, some guy who'd been sick.*

Was that guy Wyatt? What on earth did it mean if it was?

Tony turned to Sharon. "Let's go. Christopher, you lead the way."

They proceeded downhill, Christopher up

483

front, Sharon and Maggie behind him, Tony taking up the rear. The ground was sodden with a layer of wet leaves, and Tony hoped that Sharon was right when she said "wetter is better" — they were going to be slogging through plenty of it.

Christopher halted and looked around. "There's the dump. We went around it and over the hill."

"We're right behind you," Sharon said encouragingly.

When they topped the rise, Christopher pointed. His breathing was rapid and shallow, and he reached up to open the collar of his coat as if he were hot. "There. Under that dead tree. That's where I pushed her down."

Tony put his hand on the boy's shoulder. "I want you to stop here, Christopher. If Maggie picks up the scent and we take off, go on back to the road and wait with your mother. Will you do that?"

Christopher nodded, and Tony thought the boy looked relieved.

Tony and Sharon made their approach. "Watch your step," she said. "If Maggie catches this, she's not going to waste any time, and it's easy to lose your footing. You much of a runner?"

"Used to be," Tony said.

"Get ready." She shrugged out of her backpack and unzipped it, removing the plastic bag with Emily's T-shirt in it. "I have a feeling about this one. Sometimes I think I've trained my own sniffer." She pulled a piece of gauze from the bag and held it under Maggie's nose. Maggie, already quivering with excitement, lifted her head and bayed, a sound that sent a shiver down Tony's spine. Maybe he was just suggestible, but this time felt different to him, too. It was like all of those moments at bat, when he had known before the pitcher even wound up what the throw would be and the kind of contact he'd make with the ball. He had learned then, and somehow forgotten in the intervening years, that there were times when skill turned into something else. Instinct. Precognition. It was as close as he'd ever gotten in his life to a spiritual experience.

Sharon unwound the lead from her arm and dropped the slack. "Maggie," she said. The dog was tense, fairly pulsing with energy and desire. "Ready. Find."

The dog put her nose to the ground. She circled, head bobbing, backtracked, circled some more, jowls and ears swinging. Her long tail arced above her hide like a question mark, and her heavy paws fell. There was a noble rhythm to her gait, and when she lifted her head and bayed again Tony felt himself nodding, as if he were agreeing or encouraging her. The ground where she was sniffing was visibly disturbed, the surface of the earth turned instead of worn flat. Tony had had just enough time to notice this when Maggie shot forward and raced deeper into the woods.

"Go on back, Christopher!" Tony called without turning around. He had barely started after Sharon when his toe snagged a root and he stumbled, nearly falling. His face and shins popped with heat as he caught himself, and then he was on the move again, darting his eyes between the way ahead and the ground below. He ducked under a branch and caught up to Sharon, who was groaning with frustration; Maggie had somehow wound her lead around a small trash tree, and she was trying as rapidly as she could to pull it free.

"Can you let her off leash?" Tony said breathlessly.

"I don't trust that I could keep up with her," Sharon said.

Tony lost any sense of time. His weariness from before was gone, and the muscles in his legs felt warm and easy; he ran like he hadn't run in years, springing over fallen logs and a tiny stream, breath coursing in and out steadily, though there had been days lately when he wheezed going into a second flight of steps. The three of them were a locomotive of rapid breath and purpose, moving deeper and deeper into the woods, so that Tony began to wonder if Emily hadn't perhaps cut through and emerged over at Grant Road, where all of those skeletons of houses stood half-erected, or even to the bypass to hitchhike. For a dark second he imagined reaching another road, another dead end to the scent trail, and he shook the thought away.

Then the dog was baying again and prancing in place, and Sharon was pulling her back, saying "Good girl" over and over, and Tony looked down and saw, with equal parts joy and terror, the comma-shaped figure of a person. "Good girl" Sharon was saying, digging around in her bag for treats, and Tony dropped to his knees and put his ear to the girl's lips. He couldn't hear anything over the dog's triumphant wail and Sharon's cheerful reassurances, and so he plugged a finger into his left ear and also grabbed the girl's wrist with his free hand, pressing his fingers so hard between the tendons that she would bruise there, if she lived. There may have been breath — he was panting too hard to say. But beneath the pads of his middle and ring fingers he felt a surge; and then, long enough apart that he registered waiting for it, another. "She's alive," Tony said, and Sharon, hugging Maggie around the neck, started to cry.

"Oh, thank God," she said. "Thank God."

The girl was filthy. Her bare hands were covered in soil, and dirt was streaked across her face, too; a sooty mark, like a thumbprint, smudged her lower lip. He touched her face and winced at how cold it was, then ran his hands along her arms and legs, trying to feel for moved bones. "I think she just lay down here," he said, more to himself than to Sharon. "I think it's best if I just carry her back. It'll save time."

"Sure it's safe to move her?"

"Think so," he said. He balanced his weight over his hips and his hips over his knees, then leaned down to put the girl's left arm around his neck. His right side was stronger, and so he slipped his left arm under her knees, then shifted her toward him a little, gritting his teeth against a little sting of protest in his scar. *Please don't let me drop this child,* he thought. *Please don't let me blow my back out between here and the road.*

"Tony," Sharon said.

"Just a minute," he grunted. There was a smell on the girl, an awful smell, and he pinched his lips shut against it. How much did she weigh? He had been imagining a child all this time, though his memories of eighth grade, of girls who were taller than him, of snapping bra straps when the teacher wasn't paying attention, should have prepared him to expect a woman's body. He hefted her gently, testing. One thirty, at least. Would have been nothing back in the day — he remembered carrying Stefany to the bedroom, swinging her around playfully, tossing her onto the mattress.

"Tony," Sharon said again, and he didn't even bother replying this time. He had as good a hold on Emily as he'd ever have, and so he set his back straight, bit his bottom lip, and tried to unfold his knees. There was the pain he'd been eluding all morning; it clawed his lower back, making tears spring to his eyes.

"Darn it, Tony, I'm sorry, but you're going to want to look at this," Sharon said as he finally lifted to full height and locked his knees. He was sweating, and he was thinking that he might have to get Sharon to help him with Emily, little as he wanted to admit it, when he saw the woman's face, the horrified confusion on it, and let his gaze follow the line of hers.

Maggie was pulling frantically on the end of her lead, but Sharon was holding her back, first with steady pressure, as if playing a tug-of-war, then with exasperation, yanking the leash shorter and shorter in harsh, arm-length increments. "Back," she said sharply. "Down, Maggie. Back." The dog's panting took on a strangled, raspy sound as she strained against her harness, digging her toenails into the soil for purchase, and then Tony saw what she was trying to get at.

There was a ragged hole in the ground about ten feet away. Emerging from it was what looked to Tony in the gray daylight like a plastic garbage bag. It was stuffed full to bulging, the surface marred by a small dot of white.

"What is it?" he said.

Sharon looked at him unblinkingly.

He couldn't put Emily down — he would never be able to lift her again. But he took an unsteady step forward, then another, then another, wanting to go only as far as necessary to bring that dot into focus. Then it happened. He stopped, squinted, closed his eyes. When he opened them it was still there.

The dot was the tip of a finger. It had

pushed through a strained spot in the plastic bag: the sharp edge of a long fingernail, too thick and brightly peach to be anything but artificial. It seemed to be pointing at Tony, and he nearly dropped Emily in his desperation to back away from it.

Maggie lifted her head and bayed again.

2.

He put on a brave face for the ambulance tech, who kept asking about his back, and gulped down a single Darvocet as soon as he'd seen Emily off. He might as well have spit in the ocean, but the next hours were critical, and he couldn't fuck this up.

"We need to call in the state police," he told Pendleton. Another officer had arrived to drive Christopher and his mother to the middle school and Sharon and Maggie back to the Best Western, and so they were alone on the side of the road, trying to ignore the conspicuously slow crawl of passing cars. "We don't have the resources to process the scene down there."

"You think it's Ronnie?"

"I don't know who else it could be," Tony said. He was sweating with the pain now.

Pendleton waved a car by irritably. "What in the hell was that girl doing down there? I mean, shit." He shook his head, obviously not wanting to say what he was thinking.

"Maybe it was coincidence," Tony said.

"Ain't no such thing."

Tony lifted his hands and looked at them. He could still smell the rotten stench that had clouded the girl, which was now on him, and he rubbed his tongue roughly across the roof of his mouth to keep from retching.

There was no time to rest, barely time to think. While they waited for the first state officer to arrive, Pendleton's wife came by with a bag of hamburgers from McDonald's, and so Tony and Pendleton sat in Tony's car with the heat running and had a fast and awkward meal. Tony had left his appetite behind in the woods, but he chewed the food as if it were medicine, knowing that if he took another Darvocet on his empty stomach he'd not be able to keep it down.

Pendleton put away two of the burgers, then offered the last to Tony, who shook his head. "I can't have this shit in front of me," Pendleton said apologetically, wadding up the bag with the leftover burger in it and throwing it quickly into the backseat. He stuck a cigarette in his mouth immediately. "I don't know why she buys that junk. She just don't think."

"It was nice of her to come by," Tony said.

He slurped the big cola she'd brought him, enjoying that more than he had the food. He didn't drink soda much, and it always came as a shock to him — so sweet, so much bite from the carbonation. He felt a surge of energy, which he knew would be short-lived, and was glad when the brown state car arrived and pulled off on the shoulder ahead of him. Maybe the sugar rush would last long enough to get him back down to the body, long enough for him to hand the case over and work on a way to tell Susanna the thing he suspected, which was the thing she must have already known was true, somewhere deep down: that Ronnie was never coming home.

It was almost five o'clock before he finally begged off. The forensic team had arrived from Madisonville, Pendleton had gone back to the station to file a report, and Tony had told Lieutenant Brice most of what he knew about the remains and the chain of events that had led him to them. He showed him the location of the body and where Emily had been found in relation to it, and he helped Brice string up yellow warning tape in a perimeter around the scene. On their way back through the woods to Hill Street, Tony had to stop for a moment and catch his breath. It was embarrassing, all the more because the lieutenant was probably at least a couple of years younger than him, tow haired and toothy — he looked like the high school quarterback. Tony didn't want to hand this case over to him, even though he knew it was the right thing to do, maybe the only thing. He was so tired that it had become an effort just to string words together. But he'd done some good work today, damned good work — the kind of work that might make a difference a few years from now, when Sheriff Coe finally retired — and he didn't want someone else getting credit for it.

"You all right, Tony?" Brice asked.

"I'm fine," he said roughly, then regretted it. He hadn't sounded strong or in charge; he'd sounded defensive, desperate. "I'm sorry. I haven't slept since getting up yesterday morning."

"Well, you've earned some rest. Go on home for the night. We'll catch you up tomorrow."

They resumed their walk. Tony felt as if he were wearing cement boots; every step required effort and thought.

At the road, Brice smiled and shook Tony's hand. "Thanks for all your efforts, Mr. Joyce. I'm looking forward to talking with you more in the morning."

"Likewise," Tony said. "I'll be at the station no later than seven o'clock."

"Eh, make it nine o'clock. We won't have any lab results before then, anyway." He waved to another officer, who was waiting at a second state car. "Wanda, we're ready down there. Grab the camera."

She popped the trunk and started shouldering equipment. Tony found himself staring at her in a dazed way.

"See you, Tony," Brice said pointedly.

He nodded. He got it.

In his car, he found some old fast-food napkins in his glove compartment and mopped his face dry, then gulped down the watery dregs of his soda from lunch. Tired as he was, he couldn't yet go home and sleep — not until he'd talked to Susanna. But how could he say this to her? And what could he even tell her at this point? He wanted to offer her something, anything, as consolation, but he didn't want to be premature, and he didn't want to compromise the investigation at such a critical juncture.

His car was already pointed north, so he started it and went ahead and drifted downhill, not even having to apply the gas, into Wyatt's subdivision. There was an unrest in him, a ticklish sense of elements beyond his control. All his life he'd had a habit of sinking into sudden gloom over things that he couldn't at first remember, or hadn't even yet realized. He'd be moving through a day, fine, and then suddenly he'd feel an acute wrongness, and all he could do was work on tracing its source. What had he just been thinking? What had he seen to provoke it? More often than not, the gloom's root was trivial, and the cure was just to remember it: a bill he'd dreaded paying, some minor annoyance in a conversation with one of his colleagues. Nothing worth being upset over. Sometimes, the source was more of a tangled knot, an accumulation of details that eventually sent warnings up to his conscious brain. These moods always lasted longer, weeks and even months, and the realizations they signaled were harder to accept. Like the end to his relationship with Stefany. Or his decision to come back to Roma to keep an eye on his parents, because he simply understood one day that his dad's health was on a steady decline, that it would be a moral failing for him not to take care of them when their time of need came.

What he was feeling now — this tickle — was similar but not the same. It was like doing a long-division problem, getting to the end, and realizing that you must have made some trifling error along the way. So he wasn't surprised, exactly, when he pulled past Wyatt's house and saw what he saw.

Wyatt's truck wasn't in the driveway.

"Damn it," Tony muttered. He idled in front of the house, wondering if he should call Brice. But what could they do without an indictment? Wyatt was probably just out on an errand. He'd run out of groceries. He was going stir-crazy and needed a few minutes outside. He was a fifty-five-year-old man recovering from a major heart attack, living on a factory worker's salary. Tony was pretty sure he didn't have the health or the resources to make a break for it.

Tony, in the meantime, still had Susanna to talk to and two nights' sleep to catch up on. He decided that Wyatt could wait until morning.

CHAPTER TWENTY-NINE

1.

Wyatt wasn't at the grocery store or running an errand. He wasn't out for a drive. He was, in fact, parked in the middle of the employee lot at Price Electric. His hands, still bruised red and black from the IV, were folded neatly in his lap, and his eyes were fixed on the entrance used by the factory's laboring class: the men and women who funneled through that door each morning, tiredly punching their cards, buffing the concrete floors to a shine with their shuffling steel-toed boots; the same men and women who funneled back out eight and a half hours later, talking, lighting cigarettes, their eyes dimly lit, too, with the relief of another day passed. For almost forty years Wyatt had been one of them. It was strange, sitting here, trying to make sense of the passage of time. He had never stopped to consider it. He had never parked in this lot and not gone immediately into the building, which was a low, sprawling series of metal-sided boxes abutting a brick-clad front office. A corner was marked off with chain-link fencing; behind the fence, half a dozen men smoked and wandered back and forth, looking like prisoners getting their ten minutes of sunlight.

No, he'd never sat here like this, contemplating the place where he had spent most of his adult life. What a waste it was. You worked to live and lived to work. Price Electric had put sausage in his skillet and gas in his truck tank, but the fuel kept bringing him back here, to toil under the buzzing fluorescent lights, alongside men whose language he didn't speak and boys who didn't respect him. He came in wishing the day over. He went home dreading five A.M., when his body, whether he wanted it to or not, would jolt suddenly to wakefulness. And yet now, as he imagined that he was looking at the factory for the last time, that he would never enter that front door again and punch his card, he felt lost.

He'd had a bad night — tossing and turning, the bed hard beneath him, Boss getting up and down, up and down, whining about some kind of disturbance outside. Wyatt had finally risen, crept to the living room, and parted the curtains of the picture window. He hadn't been able to make sense of what he was seeing: a pack of men, perhaps half a dozen, walking along the street and shining flashlights at the homes on both sides of the road. As he watched, the men with the flashlights passed, and the street grew calm once more. He had returned to his bed and drawn the covers over his head, like a child afraid of monsters. At some point he slipped into a half sleep, a kind of anguished limbo in which the men with the flashlights kept coming back, he kept watching them approach, and then his conscious mind interceded just enough to remind him that they'd passed his door.

He spent most of the next morning trying to work up the courage to call Sarah and ask her why she had not come over as she'd promised. Her silence told him everything he needed to know — and yet, he wanted to hear her voice again. He thought that if he could speak to her, if he could tell her how much he needed her, she would at least let him explain his side of things. There was a story he had started to tell himself, a story that he was starting to believe. In it, the woman at Nancy's, the one who'd helped pay his tab and given him the ride back to Roma, had admitted to him how unhappy she was. She hated her job, the sameness of it, the thanklessness. She hated her rental house. She hated the boyfriend she'd gotten into an argument with. *I've had a rough night,* she had said. *Hell, I've had a rough life.* In this story, she dropped him off at home, thanked him for the company, and told him that she'd finally had it — that she'd fantasized more than once about just getting on the road and driving and driving, leaving and never returning. He hadn't believed her at the time. It was just one of those things people said to each other in the dead of night, when they'd been drinking and confiding in one another. But, looking back, there was something in her eyes. Determination. Recklessness. A part of his mind snagged on the fact of her car, but in the story, the story that he was telling himself, he navigated around the inconsistency the way the mind moves through inconsistencies in a dream, always improvising, accommodating, until enough of them pile up that the sleeper is forced to awaken. In the story, she drove off perched on her seat cushion, hand making little waves on the air rushing through her window, and she found happiness somewhere that wasn't here. The story was for him as much as it was for Sarah, or the police. He needed it to be true. He couldn't be the man he thought he was if it wasn't.

At last he pulled the telephone book out of a drawer on the phone table, flipped to the number for the hospital, and dialed. He still rented a rotary phone from South Central Bell, had never seen the point in replacing it, and so each number took time; he had the length of those zeros and eights to listen to the tick of the dial as it rotated back into place, to wonder if he was doing the right thing. At last the other line started to ring, and an efficient female voice greeted him: "Roma Memorial, how may I direct your call?"

"The nurses' station, please," he said. His throat was so dry it came out as a whisper, and so he coughed and repeated himself, then added, "I need to talk to Sarah Baldwin."

"Please hold."

An automated voice picked up midsentence: "— choosing Roma Memorial, a proud member of the Tri-Health family of hospitals. At Roma Memorial, we understand that patient care means —"

Her voice cut in so abruptly that he nearly dropped the phone. "Sarah speaking."

He opened his mouth but couldn't produce a sound. His face crumpled, and he knuckled tears away as silently as he could.

"Hello?"

Those few words — *Sarah speaking. Hello?* — how they made him ache. He could hear in them her strength and smarts, her kindness and sensibility. Her head was on his chest, and he could feel the movement of her jaw as she spoke. Her head was on his shoulder, breath hitting his neck as they danced. He wanted her — but he wanted to do the right thing, too. Was it right to love her, to demand love from her in return? Had it been right to let things progress this far?

"Wyatt?" The quiver in her voice was unmistakable.

"Yes," he said, the word coming from the back of his throat, choked by the swell in his sinuses.

"I can't do this." She was speaking lowly but with intensity, and he guessed that there was someone else in the room with her. "I'm so sorry. I want nothing but the best for you. But if you care about me at all, you'll leave me be. I can't get dragged into this. I'm sorry."

"Sarah —" he started. If only she'd let him explain, but his mouth was stupid and numb, and he couldn't figure out where to begin. *I didn't. I wouldn't.*

There was a click. After a moment, the dial tone sounded.

He had barely placed the receiver back in its cradle when the phone rang in his hand, and his chest swelled up painfully with hope. He snatched it back to his ear. "Yes, hello?"

"May I speak to Wyatt Powell, please?" The voice was smoothly southern, male.

He said, out of reflex, "This is Wyatt."

"Wyatt, my name is Johnny Burke," the man said. The name registered with Wyatt as vaguely familiar, but he couldn't place it. "I hope you'll forgive this intrusion on your time. I understand you're not in your best health right at the moment."

"If you're selling something, I'm not interested," Wyatt said.

Johnny Burke laughed. "No, I'm not selling anything. Please don't hang up. I have a very serious matter to discuss with you."

Wyatt wasn't sure why he kept listening. There was something slick and false about the way the man talked, and it reminded Wyatt of every car salesman he'd ever haggled with. But the name tickled him like an itch that needed scratching, so he hesitated. "What is it?"

"I'm a lawyer in town, Wyatt. I have an

office on the square — you've probably seen it?"

"By the bank?" He thought he remembered now: the old two-story storefront with the hanging wooden sign that creaked when a strong breeze hit it.

"That's right, Wyatt. That's it, indeed. Now, I'm going to say what follows as delicately as I can, and I want you to remember when I say it that I'm on your side. Can you do that, Wyatt?"

He was too confused to even brace himself. "What? What is it?"

"First, I'm going to tell you the most serious thing. I tell you this so you'll pay attention when I say the rest of it."

Wyatt was going to punch a hole in the wall if this guy didn't make his point. "What?"

"I have it on excellent authority that the police found a body out in the woods off Hill Street. Well, let me rephrase that. I'm being a bit too delicate. I have it on excellent authority that the police found bits and pieces of a body out in the woods off Hill Street. These earthly remains were, in fact, divided among three different Hefty bags and left in a hole to rot. Does that sound about right?"

Wyatt flushed with heat. *Nothing,* he

thought. *It was all for nothing.* Finally, he muttered, "I — I have no idea what you're talking about."

"Good!" Johnny Burke said. "That's good. I hoped you didn't."

"I'm hanging up now," Wyatt said, but he held on to the phone.

"I wish you wouldn't. I started with the worst news, but I promised you something else. Will you listen to it?"

He sat very still, breathing raggedly into the phone.

"You there? It sounds like you're there. So here I go, Wyatt. Here's my spiel. I hope if you find yourself in need of the services of an attorney sometime in the future, you'll consider me for the job. I'm very good at what I do. I think you'll find that I'm just the man you want on your side in a difficult time."

"I don't have any money for a lawyer," Wyatt said.

"Don't you worry about that. Each according to his ability and needs, that's my motto. If you believe in the justice system, you believe that a man's entitled to a good defense, and that's what I'm offering you, Mr. Powell. If there are particulars to work out, we'll work them out later."

Wyatt looked at Boss stretched out on the

floor across the room and remembered how it had been not so long ago, him on the couch, Boss lying down beside him so that Wyatt could rest his hand on the dog's warm side. It occurred to him for the first time that maybe the dog didn't avoid him now for what it smelled on him or sensed about him, because he didn't think that a dog knew that much about a person. Not really. Maybe Boss avoided him because Wyatt came home that night a different person than the one who'd left, and this new Wyatt had done a piss-poor job of taking care of him. Of treating him like he was loved.

"I don't know what you're talking about," Wyatt said again.

"That's OK," Johnny Burke said. "That's quite all right. Just holler if you need me. The number's in the phone book."

Wyatt put his finger on the hook switch, then replaced the handset before he could hear the dial tone sound.

He told himself the story again, the story of that night with the nice woman from Nancy's. That woman, so filled up with sadness and anger, who had needed a friend that night as much as Wyatt had needed one. He told himself again about how she dropped him off and what she said: *I've*

finally had it with Roma. I might just get on that road out of town and never come back. And how he hadn't believed her, but he believed it now, and perhaps she was finally happy wherever she was, or getting to wherever she was going, perhaps she was —
— *divided among three different Hefty bags and left in a hole to rot.*

That was when he had risen and gone to the kitchen. He refilled the dog's water dish to the brim, dumped out a big scoopful of Ol' Roy. There was some sausage left in the refrigerator, gray but not yet stinking, and he unpeeled what was left of the tube into the cast-iron skillet, set the burner to high, and broke the meat up with a fork until it was cooked through and the grease was smoking. He added all of this to Boss's kibble, and the dog, bribed, allowed Wyatt to stroke his back as he ate. He felt for a moment almost happy, almost like himself. His eyes watered with the tang of red pepper. Then he opened the back door and let Boss out to do his business. It had only been a couple of hours since the last time, so the dog wandered a bit, circled, urinated on a fallen branch. Finally he stood staring at Wyatt, as if waiting for another instruction.

"Are you coming back inside?" Wyatt

508

asked. He was huddled in the doorway, arms crossed for warmth.

The dog backed down on his haunches and stretched his forepaws out.

"That's all right, then," he had said, retreating to the kitchen. He let the storm door slam, gazing lovingly through it at his dog: the drooping, mournful eyes, the rust-colored fur that had been, in Boss's prime, brilliant as satin. "That's OK. You can be wherever you want."

2.

A horn sounded, signaling shift change. Wyatt shook himself alert, started his truck, and fixed his gaze on a red Dodge Ram pickup near the door. Its owner had parked it, as always, so that it took up two spaces instead of one.

He'd gotten cold with the engine off, and the cold had made him sleepy. He rubbed his hands briskly across his face and turned up the sound on the radio. The station was still set to AM WRKY, and it sounded like he'd caught the second half of *Open Air* with Spencer Downs, the part where people could call in to request or advertise an item for sale.

"I was hunting through my basement for some old pictures, and I came across a box

of postcards of my father's. These are real pretty postcards from the war. Real pretty colors. I would say you could call them antiques. They have stamps from England, Germany, and Italy. You could say they're a real piece of history."

"That's a neat find, Mary Sue! What are you asking for them?"

"I'll take five dollars for the box."

The door opened, and the first shift started streaming out; There they all were: Morris and Jusef, Daniel Stone, Gene Lawson; Mitchell O'Leery, who came on just two years after Wyatt and had moved up long ago to shift manager; Becky Wilkinson, who was always sweet to him, and brought him peanut brittle in a tin each Christmas; Meg Stevens, who was not, and glowered at him every time he crossed the floor for a bathroom break, as though she were keeping notes on the minutes he spent away from his station. There was Enrique Ramirez, who let you call him Ricky and had taught him a few Spanish words. *"Pendejo,"* he would say, grinning, wagging his thumb at Mitchell as he passed, and Wyatt couldn't help but like him for it, though he clung to suspiciousness about Mexicans more generally. And Franklin Hardin, seventy-five and still not retired; he claimed that he'd keep going until he dropped, that he'd wring every thin dime he could out of Price Electric. "You'll be rolling me in and out of here in a wheelchair one of these days," he had told Wyatt more than once.

Wyatt felt a little left out, watching them. The best time of day was leaving. Everyone's mood improved; everyone was capable of kindness, or at least neutrality. Wyatt had never been asked to come home with Morris for supper or out to the VFW with Franklin, but he'd always been warmed by the thought of the people he knew in those places, gathered around tables with their children or clinking beer glasses with friends. Maybe it was sad, taking pleasure in imagining the happiness of others. But imagining it had been safer than seeking out happiness of his own.

At last Sam Austen emerged. He was always near the back of the pack because he never left Price in his work boots; he would go to the break room, change into cowboy boots, and then stop in the bathroom to fuss with his hair and reapply cologne. Everyone knew it, everyone snickered about it behind his back. No one ribbed him to his face. It amazed Wyatt that he had been — well, he might as well admit it to himself — scared of this boy. Intimidated by him. Worried about what Sam thought of him, worried what he might say in front of others. He remembered what Morris had told him on the day of his heart attack, after Sam and his gang had been teasing him by the vending machines: *They're not your friends. They're not good people . . . You don't want this guy and his buddies jumping you in the parking lot.* Wyatt laughed out loud. What a chill he'd felt! Even after Ronnie, after what he'd learned he was capable of, he had quaked at the thought of Sam confronting him, threatening to use his fists. Now, Sam was sidling up to Sue Petty, who had a plump little body but an achingly pretty face; he dropped his arm flirtatiously around her neck, letting the hand drift down just a bit too far so that his fingertips were within grazing distance of her right breast. Wyatt could see from here her flush of cautious pleasure and Sam's look of amused good cheer. This was the kind of girl, Wyatt thought, that Sam would flirt with for the sake of his own ego, talk into sleeping with him, and never once take out on a real date. She was too smart to fall for it, but she would — they all did. Sam was too charming, too suffused with life. He had a way of making his attention feel like a gift, and Wyatt knew that firsthand.

Sue twisted out of his embrace, beaming despite the no-nonsense set of her lips, and crossed her arms. Sam dropped his head to the right in an imitation of disappointment and wounded pride. He put his hands out, palms up: *Aw, come on. You're not busy, are you? It'll be fun. I promise.* That is what he'd said to Wyatt. Sue laughed and shook her head. He reached out and stroked her upper arm almost tenderly, and her chin drooped shyly, and then she was nodding. Wyatt's sigh was more like a hiss.

"I'm looking for a photograph of slaves picking cotton, somewhere right here in Wilke County. I'll know if you try to pass off somewhere else as here."

"That's awfully specific. What are you offering?"

"Depends on the picture, but upwards of ten dollars."

They split at her car, a Nissan Sentra. Sam, grinning, shoved his hands into his pockets and strutted toward his truck. Wyatt's heartbeat picked up a bit.

"Thanks for having me on, Spencer. I'm selling an '87 Ford Tempo with only sixty-five thousand miles on it. Automatic transmission, windows, shoulder straps — it practically drives itself. And if you call right now, we'll —"

"All right, all right. Mister, you know we don't

let dealerships on here. Sorry, listeners. This happens when you're your own producer. Just a reminder, folks, if you're a business owner, you can talk to the nice folks in WRMA's advertising office, and they'll fix you up at a reasonable price. OK, let's try this again. You're at the Swap Meet, caller, what are you swapping?"

Sam peeled out of his parking spot with a rev and a squeal, tooted his horn at Sue, who hadn't even started her car yet, and pulled into the line of exiting vehicles. He passed behind Wyatt, and Wyatt watched him in the rearview mirror. He didn't duck. He knew that Sam wouldn't notice him. When the truck had passed, Wyatt backed smoothly out of his spot, pulling into the line before anyone else could intercept, and followed.

CHAPTER THIRTY

1.

In fifth period, the bell signaling an address over the PA system sounded, and Wally Burton's nasal tones of reassurance echoed in classrooms across Roma Middle:

"Faculty, staff, and students, I'm pleased to be able to tell you that Emily Houchens has been found. She has been admitted at Roma Memorial Hospital for the night for observation, but she's expected to make a full recovery. I want to thank you all for your cooperation and sensitivity on this difficult day. We'll be distributing 'get well soon' cards in each of the classes for you to sign, so that Emily knows we're thinking of her. We will also follow through today and tomorrow with the new safety procedures, at least until we have more information from the police department."

Susanna exhaled shakily. She did not realize how tightly clenched she had been all afternoon until she relaxed, and an almost pleasant soreness crept into her neck and back.

The students were already whispering, analyzing, deconstructing. "She just did it for attention," Kristy McKenna said loudly to Tara Dunn, and Tara shrugged.

"Kristy," Susanna said. "Keep your thoughts to yourself. Show a little compassion."

Kristy's brows were furrowed, her lips puckered. She looked as if she'd taken Emily's reappearance as a personal affront, and Susanna realized that she was disappointed. Emily was more interesting to the eighth grade lost than found, and in being found she had stolen from them days of exciting speculation and breaks in routine. Yes, that was it, and many of the students seemed to share Kristy's attitude; the day passed, not with celebration or widespread relief, but with an air of deflation, all of the electric charge from the morning spent. The movie had been stopped midreel, the picnic rained on.

Susanna didn't know what to feel, exactly. She wanted to talk to Tony but understood why he hadn't come to her — he had plenty to worry about, getting Emily to the hospital and figuring out how and why she was lost in the first place, and it wasn't as if Susanna could slip out of her classes to have a conversation with him, anyway. She was glad, of course, that they had found Emily. More than glad. She was tenderhearted toward the girl. Emily was not, like Christopher, a natural writing talent with abundant style, but she was a hardworking student, one of the hardest working in the class, who read every story and poem and play with an earnestness that broke Susanna's heart. Susanna remembered being thirteen and feeling sometimes that the books she read were more real to her and more valuable than the life she lived. She had read the things she loved most, such as *Pride and Prejudice,* over and over and over, until she knew whole paragraphs by heart, and she remembered her affection for Elizabeth and her passion for Darcy, how desperately she wished them real, how cruel it seemed to her that they weren't. Emily was like that, lingering after class to talk to Susanna about characters, telling her what she thought would happen to them after the book's end, even speculating about how characters from entirely different works would relate to one another. She thought that Finny from *A Separate Peace* would be friends with Leslie from *Bridge to Terabithia,* because they were both leaders who didn't care what other people thought of them. She seemed to feel an almost profound connection with Jess from *Bridge to Terabithia,* and it wasn't hard to see why: he was the grade's poor kid, its outcast. It struck Susanna, as the students worked on a grammar quiz at the end of the period, that it was interesting, maybe not even coincidental, that Emily had drawn Christopher into the woods with her yesterday. Was Christopher not, like Leslie, a transplant from outside of the community? Didn't Leslie and Jess have to go into the woods together to find Terabithia, their kingdom away from the school's bullies and the pressures of their home lives?

But Emily had said something to Christopher about a body, Ronnie's body, and this was the fact Susanna's mind kept snagging on, the reason that her cheer over Emily's being found was qualified. He was almost certainly right that Emily had lied to him, that she had fixed on the body as a means for attracting his curiosity and making him notice her. Her cheeks warmed a bit with anger at the thought of Emily's manipulating him that way, and using Ronnie's disappearance to do it.

Dale was late picking her up after school let out. This was typical, and so she graded quizzes at her desk, checking the clock intermittently and watching the minute hand move to 3:45, 3:50, 4:00, ten after. They used separate cars during the band season, when Dale had to stay after most days of the week for practice, but the rest of the time they took his Blazer and he did the majority of the driving, since the campuses were only about a mile apart. Without fail, though, he got caught in some kind of conversation between the band room and the car and arrived making excuses or — worse — not even realizing he was half an hour late. This was partly just because he was a good teacher, and high school students, with their own cars to get them home, could keep him occupied past the bell in a way that middle school students generally could not. It was also because he was social, willing to make the effort with his colleagues Susanna so rarely made, and in that way he was perhaps doing them both a favor. His goodwill within the system made up for whatever Susanna cost them by being quiet and keeping to herself. Small-town administrators appreciated glad-handers, and Dale was a glad-hander.

But now it was almost four thirty, and that was unusual. When he stuck his head in her classroom door, she almost snapped her pencil in half.

"Susanna," he said. "I'm sorry. I know I'm late."

"Are you all right?"

"Yeah, I'm OK."

She started wearily packing her tote bag with the ungraded quizzes and her teacher's edition of the class reader. She didn't have the energy to be annoyed with him. "Well, that's good."

"Hey. Sit down for a sec, please."

She looked at him. "We have to go get Abby."

"Abby can wait a little while longer. Sit."

Susanna took a nearby student desk, just as she had that day — how long ago it seemed now — when Christopher Shelton's mother came in to complain about the open-response questions. Dale took the adjacent seat, long legs bumping up against the desktop.

She wondered for an instant if Dale knew about her and Tony, if he was about to tell her that he was going to leave her. A part of her yearned for this; another felt a first flutter of panic. Where would she live? How would a judge split custody of Abby? Her mother's words echoed: *If you're going to leave what you've got, you better know what you're getting.* This thing with Tony had developed so quickly, too quickly, but it forced a question she hadn't yet allowed herself to consider: What had she been waiting for? Even in the lowest depths of her unhappiness with Dale, she'd harbored a certainty: that this was the life she'd chosen, the commitment she'd made. Perhaps it wouldn't get better. Perhaps it would. And if there were too many days strung together when she felt she was living in silent contempt of her partner, of the father of her beloved child, what could be done about it? There were days, too, when she liked him well enough, when they enjoyed each other's company. Days when she registered the ways that their partnership had, if nothing else, simplified her life. She hadn't even missed the romance much — not until seeing Tony again and remembering how it had been to be her younger self. The joy of being love-struck. Of being rendered stupid with longing.

But Dale took her hand and looked at her earnestly, and she knew he wasn't leaving her.

"They found Emily Houchens over in the woods by Harper Hill."

"I know they did," Susanna said. "My student Christopher is the one who led them there."

He looked surprised at her knowledge, even a little ruffled by it. "What else have you heard?"

"Just what Wally Burton announced. That she's at the hospital for observation and should be all right. Why?"

"I drove over to Harper Hill after school to check things out."

"To check things out," she repeated. There was the annoyance — she wasn't too tired for it, after all.

He cleared his throat. "Yeah. There were state police cars parked on the side of the road, not just town cop cars. And there was a van that was marked 'KSP Forensic Labs.' That didn't make sense to me, because they'd found Emily, and by all accounts she's OK."

"Oh my God," Susanna said. She knew all at once what he was getting ready to say, and her breath started hitching.

Dale squeezed her hand. "Listen to me. I went home and made some calls. There's nothing definite yet, but the word is that they turned up a body when they were hunting for Emily. I didn't want you to hear it from anyone else first."

"Oh my God," Susanna repeated. This thing Dale had told her — it was too big for her to see or understand. It was like trying to look through a gap in the trees and make out the curvature of the earth.

The pressure of his hand increased, almost hurtful. "What do you want to do? We can take Abby to your mother's and go to the police station. We can call that detective, that Tony guy. We can go home and wait and trust that they'll tell us when they have something to tell us. What do you want to do?"

Susanna snatched her hand away. "Why are you pummeling me with questions? Why can't you give me a minute to think?"

"I'm just trying to help."

"Sure, you're trying to help. You didn't care about Ronnie. You told me that she'd probably just run off somewhere. Now you're suddenly interested . . . and concerned . . . and I'm just supposed to, what —" She stood, hanging her hip in the desk and hurting, probably bruising, her hipbone. "Damn it," she muttered, tears of pain springing to her eyes, and she rubbed furiously at the spot she'd hit.

"Susanna," Dale whispered, "there are still people in this building."

"I'm supposed to let you comfort me?" She felt utterly empty and sorrowful, and she realized as she asked the question that she meant it honestly. That it wasn't rhetorical, wasn't just a cheap shot.

He removed his glasses and rubbed his eyes, then covered his mouth, so that his thumb pressed up against his cheekbone and his nose rested on his forefinger. When he spoke, his voice was muffled. "I don't know. I want to comfort you. But I don't know how."

"You say, 'I'm sorry, Susanna.' You say, 'I'm sorry about Ronnie.' "

"I *am* sorry about Ronnie," he said fervently.

"But see, I don't believe you now," she said. "Not after you didn't believe me. And not after how you treated Ronnie when she was —" She couldn't bring herself to say the word. Not yet.

"Ronnie had problems. You and I both know it. And I'm not just talking about the drugs and the sleeping around. She was a user, Susanna. She used people. She used you and she used your mom, and I didn't like it, and I never will like it, no matter what." He had put his glasses back on, and his eyes were damp and magnified through the lenses. "But I'm not glad she's gone, and I'm not glad you're suffering, and I'm so sorry I didn't believe you. I am."

"She might have been a user," Susanna said, "but at least she wasn't a phony."

"You think I'm a phony?"

"I think we both are." She had been clutching her tote bag so tightly her fingers were numb. She relaxed them, drew the strap over her shoulder, then wiped her face as clean as she could with her shirtsleeve. "I want you to take me home so that I can get my car. Then I want you to get Abby and keep an eye on her until I can come back. If you really want to comfort me, that's the best way you can do it."

"OK," Dale said.

She went to him, put her hands on his cheeks, and kissed his lips — a slow, soft kiss. Then she put her forehead against his. The tears were spilling again, but she didn't move. "I'm sorry."

"I'm sorry, too," he said. Not understanding.

He drove her home, and she didn't kiss him again when she said good-bye. She just climbed out of his car and got into hers, thinking that this is what she had been waiting for: a conclusion so terrible that it eclipsed her everyday unhappiness — so terrible that it showed her the stupidity of thinking all this time that she had to live with it.

2.

Tony went to the door, took a deep breath, and knocked.

He had stopped at the Fill-Up on the way out of Wyatt's subdivision and purchased another soda, a package of cheese crackers, and a box of Vivarin. In his car, he ate the crackers, drank half the soda, and then took one Darvocet and two of the caffeine pills. Then he finished the soda. He got out of the car and walked briskly around the block, noting how the pain in his back gradually receded, so that each step stopped feeling like it was setting off a thunderbolt through his torso. He worried about the pills; he didn't want to get to Susanna's jingling and jangling. But the walk helped. It reminded him, in a way, of his Bluefield days of trying to guess that exact right moment in a night of partying to approach a girl. Too early, when his buzz wasn't quite buzzing, and he was stiff, flat. Too many drinks in and he was liable to slobber all over her. The trick had been drinking right up to that moment when he felt smooth and easy and right with the world, and then making his approach. Now the trick seemed to be walking until he'd worn the sharp edge off his nervous energy. He had walked a lot today, not to mention that first sprint through the woods that morning when Maggie was tracking. He could smell the musk of exhaustion and exertion on himself, and his skin was clammy under the weight of his long-sleeved shirt and wool jacket. He wished he had time to go home and shower before seeing Susanna, but he understood that it didn't really matter, considering the news he was delivering. That she wouldn't be noticing him much one way or the other.

There was the click of a turning deadbolt, and the knob rattled. Tony stood very straight and folded his hands in front of him. He had thought it possible, even likely, that her husband would be home, but he hadn't imagined Dale answering the door; nor had he once, forming this plan in his head, remembered Susanna's child. But here they both were, husband and daughter, Dale holding the girl on his hip, though she was big enough that her legs dangled almost to his knees, and the little girl narrowing her eyes at Tony with what seemed to him righteous distrust. She was unmistakably Susanna's: the same large eyes that were set just a bit too far apart, the same heart-shaped face and dwindling chin. Her brown hair was fine and limp and had been trimmed into a chin-length cap, and she was wearing thermal pajama pants that cuffed at the ankles and a stained T-shirt. He saw all of this in just a matter of seconds, but it felt to him like he couldn't take his eyes off her, this person who had been, until this moment, theoretical and therefore unimportant to him. You couldn't look at her without seeing evidence of love and effort and exasperation, a whole life behind the closed door of this house that he hadn't really thought about, even when he was turning that pink-skinned baby doll over on its stomach with his foot.

Dale shifted and bounced, scooting Abby higher up on his hip, and stuck out his free hand. "Detective Joyce. I thought you'd probably come."

"You did?"

Dale nodded. He took Abby by the armpits and lowered her to the floor. "Go play in the kitchen, Ab. I need to talk to this man for a minute."

"Can I go get an oatmeal pie?"

"Yeah, go to the kitchen and eat an oatmeal pie." He waved Tony over to the sofa. "Have a seat if you want. Susanna's not here. She's probably out looking for you, or maybe she went to her mother's. We heard about the body."

Tony shook his head with disbelief. "I'm so sorry. I came over as soon as I could."

"Is it her? For sure?"

"Not for sure," Tony said. "The lab is fingerprinting and comparing dental records tonight. There were a couple of clothing items in the bag, and we may need Susanna or her mother to come look at them tomorrow to see if they recognize them. But the lab tech told me that the state of —" He had been about to say *decomposition*. "The state of the body, given the condition we found it in, suggests it's been there no more than a few weeks. At the most. And that's consistent with when Ronnie went missing."

Dale, hunched forward in his chair so that his elbows were resting on his knees, rubbed his palms together and nodded. "Hey," he said suddenly, sitting upright. "She had a tattoo. Here." He pointed to the nape of his neck. "Just under the collar, so you couldn't see it unless she had a tank top on."

"Susanna put it in the missing-person report," Tony said. "A four-leaf clover, right?"

"Yeah." Dale's mouth contorted into a slanted smirk, and he sighed through his nostrils. "Yeah. Anyway, I thought it might be something to look for."

"Well, there's another thing." Tony hesitated. It seemed to him, in talking to Dale this way, that he was shrugging off some of his responsibility, ceding it to Susanna's husband. "The body was not . . ." Again, he searched for a word. "Intact."

"Intact?" Dale looked over his shoulder at the kitchen, but Abby was still out of view. "What does that mean?"

Tony lowered his voice to almost a whisper. "There were three garbage bags at the scene. I didn't get a close look — I couldn't. But it's bad."

"Dear Lord," Dale said.

Tony felt an immense, guilty relief at unburdening himself of that secret. You had to love the person who told you a thing like that, because otherwise you would come to hate him. He didn't want Susanna to hate him.

"I'll tell her," Dale said. He said it with force, as if to steel himself for the task, and Tony was struck by a wave of pity for him. He had known before the wrong of what he and Susanna had done, but he hadn't truly felt it. Perhaps Dale was all of what Susanna had implied about him — self-centered, insensitive, more worried about what people thought of him than his wife's feelings — but Tony didn't think he was a bad man. He plainly loved her. Who had he been to come into this man's own home and make a fool of him? If Tony had really wanted to be with Susanna, to love her, to take her away from this life, that would have been one thing. And maybe that was the story he had been telling himself these last few days. But he didn't love her, he realized. What he wanted was to find her sister's killer. For her, yes, and for Ronnie's spirit, if such a thing existed, but also for himself. Because maybe he wasn't through with all of those major league dreams, after all.

"I'm so sorry," Tony said.

"Don't be sorry for me," Dale said. "Be sorry for my wife."

They stood and walked together to the front door, then shook hands again. Tony could see the little girl peeking around the door frame and wondered how he must have appeared to her. Big, dark. Bringing with him an air of sorrow.

"I'll call tomorrow about having Susanna come by to identify those clothing items," Tony said. He thought for an instant of mentioning Wyatt, then stopped himself. He still had that paranoid, almost superstitious feeling from before, and he wondered if anything short of getting a search warrant tomorrow would rid him of it. He figured that he'd drive back by Wyatt's house again on his way home; if he wasn't there, Tony would perhaps try to find an inconspicuous parking spot and wait him out awhile, since he was still feeling a boost from the soda and caffeine pills. Seeing the truck in the drive wouldn't completely ease his mind, but it was a start.

CHAPTER THIRTY-ONE

1.

Sam Austen's Dodge Ram stopped at a red light, then pulled out to the right without signaling. Wyatt did the same.

"I got two boxfuls of boys' baby clothes, all of it in good condition. I've also got a crib with a good mattress and all the bedding, a stroller, and some other odds and ends. I'll sell it all for a hundred dollars, but I can negotiate on just the furniture, too."

"Sounds like a great deal, listeners. Amanda, are you sure you'll never need that stuff again?"

"Lord, I hope not!"

Wyatt had always liked the Swap Meet. He never called in and bought anything, and he'd sure as heck never tried selling, though it had crossed his mind a few times that he might fetch a few dollars for his mother's old serving ware, the stuff that had always seemed too impractical to him to actually use: the jade mixing bowl set, the sterling coffee urn, the crystal punch bowl with wispy little cups that hung from it on crystal hooks. He liked hearing what people wanted, what they were trying to get rid of. He liked imagining the dramas of their lives. Occasionally some desperate soul called in offering his television set or VCR, or something random and of little value such as a used vacuum cleaner, and you could tell in his voice that he needed cash, any he could get his hands on. These calls inspired in Wyatt a coarse curiosity. Maybe they were about to get turned out of their house, he'd think, and he'd feel more content with the home he was driving to. Maybe they were addicted to drugs or drink, and he'd send up a little prayer of gratitude that he'd never taken to an addiction himself, not even cigarettes.

He knew, in the way that everyone at Price knew, that Sam still lived with his father and mother at their farm out on 68–80 heading toward Hopkinsville. Russell Austen was a magistrate, and he was a district manager for Valu-Ville, the regional chain of grocery stores, so the house was practically a mansion by local standards: built new in the eighties, two stories, a kind of hybrid in style between a German timber

frame house and a horse barn. When Sam
turned left going out of the factory, Wyatt
knew he wasn't going home — or not yet,
at least. Wyatt, too, signaled left and followed him, not bothering to fall back and
try for inconspicuousness. His only object
was to keep Sam's truck in his sights, and
the consequences beyond that did not
concern him. He had wondered since leaving home today if he could trust this sudden steadiness, this acute sense of purpose
that had fallen on him after Johnny Burke's
phone call. If what had happened that night
after Nancy's proved anything, it was that
Wyatt didn't know himself, that maybe no
man knew himself, and so the emotions of
a moment were fragile, shifty, untrustworthy
things. You could only ride them as long as
they let you.

*"Let's get a couple more buyers on here
before we wrap up for the day. Call me at 726-
WRMA if there's something you want, and
who knows? Maybe one of our listeners will
have it. What do you want, listeners?"*

Left. Right. Right. The truck glided
through a stop sign, and Wyatt also glided,
unconcerned that his path might cross with
that of another unsuspecting driver, or that
a police officer parked just out of sight
would notice him. He was invisible. Un-

touchable. The truck sped up to sixty in a thirty-five, and Wyatt pressed down on his own gas. An almost sleepy calm had fallen over him. It was only four o'clock, but the sky was already getting gray, the sun low and distant and obscured by a haze of clouds. A single band of bright pink cut through them, visible in his mirrors. They were driving east now, back toward town. Sam had made a circle.

"It's me again, Spencer. I figured it couldn't hurt to try."

"Go ahead, Mrs. Miller. You never know."

"Well, I've been looking for a long time for a baby doll like I had as a little girl. My sister and I both had one, and we lost them when our daddy moved us to Kentucky in 1935. I've always missed that baby doll. It was a Kewpie doll with a ceramic head and a soft body, looked like it was wearing onesie pajamas. It had a hood on and a long tassel coming off the top, like a sleep cap. I have been looking for a baby doll like that all my life."

"Our regular listeners will know that Mrs. Miller has been calling in to Swap Meet for — how long is it?"

"Probably ten years."

"Ten years! So if you know of a doll like that Kewpie, call in. I'll take up a collection to pay for it if I have to."

"It's all I can think about now that my sister's passed. I'd really like to have that baby doll."

The Ram braked suddenly and whipped into the parking lot of an Advance Auto. Wyatt turned in, too, shifted to neutral, and set the key to "Accessories" so that the radio could still run. He'd heard Mrs. Miller many times, and he thought that she sounded like a good person. He sometimes went to the flea market on weekends — it was something to do — and he always looked at the dolls, hoping to see the Kewpie with the pajamas and the sleep cap, wishing that he could be the person to call in one day and tell her he'd found it, that he was making it a gift to her.

"I've never got over the loss of that doll. I miss it every day."

He waited, not wanting to emerge before Sam did. Finally, the door on the Ram opened and Sam stepped out, looking furious at first and then, recognizing Wyatt, perplexed. Finally, something else settled on his face. He was trying for amusement, for the same shit-eating grin he usually wore when he was teasing Wyatt, but there was a flicker of something else. Uneasiness. Perhaps even fear. Wyatt felt a surge of pleasure. He shut the radio off, pocketed his keys, and exited his truck cab. The lot was quiet, not secluded. There were two other cars, lights on in the building.

"Tubs," Sam said. "What the fuck do you think you're doing?"

2.

That night — the night that ruined everything — Wyatt had sat at the kitchen table in Ronnie's little house, eating from his paper basket of livers and gizzards methodically with both hands; every now and then he stopped to lick his fingers, hesitated, and wiped them on a napkin instead. Ronnie had gotten strangely quiet, all of her earlier playfulness dissipated, as if Wyatt had imagined it in the first place. *You brought me here,* Wyatt wanted to blurt out. *It was your idea.*

"I'm going to pay you back that money," he said for the third time. Maybe she was brooding over it. Maybe she hadn't had it to give.

"Hon, it's fine." Her voice was flat. She popped a liver into her mouth and chewed, her eyes fixed on some point behind and to the left of him. He craned his neck blearily, thinking she might have turned on a television, but saw nothing. Just the paneled wall of her living room, the back of the couch. An old clock hung on the wall, its pendulum swinging jauntily.

"Thanks for bringing me here." He had said this already, too.

She lit a cigarette and took a deep drag, her foot jogging a little under the table. He could feel the vibration through the soles of his shoes. "Yep. It's no problem."

He finished the basket and sat back. "Well, I'll probably regret that later."

"It's good for you," Ronnie said with what felt to Wyatt like forced cheer, like a last surge of perfunctory politeness from an otherwise rude DMV or fast-food employee, but even forced cheer was better than none at all. "Grease soaks up the alcohol."

He looked down at his empty container, embarrassed. He hadn't even been hungry, really — just nervous, unsure of what to do with himself. The salt and grease roiled in his stomach. He imagined it as a shiny slick on an ocean of beer.

Ronnie yawned pointedly, and Wyatt felt the motion of the clock's pendulum behind him. "You said you'd had a bad night," he said in a rush, hoping to restore that little pocket of intimacy from before. "What happened?"

"Nothing," she said. She crooked a shoulder. "A fight, sort of."

"With a friend? A boyfriend?"

"I smacked the closest thing I ever had to a boyfriend upside the head tonight." She blurted this out with forced bravado, daring Wyatt to chastise her. But he laughed stupidly, playing along.

"Smacked him, huh?"

Ronnie finally met his gaze. Her eyes, so wide and round, glittered within their dark frames of mascara. "Yeah," she said. "I did. Anyway," she added, blinking rapidly, "we'll probably make up. We always do."

Wyatt leaned forward a little, put his hand on the tabletop. It was a plump, almost feminine hand, even after all of those years he worked in the winding room, the bones delicate, the skin milky. He hated his hands, had always felt that they gave away his weakness the way some people were betrayed by blushes or nervous tics. No wonder he was pushing sixty and alone. No wonder those boys from work had known they could make a fool of him.

"Maybe that's not a man worth making up with," he said, the hand beached awkwardly between them. He tweezed a plastic Fill-Up bag between his index and middle fingers, as if that had been his intention all along. "What did he do? Cheat on you?"

"It wasn't like that," Ronnie said.

"Hit you? You don't want to be with a man

who hits."

Ronnie laughed. "Did you even hear my story? I hit *him.*"

"Whoever he is, he's a fool to piss off a beautiful woman like you," Wyatt said in a rush. "If you were mine I'd treat you right. I'd take care of you."

"I can take care of myself," Ronnie said. The corner of her mouth twisted a little.

There was a silence. Ronnie stumped out her cigarette, and Wyatt noticed it was only half-smoked.

"You getting tired, Wyatt? You look tired. Why don't you let me take you home." Her leg was jogging again, making her half-empty bottle of High Life rattle on the Formica tabletop, and Wyatt felt the first tremor of something other than shame and desperation, thinking again, *You brought me here,* wondering what kind of woman would invite a man home only to sneer at him, to show him to the door. What kind of woman would do that to a man on a night like this one, when she'd already witnessed his humiliation? He wondered suddenly if she was in on it, if the joke was still happening. He looked over his shoulder again, where she'd leveled so much of her gaze this night, and saw the old clock, marking off the remaining moments between them, and a picture window off to the side. Lace sheers hung down, obscuring his view of the driveway, and Wyatt imagined Sam and the rest out there waiting for him. Getting ready for one last laugh.

"I thought you said something about me taking the couch," Wyatt said.

"I did. But, you know, sometimes it's better in your own bed. More comfortable."

"Maybe you could show me your bed," he said. His voice was hoarse — he hardly recognized it. *It was your idea,* he thought, and then he found himself saying it aloud: "It was your idea."

"What did you say?" The expression on her face wavered between amusement and annoyance, not committing to either.

"Your bed," he said. "You could show me your bed." He added, almost wonderingly, "You brought me here," because that was the part that got him, the part that made him want to draw his smooth, weak hand into a fist, to make at least one part of himself hard and powerful and impervious to harm. He knew she would say no. He knew, though she had invited him into her home, that he had no claim on her body, her favors. He wasn't entitled to anything but her respect, he thought. And she owed him that. *Respect,* he lectured in his head, thinking of not just Ronnie but Sam, Gene, Daniel Stone, all of those guys. Thinking of Jusef, who would sometimes shove him to the side to get a pallet loaded, and Meg Stevens, glaring at him for taking a bathroom break, too young to understand the reality of a fifty-five-year-old prostate, too young to give a damn. *Respect. Not just because I've earned it. But because you owe it. Because I'm another goddamned human being, and I need it, and it don't cost you nothing to give it.*

"Old man," Ronnie said, "I'm not interested." She pulled a fresh cigarette from her pack, smiling around the filter. Lit, puffed. "I'm not even the least bit interested."

His face prickled with heat; it streaked across a wedge of his scalp like a grass fire. "You asked me here," he repeated. "You drove me here."

"Yeah," Ronnie says. "And now I'm asking you to go."

"And you'll drive me?"

"I would have." She pushed back her chair and stood. "But I think it might be best now for you to just hoof it. I need my sleep."

Wyatt was still sitting. His fingers extended a bit and grasped more of the plastic grocery sack that the food came in; there was a crackling as he worked the bag between his fingers and thumb.

"Wyatt," Ronnie said. "Do you hear me? Time to go."

"And you can't even give me a ride," Wyatt said. "I live on the other side of the hill, at least a couple of miles. And you can't even stand me long enough to get me there?"

In the quiet that followed Wyatt could hear his own breathing, the eerie speed of it. As if there were a third person in the room. He was panting like a dog.

"No," she told him, her voice softening a little, becoming almost tender. Pitying. "I couldn't stand you that long. I can't stand you another minute."

He swallowed against what felt like a knife blade, and when she leaned down to ash her new cigarette, his fist closed around the plastic sack. "You shut up," he said.

"Get out," she said. "I'm not kidding."

He squeezed the bag — it seemed to sigh, and then a little bubble within it burst like a popcorn kernel. His only thought when he felt himself moving toward her was that he would shut her up, that he wanted to know what her cruel, leering face would look like if he scared her, if he hurt her like she had hurt him. The beer and food sloshed in his belly, and his heart seemed to be rapping on his chest from the inside, protesting, but he grabbed her by the jaw and pushed her against the wall, and she managed to shriek once before he remembered the bag in his hand — it was there as if he'd known all along what he'd need it for — and then her cries became muffled, their grappling strangely quiet, so that Wyatt could hear the cartilage in her nose shifting under his palm, and what he would remember most, later, was the way the bag between her lips crackled, and then three high, sharp inhalations, and then the strangled sound of her gorge rising. Her long fake nails scrabbled against his shirt collar and sliced a painful line across the tender skin of his collarbone, and then, after a long while, the hands simply quivered against his chest, and she was sliding heavily into the floor. Then nothing.

When he emerged from the house thirty minutes later, her body slung over his shoulder, he remembered his sudden certainty that Sam and the guys would be waiting. They weren't, of course. No one was.

3.

"What are you doing?" Sam repeated.

Wyatt rubbed his chin. He hadn't shaved this morning, he'd forgotten to, and his whiskers rasped against his hand. "I'm just out for a drive," he told Sam, whose hands had drawn into loose fists at his sides.

"You're tailing my ass, is what you're doing. I didn't know what the hell was going on."

Wyatt appraised him silently.

"Aren't you supposed to be laid up?" Sam's eyes darted between Wyatt and the building. "That's what I heard."

"I've had a rough week."

"That's too bad," Sam said. "Folks have been asking about you."

"I hear," Wyatt said, "that you've been telling them all about me. That was real helpful of you."

Sam swallowed, looked at the Advance Auto again. He backed up a step. "I've got to go, Wyatt. I've got to meet a girl."

"You called me Wyatt."

"Well, that's your name, isn't it?"

Wyatt placed his hand on the lip of his truck bed. "I thought it was Tubs."

"That was a joke."

"You like jokes," Wyatt said. "You should have been a stand-up comedian."

Sam licked his lips and took a shaky breath. "You're giving me the creeps. And this ain't a good time for you to go around giving people the creeps, if you know what I mean. I'm just saying."

Wyatt grinned. "I'm sorry, Sam, but that's funny. I give you the creeps. I had no idea I had that power over you."

"You ain't got power over shit."

"Maybe I don't." Wyatt turned, leaned over the side of his truck bed, and inspected its contents. "But I have got absolutely nothing left to lose, either. You know that?" He grasped the handle of his shovel and pulled it out, enjoying the way Sam's lips parted at the sight of it.

"Put that thing down."

Wyatt dropped it, lifted his hands. "All right, then. Fight me fair."

"I'm not fighting nobody."

The calm had seeped away, but it had not been replaced by the old cowardice, nor was Wyatt feeling exactly what he'd felt that night with Ronnie, when his loneliness and humiliation had sparked something hidden and dormant within him, a thing that might never have awakened if not for Sam Austen. It was Sam's fault, all of it. He would never have been at Nancy's. He would never have been left behind. He would never have met Sarah, true, but he never would have lost her, either. He never would have taken that ride with Ronnie, and he never would have hoped for more than his quiet life of observing and imagining the pleasures of others.

"If only I had known then what I know now."

Sam narrowed his eyes. "And what's that?"

"What a chickenshit you are. Just a spoiled daddy's boy who won't ever get out of Roma and knows it."

"You want to shut up now, you fat bastard."

"Shut me up," Wyatt said.

He let him have the first swing and took it in the shoulder. It stung, and the muscle in his bicep went hot and loose, but he could tell already that Sam didn't know what he was doing. There was no force in it. No conviction. Sam was huffing a little and bobbing in place, his hands lifted up in defense. Wyatt could smell the acrid tang of Sam's sweat — it was sudden, ripe, rising up between them like steam from a sewer grate. Fear sweat, coming in on a wave of adrenaline. His armpits were all at once dark with it.

"You've got to do better than that, Rocky Balboa," Wyatt said.

"Shut the fuck up."

He jabbed at Wyatt again, aiming for his face, and Wyatt turned to the side, catching it just barely on the ear. More heat, a bit more pain — the punch was no better than the first, but it landed in a tender spot.

"Young guy like you, can't even hit me. You can't even hit this fat bastard worth a damn."

Sam struck again, catching him on the cheekbone. Harder, much more hurtful. An ache splintered out from his sinuses to his eyeball and eyetooth. It was clarifying, even invigorating, and it steadied his nerves to have this part of it over with, to be initiated into suffering, to at last know what he had been worrying about, this worst-case scenario. It wasn't so bad. He rocketed forward, barely aiming. The worst pain yet was the sensation of his hand connecting with Sam's nose — worse than anything Sam had subjected him to. There was the unmistakable sound of rupturing flesh, kind of a doughy pop, and the bones in his hand seemed to shift, as though he'd driven a spike between his knuckles.

Sam shrieked. "Son of a —" he started, and Wyatt hit him again in the mouth to stop his talk, sending another spike up through his hand and arm. Sam backed away from him, head down, hands on his face. A runner of blood was spilling down between his fingers and soaking into the gravel, and Sam stomped, making Wyatt think of that night at Nancy's, his little thigh-slapping boogie on the dance floor. He mumbled something, but it was muffled, guttural. Probably a curse.

Wyatt's hand was shot now. He picked up the shovel again.

"Hey! Hey, put that down!" The voice was from behind him.

Sam looked up. His eyes were bright and damp over his red fingertips, and they widened as Wyatt advanced. He held out a hand and shook his head, then turned to run, stumbling, gaining his feet. Wyatt swung the shovel head in a neat arc and clipped Sam right between the shoulder blades, knocking him forward. Sam landed on his palms and rolled over quickly, arms raised in defense.

"No, man, no! You can't do that! Shane, call 911!"

Wyatt brought the shovel down again, and it landed on one of Sam's knees, ringing cheerfully. The vibration went all the way up to Wyatt's shoulders. Sam screamed, and he curled up with his chin tucked down and his knees up to his chest, elbows hiding his face and forearms over his ears. Wyatt hadn't actually come here to kill him. To hurt him, yes, and to scare him, yes, and to make him pay — but not to kill him. But it seemed suddenly, as he pulled the shovel back again to swing, that Sam's life was worth half as much as Ronnie's had been, and so what did it matter? He let the shovel fall, and Sam howled. He swung it again. And again.

He was gasping, heart jackhammering, when he brought the shovel up a last time. He only had the strength for one more, and he wanted it to be a good one.

A familiar ache raced up his left arm, and his knees buckled. He seemed to fall backward and forward all at once and landed on his side, legs bent somehow beneath him, and he squeezed his eyes shut against a nauseating wave of pain so intense that the world went far away for an instant and a high tone sounded in his ears. He couldn't breathe. He tried rolling onto his back, was stopped by something, and so only turned his torso. He was able to take one very slow, very thin breath, and then groan the air just as slowly out.

What happened to him? Is he down? The voice seemed to be coming from across an empty ballroom. It was clear enough, but small, flat.

Looks like it.

Wyatt blinked several times but his vision didn't clear.

What about him?

Lord, I don't know. He beat him to a pulp.

Was he listening to the radio again? The program had gotten very strange.

Oh my God. Oh my God. We should have gotten out here sooner.

What on earth were we supposed to do? The guy's obviously crazy.

Oh my God. I think they're dying.

They were gray blurs above him.

He looks familiar.

4.

The night he moved the body, he had found a child's red glove. He tossed it unthinkingly into one of the garbage bags, assuming it had been there all along.

CHAPTER THIRTY-TWO

1.

On Main Street, Christopher Shelton's mother is making cocoa and trembling with relief that Emily Houchens has been found alive. There was a moment today, so brief that she can almost convince herself it didn't happen, when she wondered about her son, doubted him. Thought him capable of horrors. She whisks the chopped slivers of chocolate into the cream vigorously, stomach clenching at the thought of so much sweetness. But what else can she do? What more can she offer him? Chris retreated to the guesthouse as soon as they arrived home from the police station, and Nita doesn't know how to go to him without some kind of offering in hand. *I'm sorry, I'm sorry, I'm sorry,* she thinks, stirring, almost praying. Praying to her son. He is as distant as a star right now. She doesn't know what it would take to reach him.

At the police station, Sergeant Pendleton fills out a report on his typewriter, working with such slow concentration that the point of his tongue peeks from the corner of his mouth. He took a semester of typing back in high school, but he is better off using his index fingers — faster, more accurate. "I RESPONDED TO CALL AT APROXI-MATLY 7:10 PM AND WENT DI-RECTLY TO PARENTS HOME," he types, legs restless beneath his desktop. He is starting to feel pangs of nervousness about talking to Johnny Burke earlier — letting slip not just news of the body but also the name Tony had uncovered, Wyatt Powell. It was stupid, stupid (he jabs the return key angrily in time with his thoughts) — stupid! — to fall for Burke's little routine. How he came by, acting friendly, interested, asking Pendleton when he was going to let Johnny bring him to the country club as his guest, so they could play nine holes together. (It has never once happened. Always the jocular invitation, the phrasing that suggests Pendleton is holding out on him, when in fact Pendleton always said, "You know I'd love to come, Johnny. Just name the date." And Burke always replied, "Yes, yes. I'll call you about it. Just got to get your name down with the secretary out there first.") Then

Burke started asking questions, and he didn't even have to press Pendleton much — Pendleton just started spilling what he knew, loving the way Burke's eyes brightened with interest, thrilling each time he said something like "You don't say?" or "I'll be damned." It is just that Johnny Burke is such a big, important guy around here, was even interviewed on national TV once a couple of years ago, when CBS News came to town that time the Ku Klux Klan promised to riot at a Martin Luther King, Jr. Day parade. There is talk of his running for district judge next year. To be the friend of such a man — to get invited to the country club, or to Burke's fancy house on the outskirts of town — well, that would mean something. That could mean a whole lot. Especially if Pendleton hopes to be considered for police chief when Evan Harding finally retires.

Johnny Burke is, like Pendleton, a man of ambition — but his ambitions transcend small-town politics. Sure, he'd once set his sights on district judge. Had once thought a position like that mattered. But then CBS came down to Roma and put him on television, and he watched himself on the news that night, handsome and ruddy, his prematurely graying hair swept back pleasingly from his forehead, and he thought, That, *that is what I'm meant to do. That is the kind of life I ought to be leading. But how?*

Now, rocking gently in his leather office chair, watching through his window the procession of traffic around the square, he smiles a little, thinking of Wyatt Powell. He wasn't convinced of the man's guilt when he called — Pendleton isn't the sharpest knife in the drawer, and his eagerness to please sometimes moves him to exaggeration — but he is convinced now. The knowledge came to him, fully formed, in that too-long pause between Johnny's speech and Wyatt's denial: *I — I have no idea what you're talking about.* Scary, really, to think of a man like that living in your community, shopping at the same supermarket as your wife, maybe commuting to work on the road that runs past your daughter's school. He'd have to be a monster to not consider these facts. But still, every accused man is entitled to a defense, and Johnny Burke has no reservations about providing Wyatt Powell with one. This is the kind of case that comes to Roma once in a decade, maybe even less than that, and if Johnny can't prosecute it, he'll defend it. Simple as that.

While Johnny watches the square, his daughter watches the front door of her house. Her mother stepped out twenty minutes ago for groceries, and so she has perhaps half an hour — max — to make some more phone calls and try to find out the intel on Emily Houchens. She feels infuriatingly out of touch. She tried Christopher first — word had gotten around, even to the ALC trailer, that he'd left school today with a cop, shortly before Mr. Burton announced that Emily was found — but his mother answered his private line and told her, sharply, Leanna thinks, that Christopher was indisposed. "And you know he doesn't have any phone privileges this week," she added. Then Leanna tried Maggie and Anita. Maggie is in the same boat as she — friends only with the exclusive crowd that had been hidden away in supply closets all around Roma Middle — and knew nothing. Anita, to Leanna's constant mystification, has a pretty decent friend outside of their circle, a black girl named Lauren who is with her on the basketball team, but Anita isn't answering her phone. Could she call Lauren herself? Leanna pages through the phone book to the J's, chewing her lip. She can't remember Lauren's father's name, and there are, like, a hundred Johnsons. Where would she even start?

She racks her brain for names — someone, anyone. Chelsea Brodzinski? How many Brodzinskis can there be in this town? Just one, she sees, running her finger along the list of B's, and she gets ready to dial, then hesitates, thumb poised over the seven. Chelsea Buttinsky, she'd called her when she moved to town four years ago. They'd been at a birthday party together, Chelsea foisted onto the group of girls by a well-meaning parent, and Leanna hadn't been able to stop herself: *Buttinsky, Buttinsky,* she chanted, pulling Chelsea's braid as Chelsea tried to play Super Mario Bros. on Lily Peterson's brother's black-and-white TV. Chelsea's braid was thick and bumpy, because her hair was snarled with natural curls the circumference of a pinky finger, and Leanna was so repulsed by its oily texture that she'd pulled harder, observing with satisfaction how Chelsea only continued to silently play, tears rolling down her cheeks. She'd tired of this only when Lily's mother yelled "Pizza's here!" from the kitchen.

No, she probably shouldn't call Chelsea Buttinsky.

Back on Main Street, Christopher Shelton spins the dials on his foosball table. The cocoa his mother brought sits cooling by the door, untouched. Why is she always forcing that shit on him? It makes him sick to his stomach. He pops the ball halfheartedly with one of the players on the right-hand side of the table, stops it from scoring with his left-hand goalie. He likes the sound of the spinning rods, how something in them ticks when he rolls the handles off his palms. There is a hypnotic draw to this: standing, staring at the table, watching the ball move back and forth across the painted field. He lets his eyes blur, and the foos men double, triple. There is an army of foos men. He feels almost sleepy considering them, and so he closes his eyes, and then he opens them again, and then he goes to lie on his bed and closes them again.

He dreamed last night about that day at the tennis court, and in his dream he had suddenly realized that it was Emily, not Leanna, going down on him, and the feeling accompanying this realization was at first relief, and then fear. He recalls the dream now, punishing himself. What is he afraid of?

2.

Susanna drives straight to Harper Hill, but by the time she arrives, the van Dale mentioned — the one marked KSP FORENSIC

LABS — is gone. There is a single state police cruiser on the shoulder, and she thinks for a second of stopping, telling him who she is, demanding an answer. But some fear kicks in. Of authority? Perhaps. Or maybe just of getting confirmation. She won't be able to believe what a stranger on the side of the road tells her, no matter what kind of uniform he is wearing. She will only believe Tony.

She thinks then of going to her mother. She ought to. If the gossip mill came through for Dale on this one, it is only a matter of time before someone calls Susanna's mother. Better for Susanna to prepare her — to assure her that nothing yet is certain, no matter what people are whispering. That the police haven't even reached out to her. You can't know anything until the police tell you so, can you? If it weren't for Dale's nosiness, why, she'd still be in the same position she was in yesterday: wondering, yes, and worrying, certainly — but also hoping. Dale stole her hope, but that doesn't mean she has to steal her mother's.

She brakes suddenly and grips the steering wheel until she can feel the rubber parting beneath her fingernails. The sob seems to come from outside of her — or rather, she feels outside of herself, the sob lodged in the body she left behind. Had she hoped? Really?

Her thoughts race. She imagines leaning over a casket. Ronnie, her eyes closed, her small hands folded across her rib cage. Susanna wonders how she would dress her, what Ronnie would want. Not a dress — does her sister even own one? Susanna remembers a blouse, oddly prim and old-fashioned: cream-colored satin, a ruffle on the collar, a line of fabric-covered buttons along the cuffs of the sleeves. She wears it to wedding showers. She had worn it to a funeral. Always with trousers, mannish, shapeless black trousers that look almost comical with that exaggeratedly feminine blouse.

She was a user, Susanna. She used people.
Say it's Ronnie in the woods. Not a body in the hospital, the blood pressure monitor a sudden flat line, the arms snaked with IVs. Not a very old body, in bed, face slack with peace. Not a body behind the steering wheel of a wrecked car, like their father's body — a body too bruised and battered to display at the funeral but not so bad that they couldn't look at him privately, say their angry, grudging good-byes. No. Ronnie, in the woods. A found thing, a discarded thing.

There is a truth here, a terrible truth that Susanna wants to walk away from, leave buried, and it occurs to her that this is why she left home, left Dale. Not to find a cop and get answers. Not to tell her mother. So that she can hide from this truth awhile longer.

She can't go back. She can't go forward. Where does she go? The car isn't even in park; she has been holding the brake down with such force that she has to think to unlock her knee.

3.

Tony is just driving past Wyatt's, noting with a sinking stomach the still-empty driveway, when the radio crackles, then beeps: "Available units, we have a call at the Advance Auto on Sweetbriar. Please copy if you're in the area."

Tony waits. He is perhaps two miles from the Advance Auto, could be there in a minute with sirens running, but everything is close in Roma. He trusts that someone else can take it. Anyway, he isn't even supposed to be on duty right now — or is he? Maybe he has been on duty so long that his next shift has, technically, started.

"This is Eight oh eight, dispatch. I'm out by Wal-Mart."

"Eight oh four, dispatch. I'm at the Pantry on the bypass."

"Eight oh four, why don't you take it. You'll be meeting an ambulance. Situation appears to be assault and battery, two men involved, both down."

"Inside or outside the store?"

"Out in the parking lot, Eight oh four. Employees noticed the disturbance and came outside."

"Copy, dispatch. I'm on my way."

"Eight oh eight, stand by for backup."

Tony finds himself driving in the direction of Sweetbriar. It is more or less on his way, and his curiosity is piqued. He will take a look, make sure the situation is stable. Then he'll try Wyatt's again one more time before giving in and going home, to bed. He is so tired that he has to remind himself to care about all of this: his job, Susanna's feelings, his essential obligation to do the right thing. He has to remind himself that these things will be just as important to him — even more important — on the other side of that much-needed night's sleep.

4.

"Are you coming down with something?" Jan asks. "You haven't been yourself all day. Or yesterday, for that matter."

Sarah has been staring at the computer screen, eyes unfocused, and she tries to focus them now. She was about to type something into Mr. Anderson's file — something about his meds — but she has forgotten what. She pinches her eyes shut and takes a deep breath. "Um. No. I mean, I'm OK."

"You sure?"

"Just tired."

Jan points to the clock. "Go on and take off. The girls will be here in a little bit, and I can hold down the fort until then."

Sarah nods and picks up her purse. She looks around, confused, feeling as if there's something she has left behind. "Oh," she says. She waves her hand, as if beckoning Jan to supply the words that have eluded her, and Jan's brows draw in confusion. Sarah's brain is fogged; it is like a morning after too many beers. "You know. Mr. Anderson."

"You want me to log in that dose for you?"

"Yes," Sarah says, practically sighing with relief.

"You should go home," Jan says. "Take some vitamin B and scramble yourself an egg."

Sarah manages a wan smile. "You know how I feel about eggs." Her stomach clenches; she hasn't been able to stomach more than a bowl of cereal today, and nothing at all since Wyatt's call.

"That's why you're so peaked."

Sarah sketches a halfhearted wave of good-bye, slips into her winter coat, and draws her purse strap over her shoulder. She is the one feeling scrambled, her thoughts disconnected and contradictory, her body so tired and weak it seems mired in quicksand and yet restless, so that she hasn't been able to stop herself all day from jostling a leg or thumping out a rhythm on the tabletop with her thumb. The worst thing is that she feels short of breath. Her passageways aren't constricted — the right amount of oxygen is entering and exiting — and yet her chest feels weighted, compressed. When she was in her twenties, she had a tabby cat named Peggy Sue who would climb up on her breasts as she slept. Sarah would be dreaming about drowning, or about being held down in a fight, and she would struggle to wakefulness to realize that the cat was a heavy, tight ball on top of her, ridge of its bony spine tucked against her chin. "The little shit's trying to kill me," she complained to her friends, and she had to at last start putting the cat out of her bedroom at night and learn to sleep through its steady, plaintive cries. Eventually, when Peggy Sue died of old age, she had to learn again to sleep without them.

He did nothing wrong and she has abandoned him.

He did something wrong — terribly wrong — and she was foolish enough to fall for him.

The wind is very bad today; it is whistling beneath the hospital's canopies and making the three flags on the pole outside of the emergency room — American, Commonwealth of Kentucky, and Tri-Health — ripple loudly. Sarah buries her fingers in her pockets and walks to the car with her head tucked down. She has always liked the cold, thrives better in winter than in summer, but it is only anesthetizing now, not invigorating. She doesn't know where to go or what to do. She was happy to leave work, but she is not ready to confront the emptiness of her home. The library? She can't concentrate well enough to read. Out for a beer? Bad idea, she thinks. Bad, bad idea. Not now. Not feeling like this.

She is considering going by her brother's, because her nieces almost always lift her spirits, when she hears the distant whine of sirens — multiple sets, if she isn't mistaken. The sound cuts through her mental fog, barely; it stimulates something, causes the faintest twitch: of curiosity, of concern. It is like desire. There will be stretches, weeks and weeks, when it is easy for her to not think of sex, easy for her to accept that sex isn't something she needs or even cares about. Then, out of nowhere, something will light her up, spark that dormant thing within her, set her to aching. What she feels now is a different kind of desire, but she acknowledges it, tries to hold on to it. Any old lifeline out of this gloom that has descended on her, she'll take.

The ambulance rolls into the parking lot, quivering a little with the speed of its turn, and Sarah presses back automatically against someone else's car. The ambulance she expected; the two cars following it, both with lights flashing, one a marked Roma police car and the other unmarked, she did not. The three sirens overlap and vibrate so that Sarah feels the sound in her teeth, and she puts her palms over her ears. It's not completely unusual for a police car to accompany an ambulance in, especially when there's been a car accident and suspicion of DUI, but at five o'clock on a Tuesday, it makes her wonder. She watches uneasily as the ambulance parks under the emergency canopy. The unmarked car brakes and pulls abruptly into a nearby empty slot; its driver, a tall black man, runs for the ambulance. The sirens stop within seconds of each other, but the lights on the ambulance keep throbbing like a heartbeat.

The pressure on her chest increases.

"Back up, stand to the side," the ambulance driver says as he emerges from the cab and unhooks the rear double doors.

The man from the unmarked car backs up, lifting his hands a little as if to say sorry. Sarah, meanwhile, starts back across the parking lot toward them. She watches as the driver starts to pull out the stretcher. The wheeled legs drop, accordion-style, and the EMT in the back of the ambulance unhooks the safety latch, then jumps down after the stretcher to help roll it into the emergency bay. By now a couple of nurses from the emergency room, Marjorie and Ricky, have come out to assist, and the EMTs pass the stretcher on to them. There is an oxygen mask over the person's mouth, so she can't see his face, but a pair of shiny black cowboy boots with red stitching make a jaunty V at the end of the stretcher, as if the man they're attached to is just kicked back in a lawn chair, napping after a barbecue.

There's something familiar about those

boots. She knows them.

The men walk more slowly back to the ambulance, where the tall black man is waiting and looking through the gaping double doors. Sarah approaches them, and they seem at first not to notice. The man from the unmarked car points inside to a second gurney.

"What about him?"

"I had to call it," the EMT who'd been riding in the back says. "His heart stopped. There wasn't any kick-starting it. Oh, hey, Sarah."

She nearly jumps. She recognizes him now, but it's been years since she put in hours at the ER. She can't place his name. "Oh, hello."

"You working ER today?"

"No," Sarah says. "My shift just ended. I was on my way out when I heard the ruckus."

The driver is shaking his head. "I just loaded this guy up last week out at Harper Hill. I'll be damned."

It is as if she has known all along that Wyatt is dead. "Harper Hill?" she manages.

"Yeah, had a heart attack. I can't think of his name."

"Wyatt Powell," Sarah says, and the black man looks at her sharply.

"You knew him?" he asks.

She nods hard, unable to speak. She swallows past a sharp ache and feels her eyes well up with water, but she doesn't blink, and the tears do not — quite — spill. "I treated him. He was in my wing."

"Well, he had a screw loose," the EMT who knows her says. "He beat the living daylights out of that kid we just wheeled in."

"Lucky he didn't kill him," the driver said.

The black man gestures toward the building, and Sarah notices the bags under his eyes. "The young guy. Will he recover? What are his chances?"

"That's not for me to say. His heart rate's steady. It might look worse than it is."

"It looked pretty bad." The man again — Sarah guesses he is some kind of a cop.

The driver lights a cigarette, waves the pack around, gets no takers.

"His name is Sam Austen," the cop says. "I'd like to talk to him when he wakes up. It's important."

The EMT — Ryan, Sarah thinks, his name is Ryan — hops back up in the ambulance and starts working on the second stretcher, this one on a bench attached to the wall. She can see Wyatt's fine gray hair move as Ryan jostles the gurney. She remembers combing it into place with her fingertips as Wyatt slept.

"Talk to the doc," Ryan says with a grunt from inside. "That's his call."

The two EMTs get the second stretcher unloaded. Wyatt's eyes are half-open, the eyes of a child fighting sleep. The gurney straps hit him at the shoulders, stomach, and knees, pressing his arms tightly to his sides. Sarah covers her mouth, pinches her lips together. She can smell his cologne, the English Leather he wore the night they met at Nancy's and on the evening he came home from the hospital. The backs of his hands are still freckled, the curly hairs on his forearms, visible where the cuff of his shirtsleeve is pulled back, still the color of rust. The EMTs start to wheel him inside, not getting in any hurry about it. She doesn't reach out to touch him. She doesn't dare to.

"Are you OK?" the cop asks her when Wyatt — what is left of him — is gone.

"Yes," she whispers.

"You knew him," he says.

A tear slips down her cheek, and she backhands it roughly away. "I took care of him."

"You must be a good nurse," the man says. "To care this much." His voice is gentle. She doesn't think he is being sarcastic. "I bet he appreciated it."

"You care about some more than others," she says finally. "I thought he was a kind man. He was kind to me."

5.

Billy Houchens, like his sister, Emily, is a walker. Once a day — usually at four P.M., so that he can time his return home with his father's arrival from the factory — he makes a circuit of about half a mile, never altering his course, never reversing it. He starts on his street, Forsythia, and takes it until it makes a right angle at Poplar. Poplar he takes to Marigold, a name that always makes him smile, because when he was a little, little boy he thought Marigold was a kind of treasure, but now he knows that it is a kind of flower. From Marigold he cuts through an alleyway between two fence lines to reach Washington Lane, the dead-end street, which is where Emily goes to be by herself in the woods. He has hidden here many times and watched her scurry past the Potters' barking dog. He does not think he is being sneaky or sinister in doing so; he thinks only of his curiosity about Emily's comings and goings, a curiosity that has increased these last few weeks. He has not, like his parents, sensed Emily's sadness; he has not speculated about her loneliness or wondered why she, like himself, doesn't have any friends. Emily is as she has always been to him: an object of interest and bright, simplistic affection. When Emily was three and he was nine, he was her tireless playmate. He turned the crank on the jack-in-the-box as many times as she wanted him to. He pushed around a Matchbox car after hers. When Emily started kindergarten and came home with books of letters and numbers and pictures of farm animals, he sat beside her on the couch, following her progress from page to page, learning right alongside of her. At eleven he finally started reading for the first time on his own, and now he can understand comic books — if he reads the dialogue out loud, he can follow how it goes with the pictures — and *TV Guide.* He watches a lot of television. He likes to know what is coming up next.

He likes schedules, patterns. He likes his routine. And so it is not Emily's changing emotions he has noticed these last weeks but her changing habits: the frequency of her trips into the woods past the dead-end street, her tardiness coming home, her smell — there is something different there, something foul. It makes him want to keep his distance from her. He has been maintaining, in his way, a mental log of her comings and goings, a log that failed to receive its entry last night, when Emily didn't come home. Not at six, or at seven. Not at all. He didn't like it. He didn't like it when dinner cooled with nobody eating it, and he didn't like it when his parents (he always thought of them as "his," not "their") started pacing and making scared faces. He didn't like it when they got on the phone with their trembling voices, or when his father went out alone in the truck, or when the police officer came over and started looking around their house and asking questions. He didn't like the police officer with the thick mustache. And so he screamed, and he did the good bumping thing, which was how he made his head better. And his parents said, "Quiet, quiet," then, "Shut up, shut up," and it wasn't good anymore, and so he went to bed and slept as long as he could.

It still isn't good today. He knows now where Emily is: the hospital. He doesn't like her there, but he likes her there better than nowhere, which is where she was last night, and so he is a little calmer. But his parents are gone much of the day, and his mother doesn't come home to cook dinner at five o'clock. Instead, his father brings him home a bag with fish 'n' chips (which aren't chips, but French fries) from Captain D's and tells him that Aunt Bonnie will be coming over later to stay the night. He likes Aunt Bonnie, but he doesn't like her sleeping in his house, in his mom and daddy's bed, and he doesn't like eating Captain D's when no one else is around to eat it with him. He doesn't like eating at four o'clock, which is when he is supposed to have his walk, even when his daddy tells him that Aunt Bonnie will heat him up some mozzarella sticks later if he doesn't give her any trouble.

He doesn't consider not going for the walk; in his hierarchy of rituals, an outright omission is a greater sin than a shuffling of the schedule. So at five o'clock, after washing the grease from his supper off his fingers, he goes to the kitchen window to check the thermometer: 40 degrees. He trudges to the utility room, chooses his parka with the hood, and slips into it, then dons the gloves tucked into the right front pocket. None of this feels quite right, but going through the motions is calming. He thinks of it as *making even.* In his mind is a scale, and the more right he does, the more balanced the scales. When the scales are off, the good bumping can help, or rocking in his chair can help, and it's as if he's jostling the thing that's off back into place.

It is too dark and too cold out. But he starts walking.

He feels, despite himself, some fresh interest in this new vantage point. It is November; at five o'clock the sun is already low enough in the sky that the houses are illuminated from within, dioramas visible from the road. In the Clemmons house, a woman is stretching — lifting her arms, arching her back — in the picture window. The sight arouses Billy, and he pauses to watch. The stretching woman stops, drops her arms, swings them a little at her sides. Then she moves out of sight.

He moves on, too.

He is on Washington Lane and circling back toward Poplar when a large figure crosses the street in front of him. Billy, unafraid, peers ahead. The streetlights will not kick on until six o'clock, and so the road is washed in shadow.

"Boss?" Billy says.

The dog trots easily toward him, unhurried. Billy holds out the back of his hand, as his mother taught him to do, and grins as the dog sniffs it, enjoying the tickle of its whiskers. When the dog has gotten its fill it snorts out air, then shakes its head back and forth, sending jets of saliva flying. Billy groans and wipes a string of the stuff off his chest with his shirtsleeve.

"Ew, Boss. You aren't supposed to do that."

Boss looks up at him.

"Where's Mr. Powell?"

The dog's expression is comical. Billy likes Boss. His sister got to do most of the walking with him while Mr. Powell was in the hospital, but Billy and Boss were friends before Emily came home from school. He reaches out to scratch the top of the dog's head. There is a hard knob of bone, like a knuckle — Billy's father called it a "knowledge bump."

If his parents were home, he would go back and ask them what to do. But they are at the hospital with Emily, and Aunt Bonnie is still finishing her shift at Wal-Mart. Billy crosses the street to Mr. Powell's house, which, like his own, is a white, aluminum-sided rectangle with a big front window and a gravel drive. Mr. Powell has a carport, though, and Billy's parents do not. This difference interests him. He thinks that Mr. Powell must be richer than his family to have a carport.

There aren't any lights on in the house, but he knocks anyway. He looks over his shoulder. Boss is still standing in the road.

He knocks again. Then he tries the door-knob, thinking that he ought to get Boss to go back inside. Mr. Powell doesn't have a fence.

The door is locked. He returns to the road.

"I don't know where Mr. Powell is, Boss. I wonder how you got outside."

He knows the dog doesn't understand him, but he likes talking aloud to him this way.

"Well, I've got to go home."

He resumes his walk. He likes the smell out here — the moldy sweetness of damp leaves, a whiff of gasoline from somebody's running car. There is a head bobbing in the kitchen window of Jake and Lottie Summers, and he wonders if Mrs. Summers is washing dishes. He likes Mrs. Summers. When he walks by here in the summer, and she is sitting out front in a lawn chair, she always says, "How's life treating you?" and Billy always says, "Fine, just fine."

He has reached Poplar Street when he realizes the dog is following him. "No, Boss, you need to go home," he says, making a shooing motion, and the dog backs up a step. But when Billy proceeds, the dog keeps time, and there is something so appealing about the cheerful clack of Boss's toenails on the cement that Billy can't bring himself to protest again.

His mother won't be happy to see Boss. She was always saying, "Ugh, Boss stinks," and "Ugh, I think I have a flea bite." But nothing is *even* right now, nothing is normal — and if his parents can make him eat Captain D's alone at four, and take his walk at five, and have Aunt Bonnie make his mozzarella sticks, then he reckons he can have Boss, too. At least until Mr. Powell gets back home.

6.

Emily has been in and out of a fog, struggling just enough to wakefulness to wish that she were still sleeping, when she notices that Christopher Shelton is at her bedside. He looks worried, earnest; he sits up straighter when he realizes that her eyes are on him, and Emily shifts around in the bed, self-conscious in her hospital gown.

"Hey," Christopher says bashfully. "You're awake."

"Hey," Emily says. She doesn't know until she speaks how hoarse her voice is, how sore her throat. When she swallows, her tongue feels broad and stupid in her mouth. "What are you doing here?"

"My mom brought me. I wanted to check

on you."

Her chest swells with gratitude. "Really?"

"Really."

She can't stop herself from asking: "You're not mad?"

He shakes his head, and the dark curl of hair on his forehead trembles. "Of course I'm not mad. It turns out you were right all along, Emily. There really was a body. It was there, just like you said it was."

"I knew it," she murmured.

"You're a hero. Everyone at school is talking about it — about how brave you were. We've all been so worried."

Emily frowns. Something is nagging at her, tickling the back of her mind. "Where was the body?"

"Where you said it was," Christopher says.

Her mother and father are in the room — she hadn't noticed before. They smile in that bland, stupid way they can have around people they don't know well, and she is embarrassed, then confused. "Mom?" Her mother nods encouragingly. Emily looks back at Christopher. "No, I looked there. I crawled around on the ground. It wasn't there."

Her father says, "That's just because you got turned around out in those woods. You took Christopher to the wrong tree." Emily is bothered, because the answer seems somehow too right, too close to what she had wanted to hear. It's as though her father has seen into her heart, answered her thoughts.

A dark knowledge settles over her. She wishes her parents away, and they're gone. She puts out her hand, and Christopher takes it. "You're not mad at me?" she repeats, and Christopher says no, but now she doesn't believe him. A tear slides down her cheek, and a soft cloth presses it away.

"Don't cry, kiddo. We're here. Me and Daddy."

She opens her eyes. How could she be so easily fooled by dreams, by fantasies? Reality is coldly inarguable — it's there in the dark pores on the end of her mother's nose, which looks red from getting rubbed too many times with a tissue; in the smell of her father's cheeks and neck, which she can tell with eerie certainty is tinged with the remnants of his Barbasol shaving cream and his usual splash of Old Spice. It's there in their looks of desperation, how badly they need her to tell them she's all right, and she resents them for needing this from her, for wanting reassurance more than the truth.

"Go away," she says, and her mother

seems to crumple into the tissue she's holding.

"Now, don't say that." Her father has his arm firmly around her mother's shoulder, and though the tone of his voice is firm, Emily can tell that he's just as shaky; her parents are like pins she is knocking down, and she takes a small, bitter pleasure in watching them fall.

"Go away," she repeats, and she thinks of her brother, Billy, of how he acts when he is displeased, the way her parents scramble to satisfy him, to shut him up. She lifts her head off the pillow, drops it. Lifts, drops. It feels good. It feels right. Bop, bop, bop, she is being like her brother, and her parents exchange terrified glances, seem to say to one another without speaking aloud, *Please, God, not her, too.*

"Stop that, Emily," her mother says sharply.

She gets her shoulders into the motion now. She *is* crazy, isn't she? Seeing things that aren't there? The guardrail starts to rattle, and the IV rack trembles. Her eyes are open, and so the square of silver light on the ceiling becomes a bright blur streaking across her vision, and her parents are dark, frantic smudges.

"Press the call button," her mother says,

her voice choked with fear.

"Where? I —"

There is pressure across her middle, on her shoulders. She moves her head faster. She could stop, but what will happen then — what questions will she have to answer, what truths will she have to face? She is talking. She doesn't even know what she's saying. And then a new face leans over her, and the silver streak of light becomes a square again, and then it winks out.

Chapter Thirty-Three

1.

When Susanna got to the room, a man was standing in the hall. He was tall, gangly, with bulging, sorrowful eyes — Buster Keaton in blue jeans and an old flannel work shirt. He leaned against the wall, staring off into space.

"Are you Mr. Houchens?" Susanna asked gently, not wanting to startle him.

He drew up his shoulders, and his large eyes rolled tiredly her way. He nodded, attempted a smile. "Yes, ma'am. Morris." He held out his hand. She shook it.

"I'm Susanna Mitchell," she said. "I'm one of Emily's teachers at the middle school."

Some emotion passed across his features. She thought it might have been relief. "Oh. Oh, yeah, it's good of you to come. It's real good of you." He pulled a blue paisley handkerchief from his back pocket and wiped his neck with it. "Go on in. My wife's there. Emily's probably still sleeping."

She nodded her thanks and went to the half-open door, rapping softly to announce her presence. Emily was in the bed, eyes closed. A woman, her mother, was seated beside her, face in her hands. She sniffed, lifted her head; her face was damp and blotchy, her eyes obscured by thick lenses.

"Is this a bad time?" Susanna asked.

The woman scrutinized her, confused. "Oh," she said. "I know you." To Susanna's surprise she rose, stepped forward, and embraced her.

"We talked on the phone last week," Susanna said. She held the woman carefully. She could feel her tears soaking through the fabric of her blouse, an embarrassingly intimate sensation.

"I remember. You were good to Emily." She was shaking now.

"Is she all right? I had heard she was doing well."

The woman pulled back, nodding, and sat down again. She motioned to an adjacent chair, which Susanna took. "Oh — yes. She's OK. The doctor said that the main issue is dehydration, so they've got her on an IV. And she's exhausted and —" She thought about it. "Upset. Hysterical. They had to give her a sedative."

"It's only natural," Susanna said. "She just needs some time."

"I hope so." The mother lifted her glasses and backhanded away tears. "I'm sorry. It's been a rough day."

"I can't even imagine," Susanna said, and she found that she meant it. Despite everything.

The woman's face crumpled, and her voice broke. "I don't get it, I don't understand it. I keep replaying things, trying to figure out what we did wrong. I thought we were good to her. We've got our hands full with Billy, and that puts a stress on all of us. I won't say I never raise my voice. But I thought we were good to her."

"I'm sure you are," Susanna said, touching her shoulder.

"But she did run off," the woman said.

"You can do everything right by a person and still have things go wrong," Susanna said. "Emily was having a hard time at school. She got singled out for a lot of cruelty, and none of that was her fault, or yours."

Emily's mother snorted a laugh — a sharp, humorless sound. "I told her to try to be normal. That's how I supported her."

"I don't think that's such bad advice," Susanna said. "It's realistic."

"She's never been one to face reality." The woman looked at Emily lovingly, and Susanna's stomach clenched with pity. "It's my fault, because I've never been good at facing it, either. I always told her stories. Played make-believe." She stroked Emily's hand, which rested on the top of the sheet. "And then we've got Billy. Make-believe's just easier sometimes."

Susanna, feeling her own tears threaten, nodded briskly. "It sounds to me like you did your best."

"She told me she wished she was dead," Emily's mother said. "She started crying and banging her head like her brother does when he's unhappy, and she said we should have left her in the woods. She didn't stop until the nurse put something into her IV. They want her to talk to a psychiatrist."

"Teenagers say that kind of thing all the time," Susanna said uneasily. But she thought of Emily that day in the bathroom, after the incident in the cafeteria — her humming, the mechanical way she went about wiping spaghetti sauce off her face — and wondered.

"Kelly?" Morris was standing in the doorway, eyes even wider than before, handkerchief getting twisted between his two hands.

"The counselor is here."

"I should leave you to it," Susanna said. She shouldered her purse strap and stood.

Emily's mother — Kelly — looked back and forth between Susanna and Morris. "Does she want to meet in here? In front of Emily?"

A young woman, as young as Susanna, slipped into view. She was dressed in a costume of seriousness: a flowery blouse with a bow at the neck, long skirt, tailored jacket. It reminded Susanna of her wardrobe in the first year she taught at RMS, when she had the audacity to consider her round, unlined face a liability. "Mrs. Houchens, there's a conference space we can use just down the hall. I thought we could go there."

Kelly stood. She already appeared defeated; she had the confidence and posture of a person shuffling down the hall in a robe and slippers. Her hair was limp and uncombed, and Susanna noticed for the first time that she appeared to be wearing a long nightshirt over her jeans instead of a regular T. It was a thin, nubby polyester with a cracked screen print that read CAFFEINE, PLEASE!

"I don't think I should leave her," Kelly said. She held on to the edge of the bed as if she might fall.

"Go on," Susanna said softly. "She's sleeping — she won't miss you. I'll stay with her until you get back."

"You don't have any place you need to be?" Morris asked.

Susanna said no.

"Thank you," Kelly said. She followed Morris out to the hallway, and Susanna tried not to listen to the soft, awkward murmur of introductions. At last the voices dwindled. She and Emily were alone.

She felt, strangely, that there was no better place for her to be at this moment, no better person for her to spend time with. Home had not been right. Her mother's house had not been right. Not with her husband or even her own daughter. This girl — this odd, haunted girl — was the one she needed. This child whose resting place had revealed her sister's. Susanna watched Emily sleep. Her stomach moved gently under the sheet, and her lashes lay long, almost prettily, on her freckled cheeks. Her hair was coarse and limp, a light brown so joyless that it was practically green. The resting hands, Susanna noticed, looked as if they had been wiped with a cloth but not scrubbed; the fingernails had crescents of grime beneath them, and the knuckles were nicked and scraped, damp with some kind of clear ointment.

"Why were you there?" Susanna said softly. "How did you know?"

Emily's eyeballs twitched behind their lids. Her forehead creased, and she made a sound, faint, kittenish — something between a grunt and a wince.

"What did you see?" Susanna whispered.

A sound from behind her: a clearing throat. Susanna sat up with a start, turned.

"Tony," she said, standing.

"Hey there," he said.

She gave no thought to what he wanted, what he would be comfortable with. She gave no thought to appearances. She went forward, arms opened, and made him envelop her — bold because she knew now she could be, that it didn't matter any longer. Or didn't matter in the way she had once thought it might.

His bright-smelling cologne was a distant note, an afterthought. The spice of his skin was stronger, ripe, and she knew without asking how tired he was, how hard he had pushed himself today. It was on his face when he pulled back: the red threads running through the whites of his eyes, the gray cast to his skin. The planes of his cheeks above the neat line of his goatee were grizzled faintly with hairs.

"I already know about Ronnie," she said. "I already know, Tony."

He touched her cheek; she could feel the rough callus on his thumb. "I went to your house," he said. "Your husband was there. He told me you'd heard." She blinked, and a tear spilled toward his hand. "It shouldn't have gotten to you that way."

"There was no good way."

"Nothing is certain yet," Tony said. "We won't know until they finish the lab work."

"Did you see it? The body?"

His eyes darted to the side. "I didn't see much. Enough to know what it was."

Her breath hitched, and she pressed her palm to her chest. "And it looked like it could be her?"

He was still staring at some point to the left of her. "You have to believe me when I say I can't answer that."

"You mean you won't. You're not supposed to."

"I mean I'm not able to," Tony said. There was something in his face. Fear. Weakness. She wondered for the first time if she could trust him.

"It's her," she said. "I feel it. I know it."

He didn't reply.

"And you know it, too," Susanna said, at last believing. She had wanted to elicit in

Tony some reaction of surprise or refutation. Something to make her hope. But there was no hope on his face.

"I think it is, yes," he said. "I'm so sorry. But I think it's your sister. There aren't any other missing persons reported in the area."

"And somebody put her there," Susanna said.

"Yes," Tony said.

"Somebody put her there," she murmured to herself. "Tony, you've got to find out who. You've got to find him."

Tony stepped abruptly around her and looked down at Emily. "How is she? I was here — and I had some time. I thought I'd check in."

"As well as can be expected, I guess," Susanna said. "Medically, she's OK. Her mother told me she woke up pretty upset."

"It's no wonder," Tony said.

"Was she with the body?"

His hands were in his pockets, his shoulders slumped. "Nearby. Ten or fifteen feet from it."

"You think she found it?"

He shrugged. "She was within sight of it. But I'm not sure. Maybe it was a coincidence."

"I wish she would wake up," Susanna said.

But the child slept on, her breaths long

and steady, her features smooth. If she had been dreaming before, she didn't seem to be now. The monitor at her bedside beat out a steady time. Somewhere down the hall, a television blasted the laugh track to a sitcom. Susanna sat again in the chair Kelly had vacated, thinking that she could almost be jealous of Emily right now, despite all of the hard truths she was about to awaken to. In this moment, the girl had found a hiding place. She was still young enough that the world would allow her that.

"You'll go home?" Tony asked. "Your husband seemed worried about you. Genuinely."

She smiled a tiny, rueful smile. She understood what he was really saying.

"What I mean to say is that he seems to love you."

But you don't, Susanna thought. She was gripping the edge of the rough-woven thermal blanket on Emily's bed, and she unwound it from her fingers.

"And your daughter," Tony said. "I saw her. He seems like a good father to her."

"Well, then, I guess I've got all a girl could hope for."

He shuffled uncomfortably.

"I know that's not what you meant," Susanna said hoarsely.

Tony went to the door, halted. "I'll call you tomorrow, when we hear from the lab. It's possible that we'll need you to come in and identify some clothing items."

"Perhaps you could have that Pendleton guy take care of it," Susanna said. She turned and looked over her shoulder at him. "Just for now. For this part of things."

"Are you sure that's what you want?"

She nodded, lips pressed tightly together.

He was propped against the doorpost stiffly, as if he needed holding up, and she wondered if his back was paining him. His temples and forehead were damp.

"Try to get some rest tonight, Suzy."

She lifted her fingers in a little wave. It was all she could manage.

2.

She looks down at Emily Houchens, not seeing her. She is thinking about what comes next. She will go home and pack a bag. She will pack a bag for her daughter. She will take Abby to her mother's, and she will try to explain to the both of them about Ronnie, and then they will face the rest of it together. She knows now what she is getting, which isn't much — and what is left, which is enough. Just enough to keep her going. She suspects that this is a decision she will have to make not just now but every day of her life, each time she passes her daughter off to Dale for a visitation, each time Abby asks her the difficult questions, each time her mother draws her lips in disappointment. Am I right? Is it worth it?

Ronnie, she thinks, is the only one who would have understood. Who would have told her, each time she needed to hear it, *yes.*

■ ■ ■ ■

THANKSGIVING

■ ■ ■ ■

Ronnie had come with a bottle of white wine, because Susanna liked it, though Ronnie had known she was baiting Dale — that he would spend the rest of the day silently angry about it. And she was right, of course; he scowled when Susanna dug out a corkscrew before serving dinner, scowled when she poured equal portions into two of her crystal water goblets, the only glasses she owned with stems. His disapproval was only matched by their mother's. "I don't see how the two of you can tempt fate that way after what your father put us through," she said. "They say it runs in the family."

"What?" Ronnie said. "Crazy? We got that from your side."

Susanna laughed.

"Oh, hush," their mother said. "You know what I'm talking about." But she wouldn't say the word. She never said the word.

When they'd finished eating, Dale stood and tucked his cloth napkin under the lip of his plate. "It was good," he told Susanna. "I'm going to watch the game in the bedroom, if that's all right with you."

"We were about to play hearts," Susanna said. "You don't want to? We need a fourth."

"Just deal out an extra hand and don't do pairs. It's not a big deal."

Susanna snatched his plate from across the table and started scraping it roughly into hers. "Fine," she said, and Ronnie couldn't help but wince a little. Dale was an asshole, behaving in characteristically asshole fashion, but she hated seeing her sister this way, so prissy and petty.

"Calm down, Sister," Ronnie said. "I'll help you with the dishes. Let Dale take off." She threw him an exaggerated smile. "We'll just finish this bottle of wine and yak."

He left the room without speaking again, and it was better, really. Even their mother seemed to feel the difference, and she didn't object when Ronnie poured a small amount of wine into her empty water goblet, or when she poured her own and Susanna's back to full.

"Well," their mother said, taking a tentative sip, "it *is* Thanksgiving."

They all went to the living room. Abby

hunched down at the coffee table to play with Matchbox cars, and Susanna set the television on a cartoon, something the grown-ups could ignore. It was so rarely like this: the three of them together, enjoying each other, talking about something besides old grievances. How many holidays had they spent rehashing their father's sins against them and their sins against one another? The most terrible days of Ronnie's and Susanna's youth had taken on a kind of legendary status among them, and they each had their pet stories: Ronnie's was the time that Dad had slapped her so hard her ear bled, and how Mama's reaction was to flee the room weeping instead of tending to her. Susanna's was when she came in from school to find their father passed out naked on the couch, and though Ronnie never said so, she thought that Susanna was being a bit dramatic about the whole thing. *Ever been socked in the ear?* she wanted to say. *I'd have rather gotten a look at the old man's pecker any day.*

Their mother didn't have stories so much as she did favorite excuses, even accusations. "You girls don't know how much I protected you from," she liked to tell them. "You don't know how many times I took the punches so you wouldn't have to." By the end of it she was the victim, and Ronnie and Susanna were the ones apologizing. That's how these powwows always went: storytelling, accusations, apologies, tears. By the end they would convince themselves that they'd really and truly cleared the air and gotten closure; they weren't angry anymore; they just loved each other *so much.* And yet, when the next holiday came, they were ready for another round.

But maybe they really had gotten it out of their systems last time, because here they were, bellies full, talking about Christmas shopping and decorating, and Susanna was saying that it was going to be the first year that Abby could really appreciate the idea of Santa. This got them into some old memories, but only the good and funny ones: The year Ronnie had gotten a bike and Susanna had gotten roller skates, and they were each so sure that the other's present was the superior one that they screamed for a solid hour. The one time Dad dressed as Santa, because a guy he worked with loaned him a costume. The year Dad drove them way out in the country, parked them on the side of the road, and led them through a stranger's woods with an ax and some rope, and how they didn't realize until they were adults that they'd trespassed and stolen a tree. "I don't know about that. Are you sure that's what happened?" their mother said, and Ronnie and Susanna said "Yes, Mother" in sync, in the same droll tone of voice, and they all laughed. They were feeling the wine in that really good way that was warm and tickly and innocent, which was when Ronnie would usually open another bottle or dip into the whiskey, because she was always so afraid of losing the good feeling that she ended up killing it by having too much. But here, now, this was enough. She was comfortable on her sister's ugly sofa, with her foot propped up on the coffee table; Abby kept crawling under her leg and driving the Matchbox cars along her shin.

Susanna went to the kitchen and returned with a camera. "Smile, Mom," she said, and their mother grinned in that tortured way she had, so that the bones in her face stood out more and her eyes narrowed to lines. "Okay, now you, Ronnie."

Ronnie held a hand in front of her face. "Put that thing away. We were having a good time, for God's sake."

"You can do this one thing for me," Susanna said. "I made green bean casserole for you. No one else even eats it."

Ronnie huffed and set her shoulders. "All

right, all right," she said. "Get it over with."

"Smile," Susanna said firmly.

Ronnie crooked her lip a bit and then blinked away the flash. She hated taking pictures, hated how vulnerable it made her feel to put herself on display like that, not knowing if her expression was pretty or if she was dropping her chin in that way that made it seem as if she didn't have one. She beckoned Susanna briskly with her right hand. "Here, give me that," she said. "Let me get one of you and Mom and Abby together. Three generations of Eastman women."

"OK," Susanna said. "Abby, come here to me. Let's take a picture with Grandma."

"You can all get on the couch," Ronnie said.

Susanna and their mother sat on the couch together, close, and put Abby awkwardly between them, so that one of her legs was on each of their laps. Abby still had a grip on a Matchbox car, and Susanna tried to pry it out of her hand, but she grunted as if she might cry. Ronnie boxed them in the camera's viewfinder, putting its red crosshairs on her niece's face. She felt something, seeing the three of them like that. She wasn't sure what, but it was like a flutter in her chest, something that would take flight and stick in her throat.

"Wait a minute," Susanna said before Ronnie could snap the picture. "Ronnie, we can't do this picture without you in it. Let's get Dale in here to take it. Dale!" she yelled. "Dale, come in here a sec and take our photo!"

There was a split second when Ronnie would have posed for the photo, when she wanted very much to be part of it, and then Dale yelled back, "Does it have to be right this minute? I'm going to miss this play," and she just shook the want away and said, "Never mind that and smile. I'll be in the photo next year." Then she snapped it.

Something changed then. Abby's cartoon ended, and Susanna spent five minutes flipping channels, trying to find something else that would satisfy her. Ronnie's wine buzz dissipated. Their mother started making noises about leaving, and Susanna said, "If I don't get those dishes in the washer soon I'll have to scrub them."

Ronnie went to the porch for a cigarette. It was a gray, drizzly day, temperatures in the forties, and she hadn't thought to slip into her coat before stepping out. She sat on the front stoop and smoked her first cigarette almost immediately down to the filter. She flicked it off her thumb into the yard, thrilling a little at the sight of it littering her sister's neat lawn, and wondered where this anger had come from. She had looked through the camera lens and there it was. She couldn't explain it. But anger was always sneaking up on Ronnie, appearing at the bottom of a glass or around a bend in the road or in a song on the radio.

The door behind her opened just as she was lighting her second cigarette. "Here," Susanna said, and Ronnie looked at what she was offering: her jean jacket. She slid into it and grunted a thank-you.

"Want one?" She offered the pack.

"Guess not," Susanna said. "Though it might be fun just to piss him off."

"He'll smell mine on you," Ronnie said. "That's enough to do it."

"I'm sure you're right."

They watched as a car pulled in at the house across the street, where a half dozen other vehicles were already parked in the drive and lining the road in front of the house. That was what Thanksgiving was supposed to look like, Ronnie thought as a graying couple emerged and pulled foil-covered pans out of the backseat; she could make out the steam rising off of the dishes from here. It was supposed to be big and rowdy and chaotic, not five sullen people gathered around a table with room to spare.

"How's work going?" Susanna said.

"Like it always goes. I do the same thing every day. There ain't exactly highs and lows." Sensing Susanna's discomfort, she tried to soften her voice a little. "It's fine. I can do it in my sleep now. How about you?"

Susanna laughed a little. "The same, in a way. I teach the same lesson five times a day, and then the next year I start the whole thing over again."

"It's not the same," Ronnie said flatly, and they were silent for a moment.

"I guess it isn't."

Ronnie pulled on the filter and blew smoke through her nostrils. "What are the kids reading?"

"They just started a unit on tragedy, so we'll do *Oedipus Rex* and *Death of a Salesman,* and then we'll do *The Diary of Anne Frank* right before Christmas."

"That sounds awfully fucking cheery. Merry Christmas."

"Eighth graders love this stuff. They really do. It appeals to their already heightened sense of drama."

"OK, what else?"

"Well," Susanna said, "we just finished that John Knowles novel I told you about, *A Separate Peace.*"

Ronnie thought. "Remind me what that's about?"

"It's set at a boarding school during World War II. There are these two friends, Finny and Gene. Gene is the serious, studious one, and Finny's just this really vibrant character, full of life. He has this magnetism that everyone responds to."

"He sounds like fun. What happens to him?"

"He dies."

Ronnie laughed sharply. "Now see, this is why I don't read novels. They always kill off the people you'd actually want to spend time with and stick you with the bores."

Susanna shook her head and huffed with exasperation. "I think you'd like the book if you read it. I honestly do."

"Well, maybe. Eventually. Even though you told me how it ends."

"That's the only way I've ever been able to get you to read something, is telling you how it ends."

"You know, that's true," Ronnie said. "I guess I don't like not knowing. I don't like the stress of it." She popped to a stand and wiped the grit of the porch off her bottom. "All right, I guess I'll take off. I think I've hit my family bonding quota for the month."

"Thanks a lot," Susanna said. "I thought

you were going to help me with dishes."

Ronnie groaned. "Do I have to? I'll do them at Christmas, promise. Or better yet, get Dale to do them. He needs something to distract him from being a prick."

"You realize that the two of you are just alike, don't you? It's occurring to me for the first time."

Ronnie bent down and kissed the crown of Susanna's head. She was already cheering up — she'd just needed to get into motion, to decide to change the scenery. "That's pretty sick, Sis."

"Can you at least give Mom a ride home?"

But it was no good. The restlessness, when it took hold of her, was sudden and decisive, and she felt like she might jolt apart into halves if she kept herself rooted in this spot even a moment longer. "There's no time, hon. I've got to get to Fort Campbell by six o'clock. I told Sonny we'd hang out."

"You never mentioned this before."

"I'm mentioning it now."

"Are you even going to tell Abby goodbye?"

"Give her a kiss for me," Ronnie said. "OK? Tell her I'll have a surprise for her the next time she sees me."

"All right, Ronnie." Her voice was tired. "Just be careful."

"I'm always careful," Ronnie said.

In her Camaro, on the road, with the window down and freezing air blowing in and her left hand making little waves as she raced along, she could be herself, finally. She would rather be leaving than coming, driving than arriving; she lived better in the in-between than she ever had sitting still. Which was why she didn't belong in any photograph. She had looked through the camera's lens and seen not her family but her own absence, and it had seemed to her for a moment that she was a ghost, that she didn't really exist and wouldn't be missed.

When she cleared town and made it to 79 she popped the clutch, shifted into fifth, and laid down on the gas. Stubbled cornfields rolled out on either side of her, and she passed a farmhouse that was already decked out in Christmas lights, cheerful against the beige-colored gloom. She didn't know if Sonny would be home or if he would be glad to see her, but the day was so full of possibility right now that it almost didn't matter. The drive was enough.

ACKNOWLEDGMENTS

Warmest thanks to this book's readers, who offered me insights and support across the various drafts: Erin McGraw, Danielle Lavaque-Manty, Jolie Lewis, Risa Applegarth, Matthew Loyd, and Francis Kelly.

Thanks also to Mary Lou Stevens and Polly Duggan of Triad Bloodhounds, and their dogs, Otis and Ellie, who helped me understand canine search-and-rescue operations. What I got right was their doing; what I got wrong was mine. The same goes for my father-in-law, Larry Jones, who is my go-to expert on all matters pertaining to law enforcement.

I am honored and lucky to still be working with Gail Hochman and Sally Kim, who are, respectively, the wisest, kindest, and most endlessly patient agent and editor I could hope for.

To the communities of colleagues, students, and fellow writers I've made at home in Greensboro and summers in Sewanee, thanks for the friendship, inspiration, and stiff drinks.

Finally, as ever, to Brandon: I love you so much. I could not do this without you.

ABOUT THE AUTHOR

Holly Goddard Jones is author of the short story collection *Girl Trouble.* Her work has appeared in *The Best American Mystery Stories, New Stories from the South, Tin House* magazine and elsewhere, and she was a 2007 recipient of a Rona Jaffe Foundation Writers' Award. She teaches in the creative writing program at the University of North Carolina at Greensboro and lives in Greensboro with her husband, Brandon, and two rowdy dogs.

The employees of Thorndike Press hope you have enjoyed this Large Print book. All our Thorndike, Wheeler, and Kennebec Large Print titles are designed for easy reading, and all our books are made to last. Other Thorndike Press Large Print books are available at your library, through selected bookstores, or directly from us.

For information about titles, please call:
(800) 223-1244

or visit our Web site at:
http://gale.cengage.com/thorndike

To share your comments, please write:
Publisher
Thorndike Press
10 Water St., Suite 310
Waterville, ME 04901